The Emerald Voyage

"An adventure of the heart on a voyage of a lifetime"

Majesty Everleigh

Nelom Publishing, LLC

This book is dedicated to Drusilla, the love of my life.

Introduction

This is a story of a beautiful young couple each getting away on a luxury cruise to restart the next chapter of their life. Their meeting is a story of intense romance, intrigue, and danger.

An adventure of the heart on a voyage of a lifetime.

THE EMERALD VOYAGE

"An adventure of the heart on a voyage of a lifetime."

By Majesty Everleigh

Chapter 1

A New Beginning

Drusilla Pennington stood in the corner of the elegant cocktail reception, a few blocks from Times Square, at the Manhattan Cruise Terminal, watching the crowd mingle. The hum of conversation was punctuated by the clink of champagne glasses and the soft jazz music playing in the background. She had never been one for these kinds of events, but the cruise was a gift from her mother, a chance to escape and start fresh after leaving a long term relationship. The idea of traveling the world was a tantalizing one, and yet, there was something else pulling at her heart—an ache she couldn't quite define.

She smoothed the fabric of her dress, a deep navy that accentuated the pale skin of her arms and neck. Her long brown hair cascaded in loose waves, the soft curls framing her face in a way that made her feel elegant, even if she didn't quite feel that way today. She had always preferred the solitude of her art studio to events like these. Still, it was hard to ignore the charm of the glamorous setting and the allure of new faces.

As she turned, her eyes met his.

The tall, handsome, broad shouldered guy in the sharp tailored suit was drawing her gaze like a magnet. He was looking straight at her, his blue eyes intense and curious. Something flickered between them, something she hadn't expected. She smiled politely, her hand tightening on the champagne flute as she walked toward him.

"Drusilla, right?" His voice was warm, deep, and confident, the kind of voice that made her feel like he was speaking just to her, even though there were other people around.

"Yes," she replied, offering a shy smile. "How do you know my name?"

"I was behind you as we were checking in. I thought, what a beautiful name."

"I'm Jonathan, Jonathan Anderson," he said, his lips curling into a half-smile, "my friends call me JT."

She nodded, feeling a strange pull in her chest. There was something about him—his calm demeanor, the quiet strength he exuded. He wasn't the type to flash a charming grin or make small talk just to fill the silence. No, JT was more of a listener, a man who seemed to take his time with every word.

"I'm glad we have a chance to talk," he continued, taking a sip of his drink. "It looks like we're both headed for the same adventure."

Drusilla's brow furrowed slightly. "I guess so. This is my first cruise."

"Mine too. I'm not one for these types of things, but I think it will be nice to get away for a while."

She raised an eyebrow. "I agree. It's why I'm here."

JT chuckled softly. "So, tell me, what brings you on a cruise like this?"

She thought for a moment. "I needed a change. My life... it was time to do something different. My mother sent me on this cruise. Said it would help to get away from my art studio and try to reset."

"Reset?" JT's smile softened, and he leaned in just a fraction closer. "That sounds intriguing."

She felt a flicker of heat in her chest, but she quickly pushed it away. She didn't come here to get caught up in distractions.

"And what about you?" she asked, trying to divert the conversation away from her personal life.

JT's expression shifted slightly, the corners of his mouth tightening as if the question had caught him off guard. "A bit of the same, I suppose," he replied after a beat. "I've been working non-stop, and my family encouraged me to take this trip. It's... a way to unwind."

"Unwind," she repeated softly, then added, "We could all use that, I think."

He nodded, and they both fell into a comfortable silence, the kind that felt natural and easy, as though they had known each other far longer than the mere minutes that had passed.

"Well," JT said finally, his smile returning, "I'll let you get back to your evening. But perhaps we could get together for a coffee or a drink tomorrow? I'd like to hear more about your art. I've always admired people who can create something beautiful from their imagination."

Drusilla's heart skipped a beat. She wasn't sure why, but the idea of talking with him again felt like an invitation to something more. Something new.

"I'd like that," she said, her voice barely above a whisper.

As the reception winds down, JT and Drusilla exchange one last look before parting ways. They both have that lingering sense of curiosity, knowing they'll see each other again soon.

As Drusilla turns to walk away, she feels a slight flutter of nerves. The reception was short but charged, and she's unsure if she should have stayed in the conversation longer. Just as she reaches the door, she glances back, almost without thinking. JT is still standing by the bar, his posture relaxed but his gaze fixed on her as she walks away. Their eyes meet briefly, and there's an unspoken acknowledgment between them—something that hints at future possibilities. Drusilla

7

feels a small twinge of heat in her cheeks, but she quickly looks away, trying to mask the effect JT's gaze had on her.

As JT watches her leave, noting how her posture shifts when she looks back at him. He doesn't feel self-conscious about it; instead, he's intrigued by the way she carries herself, the spark in her eyes, and the mystery she seems to radiate. He catches himself staring a little longer than he intended but justifies it as curiosity. She is a very beautiful woman. He wonders if she will seek him out again, or if their initial meeting was a fluke. Something about her stuck with him, though— her wit, her independent air. He tells himself it's probably just another passing encounter, but deep down, he's eager to see where it goes. After all, he's only been single for a few months.

Chapter 2
The Ship Sails

The first day at sea is full of new experiences—exploring the ship, getting to know the other passengers, and soaking in the excitement of the adventure ahead. But throughout the day, Drusilla finds herself glancing around, half-expecting to see JT somewhere on the ship. When evening falls and she's retired to her cabin, she feels a bit of disappointment at the missed opportunity to run into him. *Maybe it was just a fleeting attraction, nothing more. I shouldn't have expected to see him again so soon, but... something felt different. It would've been nice to see him again...*

JT, equally busy with the start of the cruise, had imagined that he would run into Drusilla at some point during the day. He could even picture the easy conversation they might have shared. But as the day draws to a close and he finds himself alone in his cabin, he feels the same slight sense of letdown. He didn't want to admit it, but he had been looking forward to seeing her again. *I guess it was just a one-time thing... it's not like I expected us to meet every day. But still, it would've been nice to have that second chance to talk to her. Maybe tomorrow...*

The Poolside Encounter

The following morning, JT grabs a coffee and heads to the pool deck, the warmth of the sun on his skin and the gentle sound of the water lapping at the edge. As he walks toward the pool, he scans the area, his eyes landing on Drusilla. She's lounging in a chair, a book in hand, her face relaxed and content. The sunlight catches her features just right, and for a moment, JT's breath catches in his throat. His first thought is simple: *She's so beautiful. There's something about her... she's got this effortless grace. Even here, under the sun, she seems... untouchable.*

Drusilla is so absorbed in her book that she doesn't notice JT approaching. Her focus is on the pages in front of her, her mind wandering in the peaceful silence of the moment. But when she finally looks up and sees JT standing there, a slight smile plays at the corners of her lips. *So, he finally found me. Maybe this isn't such a coincidence after all...*

JT, not one to hesitate, flashes her a warm, easy smile as he steps closer. "I didn't think I'd find you here. Looks like I'm not the only one who enjoys the morning sun." Drusilla raises an eyebrow playfully, closing her book and shifting slightly in her chair. "You've got good timing. I was starting to think this cruise was a little too big for two people to ever cross paths again." JT smiles and says, "Guess we're lucky then. Mind if I join you?" Drusilla quickly replied, "not at all."

JT slides into the chair next to her, setting down his coffee and towel. The conversation starts off casually. They've both noticed the attraction between them, and the atmosphere around the pool seems to heighten that. JT asks, "What's the book? You seem so lost in it." Drusilla smiles and says, "It's just something light, a romance novel."

The banter flows easily between them as they talk, their chemistry more evident than before. JT's relaxed demeanor allows Drusilla to feel more comfortable, and she starts to open up more, sharing her thoughts on the cruise and her art.

"Are you from New York," Drusilla asks. Yes, I've lived in the city for the past 17 years. "How about you?" "No, I'm from Boston. I've lived there my entire life." You know, New York's not so bad... for a city," Drusilla says playfully. JT responds, "I'll take that as a compliment. What about Boston, though? Is it really as cold as they say?" Drusilla replies, "Only in the winter."

After more lighthearted banter, JT shifts the conversation to something more personal. "So... you're here for a new start, right? You must have been through a lot before all this." Drusilla responds, "Yeah... It's been a difficult few months. My mother thought that I needed a change of scenery, so here I am."

JT feels the weight of her words. He wonders what she means by "difficult few months."

Getting a bit more serious, JT says, "It's funny, isn't it? How life can throw you into situations that leave you questioning... everything. I was married for 17 years." He pauses, reflecting for a moment. "I thought it was forever, but in the end, I guess I was wrong."

Drusilla paused for a moment, then said, "I get it. I was in a committed relationship with someone for eight years. We had a good thing going, but... he wasn't ready for anything more, and I... I was ready to move forward. We weren't on the same page, you know? I didn't want to wake up in ten years and wonder why I wasted so much time in a relationship that wasn't going anywhere."

As they both shared their stories, they realized the common thread between them: They both wanted more in their relationships, and neither partner was willing to compromise as much as it would take to make things work.

Drusilla added, "He never wanted to take that next step. I wanted more... but he was fine with the way things were. Maybe that's what really got to me. I needed to know I was wanted in a way that felt real, that felt special, that felt like I wanted this for the rest of my life."

JT responded, "I hear you. That's what I felt too. It's not that I didn't love her, but I think I started feeling like I wasn't really seen anymore. Like... I wasn't part of her world. Like her mind was always somewhere else. In the beginning, I felt like it was going to be that way forever. As it turned out, I was wrong. I didn't want to waste any more of my time or hers in a marriage that felt so empty."

10

There was a pause in the conversation, then Drusilla responded, "Yeah... it's that feeling of being invisible, even when you're right there. Like you're two people living separate lives."

There's a quiet understanding between them now. Their shared experiences of being in long-term relationships that didn't work out because they weren't truly seen or valued by their partners allow them to relate in a way that feels deeper than just surface-level attraction.

This moment of shared vulnerability helps solidify the connection between them. The initial attraction is no longer just physical; it's emotional and intellectual. They've both been through something similar, and that mutual understanding sets a solid foundation for their relationship to grow.

After their deep conversation by the pool, there's a comfortable silence between them, and the time feels right to suggest continuing their connection. JT, eager to keep the momentum going, breaks the silence with a casual suggestion, "I'm really enjoying our conversation, Drusilla. How about we meet up for a drink later, before dinner? Just a little more time to chat." Drusilla smiled and said, "I'd like that. It's nice to talk to someone who actually listens." JT happily responded, "Same here. Let's say... around six, before the dinner crowd hits? The bar up on the deck sounds perfect." "It's a date," Drusilla said with a playful smile.

As they agree to meet later, there's an unspoken sense of anticipation. They both know this isn't just a casual drink—it's a chance to get to know each other more, to see if the connection they've felt so far could turn into something more.

As they part ways to head back to their respective cabins and get ready for the evening, there's an excitement in the air. Both of them think about what their time together could lead to, but neither wants to rush into anything. They're both savoring the slow buildup.

First Spark

JT arrived a few minutes before Drusilla and took a seat at the end of the bar. He glanced around the room to make sure she hadn't arrived before him. Just then, Drusilla enters the bar, the room seems to quiet for a moment. JT's eyes lock on her immediately. The soft, golden light of the bar creates an almost ethereal glow around her. She's wearing a simple, yet stunning black dress that flatters her figure, her hair falling in gentle waves around her shoulders. He feels like the entire room stops to watch her walk in. She is, without a doubt, the most beautiful woman in the room. He thinks: *She's incredible... I've never seen anyone quite like her before. It's not just her beauty—it's the way she carries herself, the way she doesn't try to impress anyone. She's effortlessly captivating and so sure of herself.*

As she spots him, their eyes meet, and she smiles, making her way over to him with a graceful stride. This is the first time she's truly felt attracted to someone since her breakup, and the realization gives her a little thrill. She can't help but noticed that he was dressed to perfection in a crisp white shirt and dark blazer, a sophisticated yet approachable look. "You look stunning," he said, his voice warm and sincere. It was the kind of compliment that made her feel like the only woman in the room.

For a brief moment, her mind drifts to Sam, and she can't help but compare the two. Her ex was athletic, always in casual sportswear, often dressed like he'd just come from the gym. That had been fine at the time, but now, seeing JT, she realizes how much she appreciates the subtle elegance he exudes. There's something about the way he presents himself that feels... different.

"Thank you," Drusilla replied, her voice soft, as she returned his smile. Her heart skipped a beat at his words, and it only intensified when he reached forward to touch her arm as she took a seat next to him at the bar. His touch sent a shiver of excitement through her, and she realized how much she had been hoping to feel that connection between them.

They ordered champagne, and the conversation quickly fell into a comfortable rhythm. They spoke about the cruise, about places they wanted to visit, and then, as the night wore on, they began to open up about themselves. It was a conversation that felt surprisingly intimate, given how little time they had spent together.

When the waiter arrived to take them to their table, JT, always the gentleman, stood first, offering his hand to Drusilla. "Shall we?" he asked, his voice low but filled with promise.

She smiled, feeling something stir inside her as she placed her hand in his. As they approached their table, JT stepped forward to pull out her chair, his manners impeccable. He had no idea how much the gesture meant to her, but she appreciated it more than he could know. It was a small thing, but it made her feel like she mattered, the kind of simple act that feels thoughtful and respectful. She's not used to this kind of treatment. *This... this feels different. It's not just what he does, but how he does it. It's respectful. Thoughtful. I love that he's a gentleman in ways I didn't even realize I missed.* Sam had never been one to make such small, considerate gestures. His actions were always about convenience, not care.

Drusilla smiles as she lowers herself into the chair, catching JT's gaze. There's a warmth in his eyes, a quiet confidence that makes her feel at ease. She can't help but appreciate this side of him—the side that's careful, kind, and genuinely attentive. "You know, not every man would do that these days. I'm impressed." Smiling, JT said, "I was raised to believe in manners. I think the little things matter."

Their conversation flows easily after that, and Drusilla can't help but feel more at ease, noticing JT seems to be the kind of man who values respect in even the simplest actions.

After sitting down, their conversation picks up right where they left off, this time with a more playful and relaxed vibe. The earlier heaviness of their shared stories is now replaced with a lightness. The chemistry between them is undeniable, and they begin to banter about their favorite parts of the cruise so far.

"I never thought I'd enjoy a cruise this much. I thought it'd just be a break, but it's... kind of magical," Drusilla said.

JT responded, "Yeah, the whole world feels different when you're out on the water. Like, anything's possible. It's strange, but it feels like a fresh start."

Drusilla laughs softly, "Funny, I thought the same thing. It's like the world's smaller in some ways, but there's so much more to discover."

"Exactly." He pauses, then adds, almost casually, "Do you think this is your fresh start? The cruise, I mean?"

Her smile softens, and she takes a moment to think, "I hope so. I'm not running away from my past, but I think I'm ready for something new. To figure out what I really want, not just what I've been comfortable with."

Nodding in understanding, "I get that. I feel the same way. It's not about escaping, but about... rethinking everything. Looking forward."

After this exchange, there's a quiet moment between them. The sound of soft music from a nearby lounge and the sound of other passengers creates a peaceful atmosphere, and they both settle into the ease of being in each other's company. Their connection feels deeper now—not just based on attraction but on mutual respect for what they've been through and what they're both looking for.

Dinner was a slow indulgence, the kind where the world around them faded, and it was just the two of them sharing stories, laughs, and more than a few meaningful glances. By the time the main course was finished, they were both a little tipsy from the wine and a lot more comfortable than either had expected. Their laughter filled the room, and for once, they didn't care that they were being a bit loud. Their connection had become undeniable, and neither could ignore it.

As they sat back after dessert, JT glanced at his watch and smiled. "I think we've made enough of a scene for tonight," he said, his tone teasing but affectionate.

"I think it's because I'm so fascinating," Drusilla replied with a flirty grin, feeling a warmth spread through her at the way he was looking at her.

"I wouldn't argue with that," JT said, his voice low and sincere. He reached across the table to touch her hand, and when their fingers met, Drusilla felt the spark once again. *What is this? It's like a spark every time he touches me. I haven't felt this... this alive in so long. It's almost like I'm rediscovering how to feel this way.*

JT, too, seems to be enjoying the easy camaraderie, his occasional touches causing a warmth to spread through him. There's something about Drusilla—her humor, her grace, the way she lets her guard down just enough for him to see the real her—that draws him in deeper. He can't help but smile at the ease between them. *She's amazing... funny, smart, and so... beautiful. I can't believe how easy this is. I haven't had a conversation like this in years.*

By the time dinner ends, neither of them wants the night to be over. The connection they've built over the course of the evening has left them both wanting more. As they leave the restaurant, JT offers to walk Drusilla back to her cabin, and she agrees with a soft smile.

As they wandered out onto the deck of the ship, the night was cool and the sea breeze made her hair flutter around her face. JT seemed to notice her shiver and, without a word, slipped off his jacket and placed it over her shoulders. The warmth of his jacket surrounded her, and for a moment, she simply closed her eyes, feeling the weight of his gesture settle in her chest.

"Better?" he asked, his voice gentle.

"Much," she replied, leaning a little closer to him. There was something about his presence that made her feel safe and desired all at once.

They walked together in silence for a while, both lost in their thoughts, the moonlight glistening off the water and the sound of the ship's engines in the distance. When they reached her cabin, Drusilla paused, wondering what would come next. She turned to face him, feeling an almost magnetic pull between them.

JT took her hands in his, his grip warm and steady. "I really enjoyed tonight," he said, his voice soft but sincere. "I hope we can do it again."

Drusilla smiled, her heart thumping in her chest. "Me too," she said, her voice quiet but filled with meaning.

He leaned in and kissed her lightly on the cheek, his lips warm against her skin. For a moment, she felt a twinge of disappointment—was that all it was going to be? But then, she realized how much she appreciated the gentleness of the moment. It was something she hadn't had in a long time.

"I'll see you tomorrow," she said, her voice steady as she pulled back slightly, her fingers brushing his chest. The touch was enough to make her heart race all over again.

JT smiled, a little unsure of what was going through her mind. "Goodnight, Drusilla," he said, "I had a wonderful time tonight."

As the door clicked shut behind her, Drusilla leaned back against it, trying to steady her breath. The night had been perfect, and she knew that tomorrow, it could be even better. She hadn't expected to feel this way so soon, but there was something about JT that had drawn her in completely.

As JT walked away, a wave of regret washed over him. He had felt such a connection with Drusilla, but he hadn't wanted to rush anything. He didn't want to seem presumptuous or pushy, but part of him wondered if he had made a mistake by not staying with her.

He takes a deep breath, trying to shake off the feeling of second-guessing himself. Tomorrow, he tells himself....is another day.

Chapter 3

Port of Call: Bermuda

As Drusilla woke the following morning, the soft light of the early sun streamed through her cabin's window. She rose from the bed and made her way to the balcony, drawn by the peaceful view of Hamilton, Bermuda. The town looked like something out of a painting, with its charming pastel buildings bathed in the golden glow of the sun. It was as if the entire town was waking up to greet her.

The faint sound of waves against the ship's hull created a calming backdrop as she took in the view. She breathed in deeply, savoring the fresh ocean air. There was a sense of possibility in the morning light, a promise of new adventures, and Drusilla couldn't help but smile.

Just then, an announcement crackled over the intercom, echoing through the ship.

"Good morning, everyone! We're approaching Hamilton, Bermuda. We will be anchoring offshore. There will be three shuttle boats departing shortly for day trips into town. We look forward to a wonderful day on the island!"

Her heart fluttered with excitement, and she had already begun to plan what she might do once onshore. Before she could think too much about it, the phone on her desk rang.

"Good morning, beautiful, it's JT. Would you like to join me for breakfast on deck? I'd love to start the day with you."

Drusilla's heart skipped a beat. She was excited, but at the same time, a flutter of nerves danced in her stomach. "I'd love that. I'll meet you there."

Within minutes, she was dressed and ready, the idea of spending more time with JT making her feel both giddy and excited. She made her way to the outdoor dining area, and when she arrived, she saw him right away. JT was already seated at a small two-top table next to the rail, his face lit by the morning sun as he looked out over the island.

As Drusilla approached, JT stood with a warm smile. He kissed her lightly on the cheek, and as always, pulled her chair out for her, making her feel like the most important person in the world. She loved that he was so thoughtful and considerate, a refreshing change from what she had been used to.

"Good morning," he said. "I'm so glad you could join me."

Smiling, sitting down, Drusilla said, "Thanks for inviting me."

They exchanged smiles before settling into comfortable conversation, their laughter and easy chatter filling the air. As they sipped their Starbucks coffee and broke off pieces of flaky croissant, the world seemed to fade away. The beauty of the island, the warmth of the morning, and the undeniable connection between them made for the perfect moment.

The stillness of the morning was only broken by the occasional sound of the ship's horn or the distant chatter of other passengers, but even with all that, Drusilla couldn't help but feel that she and JT were in their own little bubble, sharing something special.

As they sipped their coffee, the conversation shifted from easy pleasantries to plans for the day ahead. Drusilla listened intently as JT described the sights and experiences of Bermuda, a place he had visited before. He was quick to mention the famous beaches, the vibrant colors of the island's colonial architecture, and the charming streets of Hamilton.

JT said, "There's a little cafe I like near the docks, where they make the best iced coffee. If you're in the mood for something simple, I'd recommend that. But for a day like today, I think you'll want to explore a bit more of the island."

"I'm excited," Drusilla responded smiling. "I've never been to Bermuda before. It all looks so beautiful, like something out of a dream."

Her eyes scanned the view again, taking in the pastel-colored buildings, the lush greenery, and the clear blue waters beyond. It was everything she had imagined and more.

JT, happy to see her so excited, said, "I think you'll love it here. And we have plenty of time to wander. The last shuttle back to the boat is at 9:30 pm, so we can make a day of it."

The idea of spending the entire day with JT felt like the perfect way to immerse herself in the island's charm. She felt a flutter of excitement at the thought of exploring it all—especially with him by her side.

"That sounds wonderful. What do you suggest we do first?"

JT was happy to take charge. "We could take a stroll through the town—there's a few shops and galleries that I think you'd really like. I know you're an artist, and there are a few local painters whose work I think would inspire you. But if you'd like something a little more... adventurous, there's a spot where you can rent scooters or bikes and ride out to the beaches. It's a bit more free-spirited."

Drusilla grinning, "I think I like the sound of that. Let's do both. We can take a stroll through the shops first, and then head out to the beach after that."

JT nodded, happy to see the excitement in her eyes. As they continued discussing their plans, he paused for a moment, his eyes scanning the horizon before turning back to her with a smile.

"There's also a place I'd like to take you for dinner later—Four Ways. It's one of the best restaurants on the island, five stars. It's got a great atmosphere, and the food is incredible. I thought it might be the perfect way to end the day."

Drusilla responded, "It sounds perfect. I've heard of it. A little fancy, but I think it will

be fun."

JT smiled, visibly relieved. He wanted the day to be special—after all, this was the kind of memory he wanted to create, not just for himself, but for Drusilla as well. He had a feeling that this was only the beginning of a very memorable journey. "I think we'll both enjoy it. It's nice to mix a little adventure with a little luxury."

The two of them finished their croissants and coffee, their minds buzzing with the possibilities of the day ahead. There was a sense of anticipation in the air, the feeling that the island was waiting for them, ready to offer its secrets to the two of them as they discovered it together.

After breakfast, Drusilla and JT made their way off the ship, feeling the warm Bermuda breeze as they stepped onto the dock. The town of Hamilton was just a short distance away, its pastel buildings reflecting the sunlight as they strolled down the charming streets. The air was filled with the scent of saltwater and blooming tropical flowers, a perfect day for discovering the island.

Drusilla and JT dressed for both comfort and style, perfectly suited for a leisurely stroll through the charming streets and shops. Drusilla opts for a breezy, flowy summer dress, in a soft pastel that hits just above the knee. The light fabric will keep her cool under the warm Bermuda sun, and her chic, comfortable sandals will make it easy to walk around. She completes the look with a wide-brimmed hat to protect her from the sun, oversized sunglasses for a touch of glamour, and a structured handbag in a neutral tone, practical yet stylish. Simple gold jewelry, a delicate necklace and hoop earrings, add the finishing touch to her ensemble.

JT, on the other hand, keeps things relaxed yet polished with a well-fitted short-sleeve linen shirt in a soft blue. His slim-fit chinos in beige offer the perfect balance between casual and sophisticated, while his stylish boat shoes ensure comfort as they walk through the town. A pair of aviator sunglasses shield his eyes, and a classy wristwatch adds a subtle touch of luxury.

JT tells her, "This is one of my favorite islands. The architecture here has such a unique charm, don't you think?"

Drusilla nodded, taking in the vibrant colors of the buildings that seemed to leap from a postcard. She couldn't resist snapping a few pictures, her artist's eye caught by the way the sunlight played across the town's buildings.

Drusilla: "I love how everything looks so alive here. It's almost like stepping into a painting."

They wandered through the local shops, Drusilla admiring the intricate crafts and jewelry that lined the windows. She stopped to chat with a local artisan, who showed her a selection of handmade ceramic pieces, which made Drusilla smile. She felt an instant connection to the work, and the artist, sensing this, encouraged her to try her hand at a pottery workshop on the island.

Drusilla: "Maybe I'll try it out before we leave. It would be amazing to create something inspired by this place."

20

JT: "I think you'd like that. Plus, it'd be something special to take home with you."

The two of them continued exploring, eventually finding a small park with benches under a canopy of trees. They sat and chatted about everything from their travels to their favorite types of food. JT mentioned how much he enjoyed exploring new places but hadn't had much time for relaxation recently. He was surprised by how easy it was to talk to Drusilla, a refreshing change from his more guarded nature back home.

JT: "It's been nice, this quiet pace. I don't know why I waited so long to take time for myself."

Drusilla: "Sometimes, it takes something like this to shake us out of the routine. I'm glad we're both here now."

As they finished their drinks, Drusilla's eyes sparkled with excitement.

Drusilla: "What do you think about renting scooters or bikes like you mentioned earlier?"

JT grinned, happy to see her excitement.

JT: "Let's do it. I know a spot where we can pick them up. The views from the coastline are amazing—you'll love it."

They rented two scooters and set off, weaving through the narrow streets of Hamilton and out toward the more secluded beaches. The wind in their hair and the sun on their faces, the ride felt liberating, and they both couldn't help but laugh as they tried to keep up with each other.

As they approached the beach, the sight took Drusilla's breath away. The water was a brilliant turquoise, the soft white sand stretching out before them. They parked the scooters and walked down to the shore, dipping their toes into the cool water.

Drusilla: "This is perfect. It's like Paradise."

They spent the next few hours lounging on the beach, chatting, and enjoying the beauty of the island. Drusilla buried her feet in the sand, feeling the stress of the past months fade away with every wave that rolled in. JT watched her, mesmerized by how at peace she seemed. He had never seen someone so completely lost in the moment.

As the afternoon sun began to dip lower in the sky, they packed up and rode back to Hamilton. Their hearts were light, their minds full of memories from the day together.

JT: "How about we head back to the ship to freshen up before dinner? We've got a little time before our reservation."

Drusilla: "Sounds like a plan. I'm looking forward to it."

They made their way back to the ship, both content with how their day had unfolded. Drusilla couldn't help but feel a growing affection for JT. Something about the way he cared for her, made her feel special, and showed her new places she had never been before—it was all so natural.

After a day spent exploring the vibrant streets of Hamilton and relaxing on the beach, JT and Drusilla return to the ship to prepare for a memorable dinner. Drusilla, wanting to look effortlessly chic for the upscale evening, chooses a sleek, sleeveless black dress that falls just below the knee. The dress hugs her cute figure, but the soft, flowing fabric adds a touch of movement as she walks. She pairs it with a pair of strappy, high-heeled sandals in silver, the metallic shimmer adding a bit of glamour to her look. Her hair is styled in loose, soft waves, and she wears a subtle touch of makeup—just enough to highlight her features. She accessorizes with simple yet elegant jewelry, opting for a pair of drop earrings and a delicate bracelet that catches the light. To complete the look, she carries a small clutch in a soft, neutral shade.

JT, wanting to match the restaurant's sophisticated atmosphere, goes for a sharp, well-tailored look. He wears a dark navy blazer over a crisp, white dress shirt with a slight sheen to it, giving off a polished, refined vibe. The blazer is perfectly fitted, and he leaves the top button of his shirt undone for a relaxed, approachable touch. He pairs it with dark gray trousers, slim-cut and tailored to perfection. His shoes are sleek black leather oxfords, polished to a high shine, and he wears a classic black leather belt to match. His wristwatch, understated yet elegant, peeks out from under his cuff, and his hair is neatly styled, adding to his dashing appearance. Together, they look like the perfect pair—Drusilla in her elegant black dress and JT in his refined yet effortlessly cool ensemble—ready to enjoy an unforgettable evening at Bermuda's finest restaurant.

They meet in the ship's grand lobby. JT asks, "Ready for a little luxury?"

Drusilla smiled, her heart fluttering. "Absolutely. I think we've earned it."

As the sun began to set, painting the sky with vibrant hues of orange and pink, Drusilla and JT stood at the rail of the shuttle boat, gazing out over the shimmering water. The island of Bermuda, now bathed in the soft light of evening, looked even more magical than it had earlier in the day. The gentle hum of the boat's engine and the salty sea breeze made the moment feel suspended in time.

JT turned to Drusilla, the look in his eyes soft yet intense, and for a brief moment, it felt like the world had narrowed to just the two of them. The closeness between them was undeniable—something unspoken that had been building throughout the day. He reached out, his hand cupping her chin gently, guiding her gaze back to him.

For a heartbeat, they both paused, just taking in the closeness, the shared warmth between them. And then, with the ocean as their witness and the sun's final rays casting a golden glow on them, JT leaned in, pressing his lips gently against hers.

Drusilla's breath caught at the unexpected tenderness of the kiss. She hadn't expected it to feel this right, this perfect. She felt the pressure of his lips, soft yet lingering, holding her in that perfect moment. The world seemed to stop. She closed her eyes, allowing herself to savor the moment, to feel every second.

After a few seconds, JT pulled back slightly, just enough to look into her eyes, his lips still so close to hers.

Softly, he said, "I've wanted to do that all day."

Drusilla's heart raced as she smiled up at him, a mix of excitement and warmth flooding her chest. Without thinking, she reached up and pulled him toward her again, this time kissing him

23

more urgently, more passionately. It was as if the kiss itself was a release—a way to express the emotions that had been building between them all day.

JT responded with equal intensity, his arms wrapping around her, pulling her closer against him. The cool breeze of the evening kissed their skin as they stood there, locked in the kiss, their connection deepening with each second.

Time seemed to slow as they snuggled against the rail, the only sounds the gentle splash of water against the boat and the rhythmic beat of their hearts. The world around them was slipping away, and all that mattered was the warmth of each other's embrace, the feeling of something new and exciting blossoming between them.

The shuttle docked, the soft thud of the boat against the pier marking the end of their boat ride. But it wasn't the end of the evening; it was just the beginning. They still had dinner to look forward to.

JT *(with a smile)*, "Shall we? It's a short walk to Four Ways."

Drusilla *(grinning, a little breathless)*, "I can't wait."

They walked together, hand in hand, as the evening unfolded before them. The island lights twinkled in the distance, and they both knew that the connection they had just shared was only the beginning of something special.

As they walked toward the restaurant, hand in hand, Drusilla's excitement began to fade for a brief moment. A nagging thought crept into her mind—*Is this just happening because we're both rebounding from our past relationships?* She had been through so much with her ex, and JT's situation seemed just as complicated. She had to admit that part of her wanted to believe in what they were building, but there was still a flicker of doubt. Was this just the need to fill a void?

For a second, she felt a little unsure of herself, wondering if her feelings were clouded by the past. But just as quickly, she felt JT's arm slip around her shoulders, pulling her closer to him as they walked. His touch was warm and comforting, and the slight pressure of his hand against her back reassured her.

No, this is real, she thought, pushing away the doubt. She looked up at him and smiled, the warmth of his embrace melting away the uncertainty. There was something about him—something that felt more genuine than just a simple distraction from the past.

JT turned to her, noticing the brief change in her expression. Without missing a beat, he squeezed her shoulder gently, his eyes soft and understanding.

He asked, "You okay?"

Drusilla nodded, feeling a rush of warmth at his concern. "Yeah. Just thinking. It's been a whirlwind today."

Smiling, JT responded, "Well, let's keep the whirlwind going. Dinner's going to be great."

Her heart fluttered again as they continued toward the restaurant. The earlier uncertainty was gone, replaced with the certainty that whatever was happening between them was more than just a rebound. If it was a fresh start, she was ready for it.

As they approached the host stand to check in, Drusilla's eyes were drawn to the walls, which were adorned with black-and-white photographs of dignitaries and celebrities. Kings, presidents, and even one of Princess Diana with Prince Charles. Smiling, Drusilla paused for a moment, taking in the history of the place.

Now it all made sense. *No wonder JT had suggested this spot,* she thought. The place was clearly a landmark, an institution where the rich and powerful dined. If these pictures were anything to go by, it was a place that carried weight, a place where memories had been made by people who knew the value of fine dining.

(murmuring, more to herself), "Wow, look at all these photos."

JT, grinning, clearly pleased by her reaction, "Yeah, it's a pretty special spot. It's been around for years."

Drusilla smiled at the thought of this being one of JT's favorite places. *It must be good,* she mused. If kings and celebrities ate here, it was definitely something to experience. She was already excited, knowing that the night was going to be even more memorable than she had imagined.

As they checked in, the host smiled warmly and led them to their table, tucked in a quiet corner with a perfect view of the island's twinkling lights. The ambiance was intimate and elegant, with soft lighting casting a romantic glow over the room.

As they settled into their seats, the waiter handed JT the wine list, and he made his selection with confidence. Smiling at Drusilla, "We'll have a bottle of Cristal, please. And we'll need to be out by 9:00 to catch the last shuttle back to the ship."

The waiter nodded, confirming their request and noting the time. Moments later, a sommelier appeared, holding the bottle of champagne. He expertly uncorked it with a soft pop, pouring a small amount into JT's glass for him to taste.

JT took a careful sip, savoring the crisp bubbles before nodding in approval. "Perfect, thank you."

The sommelier proceeded to pour a generous amount into their glasses, and as he left, JT turned to Drusilla with a grin, "This is one of my favorites, but it's better sharing it with such a beautiful woman."

Drusilla smiled, watching the bubbles rise in her glass. The elegance of the moment wasn't lost on her. She clinked her glass lightly against his, "To new beginnings."

They both took a sip, savoring the crisp, refreshing taste of the champagne. As they glanced out the window at the twinkling lights of Bermuda, the soft hum of conversation and the clink of glasses in the background, Drusilla felt herself relax into the moment, letting go of any worries. This was exactly what she needed.

As the evening progressed and their conversation flowed effortlessly, Drusilla felt a sense of peace she hadn't experienced in a long time. The warm glow of the restaurant, the clinking of silverware, and the soft hum of conversation around them created a cozy, intimate atmosphere. But then, just as she was taking a sip of her wine, her phone buzzed from inside her purse.

Startled, she grabbed her phone and was surprised to see a message from Sam.

"I miss you. Can we meet up? I've been thinking about you..."

Drusilla's heart seemed to stop for a moment as memories of the past flooded her mind— the long nights spent wondering where he was, the gut-wrenching feeling of never being enough. Her fingers hovered over the phone, the temptation to reply briefly taking hold. But then she set the phone down, feeling the weight of the moment. She knew better now.

She turned back to JT, offering a warm smile despite the rush of emotions. "I'm sorry, I didn't mean to interrupt our evening."

She reached for her glass of champagne, trying to shake off the tension. "How about a toast? To a wonderful day in paradise. And what a perfect way to start a weeks-long voyage."

JT smiled and raised his glass, their eyes meeting in an unspoken connection. "To new beginnings."

They clinked their glasses, and Drusilla took a deep breath, letting the cold taste of the champagne fill her. Her thoughts returned to JT—how easy it was to be with him, how he made her forget everything else and simply enjoy the moment. She felt lighter, happier than she had in months.

After finishing their meal, JT called for the check. He paid with a quick, practiced gesture, and then, as if the evening had been one big adventure, they stood up together.

The wine had gone straight to their heads, and they both found themselves laughing as they made their way out of the restaurant, a little tipsy and giddy from the evening. They hustled toward the port, holding hands and stumbling slightly as they tried to keep up the pace, still caught in the joy of the night.

Grinning, his arm around her waist as they hurried along, "Guess we better make sure we don't miss the boat, huh?"

Drusilla laughed, her heart light as they rushed toward the shuttle, eager to continue the night. The city lights of Bermuda glimmered in the distance, and Drusilla couldn't help but feel like everything seemed to be falling into place for her.

As the shuttle arrived back at the ship, the night air was still warm, and the excitement of their day ashore lingered between them. The lights from the ship illuminated the harbor, casting a soft glow over the water. Drusilla turned to JT, a playful smile on her lips, "I'd love to freshen up before we continue the night—maybe the nightclub?"

JT nodding, his eyes lighting up at the thought of more time together. "Sounds perfect. I'll walk you to your cabin."

They walked side by side, the sounds of the ship's engines softly humming in the background. As they approached her cabin, Drusilla slowed her steps and glanced over at JT, her heart racing a little faster than usual. There was something about the night, about him, that felt different, and she couldn't ignore the pull between them.

Drusilla wondered if this would be the moment they take the next step with their budding relationship, but she didn't want to rush anything and certainly didn't want to do something that would make him think that she was just interested in a "one night stand" type of thing.

When they arrived at her cabin, JT also wondered if this would be the time that they took the next step in their relationship. After seventeen years with the same woman, he was a bit out of practice at this type of thing. He wanted to show Drusilla that he was a gentleman.

Drusilla took her key card out of her purse, turned to JT and as their eyes met, he put his hands on her waist, leaned in and kissed her softly on her lips. When he pulled away, he said, "I had a wonderful day. I'm so looking forward to spending more time with you. I'm not used to this kind of thing. I know that I don't want to do anything to change the direction this all seems to be going. Can we meet for breakfast and plan another day together."

Drusilla was a bit relieved. She too had only been with one other guy for the past eight years and wasn't sure how to react to the moment. She enjoyed JT so much. She felt something in her heart for him and anticipated what would come next, but she wanted to get to know him better, to understand more about his past. She also wanted him to know her better. She put her arms around his shoulders, reached up on her tip toes and kissed him. "I'd love that," she replied.

As the door clicked shut, the sudden silence in the room hit Drusilla. Her eyes misted over, and before she could stop it, the tears came. She wasn't sad—far from it. It was a mixture of joy, excitement, and gratitude that overwhelmed her, the kind of cry she hadn't had in years. She felt an intense rush of emotions, each tear a reflection of how deeply she was falling for this man in such a short time.

She wiped her eyes with the back of her hand and laughed softly to herself. Who could have predicted this? When she booked the cruise, she was simply looking for a fresh start, a way to escape the rut she'd been in, and perhaps gain some clarity about her future. She never imagined she'd meet someone like JT, someone who made her feel so seen, so wanted, so alive.

In the short span of just 48 hours, it felt like she had experienced more joy, more excitement, more connection than she had in the previous eight years of her life. Eight years spent in a relationship that was comfortable, yes, but ultimately unfulfilling. Was this what real love felt like? It was intense, all-consuming, yet so natural. Every touch, every word, every moment they shared felt like it was meant to happen.

Drusilla stood up and moved to the window, looking out at the sparkling blue water. She felt a sense of peace wash over her, mixed with the fluttering of something new, something she hadn't felt in so long. She didn't know where things were going with JT, but she looked forward to finding out.

With a smile on her lips, she took a deep breath and wiped the last of the tears from her eyes, feeling more certain than ever that this trip could change everything.

As Drusilla stood by the window, a thought crossed her mind that brought a warm, grateful smile to her face. She was so very thankful to her mother for treating her to this trip. It was

29

something Drusilla could never have afforded on her own. The idea of spending this kind of money on herself—traveling the world, staying in beautiful accommodations, dining at five-star restaurants—seemed like a far-off dream just a few weeks ago. But here she was, living it. And to think that her mother had made it possible, just because she wanted her to have an experience that could change her life.

Drusilla felt a deep sense of appreciation for her mother, who had always been her greatest supporter. They had always shared a special bond, but this gesture—this incredible gift—was something Drusilla would cherish forever. Her mother had been so generous, and Drusilla couldn't wait to tell her about everything that had already happened. She wanted to tell her how, just days into the trip, she had met someone who made her feel alive again—someone who understood her in ways she hadn't thought possible.

Her thoughts of JT were interrupted by the sudden rush of emotion that overcame her. She hadn't expected any of this—certainly not so soon. But she felt a sense of warmth in her heart. She had taken a leap, stepping out of her comfort zone, and it was paying off.

She picked up her phone and scrolled through her contacts until she found her mother's name. Her thumb hovered over the screen, and she smiled to herself. She wanted to share everything: the beautiful island, the incredible food, but most of all, how she was starting to feel like she was finally experiencing the life she'd longed for. But she didn't want to just tell her. She wanted her mother to feel the excitement, the joy, the newness of it all—just as Drusilla was feeling it.

After a moment's hesitation, she tapped out a message:

> *"Mom, you won't believe what's happening here! This trip is already more than I ever imagined, and I'm so thankful for this opportunity. I've met someone who makes me feel like I'm finally living again. Can't wait to share everything when I get back! Love you."*

She hit send, feeling a surge of excitement and anticipation for the conversation they'd have when she returned. Her mother would be thrilled.

With a deep breath, Drusilla glanced around her room, feeling the flutter of new possibilities in the air. Everything was changing—her heart, her world, her future. And it felt like the beginning of something extraordinary.

The next morning

When Drusilla arrived at the rooftop café for breakfast, the atmosphere felt entirely different. There was a sense of ease, a quiet understanding between her and JT that hadn't been there before. They were becoming a couple now. No more wondering, no more questions. It felt natural, like they had already known each other for years, even though their time together had been so short.

As she approached the table, she couldn't help but smile, a soft, contented smile that reached her eyes. JT stood up to greet her, as he always did, but today, there was something more intimate about the way he held her gaze, the way his smile lingered. After the closeness of their evening together, the connection they shared now was deeper, more grounded. It wasn't just about attraction or chemistry anymore. It was about a shared experience, a new chapter unfolding. He kissed her cheek, "Good morning."

They sat down, and as they looked over the menu, the conversation flowed effortlessly between them. There was no need for the tentative small talk they had shared the previous few days. They both knew what they wanted now. JT took Drusilla's hand across the table, his fingers gently wrapping around hers as if he'd been doing it for years.

Their laughter was more comfortable now, less shy, more in sync. As the server approached, they ordered without hesitation, both deciding on coffee and fruit to keep it simple.

"Do you believe this?" Drusilla asked as she sipped her sparkling water, a playful tone in her voice. "I feel like we've known each other for much longer than just a couple of days."

31

JT chuckled softly, nodding. "I know exactly what you mean. It's crazy, but… it feels right, doesn't it?"

She nodded in agreement. "Yeah. It does. I've never done anything like this before."

"I'm glad we're taking our time," Drusilla says, her eyes warm as she meets his gaze. "We don't need to rush anything. It feels nice… just being with you."

JT smiles, feeling the truth of her words settle into his chest. "I agree. There's no rush. I like this. I like getting to know you. There's a whole world out there for us to discover, right?"

They sit in comfortable silence, the weight of their pasts and the expectations they've carried for so long seeming to melt away with the gentle sway of the ship.

The words hung in the air for a moment, but there was no need to say anything else. They both understood. They had shared their thoughts and feelings like they had never done before. The closeness they had experienced the night before—of being completely vulnerable and connected—was something neither of them would ever forget.

"I'm glad you're here, Drusilla," JT said softly, his thumb brushing against her hand as he spoke. "I can't imagine being anywhere else."

Drusilla felt her heart swell at his words. She felt in that moment that this wasn't just a vacation romance. This was something real. Something that could last.

"I'm glad I'm here too," she whispered, squeezing his hand. "This has been the best thing that's ever happened to me."

As they finished their breakfast, they shared a look that spoke volumes. No need for words anymore. They were both ready to see where this journey would take them, together. JT's mind wandered for a moment. A small flicker of doubt crept in—was he coming on too strong, too fast? This whirlwind romance, this connection they shared—it felt so right, but it also felt overwhelming at times. He wasn't a player. This was all so new to him.

The last thing he wanted was to come off as fake, as if he were trying too hard. Drusilla had made it clear she didn't want to settle for anything less than real. And JT wanted to show her that he was the real deal, that he could offer her something genuine. But how could he do that when he hadn't shared with her, who he was and what he was doing there.

He'd kept so much of himself hidden for so long—years of marriage, years of feeling invisible. How could he open up to Drusilla without making things complicated?

There was something he needed to share with her, something that had shaped him into who he was today. It wasn't a dark secret, but it was personal—something he hadn't shared with anyone outside his family and friends.

As he looked at Drusilla across the table, laughing and sharing her thoughts about the upcoming days of the cruise, he felt that familiar pang in his chest. He wanted to share everything with her, wanted her to know the real Jonathan Tisdale Anderson. The real, vulnerable side of him. But would that ruin the magic they were experiencing? Would it interfere with this feeling they had between them?

His fingers tightened around her hand. He didn't want to hold back, but he also didn't want to rush into anything too serious, too soon. It was still so early in their relationship. They were still getting to know each other, still savoring the exciting, new energy of their connection.

But at the same time, he knew that if he didn't share this with her, if he didn't trust her enough to be fully open, it could create a distance between them. The truth was, JT wasn't sure he was ready for that kind of honesty just yet. He didn't want to seem like he was bragging about who he was or where he came from, but he wasn't sure how long he could keep it inside.

For now, he let out a quiet breath and decided to let the moment unfold naturally. They were still in the early stages, still finding their rhythm. Maybe there would be a time later when he could tell her everything without worrying about scaring her off.

He squeezed her hand gently. She smiled back at him, her eyes full of warmth and understanding, and for a second, all of his worries melted away. Maybe they didn't need to rush into everything. Maybe, for now, it was enough to just enjoy being with her.

As the sun set, casting a warm glow over the ship's deck, JT and Drusilla found a quiet corner away from the bustle of the crowd. The day had been filled with laughter and lighthearted conversations, but now JT's expression shifted. There was something weighing on his mind, something he needed to share with her.

"Drusilla," he began, his voice soft but steady, "there's something I've been meaning to tell you. It's not easy for me to open up about this, but I feel like you deserve to know who I really am, beyond what you see on the surface."

Drusilla looked up at him, her heart racing slightly at the change in his tone. "You don't have to tell me anything you're not ready to," she said gently, her eyes searching his.

JT shook his head, a slight smile tugging at his lips, as if reassuring himself. "No, it's not that. It's just... I've spent most of my adult life keeping certain parts of my life private from people I meet, and I guess I'm afraid of coming off as something I'm not."

He paused for a moment, collecting his thoughts before continuing. "I don't want to sound arrogant or boastful. My father... he was a farmer in Ecuador, and when I was a kid, he stumbled upon something that would change our family's lives. There was an old, closed-down mine on our property, and rumors had it there were emeralds deep in the earth. My dad saved enough money to hire a company to do some digging, and sure enough, they found something—more than we ever expected.

"Two years later, a massive deposit of raw emeralds was discovered and it changed our family forever. We became one of the wealthiest families in Ecuador. When my Father retired, I became the company's Chairman and CEO. I took the company public and we had a very successful IPO. We recently completed a merger with the largest mining company in Latin America and it more than doubled the size of our company. It's been a wild ride, but it came with a cost. I can no longer come and go as I please. I am always surrounded by security and staff."

Drusilla's eyes widened slightly, but she remained calm. "I had no idea," she said, her voice low. "I mean, I knew you were successful, but not... like this."

JT shifted uncomfortably, running a hand through his hair. "It's not something I talk about. I don't want people thinking I'm some spoiled rich guy. But this is who I am. And I didn't want you to feel like I was hiding something from you. This is the first time since I took over the company that I've traveled without security. It was my idea. I just wanted to get away...away from the office, the staff, the attorneys, shareholders, the SEC. The merger took a lot out of me. The head of my security team suggested a cruise, thinking we would be someone contained and that I'd be safe. They are concerned because there was a failed kidnapping attempt on my Father just before he retired. Things are different in that part of the world. That's one reason, I moved to New York."

Drusilla gave him a soft smile, her eyes thoughtful. "I don't see you as arrogant in any way, JT. It's an amazing story, but I don't care about money. I don't need any of that. I'm here because I like you—because of who you are, not what you have."

JT let out a breath he hadn't realized he was holding. "Thank you. I was worried how you might see me after I told you all of that."

Drusilla reached out, touching his arm. "I see you, JT. And I'm glad you trusted me enough to share this. It doesn't change how I feel about you."

Drusilla's mind races with questions and curiosity. She wants to know everything about this man who has become such a part of her world in such a short time. His wealth, though, doesn't change her feelings for him; she wonders if it explains some of his guarded behavior or why he hadn't shared this part of his life sooner.

As she reflects on what JT told her about his family and the company, she's eager to learn more about his history. Did his father ever expect him to take over the company sooner? Did JT always feel the pressure to succeed? And she can't help but wonder about his marriage. Why didn't they have children? Was that a mutual decision? And why, after seventeen years, did it end? There's so much she wants to ask, but she doesn't want to overwhelm him.

She smiles to herself, recalling their dinner at Four Ways. It had been such a beautiful evening, and she had been impressed with how humble JT had been, despite his wealth. He didn't flaunt it. When she suggested they split an entree, he didn't hesitate, and she found it endearing. It wasn't about money for him, it was about the experience.

Her heart warmed as she thought about the man who had become so important to her so quickly. She knew she had her own questions to answer too—how far would this relationship go? Would it last beyond the cruise? And, more importantly, what did she want from it?

For now, though, she was content. JT had shared something deeply personal, and in return, she needed to think carefully about what she would share with him.

That afternoon, while JT was busy with a video conference, Drusilla found herself alone in her cabin. She settled into a quiet corner, her book in hand, but her mind was restless. She tried to focus on the cruise itinerary, letting the details of the upcoming ports of call distract her from the whirlwind of thoughts racing through her mind.

More from Sam

As she turned the pages, her phone beeped, pulling her attention away from the printed pages. It was another text from Sam.

I miss you. Can we talk?

Her heart skipped a beat, the weight of his words sinking in. For a moment, memories of the good times they'd shared flooded her mind—the laughter, the intimacy, the plans for a future they'd never built together. She thought about how they'd spent nearly a decade together and how, at one time, she'd truly believed they would last forever.

But then reality crept in. The long nights when he'd been distant, the feelings of loneliness, the doubts that had crept into her mind about where his heart had truly been. She had left him for a reason, a reason that had only become clearer over time. Even still, a part of her felt compelled to respond.

She typed back:

I'm out of town and won't be back for a while.

Almost immediately, he replied:

Where are you?

She stared at his message, the familiar feeling of uncertainty creeping back in. She hesitated, her finger hovering over the keyboard. She didn't want to tell him where she was. She didn't owe him an explanation, and yet, a small part of her wanted to reach out, to tell him the truth. But then she thought of JT, the man she'd been spending so much time with.

The man who, in such a short time, had made her feel alive, understood, and valued. She wasn't sure what the future held with him, but she knew that right now, this moment, she didn't want to go back to the past. She didn't want to drag her ex's shadow back into her life.

Drusilla typed quickly:

Let's talk when I get home.

Then she hit send, feeling a strange sense of relief wash over her.

She set the phone down and took a deep breath. JT was still on his video conference, and she was free to spend the afternoon however she wished. She had made a choice, even if she wasn't sure exactly where it would lead, and that felt like the first step toward moving forward.

As the minutes passed and the ship rocked gently in the water, Drusilla turned her attention back to the itinerary, her thoughts drifting to the future—the unknown adventures, and the possibility of what might come next with JT.

Building Trust

The following days pass in a blissful blur of moments shared between them. The ship sails toward their next destination, but neither JT nor Drusilla is concerned with where they're going.

37

The journey has become one of getting to know each other in ways that feel deeper and more meaningful than the rush of passion.

They spend afternoons lounging by the pool, talking about the things they never shared with anyone else—Drusilla opens up about her childhood in Boston, the struggles of living up to her mother's high expectations, while JT confesses the quiet pain of his divorce, the loneliness of feeling unseen in a relationship that once felt like everything.

Drusilla finds herself growing fond of JT in a way she hadn't expected. There's something about the way he listens to her, the way he makes her feel heard and valued. She can't help but admire his patience and gentleness, the way he respects her boundaries while still showing his desire. It's the way he touches her hand as if he's trying to memorize the feel of it, but never pushing beyond what she's comfortable with.

The next few days are filled with tender moments: long walks, quiet dinners where they share their hopes and dreams, and more stolen kisses under the stars. They both find themselves falling deeper into a rhythm, a slow, steady dance of closeness that feels natural and right.

On their last evening before they dock in their next port, they sit on the balcony of JT's suite, watching the stars reflect off the dark ocean. JT turns to Drusilla, his gaze filled with sincerity.

"I've never felt this at ease with someone before," he says softly. "It's like I can be myself around you. No pretenses, no rush. Just... being here with you."

Drusilla leans in, brushing her lips against his, her heart full. "Same here," she whispers. "It's rare to find something this... real. I don't want to let it go."

And in that moment, both of them know they're on the right path. The sex will come when it feels right, but for now, they're content to enjoy the emotional intimacy, the trust, and the joy of each other's company. They have time, and they're in no rush. Their connection, slow and steady, is already something special—something worth holding onto.

Chapter 4

A Relaxing Day at the Spa

The morning light spills through the large windows of Drusilla's cabin. After a few days of wandering the ship, enjoying romantic dinners, and endless conversations, today is about something different. Today is about relaxation, both physical and emotional.

As they share a quiet breakfast on the balcony of JT's suite, a soft knock on the door interrupts their peaceful morning. The ship's spa staff has arrived with a personal invitation for a couple's treatment, and JT, with a smile, suggests they indulge in a little luxury.

"I think we've earned a day of pampering," he says, his eyes twinkling as he sets down his coffee. "What do you think?"

Drusilla smiles, the thought of a calming spa experience feeling like the perfect way to spend the day. "I couldn't agree more, I'm so excited," she replies, her voice light but filled with anticipation. "Let's go.

The spa area of the ship is a sanctuary of soft lighting, tranquil music, and the faint scent of lavender and eucalyptus. They're led into a private suite with floor-to-ceiling windows, offering an uninterrupted view of the endless ocean stretching out beneath the sun. The soothing sound of water lapping against the hull of the ship creates a natural soundtrack to their serene surroundings.

After changing into their robes and slippers, they both meet in the treatment room, where the spa staff offers them a brief consultation. They decide on a *couples' spa day*—a combination of deep tissue massages, facials, and a soothing seaweed wrap to detoxify and rejuvenate their skin.

"Are you sure you're not going to fall asleep halfway through?" Drusilla teases, as JT sinks onto the plush massage table.

He grins. "I'm not that easy to put to sleep, but I'll take your word for it. I have a feeling this is going to be exactly what we need."

The first hour of the experience is a blissful deep-tissue massage. The therapists work in silence, their expert hands easing the tension from their muscles. Drusilla sighs contentedly, her body relaxing beneath the rhythmic touch, while JT feels a deep sense of peace settle in his chest.

There's a moment, mid-massage, when Drusilla turns her head toward JT, catching his eye. She smiles softly, a quiet understanding between them. It's a simple moment, but the connection feels deeper than words.

After their massages, they lie side by side, covered in a calming seaweed wrap that cools and soothes their skin. The silence between them is comforting, the kind of quiet that speaks volumes. Drusilla closes her eyes and feels a sense of calm wash over her. The weight of her past relationships—of all the emotional baggage—seems so far away in this serene space, with JT beside her.

"So," she says softly, breaking the silence, "how does it feel to have nothing to do but relax for a few hours?"

JT chuckles, his voice low and relaxed. "Honestly? I don't think I've ever had a chance to just... stop. I'm so used to constant motion—work, meetings, responsibilities. This, though... this is a kind of peace I didn't know I needed."

Drusilla nods, her fingers absently tracing the edge of the towel around her waist. "It's strange, isn't it? How hard it is to slow down, even when we know we need it."

They share a quiet smile before returning to the calm of their spa treatments, letting the sensation of relaxation deepen between them.

After the wraps are removed and their facials are complete, their therapists offer them a soothing herbal tea. They sit together in the soft, plush lounge area, sipping the tea and chatting softly. The conversation flows easily, from the wonders of the ship to their favorite places in the world and what they hope to do next. They laugh, reveling in the simple joy of being present with each other.

When their treatments come to an end, they are both in a peaceful, contented state, their skin glowing and their minds cleared of the everyday stresses they've been carrying. As they change back into their clothes, JT takes a moment to look at Drusilla across the room, her face relaxed and serene, the natural beauty she's always had now shining even brighter.

"You look incredible," he says quietly, his gaze lingering on her.

Drusilla smiles, a soft blush coloring her cheeks. "You too. I think this was just what we needed."

"Why don't you come by my cabin after you change for a glass of wine and to watch the sunset?" JT suggests.

"Great. I'll see you shortly." She responds with a smile.

Later, as the sun sets, they find themselves sitting side by side on the balcony in JT's cabin, wrapped in plush blankets, watching the sky turn brilliant shades of orange and pink.

The spa day has brought them closer—not just because of the relaxation, but because of the space it created for them to be vulnerable, quiet, and at peace together. They've shared a day of indulgence, but also of reflection. The intimacy between them is deepening, but it's not just the physical connection that's growing; it's the emotional bond, the quiet understanding that, even in silence, they are completely content with one another.

"What's next for us?" Drusilla asks, her voice soft and curious as she looks out over the sea, her fingers gently tracing the rim of her glass.

JT takes a deep breath, contemplating her question. "I think we'll just keep taking it one step at a time. No rush. No pressure. Let's just enjoy this moment... and see where it leads."

Drusilla nods, her heart light. "I like that. No pressure. Just... us."

They sit in companionable silence, the peace of the moment wrapping around them like the softest embrace. The ship continues to sail onward into the night, but for now, they are perfectly content—together, without haste, letting their connection deepen and unfold as it will.

The last rays of the sun fade behind the horizon, leaving a soft, dusky glow in the sky as JT and Drusilla linger on the balcony, the quiet hum of the ship beneath them. After a few moments of comfortable silence, JT turns toward her, his eyes warm with the evening's lingering calm.

"So," he says, breaking the quiet, "What would you like to do for dinner tonight?"

Drusilla stretches slightly, her hand resting on the rail, and looks out over the ocean as she thinks. She smiles to herself, the soft breeze lifting her hair. "I've heard the seafood restaurant on the top deck is incredible. It seems like the perfect place for a night like this."

JT nods, already pulling his phone from his pocket. "That sounds perfect. I'll make a reservation for us."

She watches as he taps away on his phone, admiring how seamlessly he transitions from relaxed to ready for action. He's all business when it comes to making sure their evening goes smoothly.

"Casual, right?" she asks, turning to face him, her eyes gleaming with the anticipation of the evening.

"Absolutely," he replies with a grin. "Nothing too stuffy."

As JT begins the process of securing their dinner reservation, Drusilla heads back to her own cabin, her thoughts still lingering on the serene moments they shared earlier. The quiet comfort between them feels almost surreal—like a slow dance that they're both fully enjoying, letting each step unfold in its own time.

Once inside her cabin, she closes the door behind her, pausing for a moment to take in the peaceful quiet. It's just her now, but in the calm, her thoughts turn toward JT. There's a lightness in her chest when she thinks of him—of how easy they've fallen into this rhythm together, no pressure, just moments that flow effortlessly from one to the next.

She smiles to herself and heads straight for the shower, shedding her casual clothes as she goes. The cool tiles beneath her feet and the soft spray of water quickly relax her, washing away the tension from the day. The hot water feels like an indulgence, and she lets it run over her skin for a few moments longer than usual, enjoying the sensation of being completely at ease.

As the steam rises around her, she mentally goes over the evening ahead. She wants to look good for JT, but not in a way that feels forced. She's not looking for anything flashy—just comfortable and chic. She enjoys getting ready, the ritual of it, the way it lets her slip into a different version of herself, even if it's just for a few hours.

She reaches for the shampoo and conditioner she's come to love during the trip, the scent of them familiar now. She lets the conditioner sit in her hair a little longer, feeling the silkiness that only comes from the high-end products the ship offers. The water droplets bead in her hair as she rinses, and when she steps out of the shower, she feels refreshed and energized.

She dries off quickly with a fluffy white towel, then wraps it around her hair to soak up the excess water. She steps over to the vanity, where she begins her routine with a light skincare regimen—a gentle cleanser, a soothing toner, and a rich moisturizer. Her skin feels soft and well-hydrated after the spa treatments, and she takes a moment to appreciate how smooth and clear it looks. She knows she has a bit of a glow from the day's relaxation, and she's happy for it.

Unwrapping the towel from her hair, she looks at herself in the mirror for a moment. Her hair has a natural wave to it, the curls soft but defined from the humidity of the day. She picks up a blow dryer and begins to dry it slowly, using a round brush to create volume and smoothness. The process is meditative, and as she works, she imagines the evening ahead—dinner with JT, the way he'll look at her as they sit across from each other, sharing their quiet conversations and soft laughter.

When her hair is dry, she runs her fingers through it, giving it a more natural look, letting the waves fall loosely around her shoulders. It feels effortless and easy, like her style lately, like the way she's been feeling with JT.

She moves on to makeup. Drusilla doesn't go overboard; she prefers a more subtle approach. A light foundation to even out her skin tone, followed by a hint of concealer to brighten under her eyes. She adds a soft pink blush to her cheeks, just enough to give her face a healthy flush. A sweep of bronzer along her cheekbones adds some depth, and she finishes with a light touch of highlighter on the tops of her cheekbones, making her skin look dewy and fresh.

For her eyes, she keeps it simple—a soft brown eyeshadow to accentuate her lids and a delicate flick of eyeliner at the outer corners. She applies a few coats of mascara, letting her lashes look full without being too dramatic. Her lips are a soft rose color, just enough to add a hint of color but still keeping the look natural. She smiles at her reflection, feeling confident and put together without overdoing it.

With her hair and makeup done, Drusilla turns to her clothing options. She wants to be comfortable, but she also wants to feel special for tonight. She settles on a pair of white linen pants—loose and breathable, perfect for the warm evening air. The pants are tailored, falling just above her ankles, showing off the delicate straps of her nude sandals.

For her top, she chooses a blush-colored silk blouse. It's soft and luxurious against her skin, with a subtle sheen that catches the light. The blouse has a v-neck, with small buttons that run down the front, and a slight puff at the shoulders, adding a touch of romance to the outfit. The fabric drapes beautifully, and as she slips it on, she feels both relaxed and elegant. It's effortless, just like everything about tonight.

She checks herself in the mirror one last time, adjusting the blouse until it sits just right. Satisfied, she picks up her simple gold bracelet—nothing too flashy, just a delicate piece of jewelry that complements the look—and slides it on her wrist. A soft spritz of floral perfume completes her look, the scent light but fresh, lingering just enough to remind her of the ocean breeze.

As she reaches for her bag and slides on her sunglasses—just for fun, even though it's evening—she pauses for a moment, thinking about JT. It's impossible to ignore the spark she feels when she thinks about him, the way he makes her feel seen and understood in ways she hasn't felt in a long time. The connection they've shared so far feels meaningful, but also delicate, like a blossom unfolding petal by petal.

Meanwhile, JT is carefully selecting his own outfit, wanting to match the mood of the evening without overthinking it. He opts for a classic look—casual but polished. A crisp, light blue button-up shirt, unbuttoned just enough at the collar to feel effortless, paired with well-fitted white linen pants. The shirt is soft against his skin, and he rolls the sleeves up to his elbows, feeling more relaxed as he does. He'll probably wear it open for a few moments as they make their way to dinner, enjoying the light breeze.

He knows that Drusilla appreciates the understated, and he's keen on looking effortlessly stylish. No designer labels tonight, just simplicity done well. As he ties his shoes, polished yet comfortable, he glances at the time and quickly checks his phone to make sure their reservation is confirmed. Once it is, he puts the phone down, letting out a quiet sigh of relief.

As he brushes his hair back, he considers the evening ahead. There's something about Drusilla that feels like a mystery, and not the kind he's used to solving. It's different. She's not guarded, but there's an air of protectiveness about her, a carefulness he can't help but admire. The connection is real—it's not a chase, not something to conquer. They're simply enjoying the moment. And he's more than okay with that.

When he's finished getting dressed, he looks at himself in the mirror—he's in his element, but there's a softness to his smile, an ease in the way he's standing that he hasn't had in years. He pulls out a simple black leather watch and slides it on his wrist, then gives himself a final look. He's ready.

When Drusilla steps out of her cabin, she feels a gentle flutter of excitement. She takes one last look around her cabin, as if to savor the moment before she walks out the door. As she moves down the hallway toward JT's cabin, her heart quickens. There's something about the anticipation—the soft thrill of being with someone who feels so right for her, someone who shares this new chapter of her life with the same openness and ease.

She reaches his door and knocks softly, feeling the cool evening air against her skin. A moment later, the door opens, and there he is—JT, looking effortlessly handsome in his casual-chic outfit, his crisp blue shirt catching the light from the hallway. He takes one look at her, his eyes widening slightly, and a smile spreads across his face.

"Wow," he breathes, the admiration in his voice clear. "You look amazing, Drusilla."

Her heart skips a beat at the sincerity in his eyes. "Thank you. You're not so bad yourself, JT," she teases with a smile.

As he takes her hand, leading her down the hallway and toward the grand staircase, Drusilla feels a quiet thrill at the connection between them, knowing that tonight will be another step in this journey they're beginning to take together—one moment, one step, at a time.

Dinner is a quiet affair at the seafood restaurant on the top deck, where the soft sounds of the ocean provide the perfect backdrop to their meal. The air is warm, and the view of the moonlight reflecting off the waves creates a romantic atmosphere. Drusilla and JT sit across from each other, their table set with crisp white linens and flickering candlelight, casting a soft glow on their faces. The menu offers an array of fresh catches, and they decide to share a few appetizers—a delicate smoked salmon tartare and buttery lobster bisque—before moving on to their entrées.

Drusilla chooses the pan-seared sea bass, its golden crust crisped just right, while JT opts for the grilled scallops, perfectly charred on the outside but tender inside. As they eat, the conversation flows easily, a mix of lighthearted banter and meaningful moments. JT listens intently as Drusilla talks about her childhood in Boston, the way art had always been her refuge, her means of self-expression. Drusilla, in turn, is fascinated by JT's stories about his family's legacy, the way his father had built a fortune, and how JT had taken on the responsibility of running the company. It's the first time they've really delved into their pasts, and each revelation draws them closer, not just as a couple, but as two people who are slowly learning to trust one another.

The evening feels easy, effortless. There's no pressure, no rushing to the next moment. Just the shared experience of good food, good company, and the quiet joy of being in each other's presence.

After dinner, they stroll around the ship, hand in hand, the soft murmur of the ocean beneath them, the twinkling lights of the ship reflecting off the waves. Dinner had been a quiet affair—a celebration of the sunset and the easy chemistry between them. The seafood was fresh and perfectly prepared, but it was the conversation, the gentle teasing and soft laughter between bites, that made the evening unforgettable.

Drusilla feels completely at ease, her hand fitting naturally in JT's. They walk in silence for a moment, each of them soaking in the tranquility, the connection that feels both new and deeply familiar. The gentle sway of the ship beneath them is almost hypnotic, like a lullaby, and she can't help but smile at the thought of how good the day has been.

"Thank you for a wonderful dinner," she says softly, breaking the silence. Her voice is warm, relaxed from the wine and the soothing rhythm of their walk.

JT squeezes her hand, his expression softening as he glances at her. "The pleasure was all mine. I'm glad we had a chance to slow down tonight."

They continue walking for a while, taking in the beauty of the moonlight, the stars stretching endlessly above them. After a while, Drusilla leans her head slightly toward him, a quiet invitation without words.

"Care for a nightcap?" she asks, her voice carrying the playful undertone he's come to love.

JT grins. "I thought you'd never ask."

They make their way to the lounge, a cozy, intimate space at the center of the ship. It's not too crowded yet, a perfect spot for a quiet drink. The bartender, a friendly young woman with a warm smile, greets them immediately and quickly prepares two glasses of chilled champagne. The soft clink of glasses and the faint hum of a jazz band playing in the background add to the relaxed, elegant atmosphere of the room.

They settle into a secluded corner, the low lighting casting a golden glow over their faces. Drusilla takes a sip of her champagne, the effervescence tingling on her tongue, and leans back against the plush cushions of the seat. The glass feels cool in her hand, a lovely contrast to the warmth between them.

"I've been thinking about today," she says, her eyes meeting his over the rim of her glass. "It was just... perfect. The spa, the time we spent together, no rush. Just... us."

JT smiles, his gaze softening. "I've been thinking the same thing. It feels like we're in our own little world right now. Everything else just fades away."

They both sip their champagne in comfortable silence, the evening stretching out in front of them like a calm sea, untouched and endless. They've been on this journey together for a while now, but it feels like every day brings them closer, deeper, in a way that neither of them expected.

There's no rush, no expectations. Just the quiet joy of being with someone who feels as right for them as the sea feels endless.

By the time they finish their drinks, the night has deepened. The ship's lights glow softly against the darkened sea, casting a gentle reflection on the water. The lounge has grown quieter, and the energy of the evening has settled into a peaceful, contented rhythm.

"Shall we head back?" Drusilla asks, her voice soft, but there's no hurry in it. She feels no urgency, just a sense of peace, of knowing they've shared something wonderful tonight.

JT nods, standing and offering her his hand. "Let's go. I'll walk you to your cabin."

They make their way through the ship's corridors, the gentle rocking beneath their feet adding a dreamy, serene quality to the moment. Drusilla walks close to him, their fingers intertwined, the warmth of his touch still lingering on her skin.

When they reach her cabin, Drusilla stops, turning to face him. The soft light from the hallway casts a warm glow on her face, and JT's heart skips a beat. There's something about the way she looks at him tonight—content, but also holding a hint of something deeper, a quiet promise of more to come.

"I had a great time," she says softly, her voice steady but filled with meaning. "Thank you."

JT smiles, his thumb gently brushing over her hand. "The pleasure was all mine. I'm glad we spent the day together."

He steps a little closer, and without thinking, his hand moves to her cheek, his thumb caressing her skin. The simple touch feels intimate, sincere. He leans in, brushing a soft, tender kiss against her lips. It's a kiss full of promise and quiet affection, one that speaks volumes without needing to say a word.

When they pull away, they both smile, but there's a peacefulness in their expressions, a calm understanding between them.

"Good night, Drusilla," JT says, his voice low and warm.

"Good night, JT," she replies, her eyes lingering on him just a little longer before she steps back into her cabin, the door closing softly behind her.

JT stands there for a moment, his hand still lingering in the air where hers was just a moment ago. He takes a deep breath, feeling the quiet satisfaction of a day well spent. It hasn't been rushed, and there's no urgency. Just two people enjoying each other's company, learning about each other, and building something that feels meaningful.

As he walks back to his own cabin, he smiles to himself, already looking forward to the next day—whatever it may bring. For tonight, he's content, and so is Drusilla. They're exactly where they need to be.

It had been a perfect day—a spa day, a day full of relaxation, connection, and shared moments that will stay with them for a long time.

The kind of day that makes you feel, deep down, that life is exactly as it should be.

The next morning

The morning sun is already high as Drusilla steps onto the top deck, the warm breeze tousling her hair. The ship is calm, cutting through the gentle waves on its way to Barcelona. The scent of the sea fills the air, blending with the light aroma of fresh coffee and pastries from the breakfast buffet. As she walks toward the table where JT is already sitting, a soft smile spreads across her face at the sight of him. He's wearing a casual white shirt and sunglasses, looking effortlessly handsome, as usual.

"Good morning," she says, her voice bright with the warmth of the day. JT stands to greet her, pulling out the chair for her with a gentlemanly flourish.

"Good morning, beautiful. I saved you a spot," he replies, his eyes lighting up when he sees her. They sit down together, the table laden with fresh fruit, croissants, and a steaming pot of coffee. The mood is light and easy, just like the day ahead.

As they eat, they talk excitedly about their upcoming stop in Barcelona. Drusilla mentions some of the art galleries she wants to visit, while JT jokes about needing to find the best tapas bar in the city. The conversation is full of anticipation, but also grounded in the peace of the moment—there's no rush, just a quiet joy in each other's company.

After finishing their breakfast, they both agree: today will be a perfect day to relax by the pool. The ship is still heading toward Spain, and with another day and a half of sailing ahead, it feels like the ideal opportunity to unwind and enjoy the serene, sun-drenched deck. They stop at their cabins to grab towels, sunscreen, and a couple of books before heading to the pool. The water looks inviting, the deck chairs lined up under wide umbrellas, ready for a leisurely day of relaxation.

The sun is high as they settle into their poolside spots, side by side. Drusilla feels completely at ease, the warmth of the sun mingling with the cool ocean breeze. She takes a deep breath, inhaling the salty air, and feels herself relax into the comfort of being with JT. The gentle hum of the ship's engine, the soft splashes from the pool, and the occasional laughter from other passengers create a peaceful ambiance.

They talk here and there, but for the most part, they enjoy the quiet company. JT occasionally glances over at her, his eyes catching the sunlight in a way that makes her heart flutter. There's something about the calm between them, the simple pleasure of being together without the need for constant conversation, that feels right.

As the hours slip by, they sip cocktails, laugh at each other's attempts to relax in the hot tub, and occasionally dive into the pool for a quick swim. Drusilla, enjoying the carefree nature of the day, feels as though the world has paused just for them—nothing to do, nowhere to be, except right here, in the moment.

Getting creative together

The afternoon sun beats down on the pool deck as Drusilla flips through the ship's website on her phone, her sunglasses perched on her nose. She's been enjoying the laid-back atmosphere of the day, but her mind starts to wander, looking for something a bit more engaging to do. Scanning the list of activities for the day, her eyes land on something that immediately piques her interest: a pottery class at 3:00 PM.

She glances over at JT, who's lounging in his deck chair with a book in hand, a relaxed look on his face as he soaks up the sun. It's been a lovely afternoon so far, but the idea of doing something more interactive excites her. Pottery—a craft that's been a part of her life for as long as she can remember—feels like the perfect way to spend a few hours, especially in such a beautiful, serene setting. She doesn't want to rush into anything, but a chance to share something so personal with JT feels special.

"Hey," she begins, tilting her head toward him as she taps her phone screen. "I just saw that there's a pottery class at 3:00. What do you think? We could give it a try."

JT looks up, eyebrows lifting in genuine interest. He's always admired Drusilla's passion for her art, the way she lights up when she talks about her pottery, and he's more than happy to indulge her. "That sounds like a lot of fun. I'd love to give it a shot. I know you're a seasoned potter, but it'll be fun to try and keep up with you."

51

She smiles at his response, touched by how easygoing and supportive he is. Sam would never want to do anything like this, she thought. "It's not about keeping up. Pottery's about enjoying the process... the messiness of it. Besides," she adds, a playful glint in her eyes, "I can show you a few tricks along the way."

JT laughs, clearly intrigued. "Okay, now I'm definitely in. Want me to make the reservation for us?"

Drusilla shakes her head, a soft laugh escaping her. "No, I've got it covered. I'll confirm our spot."

She quickly taps through the reservation system, confirming their places in the class. The idea of sharing something so close to her heart with JT feels wonderful, and she's excited about the opportunity to teach him a few things. Pottery is a tactile, intimate experience, and she's eager to see how he approaches it. Whether he's a natural or a total novice, she knows it will be fun.

With everything set, she looks up from her phone, meeting his gaze. "All set. We've got a spot."

JT grins, his eyes twinkling with excitement. "I can't wait. I'll try not to embarrass myself too much."

"Don't worry," Drusilla says with a teasing smile. "I'll be there to guide you. But if you end up with something completely abstract, I'll just say it's *art*."

JT chuckles, clearly looking forward to the experience. "I'll take that as a challenge."

As the afternoon stretches on, the anticipation of the pottery class adds a new energy to the day. The gentle rhythm of the ship's movement, the laughter of fellow passengers around them, and the promise of getting their hands dirty together makes the moment feel even more special. For Drusilla, the idea of sharing her passion with JT, in her own element, is the perfect way to deepen their connection, and she can already tell it's going to be a fun, memorable experience.

JT glances at his watch, noticing that it's nearly 2:00. He stretches lazily, then looks over at Drusilla, who's still reclining in her deck chair, her fingers lightly tapping on her phone. He can't help but smile—she's been so easy to be with today, and the idea of the pottery class makes the whole afternoon feel full of promise.

"Hey," he says, his voice gentle but with an underlying eagerness. "It's almost time for the class. How about we head back and change for it?"

Drusilla looks up, her eyes lighting up as she agrees. "Sounds perfect." She stands and gathering her things. Together, they walk toward the elevators, the sea breeze still ruffling their hair, their steps in sync, comfortable, easy.

As they approach the hallway that leads to their cabins, JT reaches out to take her hand, his fingers slipping naturally between hers. It's a small gesture, but one that feels intimate, grounding—like something deeper is building between them, even without words.

When they reach her door, JT pauses, turning toward her. He gives her hand a gentle squeeze, a quiet moment hanging between them. The air feels charged, and the softness of her eyes, the way she stands before him, makes everything seem just *right*.

Drusilla smiles up at him, a knowing look in her eyes. There's an undeniable chemistry between them that's been building all day, and the tension from the quiet moments, the shared laughter, the subtle touches—it all has led to this.

Without any warning, she reaches up to kiss him. It's soft at first, a gentle press of lips that deepens as they both lean into the kiss, savoring the warmth of each other. For a moment, the world around them blurs, and all JT can think about is how perfect this moment feels. The taste of champagne on her lips, the salt of the sea air, the warmth of her skin—it's intoxicating.

He feels the pull of desire, stronger now than ever before. He imagines pushing the door open, pulling her into the cabin, and letting everything else fade away. The idea flashes through his mind, and his body reacts to it immediately, the ache of wanting something more clear and undeniable. But then, he pulls away just enough to touch her cheek gently, almost tenderly, his thumb grazing her skin.

"Come get me when you're ready," he says, the words sounding more like a promise than a suggestion.

Drusilla looks up at him, her breath slightly uneven and her heart beating faster from the kiss. Her gaze softens, and she takes a step back, nodding with a faint smile, the tension in her eyes replaced by something warmer, something deeper. "I will," she replies, her voice just a little husky.

With one last look, JT turns to walk down the hallway to his cabin. He's filled with an ache, a hunger he can't entirely ignore, but there's also something else: patience, respect, and the sense that when the time is right, it will happen. But as he walks away, he can't help but wonder— did he just miss the chance to move things forward? Would she have welcomed it? Or is this exactly what they both need right now? The space to figure it out, to build something that feels real, without rushing.

As he reaches his cabin, he pauses for a moment outside the door, still thinking of that kiss, still feeling the heat of it on his lips. But tonight is still ahead, and he knows that whatever happens, it will be worth the wait.

Pottery, playfulness, and possibilities

Drusilla knocks lightly on JT's cabin door, her excitement bubbling up as she pulls her hair back into a loose ponytail. She's dressed simply for the class—shorts and a comfy tee, a perfect outfit for getting her hands messy. She's not one to fuss when it comes to creating art, and today, she's ready to let the clay take over.

The door swings open, and JT stands there, equally casual, in his own shorts and tee shirt, the sleeves rolled up to reveal his toned arms. He grins at her, his eyes lighting up with that familiar spark of curiosity. "Ready to get messy?" he asks, a playful grin tugging at his lips.

She smiles back, nodding. "Definitely. I'm excited to see what we come up with."

54

JT raises an eyebrow as he steps into the hallway, his hand brushing against hers as they walk toward the pottery class. The ship's interior is quiet, save for the occasional footstep or murmur of passengers nearby, but there's a lightness to their walk—something between them that feels easy and playful.

"So, I was thinking…" JT begins, a teasing smile creeping onto his face. "This is probably going to be the perfect opportunity for a *Ghost* moment. You know, Demi Moore, Patrick Swayze, the wheel—getting all romantic with the clay." His voice is light, filled with jest, but his eyes flicker with something else, as if the idea isn't entirely unappealing.

Drusilla can't help but laugh, her chest vibrating with amusement. She leans into him as they walk, squeezing his hand lightly. "I was thinking the same thing," she says, her voice low, almost teasing. The closeness between them feels natural, their banter easy. There's something sweet about sharing this silly moment, the sexual tension between them filling the air.

They continue down the hallway, the playful energy between them palpable. The pottery studio isn't far, and soon enough, they're standing outside the door. They exchange one last glance, both holding onto the lingering moment of laughter before walking into the studio.

Inside, the room is spacious, with long tables laid out with all the necessary tools: smooth clay, spinning wheels, rolling pins, and aprons. The instructor, a woman in her mid-thirties with short blonde hair, greets them warmly. She leads them to two pottery wheels next to each other, and JT shoots Drusilla a playful look.

"Let's see if I can keep up with the expert," he teases as he takes his seat at the wheel.

Drusilla laughs and picks up her ball of clay, already feeling in her element. "You might surprise yourself. Just don't expect me to be your Demi Moore," she quips, settling in next to him.

The instructor gives them a brief rundown on how to start, demonstrating the basic steps of centering the clay and getting the wheel to spin at the right speed. It's all very basic, but as they begin, Drusilla feels that familiar, comforting connection to the clay. She lets her fingers glide over the surface, finding her rhythm, feeling the pliable material mold under her touch.

55

JT, on the other hand, starts off a little less confident. He laughs at himself as the clay wobbles under his hands and flies off the wheel, a slight look of frustration on his face. "Okay, so… this is harder than it looks," he admits, looking over at Drusilla with a grin.

Drusilla watches him with amusement, her fingers gently working the clay. "It's all about getting the feel for it. You've got this."

As they work, their conversation shifts, getting quieter, more focused on the craft, but every now and then, they exchange flirty glances or soft laughs. JT's attempts at centering the clay are… less than perfect, but Drusilla's encouraging words help him stay patient. "Don't worry, it'll take some practice," she says, her voice light with humor.

A few minutes later, JT manages to make some headway, shaping the base of what might one day resemble a bowl. "Okay, not bad," he says, more to himself than to Drusilla, clearly pleased with his progress. "I think I might have the hang of this now."

Drusilla looks over at his wheel, admiring his work. "Not bad at all, actually. I'm impressed."

She's in her element—her hands moving with confidence as she molds her own creation. But she can't help but glance over at JT, watching him with a new layer of admiration. There's something about seeing him dive into something new with that same ease and openness he's shown in everything else. She enjoys watching him try, enjoying his willingness to step outside his comfort zone.

After a while, they both finish their pieces—Drusilla's a smooth, elegant vase, JT's a somewhat uneven but endearing mug. They share a laugh as the instructor comes around, inspecting their work.

"Looks like you two both created something pretty unique," she says with a smile, glancing at their pieces.

Drusilla grins, picking up JT's mug with a teasing look. "I think it might need a little more work, but we'll get there."

JT chuckles, his smile warm. "I'm just glad it stayed on the wheel."

As the class wraps up and they step away from their wheels, Drusilla can't help but feel a sense of satisfaction. The class wasn't about perfection; it was about the shared experience, the joy of creation, and the laughter that came with it.

She looks over at JT, still smiling from the class, his hands, arms, and face speckled with clay, and feels a deep sense of connection. Pottery, messy and imperfect as it was, had brought them even closer. And maybe, just maybe, the *Ghost* moment wasn't so far off after all.

After hours of getting their hands messy with clay, JT and Drusilla are both in need of a little pampering. The pottery class was fun, but they're both ready for a change of pace— something elegant, a chance to dress up and enjoy a night of indulgence. As they make their way back to their cabins, JT turns to Drusilla with a mischievous smile.

"How about we clean up and go all out tonight? Steakhouse dinner, fancy clothes, the works." His tone is light, but there's a hint of excitement behind it. The idea of seeing Drusilla all dolled up, of sharing a more formal evening together, feels like the perfect way to cap off an afternoon of creative mess.

Drusilla's eyes light up at the suggestion. She's always loved getting dressed up—there's something special about slipping into a gorgeous outfit, doing her hair just right, and stepping into a different world. "I love that idea," she says, her voice bright with enthusiasm. "A night to feel like royalty, right?"

They part ways at their respective cabin doors, both looking forward to some downtime. Drusilla takes a deep breath as she enters her room, the excitement of the evening ahead mixing with a quiet sense of anticipation. She slips out of her casual clothes, running a hand through her hair before stepping into the shower. The hot water washes away the remnants of clay, the tension in her muscles slowly easing. As she stands under the spray, she lets herself relax, thinking about the evening—about how nice it will be to share a different side of herself with JT, to step into a more glamorous version of their connection.

When she's done, she dries off, grabs her phone and relaxes in the cozy chair to check her messages.

After relaxing for a while, she starts to get ready for dinner. She selects a soft, flowy dress—a deep navy blue that contrasts beautifully with her skin tone. She adds a little sparkle with a delicate necklace and diamond stud earrings. Her makeup is understated but polished, a perfect balance of natural beauty and evening elegance.

Drusilla takes a final look in the mirror, admiring how the dress hugs her curves. It's a bit of a transformation—her hair soft waves falling around her shoulders, her expression a little more sophisticated. She's ready for a night of indulgence, ready to show JT a different side of herself.

Meanwhile, JT is in his own cabin, running a hand through his hair as he stands in front of the mirror. He's also ready for a change—a break from the laid-back vibe of the afternoon. He picks out a crisp white button-down shirt, a charcoal blazer, and dark trousers. After a quick shave and a spray of cologne, he steps back to admire himself. He's no stranger to getting dressed up for business meetings or events, but there's something different about this night. Something about the way Drusilla makes him want to look his best, to show her a side of him that's not just about casual charm.

When they finally meet outside Drusilla's cabin, the contrast between their casual afternoon selves and their dressed-up evening personas is striking. JT's jaw drops slightly as he sees her for the first time in her dress—elegant, radiant, and effortlessly beautiful. He can't help but smile, his heart skipping a beat at the sight.

"You look stunning," he says, his voice low, filled with admiration.

Drusilla returns the compliment with a teasing glint in her eyes. "Not bad yourself, Mr. Dressed-Up. Ready to go have a fantastic dinner?"

JT grins. "Lead the way."

Hand in hand, they head down the hallway, their steps more in sync than ever, both eager for the evening ahead. They're excited to share a different kind of night, one that's all about elegance, indulgence, and the joy of being in each other's company. Dinner at the steakhouse is sure to be just the beginning of what could be an unforgettable night.

The atmosphere in the steakhouse is perfect—intimate, with warm lighting casting a golden glow over the tables. Soft jazz plays in the background, the clink of silverware and quiet murmurs of other guests filling the space.

The waiter leads them to their table, and JT pulls out Drusilla's chair, his gentlemanly instincts still going strong despite the evening's playful mood. As she sits, she glances up at him, a smile tugging at her lips. "You're really into this whole 'gentleman' thing, aren't you?" she teases, her eyes twinkling with amusement.

JT gives her a mock serious look, his lips curling into a grin. "What can I say? A gentleman's got to keep up appearances." He takes his seat across from her, his eyes never leaving hers. "But I'm happy to do it for you."

Drusilla rolls her eyes, a soft laugh escaping her. "You're lucky you're so charming."

Their playful banter flows easily, the chemistry between them is obvious, but there's also an undeniable layer of respect and admiration. The conversation drifts as the waiter pours them each a glass of champagne, the bubbles catching the light as they raise their flutes.

"Here's to a night of good food, good wine, and even better company," JT says, his eyes locking with hers as he makes the toast.

Drusilla lifts her glass, her gaze steady and warm. "To good company," she echoes, the smile on her lips softening as she meets his eyes. She takes a sip, letting the cool, crisp champagne dance on her tongue. "So," she begins, leaning in slightly as if sharing a secret, "tell me more about this mysterious, quiet billionaire side of you. I'm still trying to figure out if you're hiding some big secret."

JT laughs, shaking his head. "I told you, there's no big secret. Just a guy with some good business luck and a lot of hard work." He takes a sip of his champagne, his tone light, but there's a trace of something else in his voice. "But, maybe... maybe there's more to me than meets the eye." He leans in just slightly, the playful energy of the conversation shifting to something more charged. "I think you might be curious to find out, though."

Drusilla raises an eyebrow, clearly amused. "Oh, now I'm really intrigued. Are you trying to be mysterious on purpose, or is that just how you are?" Her voice is teasing, but there's an undercurrent of interest, a genuine desire to learn more about this man who's become a constant in her life.

JT chuckles, the sound deep and warm, a small laugh that catches her attention. "Maybe I'm just trying to keep you on your toes," he says with a wink, swirling his champagne in his glass. "Or maybe I just like the idea of leaving a little mystery between us."

Drusilla leans back in her chair, considering him for a moment, the corners of her mouth curling upward. "I think I can handle a little mystery," she says, her voice low and playful, a challenge hidden in her tone. "But don't think I won't crack the code eventually."

They both laugh as the connection between them is undeniable, and each flirtatious exchange seems to build on the last. As their food arrives—the conversation continues to flow, light and full of humor, with moments of intensity slipping through.

JT watches her as she takes her first bite of her lobster, her expression one of pure enjoyment. "You look like you're enjoying that," he comments, his voice a little deeper than before, as if the sight of her savoring the food strikes something primal in him.

"Mmm, it's delicious," Drusilla responds, looking up at him through her lashes, the playful edge in her voice replaced by something more seductive. "But I think the company is the real treat tonight."

JT's heart skips a beat at her words. He leans in just slightly, his smile softening. "Well, in that case, I'll try to keep up."

Drusilla smirks, her eyes flashing with that same mischievous glint. "You're doing just fine," she teases. "But don't get too comfortable—I still want to know the rest of your secrets."

They continue eating, their conversation a mix of flirtation, stories, and quiet moments of shared laughter. The champagne keeps flowing, and with each glass, the space between them feels warmer, the tension more electric, and the attraction undeniable.

By the time dessert arrives—decadent chocolate mousse with a delicate raspberry coulis—they've both relaxed into each other's company, the easy familiarity between them almost as comforting as the luxurious setting. JT reaches for Drusilla's hand across the table, the contact sending a gentle current through both of them.

"I have to admit," he says, his voice softer now, "this night has turned out even better than I expected."

Drusilla squeezes his hand, her thumb gently brushing over his knuckles. "It's been perfect," she agrees, her gaze steady on him. "But the best part? The company. Definitely."

The words hang in the air, heavy with the weight of their shared connection, but it's clear that they both enjoy the playful dynamic of the night, even as it moves toward something deeper. As they finish their dessert, the conversation winds down, the flirtation turning into quiet, comfortable silences. They both know that tonight is just another step in a journey—one they're both eager to continue, one moment at a time.

After dinner, the evening air is crisp, the faint scent of the ocean mingling with the soft breeze as JT and Drusilla walk side by side, their steps slow and relaxed. The moonlight shimmers across the water, casting a silver glow over the deck of the ship. There's a peaceful quiet between them, but the chemistry remains undeniable—electric, charged, like they're both waiting for something.

As they make their way to the rail, JT casually drapes his arm around Drusilla's shoulders, pulling her just a little closer to him. She leans into his side, her head resting gently against his shoulder, and for a moment, they both just breathe in the serenity of the night. The ship moves gently beneath their feet, but everything around them feels still, as if time has slowed.

Drusilla looks out at the water, her fingers gently brushing against JT's arm. She remembers the last time they stood here, the way the night had unfolded—how, in that moment, she had turned to him, her heart racing, and pulled him into a kiss that felt as if it was meant to happen. That kiss had left her breathless, longing for more. She feels that same ache now, a quiet yearning that stirs deep inside her. She wonders if he feels it too.

Turning to him, her gaze is steady, full of silent invitation. She places her arms around his neck, her fingers tangling in his hair, and steps closer, feeling the heat of his body against hers. The moment is electric—there's no need for words. She looks up into his eyes, seeking permission, and he doesn't hesitate. His hand slides to her back, pulling her in as their lips meet in a kiss that is slow and deliberate, deep with desire.

The kiss lingers, and the world around them seems to disappear. There's no rush, no hurry. They are wrapped up in the feeling of each other, in the warmth that only the closeness of their bodies can create. JT pulls her tighter, and Drusilla melts into him, her hands finding their way to his chest, feeling the strong beat of his heart beneath the fabric. For a moment, they are just two souls, lost in the softness of the kiss, both hungry for more but unwilling to cross a line they're not quite ready to cross.

When they finally break apart, their breaths are uneven, but neither of them moves away. The silence stretches between them, comfortable yet full of unspoken things. They continue their walk in the moonlight, the quiet hum of the ship's engines beneath their feet, their fingers brushing occasionally as if to remind each other that they are still there, still connected.

As they approach Drusilla's cabin, she slows her steps, turning to him with a soft smile. "Would you like to come in?" she asks, her voice low, almost shy but with a clear invitation. She hopes he'll say yes, but she won't rush him—if tonight is to end here, she'll understand.

JT looks at her, his heart fluttering in his chest. He's been trying to play it cool, trying to respect the boundaries they've set, but there's no denying the pull between them. He smiles softly, his hand brushing against her cheek. "I'd love to," he says, his voice warm and sincere, though there's an underlying heat to it as he steps closer.

Once inside, the door shuts behind them, and the world feels even more intimate. Drusilla moves to turn on some soft music, the smooth notes filling the air as JT pours them both another glass of champagne from the mini bar. The quiet moments of the evening stretch on, and they sit together on the balcony, the ocean breeze cooling their skin, the sound of the water below creating a soothing soundtrack to their conversation.

They talk about everything and nothing—stories of childhood, of travels, of the things that make them who they are. Each word brings them closer, each laugh shared a bridge between their worlds. The champagne flows, the hours slip by unnoticed. They're lost in each other's company, and the connection is undeniable, stronger than ever.

As the night grows later, Drusilla feels her eyelids grow heavy. The warmth of the evening, the champagne, and the peaceful rhythm of JT's voice all combine to make her feel drowsy. She yawns slightly, trying to fight it off, but it's inevitable.

JT notices the change, his thumb brushing over the rim of his glass. "Maybe we should call it a night," he suggests softly, his voice low, like a whisper meant just for her.

Drusilla hesitates for a moment, unsure. The night has been so perfect, so effortless, and she doesn't want it to end. But she knows she's getting tired, and there's a part of her that wonders if this is just how things are meant to be—for now, at least. She looks at him, her eyes soft and a little wistful, but full of warmth. "It's been a wonderful day. The pottery class, the dinner, this time with you," she says, her voice quiet but sincere. "I don't want it to end either."

JT stands, grabbing his jacket from the chair. He's torn, wondering if he should stay, if he should take the next step, but something inside him tells him to be patient, to let the moments unfold naturally. He walks over to where Drusilla is sitting, cupping her chin gently with his hand. His touch is tender, his eyes searching hers, his heart full.

Without a word, he leans down and presses his lips to hers once more, a kiss that is soft and lingering. When he pulls back, he kisses her forehead, his voice a low murmur. "Good night, pretty girl," he says, his words carrying a warmth that seems to fill the room. "Let's do this again tomorrow."

As he walks to the door, he feels a mix of emotions—longing, satisfaction, and a small sense of regret. Should he have stayed? Should he have taken the next step? He doesn't know, but he's content with the way the night unfolded, and he hopes she feels the same.

Drusilla watches him go, the door closing softly behind him. She leans back against the chair, a smile on her lips as she lets out a soft breath. She wonders the same thing—should she have invited him to stay? There's a part of her that admires his restraint, his gentlemanly nature, and another part of her that longs for more. But for now, she's content with the way things are, knowing that tomorrow is another day, another step in the journey they're on together.

Chapter 5

Port of Call: Barcelona, Spain

The morning light pours through the cabin. Drusilla wakes up to an announcement:

> *"Good morning ladies and gentlemen. We will be docking in Barcelona at noon today, and you will have two full days to explore the beautiful city before we set sail once more."*

Drusilla smiles to herself as the words register, a thrill running through her at the thought of exploring a city she's always wanted to visit. The idea of discovering Barcelona with JT only makes the prospect even more exciting. Just as she begins to gather her thoughts, her phone buzzes on the bedside table, the familiar notification lighting up the screen.

She picks it up quickly, her heart skipping a beat when she sees the text from JT:

> *"Breakfast, 30 minutes?"*

Her smile widens, and she feels a flutter of excitement in her chest. She doesn't hesitate.

> *"ABSOLUTELY."*

Within seconds, she's in motion—jumping into the shower to wash away the remnants of sleep and prepare for the day ahead. The warm water feels refreshing against her skin, and her thoughts drift briefly to the night before—the kiss, the conversation, the quiet moments shared on her balcony.

She's ready to start the day with JT.

Once out of the shower, Drusilla gets to work on her outfit for the day. The weather in Barcelona promises to be warm, so she slips on a pair of white linen shorts that are both chic and comfortable, pairing them with a loose-fitting cotton top in a soft shade of cream. The breezy fabric feels perfect for the warm Spanish sun, and she slips on comfortable sandals, the kind that will let her stroll through the city with ease.

Her hair is pulled back into a simple, loose ponytail, and she swipes on just a hint of makeup, enough to feel fresh but not overdone. She grabs her key card and her phone, slipping them into her bag, and heads out the door with a light step, eager to meet JT.

The ship is already bustling with passengers excited for the day, but she doesn't let the noise distract her. She makes her way to the main dining area, her heart picking up its pace as she thinks about what the day could hold. As she enters the space, she sees JT sitting at a table by the window, his gaze already scanning the room for her. His face lights up when he spots her, and he stands immediately, a wide grin spreading across his face.

"Good morning, beautiful," he says, his voice low but full of warmth. He pulls out the chair for her, always the gentleman, and she smiles, feeling a little flutter in her chest at how effortlessly he makes her feel cared for.

She sits down, her gaze never leaving his. "Good morning," she replies, her tone soft but full of excitement. "How are you today?"

JT sits back down and raises an eyebrow, as if considering the question for a moment. "Better now that you're here," he says, his words teasing but sincere. He reaches for the coffee pot, refilling both their cups. "So, Barcelona... ready to explore?"

"Absolutely," she says with a nod, her eyes shining with enthusiasm. "I can't wait to see everything. We'll need to make a list of places to go, of course."

JT smiles, his hand brushing lightly against hers as he settles back into his chair. "We can make a list," he says, leaning forward slightly, "but I'd be just as happy to explore it all with you without a plan. I've been here several times and sometimes the best parts of a city are the ones you stumble upon by accident."

Drusilla laughs softly, her gaze never leaving his. There's something about him, something that makes her feel completely at ease. "I like the sound of that," she agrees, her voice warm with affection. "Spontaneity has its charm, doesn't it?"

The two of them continue to chat as breakfast arrives, the table filling with fresh fruit, pastries, and eggs, the conversation flowing easily between them. There's an undeniable connection, one that has grown steadily since they first met, and as they talk about their plans for the day, it's clear they are both looking forward to discovering Barcelona together.

After breakfast, they linger for a while, savoring the moment. Drusilla leans back in her chair, glancing out the window at the blue waters of the Mediterranean as the ship slowly nears the port. The city of Barcelona looms ahead, its beauty already evident from this distance. Her excitement builds as she imagines the cobblestone streets, the stunning architecture, and the vibrant culture that awaits them.

As they finish their meal, JT looks at her with a grin. "Shall we head out then?" he asks, his tone filled with playful anticipation.

Drusilla nods eagerly, already standing from her chair. "Let's go. I'm ready for our adventure."

They both grab their bags and head for the exit, their hearts light and their steps in sync. Together, they're about to embark on a new chapter of their journey, one filled with discovery, laughter, and the undeniable chemistry that's grown between them over the past few days.

Barcelona is waiting. And so are they.

As the ship docked in Barcelona, Drusilla felt a flutter of excitement in her chest. The city's iconic skyline, with its unique blend of modern and Gothic architecture, stood before her. JT had promised her a day of sightseeing, and she couldn't wait to explore this vibrant city with him.

JT could sense her excitement and smiled at her, his hand resting gently on the small of her back as they walked together.

They decide to spend the day wandering through the Gothic Quarter, discovering hidden alleyways filled with art galleries and cafés. Drusilla is mesmerized by the architecture, particularly the intricate details of the Sagrada Familia, the masterpiece by Antoni Gaudí. She leans into JT as they marvel at the towering basilica, and he listens intently, fascinated by her passion for art and design.

After a leisurely lunch filled with laughter and a few too many glasses of sangria, Drusilla and JT were feeling the carefree buzz of the afternoon. The sun shone brightly, casting a golden glow on the cobblestone streets as they strolled hand in hand through the heart of Barcelona. Their conversation had lightened to playful teasing, but the undercurrent of desire was undeniable. Both of them knew the chemistry between them was stronger than ever, and it reflected in every flirting glance and every smile they exchanged.

Their passion had already reached a fever pitch, a fire that neither of them could ignore. Every glance between them sparked something more, something deeper. It was clear now—what started as a flirtation had turned into something undeniable. As they walked through the vibrant streets of Barcelona after lunch, the energy between them crackled. Neither of them could pretend that the chemistry had cooled. They couldn't even walk down the street without wanting each other.

After their leisurely morning, relaxing lunch, and an afternoon spent exploring the sun-soaked streets of Barcelona, Drusilla and JT find themselves back at the ship, their energy a mixture of contentment and quiet anticipation. The day has been filled with laughter and conversation, the vibrant sights of the city bringing them closer as they shared moments of awe— whether it was at the stunning architecture of Gaudí's *Sagrada Família* or the playful chaos of *La Rambla*.

They walk along the pier, the sea breeze ruffling their hair as they make their way back to the ship. Their conversation continues, both of them reflecting on the beauty of the city—how the mix of old and new has such a unique pulse, how every corner feels like a discovery. There's something about Barcelona that feels alive, just as their connection feels between them.

After making it back to the ship, both Drusilla and JT are ready to unwind before heading out again. The ship's calm and familiarity feel like a sanctuary after the excitement of the city. They each retreat to their cabins for some time alone, to freshen up and change before dinner.

Drusilla enters her cabin and takes a moment to relax. The light from the late afternoon sun streams through the windows, casting a warm, golden glow on everything. She moves through her cabin, unpacking a few things, then heads to the bathroom for a quick shower. The cool water feels refreshing after the warm Barcelona sun. When she finishes, she wraps herself in a soft towel and sits down in front of the vanity, running a brush through her damp hair.

She decides on something simple yet elegant for dinner—a flowy, deep emerald green dress that hits just below her knees and is just the right amount of dressy for the evening. She pairs it with a pair of strappy sandals and a light touch of makeup—just enough to enhance her natural features. Her hair with a bit of curl, down around her shoulders. As she finishes, she spritzes on a hint of her favorite perfume, a subtle floral scent that she's always loved. She looks in the mirror, feeling a sense of excitement. Dinner with JT is always more than just a meal; it's a shared experience, something that means more with every passing day.

Meanwhile, JT is in his own cabin, carefully choosing his outfit. He knows the restaurant he's taking Drusilla to, and it's one of his favorite hidden gems in the city. Tucked away in a quiet corner of the Gothic Quarter, it's a place most tourists would never find, but JT has been a few times and always found the food exceptional. He likes to keep it as his personal retreat, a place where he can step out of the limelight and just be. Tonight, though, he wants to share it with Drusilla. It feels right.

He settles on a crisp white shirt and a pair of navy blue trousers, something effortlessly stylish but comfortable for the evening. He pairs it with a navy blazer, feeling the subtle weight of the fabric and the way it compliments the atmosphere of the restaurant they'll visit. After a quick glance in the mirror to make sure everything looks just right, he heads out, already anticipating the look on Drusilla's face when they arrive.

When JT arrives at Drusilla's cabin, she answers the door with a warm smile. She looks stunning—elegant yet effortless in her green dress. JT's breath catches for a moment as he takes her in, feeling a surge of admiration. "You look beautiful," he says, his voice sincere, his gaze lingering just a little longer than he means.

Drusilla smiles, feeling a flutter in her chest. "Thank you," she replies, her tone soft and appreciative. "You look great too."

He leans in and kisses her on the neck and whispers "thank you", then extends his arm toward her with a smile, and she takes it. "Shall we go, then?"

As they make their way off the ship and into the heart of Barcelona, the evening air is warm, a gentle breeze carrying the scent of the sea mixed with the city's vibrant life. The streets are alive with energy, but JT guides them expertly through the labyrinth of alleyways and narrow streets that lead to the small restaurant he knows so well. As they walk, their conversation turns to everything and nothing—the little moments they've shared on the ship, the quirky things they've noticed about the city, and their excitement about the days ahead.

When they arrive at the restaurant, tucked in a cozy corner of the Gothic Quarter, JT smiles with quiet satisfaction. The place has an old-world charm, its rustic interior filled with wooden tables and low light, creating an intimate, almost secretive atmosphere. The waiters greet him warmly, and Drusilla can sense that this is a place where JT feels comfortable, like a second home.

They are shown to a small, candle-lit table near a window that overlooks the narrow, cobbled street outside. JT pulls out Drusilla's chair with a smile before sitting across from her. The mood is relaxed, and as they settle into the evening, the conversation flows easily. JT recommends a bottle of wine, and the two of them toast to their time in Barcelona, to the unexpected joy of their journey together.

The food arrives—local Spanish specialties, each dish more delicious than the last. They share bites of paella, savoring the flavors of the Mediterranean. There's laughter between them, and moments of quiet reflection as they talk about everything from their past to the future. The night stretches on, the ambiance of the restaurant perfectly complementing the chemistry between them. As they finish their meal, JT leans back in his chair, a satisfied smile on his lips.

"I'm glad we came here," he says, his voice low but content. "There's something about this place... it's one of those hidden gems you want to keep for yourself, but it's too good not to share."

Drusilla takes a sip of wine, her eyes meeting his with a soft smile. "I'm glad you shared it with me," she says. "It's perfect. Just like everything else today."

JT smiles, feeling the warmth of her words settle in his chest. "We've got a lot more to discover together," he says, his voice quiet but full of meaning. They both know it's true—their journey is far from over, and the adventure is only just beginning.

The night air is warm as Drusilla and JT walk back to the ship after dinner, their conversation light and easy, the kind that comes when two people have spent the day together and feel at ease in each other's company. They head up to the top deck lounge, the stars above them sparkling in the clear night sky. The gentle hum of the ship's engines is the only sound beneath their footsteps. It's the perfect night for a nightcap.

The lounge is nearly empty, save for a couple of other passengers nursing their last drinks of the evening. The soft glow of ambient lighting reflects off the polished wood surfaces, creating a quiet, intimate atmosphere. They find a cozy spot by the railing, and JT orders them both a glass of whiskey—something smooth, something they can sip slowly as they talk.

As the first sip warms her mouth, Drusilla leans back against the plush cushions of the lounge seat. Her eyes glance toward the ocean, the dark, endless expanse that surrounds them. The ship is rocking gently, a lullaby in motion. There's a peacefulness to the moment, but it's only moments before Drusilla turns to JT, her voice soft but curious.

"So, tell me... how did you and your wife meet?" She's always wondered about his past, especially about the woman he was once married to. There's so much about JT she still doesn't know, and tonight feels like the right time to ask.

He takes a slow sip of his whiskey, setting the glass down gently, as if the question has taken him by surprise. But then his expression softens, and he leans back in his chair, his gaze drifting to the horizon. "We met when I was in my late twenties. I was living in Manhattan, working for my Father. She was... well, she was everything I thought I wanted. Beautiful, ambitious, with a strong sense of purpose. She came from a family of politicians, and that's what really intrigued me at first. We connected in the way you connect with someone who challenges you, who pulls you out of your comfort zone."

Drusilla listens quietly, sensing there's more to the story. "What happened?" she asks, her voice gentle, not wanting to pry too much but genuinely wanting to understand.

JT sighs, rubbing a hand over his face. "Over time, we just... grew apart. We were both so focused on our own worlds. She had her career, and I had mine. My business took off, and I locked myself into it. We didn't have kids, though we both wanted them. It just... never happened. And by the time we realized how separate we had become, it was too late."

Drusilla doesn't speak at first, letting the weight of his words settle between them. She knows what it's like to feel invisible in a relationship, to long for something more but to feel helpless as it slips away.

"I'm sorry," she says softly, her hand finding his on the armrest. She squeezes it gently, offering silent support.

JT looks at her, his eyes searching hers for a moment, before he looks down at their hands. "I never really talk about this stuff," he admits, his voice almost a whisper. "But with you... it feels different. I don't know why, but I feel like I can tell you things I've kept locked away for so long."

Drusilla smiles softly, touched by his honesty. "You don't have to explain why. I'm glad you're sharing this with me."

JT leans back in his chair, his gaze distant now, but his mind clearly working through the past. "We spent the last few years of our marriage leading separate lives. She was deeply involved in politics, traveling all the time. I was consumed with my business. There was love between us at one point, but eventually, it became more about convenience. I felt a sense of duty to my shareholders, to the people who worked for me... I couldn't walk away from that. And she... she couldn't walk away from her own career. We grew apart. But it was always the unspoken thing— both of us knowing that it wasn't right, but neither of us really doing anything about it."

He pauses for a moment, swirling the amber liquid in his glass as if searching for something in the words. "I'm not proud of it, but it's the truth."

Drusilla feels a pang of sympathy for him, for the man who carried that burden alone for so long. "It sounds like you were both stuck in roles that no longer suited you," she says quietly. "But that doesn't mean it was your fault."

JT glances over at her, a quiet gratitude in his eyes. "I guess I've always carried that responsibility. I thought I could fix it, fix everything... But in the end, sometimes you can't fix things. You just have to let go."

The conversation shifts then, from his marriage to his family, and more specifically, his father. JT talks about his father's business—the emerald mining operation that his family had inherited. He speaks of it with a certain reverence, a pride that's unmistakable. "My father... he built the business from the ground up. He's not a man of many words, but he's always believed in the value of hard work. When he retired, he passed it on to me. And I've been running it ever since."

Drusilla listens intently, her curiosity piqued. "That must have been a big change, taking over the business. Especially with your father's legacy."

JT nods, his expression softening as he continues. "It was. The transition wasn't easy, and it came with its own set of challenges. But it's not just about the money, or the business. The people who work for us... it's their lives that matter. There are entire families that depend on the mines, and when we hit a strike... when we find a big deposit, it's a huge deal. It changes lives."

There's a quiet pride in his voice, but also something deeper—something almost reverent. "I try to take care of the families of the workers. Make sure their kids have an education, that they're supported. It's the right thing to do."

Drusilla feels a lump form in her throat, touched by his compassion, the way he's not just about the business but about the people behind it. "That's... incredible, JT," she says, her voice soft with emotion. "I never would have guessed you did all that."

He shrugs slightly, looking down at his glass again. "Most people don't know about that side of me. I keep it private. But with you, I don't feel the need to hide anything. I don't know why."

Drusilla smiles, her heart full as she watches him. "I'm glad you trust me enough to open up," she says quietly.

JT meets her gaze then, his voice lower, more earnest than before. "It's not just that I trust you. I feel something with you, Drusilla. Something that... I can't explain, but it's real. And it scares me, but in the best way."

Her heart skips a beat at his words, and she feels that same pull—one she's been feeling for days now, but has been hesitant to fully acknowledge.

"I feel it too," she says softly, her voice steady but full of warmth. "We're not in a hurry, though. Let's just take it one step at a time."

JT smiles, his hand finding hers again, his thumb lightly brushing the back of her hand. "One step at a time," he agrees, his voice filled with quiet sincerity.

The night stretches on, the soft murmur of the ocean in the background, and for the first time in a long while, both of them feel completely at peace.

As the conversation winds down, JT and Drusilla both feel the weight of the day settling in, the gentle hum of the ship's engines beneath their feet. The lounge, now quieter with only a few lingering passengers, has become a perfect backdrop for the peaceful, tender moment they share.

JT stands up, offering his hand to Drusilla with a warm smile. "I think it's time to call it a night," he says, his voice low and sincere, as if he's savoring the quiet connection they've just shared.

She nods, her heart full, and takes his hand, feeling a sense of calm and closeness with him that she hasn't felt in a long time. They walk together in silence down the long, softly lit corridors of the ship, their footsteps echoing gently in the hall.

When they reach her cabin, JT stops and turns toward her, his gaze lingering on her face. "Goodnight, Drusilla," he says, his voice thick with emotion, but still holding a touch of his usual composure. "Thank you for tonight... for letting me open up."

Drusilla smiles, her heart swelling. "I'm glad you did. It means a lot to me. You're not just a story in my book anymore, JT. You're real." She steps into his arms, wrapping him in a tight, lingering hug, one that feels like it says everything they both haven't had the words to express.

JT holds her close, a deep breath leaving him as he closes his eyes for a moment, just breathing her in. When they pull apart, his hands linger on her shoulders for a moment longer than necessary. "I'll see you in the morning, then. Breakfast?" he asks with a soft smile.

"Absolutely," Drusilla replies, the smile lighting up her face. She watches as he turns to leave, her eyes following him down the hall before she closes the door softly behind her.

Inside, she leans against the door, a contented sigh escaping her lips. She's grateful for the day they've shared—yet another step closer, yet another layer peeled back. As she takes a few moments to settle into her cabin, she reflects on the conversation, on how he opened up to her. The gentle kiss he left on her lips and the hug that followed linger in her mind.

The night ends quietly for both of them. In her room, Drusilla changes into a tee shirt, crawls into bed, and lets the events of the day wash over her. Tomorrow, they'll explore more of

Barcelona, spend the last day of their stay together. The promise of another beautiful day with JT fills her heart.

JT, in his own cabin, takes a long, reflective look out the window at the starry night. His thoughts are with Drusilla—her presence, her understanding, and the connection that's growing between them.

Tomorrow is another day. He smiles to himself as he turns off the lights and settles into bed, the quiet of the ship lulling him into a peaceful sleep.

Day two in Barcelona

The early morning light spills into Drusilla's cabin, warming her skin as she wakes. She stretches lazily, savoring the quiet of the moment. Soon, her phone buzzes on the nightstand. It's a message from JT:

Breakfast at 9?

With a smile, she quickly types back,

Absolutely.

She takes a deep breath, feeling a flutter of excitement in her chest. Each day with JT seems to unfold with ease, but today, she can sense that Barcelona will be special.

She showers quickly and picks out a flowy, off-white sundress, paired with simple sandals—something chic but comfortable for a day of wandering the city. Her hair is tousled but windswept in the best way, and she leaves it loose, adding just a touch of mascara and lip gloss for a fresh look. Grabbing her key card, she heads out of her cabin and to the restaurant, anticipating another perfect day together.

As she enters the breakfast room, she sees JT waiting by the window, a casual yet elegant presence as always. His blue shirt catches the morning sunlight, and his smile, when he sees her, is enough to make her heart skip a beat.

75

"Good morning," she greets him with a smile. "You're looking well-rested this morning."

He stands and kisses her on the cheek, pulling out her chair, then chuckles, clearly in good spirits. "Good morning, beautiful. Ready for the day?" He motions for the waiter to bring them coffee and croissants, already anticipating the energy they need to take on Barcelona.

JT suggests they start with a walk along Las Ramblas—just taking in the energy of the street performers, the markets. Maybe a stop at La Boqueria for some fresh fruit."

Drusilla's eyes light up at the suggestion. "Sounds perfect. I love markets. After that?"

"From there, I thought we could wander through the city—get lost in the old alleys and history. I have a favorite little café there I've been to a few times. And we'll end with a visit to the beach," JT suggests, his voice light but with a deep fondness for the city in his words. "It's a perfect mix of culture and relaxation. What do you think?"

"I love it," Drusilla says, feeling the warmth of anticipation settle in her chest. "It sounds like the perfect way to spend another day in Barcelona—together, just exploring."

JT smiles at her, his eyes meeting hers with a deep connection. "We'll take our time. No rush. Just you and me, and the city."

They sip their coffee as the day begins to unfold, chatting about their previous travels, the places they've each visited, and the ones they still dream of seeing. Their connection continues to deepen with each passing moment. There's a sense of contentment in the air, like they are exactly where they are meant to be.

As they finish breakfast, they both feel the pull of the city calling them, the day ahead full of possibility. They stand, ready to set off, and JT takes Drusilla's hand with a confident smile. "Let's make today unforgettable."

After a busy morning walking the streets and going in and out of the various shops, they stop at the small café that JT told her about. They take a seat at a cozy table near the window. JT handles the ordering, since he was familiar with the menu.

For starters, they share a plate of *pan con tomate*—crispy toasted bread rubbed with ripe tomatoes, garlic, and a drizzle of olive oil, the simplicity of it perfect for a light yet flavorful beginning. They savor each bite, the fresh, juicy tomatoes bursting with sweetness.

Next, they both go for a classic Barcelona dish: *bomba*—fried, crispy croquettes filled with a creamy, spiced potato and meat filling, served with a dollop of spicy aioli on the side. The rich crunch of the exterior and the soft, savory interior make for an irresistible combination. Then a traditional Catalan vegetable dish of roasted eggplant, bell peppers, and zucchini layered with tomato sauce.

The meal is delicious but unhurried, giving them time to talk and enjoy each other's company, the small café offering a perfect respite from their exploration of the city. By the end of the meal, they feel content, both physically satisfied and emotionally connected, the food having added another layer to the day's growing sense of intimacy. After a couple more glasses of sangria, the heat of the day seemed to fuel the heat between them. Every look, every comment has a hint of flirtation. They can't keep their hands off of each other.

After lunch, they walk around the city, hand in hand exchanging sexually charged innuendos. Passing the Mandarin Hotel, JT paused and turned to Drusilla with a devilish grin. "How about we take a little detour?" he suggested. She raised an eyebrow, intrigued, but she thought she knew what he meant.

He guided her through the lobby, the luxury of the hotel matching the desires burning between them. At the reception desk, he quickly arranged for a room—not for the night, but for the next couple of hours. A private space where they could sneak away and be alone together, uninterrupted.

When they arrive at the room, JT opens the door with a sense of purpose, but he pauses just inside, turning to Drusilla with a look that sends a thrill through her. His lips are slightly parted, as though he's trying to find the right words, but in the end, he doesn't speak. He simply steps closer, his hands reaching for her, the space between them shrinking with every second.

Drusilla's heart races as she feels his warm touch at her waist. She knows what is about to happen. Her body responds almost instinctively, heat flooding her entire body. She lifts her face to his, and he kisses her—soft at first, a gentle exploration, before the kiss deepens, growing more urgent, more hungry.

In that moment, everything else fades—the city, the noise, the crowd. There's only the two of them, their bodies pressed together, their hearts beating in sync, and the electricity that crackles between them like an unspoken promise.

Her hands move to his chest, feeling the strength of him under the soft fabric of his shirt. He pulls away just slightly, his breath ragged, and his eyes lock with hers, searching for any hesitation. But there is none. Only the mutual recognition of a desire long building, waiting to be unleashed.

With a swift, fluid motion, JT pulls her closer, his hands sliding up her back, and her fingers brush against his jaw as she pulls him back to her lips. There's a kind of urgency in the way they kiss now—a need to erase the space between them, to melt into each other. The world outside the room becomes a distant memory as they focus solely on the feel of each other, the taste of each other, and the pulse of each other's desire.

Drusilla's fingers move to the buttons of his shirt, tugging it open, and JT lifts her effortlessly, pressing her back against the cool wall. She wraps her legs around his waist instinctively, her body eager to be closer to his. The heat between them is overwhelming, their breaths coming faster now, mingling in the air between them as their hands roam, exploring with newfound urgency.

They move to the bed, their bodies tangled together in an uncoordinated rush, each of them intent on the singular goal of feeling the other, completely, utterly. JT's lips trail a path down her neck, his touch both tender and hungry as he finally undresses her, reverently, as though she's something precious, something he's been waiting for.

When they finally reach the moment they have both been waiting for, everything feels so natural, so beautiful. The physical connection is electric, yes, but it's more than that—this moment is years in the making. It's a culmination of their shared experiences, their unspoken understandings, and the raw, undeniable sexual chemistry that has been building from the moment they met.

There are no words at first—just the sensation of their bodies moving together in perfect harmony, their hands, their lips, and their hearts connected in a way neither of them has experienced before. Each touch, each kiss, each breath shared explodes with pure excitement.

They finish together in a moment of perfect surrender, their desires laid bare, unmasked. And as they hold each other, soaked in their sweat, breathing heavily, the world outside the room fades to nothingness, leaving only the two of them—complete, united, and finally, without restraint.

As they lay together in the soft afterglow, Drusilla feels the quiet weight of everything they've shared—every word, every glance, every touch. And in JT's arms, she knows that this connection is something far deeper than just physical; it's a union of souls, a perfect meeting of two people who have found each other amidst the noise of the world.

For the first time in a long while, she feels at peace. She was so happy that this moment was not rushed, that they had taken time to know each other.

As they left the Mandarin Hotel, their faces flushed with a mix of excitement and sheepishness. They walked through the grand lobby side by side, trying to act as if everything was perfectly normal, though the secret of what had just transpired hung between them like a delicious, unspoken truth. It felt as though every pair of eyes in the lobby knew exactly what they had been up to. Drusilla couldn't help but smile to herself, the thrill of the illicit moment still buzzing in her veins. JT, for once, didn't mind the attention, though his grin was slightly more contained.

Once outside, they stopped on the street corner to grab ice cream from a cart. The sun beat down on the cobblestone streets, the air still warm from the afternoon. They laughed as they licked their cones, the shared sweetness of the ice cream a small counterpoint to the fiery heat between them. Drusilla glanced at JT, her smile reaching her eyes, her thoughts still spinning from the afternoon's passion. He caught her eye, and his grin returned, as if he couldn't believe how fast things were unfolding, yet how perfect it felt.

As they finished their ice cream, they strolled back toward the ship, the sound of their laughter mixing with the rhythmic pulse of the city around them. The streets of Barcelona seemed to glow with the memory of the day, and with every step, Drusilla knew she'd never forget this moment—the way it felt to be so close to JT, both of them so caught up in the heat of the moment, yet so comfortable with each other.

By the time they boarded the ship, their connection was undeniable, deeper than they could have imagined when they'd first met. Neither of them spoke as they made their way to their cabins, but their hands brushed, and the warmth of it spoke volumes.

As the ship set sail into the twilight, the city fading into the distance, Drusilla's thoughts raced. She couldn't wait for what the next chapter would hold, for both of them.

Chapter 6

3 Days at Sea

The next few days aboard the ship were a blend of laughter, quiet moments, and shared experiences. With no particular place to be, Drusilla and JT found themselves slipping into a routine that felt effortless. Days were spent lounging by the pool, their legs stretched out under the sun, reading their books while occasionally stealing glances at each other, their quiet companionship speaking volumes. The slight breeze and the rhythmic sound of the ocean waves felt like the perfect soundtrack to their growing bond. It was simple—no expectations, just two people who enjoyed each other's company in silence, or sometimes with a few soft words exchanged.

The casino became their nighttime playground. They laughed as they tried their luck at the blackjack table, teasing each other when one would win or lose. JT was the one with the luck, but Drusilla was the better strategist, and together they made a fun, competitive pair. They shared flirtatious glances across the table, both still in awe of how easily they slipped into this new dynamic. It was as if they had known each other forever.

Evenings in the ship's restaurants were another highlight. They didn't have to say much to enjoy each other's presence. The dinners were a little longer now, filled with deeper conversations about dreams, regrets, and the future. Drusilla shared more about her art, her passion for painting, and how she wanted to pursue a new direction. They both realized how much they had in common, even in their vastly different worlds.

There were still moments of tenderness, like when JT would reach for her hand across the dinner table, or when he would gently fix a strand of her hair behind her ear as they walked to the restaurant. They were getting closer, yet neither of them was in a rush to define it. It was nice to just be—together. Nights were spent together in JT's cabin, enjoying the excitement of waking up together and the passion they shared night and day.

And when they weren't talking, they were just there—sitting next to each other, the gentle rock of the ship, their legs brushing, a quiet acknowledgment of their growing intimacy. Sometimes, Drusilla would glance at JT's profile, the way his jawline caught the sunlight, and think that maybe this was what it felt like to find peace in someone else.

Over the next three days at sea, JT and Drusilla continue to deepen their connection while savoring their time on the luxurious cruise. The ocean stretches endlessly around them, providing the perfect backdrop for moments of intimacy, relaxation, and shared adventure. The ship's rolling deck becomes their private sanctuary as they drift between the world they left behind and the world they're creating together.

Day 1

They begin their day with a light breakfast in the top-deck lounge, the gentle hum of the ship's movement creating a peaceful atmosphere. JT and Drusilla share their plans for the day as the sun rises, casting a golden hue over the horizon. They decide to spend the morning lounging by the pool, enjoying each other's company while sipping fresh fruit juices and basking in the sun.

81

As the hours pass, they engage in easy conversation, sometimes with laughter and playful teasing, sometimes with quiet moments of just being in each other's presence. Drusilla, ever the artist, sketches the scene before them, capturing the expansive ocean and the way the sunlight dances on the water. JT watches her, mesmerized by the ease with which she flows from one moment to the next, her creativity so natural and unforced. He feels a deeper appreciation for her in these quiet moments, when she's not performing or trying to impress anyone, but simply being herself.

Around noon, they take a break from the sun and retreat to the ship's library. The air-conditioned room offers a cool reprieve, and they settle into plush armchairs with books in hand. JT picks up a novel he's been meaning to finish, while Drusilla flips through an art magazine, sharing interesting articles and snippets with him.

Later, they indulge in a long, leisurely lunch in the ship's top deck cafe. It's a mix of light conversation and comfortable silences, as both of them savor the exquisite dishes presented before them. The experience feels luxurious but intimate, like a secret only they share.

As the evening approached they opted for a private dinner on the balcony of JT's cabin, a table set for two under the stars. Soft classical music played in the background, adding to the air of romance.

They shared their meal, exchanging thoughts on the day, their conversations ranging from light-hearted musings about the cruise to more personal, deeper reflections. JT's smile never faltered as he looked across the table at Drusilla, impressed by how easily they connected. Every laugh, every shared glance, felt effortless and natural. Over wine and the delicate flavors of their meal, they discussed everything and nothing all at once, the food taking second place to the unfolding intimacy between them.

After dinner, they decided to head to the casino for a little fun. JT had always enjoyed the thrill of gambling, and tonight, he was eager to share that excitement with Drusilla. The air in the casino was electric, filled with the chime of slot machines, the crisp shuffle of cards, and the laughter of players caught up in the moment. They tried their luck at a few games, laughing and teasing each other as they placed bets, enjoying the adrenaline of the experience. Drusilla felt a sense of liberation in the moment—free, adventurous, and fully alive. She had forgotten how exciting it could be to take a gamble on something, anything.

A couple of hours later, they made their way to the ship's lounge, both of them a little tipsy, but in high spirits. The same champagne they had been enjoying in the casino was now flowing in the lounge, and they raised their glasses to a day well spent. As the night deepened, the lounge became more intimate, the hum of the crowd blending with the soft melodies of the live music. They found a quiet corner, wrapped in conversation, stealing kisses, sharing stories and laughing at the oddities of life. Time seemed to slow down, and neither of them had any desire to rush.

Eventually, they made their way back to JT's cabin. There was something comforting about being in each other's presence, a quiet understanding that whatever came next would be welcomed without hesitation.

They showered and once they were dry, they slipped into thick white robes, feeling cozy and content as they made their way to the balcony again. The night air was cool and refreshing, the ocean whispering below them as the stars shone brightly overhead. They sat in silence for a while, both of them wrapped in the warmth of the night and the comfort of each other's presence. Every now and then, Drusilla would lean her head on JT's shoulder, the silence between them peaceful, unhurried.

They talked about anything and everything, the conversation flowing freely from topic to topic. They shared little stories from their childhoods, what they dreamed about when they were younger, and the things that made them who they were now. It was moments like this—these quiet, unguarded conversations—that made Drusilla feel like she was discovering parts of herself she had long forgotten. JT listened intently, his presence calming and reassuring. He had an ease about him that made her feel safe to share things she hadn't shared with anyone else.

As the night grew later, the conversation slowed, and they found themselves simply enjoying the silence, the peaceful hum of the ocean surrounding them. JT stood up first, offering his hand to Drusilla, and together, they made their way back inside. They slid beneath the soft sheets of the bed, still wrapped in the warmth of the night, their bodies naturally drawing close. The world outside seemed to fade away, leaving only the two of them in this perfect moment.

Without words, they let their hands explore each other, the connection between them deepening as their bodies entwined. It wasn't rushed—it was slow, tender, and intimate. In that moment, there was no rush, no hurry. Just two people lost in each other's touch, savoring the feeling of being desired in ways neither had experienced in a long time.

When the passion finally settled into something softer, Drusilla curled up in JT's arms, her head resting against his chest. His heartbeat was steady beneath her ear, a comforting rhythm that lulled her into a deep sense of peace. She drifted off to sleep with a smile on her face, the softness of the sheets and the warmth of JT's embrace making it impossible to feel anything but content.

As she slept, JT held her close, the faintest smile tugging at the corners of his mouth. He wasn't sure how it had happened, but somehow, over the course of the past few days, Drusilla had become more than just a companion. She was someone he could imagine a future with—a future that didn't seem as impossible as it once had.

The night passed in perfect harmony, another night in paradise, and as the morning sun began to peek through the curtains, they woke up to a new day. But for now, wrapped in each other's arms, the world outside could wait.

Day 2

The second day is filled with shared adventures as they try out some of the more active excursions offered by the ship. After a morning of relaxation, they sign up for a cooking class together—a private session taught by the ship's renowned chefs, who guide them through creating a Mediterranean feast. The air is filled with the sound of chopping, stirring, and occasional laughter as JT and Drusilla work together, their hands brushing as they pass ingredients, their eyes meeting over simmering pots. The chemistry between them is palpable in every moment, yet neither rushes anything. There's no need to. The connection they share is more than enough.

The evening was setting the stage for something extraordinary, and JT and Drusilla were more than ready to step into it. The ship's formal dinner in *The Dining Room* was the perfect excuse to dress up and indulge in the luxurious atmosphere surrounding them.

In his cabin, JT stood in front of the mirror, adjusting his black suit. It was tailored perfectly to his frame, the sharp lines of the jacket accentuating his broad shoulders and trim waist. The crisp white shirt and thin black tie added just the right amount of understated elegance. He was a picture of class, the kind of man who belonged in a high-end movie set. As he finished fixing his cufflinks, he couldn't help but smile at the thought of Drusilla walking into the room from her cabin, the vision of her in her dress forming in his mind.

Meanwhile, Drusilla stood before the mirror in her cabin, taking a step back to admire her look. Her black cocktail dress hugged her curves beautifully, the low-cut neckline adding just the right amount of allure without revealing too much. Her diamond stud earrings sparkled softly against the dark fabric of her dress, and the black heels made her legs look impossibly long. She slipped the black sparkling clutch onto her wrist and gave herself one last look before her phone buzzed with a message from JT:

"Ready?"

She smiled at the text and replied:

"Always."

With that, she left her cabin and made her way down the corridor toward JT's. As she knocked softly on the door, JT opened it with a smile, his eyes lighting up at the sight of her.

"Oh my God. You are stunning," he said, his voice low and filled with admiration. Drusilla, with a playful grin, stepped inside.

"You look amazing yourself," she teased, letting her gaze linger on him. Her fingers traced the line of his suit jacket before sliding up to touch the lapel.

JT reached out, pulling her into a close embrace. "I don't want to let go of you," he murmured, his lips grazing the soft skin of her neck before capturing her lips in a kiss. It was deep, slow, filled with longing. Their bodies pressed closer, a heat building between them as the taste of each other lingered on their tongues.

They both paused for a moment, breathless. Drusilla rested her forehead against his, her hands still lingering on his chest. "We could skip dinner," she said with a teasing smile, her voice hushed but filled with temptation.

JT chuckled softly, his hands sliding down to her waist. "We could," he agreed, his lips curling into a mischievous smile. But then, his gaze softened, and he kissed her again. "Don't tempt me gorgeous. That can wait. Let's go show you off in *The Dining Room*, then come back and finish that conversation."

Reluctantly, they pulled away from each other. JT held out his arm with a playful grin. "After you, my lady."

Drusilla smoothed out her dress and took his arm, giving him a wink as they made their way to *The Dining Room*, each feeling the tension of the night building between them. The elegant, golden-hued restaurant was alive with chatter and the clink of glasses, the crystal chandeliers above casting a soft glow over the room. They were shown to their table by a steward, and as they sat, the anticipation of the evening hung in the air between them.

Their flirtatious banter continued throughout dinner, punctuated with laughter and stolen glances. The dim lights and intimate setting made it easy for them to lose track of time, allowing the natural chemistry between them to flourish. Between courses, they would exchange knowing smiles, their fingers brushing over the rim of their wine glasses, each touch and gaze adding to the undeniable tension that simmered just below the surface.

Throughout the evening, Drusilla's eyes never left JT. His presence was magnetic, his words engaging, but it was his every movement—his hand on the back of her chair, the way he leaned in when he spoke to her—that made her heart race.

"I could get used to this," Drusilla said, breaking the conversation's flow for a moment, her eyes meeting his. "You, me, and dinner like this."

JT chuckled, swirling his glass of wine. "There's more to this night, you know."

"I know," she said softly, leaning back in her chair.

Later, after the last course was cleared, they stood and headed toward the lounge. The evening wasn't over yet, and there was still more to be shared. The walk back to the lounge was slow, relaxed—yet the undeniable connection between them lingered in the air like an electric charge, one that both of them knew would culminate later in a private moment.

Once in the lounge, they found a quiet corner. Drusilla leaned against the bar, her eyes still sparkling from the excitement of the evening. JT stood close beside her, his hand brushing against hers every few moments.

"This has been a perfect night," Drusilla murmured, her voice thick with longing.

JT smiled, his lips curving into a soft, intimate grin. "We're just getting started," he said, leaning in to kiss her softly.

As the night deepens, they move to a quiet lounge where they share a bottle of champagne. The music is soft, and the low hum of conversation around them feels like a distant murmur. They talk about the next port of call, and JT hints at some surprises he has planned for the upcoming days, but neither of them feels the need to rush. They're content in the now, in the space they've created together.

When they finally retire to their cabin, the night feels like it's theirs—slow, intentional, and full of promise. JT slips off his jacket and tosses it on the chair. He loosens his tie, kicks off his shoes and grabs a bottle of champagne out of the mini bar. "Meet you on the balcony."

Watching this unfold and loving every minute, Drusilla slips out of her heels, grabs two champagne glasses and joins JT on the balcony.

The soft sound of waves gently lapping against the ship below them filled the air, adding to the calm atmosphere. The bottle of champagne between them was nearly empty, and the cool night air had settled in, wrapping them in a quiet intimacy. Drusilla was curled into one of the plush chairs, still in her dress, her legs tucked underneath her, the soft glow of the moonlight accentuating the delicate curves of her face. JT sat across from her, the champagne flutes now set aside as he leaned in, his gaze warm but filled with curiosity.

"So, tell me about this Sam guy," he said, his voice low and genuine. "You spent eight years with him… that's a long time. What happened?"

Drusilla took a slow breath, her eyes flicking away for a moment before meeting his. She'd been expecting this question. In fact, part of her had been wondering when it would come. She'd shared pieces of her life with him, but never the whole story—not yet. She took a sip of champagne then set her glass down and let her fingers trace the rim of it as she collected her thoughts.

"Sam was… different," she began slowly, her voice a mixture of warmth and a hint of sadness. "We met right after I graduated from art school, and I thought… I thought we were perfect together. We had similar interests, he was kind, funny, and supportive. I didn't want for anything. But after a while, I realized I wanted more. More than just coasting along. I wanted the next step. I wanted something that felt like it meant something. But he didn't. He didn't want that… and it became this tug-of-war, you know?"

JT nodded, leaning forward slightly, his eyes softening with understanding. "And then?"

Drusilla exhaled a slow breath, her gaze distant for a moment. "We just stopped fighting for it. After so long, we were just… existing. I think we were both afraid to admit that it wasn't working, but neither of us had the strength to really walk away. Eventually, I realized that I wasn't going to get what I needed from him. And neither of us was really happy. So I left."

She looked at JT then, her eyes meeting his with a depth of emotion. "I was angry with myself for staying so long, but at the same time… I don't regret the time we had. He was part of my life for a reason. And he was there when I needed him." Her lips curved into a slight smile. "I just wish I had learned sooner that what I needed he couldn't provide."

JT let the silence hang between them for a moment before asking softly, "What about Cynthia? Your cat?"

Drusilla chuckled lightly, the heavy mood lifting. "Ah, Cynthia. She's a handful. A little diva, actually. I found her as a stray when she was just a kitten. She was so small and terrified. I took her in, and she's been with me ever since. She's… I guess you could say she's my best friend.

She's always there when I come home, even if she's a bit of a drama queen about it. I spoil her, of course."

JT smiled, the thought of Drusilla with a tiny, dramatic cat warming his heart. "She sounds like quite the character," he teased. "So, no siblings?"

"No siblings," she replied with a small shake of her head. "I'm an only child. I think that's why I'm so independent. My parents... they were great, but I never had to share them. I never had to compete for attention. My mom was always very supportive, but she was very busy. She's a high-powered lawyer. She was always working, always striving for more. My dad... well, he was never around much. They divorced when I was young. I've always felt like I've had to figure things out on my own. It's always been just me and Cynthia."

JT's eyes softened as he listened. "And your mom? Is she still in Boston?"

"Yeah. She's in the city, though we're not super close anymore," Drusilla admitted, her voice quieter now. "We used to be, but after she got remarried, things changed. She's always busy, and I think part of me resented how much of her time went to her career and her new life. I understand it now, but... well, there was a time when I wished she had been around more. Don't get me wrong. She has been a very big supporter of mine. She's always been there for me. I love her very much. She is the most important person in my life. If it weren't for her, I wouldn't be on this cruise. I wouldn't be sitting here drinking champagne with an emerald CEO."

Drusilla paused, letting the vulnerability of her words settle between them. JT was silent for a moment, his gaze unwavering. He felt a deep sense of empathy for her, knowing that the wounds from childhood—though no longer as sharp—could still leave marks. He reached over and took her hand gently in his.

"I understand more than you know," he said softly. "I think we both spent a lot of time trying to make things work with people who weren't the right fit. And I think we both understand what it's like to feel alone even when we're surrounded by people. I think that's why it's so easy to connect with you."

89

Drusilla smiled at him, squeezing his hand gently. "I'm so glad we did. Connect, I mean."

JT raised his glass of champagne, his expression sincere. "To connections," he said, his voice thick with emotion. "And to being brave enough to find them."

"To being brave enough to find them," Drusilla echoed, her voice barely a whisper as she clinked her glass against his. And in that moment, with the ocean breeze around them, the champagne in their hands, and the quiet serenity of the night, everything felt right.

They continued their conversation for a few more minutes and then take turns in the bathroom getting ready for bed. Their conversation continues once they get in bed. Then they lay silent for a few minutes, thinking about the precious moments they shared, bringing them even closer.

In each other's arms, they drift to sleep, knowing the journey they've started is far from over. And tomorrow—tomorrow they'll be ready for whatever comes next.

Chapter 7

Port of Call: Monte Carlo, Monaco

The days spent sailing between ports had been filled with the kind of carefree joy that only a couple in the throes of new love could experience. Each moment seemed to be a celebration of their growing connection, from casual afternoons lounging by the pool to quiet dinners where their eyes never seemed to leave each other.

During these lazy, sun-soaked afternoons, they found themselves stealing glances across the pool or during snack breaks in the café. It didn't matter where they were; one look, one shared smile, and they both knew what came next. Without saying a word, they'd slip away to one of their cabins—escaping the public eye to indulge in a passion that was as intense as it was magnetic. They sometimes acted like teenagers, sneaking off at a moment's notice, giddy with desire and excitement. No words were necessary. The pull between them was enough.

They'd laugh afterward, always sheepish and glowing, but unable to stop the pull they felt toward each other. There was something exhilarating about it, something that felt both innocent and new, as though they were rediscovering passion for the first time. They were past the awkwardness, past the nerves, and simply living in the moment, with no worries beyond the next touch, the next kiss. Neither one of them had ever experienced anything like this and they were enjoying every minute of it. The conversations they had only brought them closer and increased their desire for each other.

It was on one of those afternoons, as the ship's grand deck swayed in the distance behind them, that they finally arrived at the glittering shores of Monte Carlo. Monaco's luxury loomed ahead, its towering buildings and sparkling marina calling them into the heart of its sophistication. For Drusilla, this was an entirely new world—one that felt both exciting and intimidating in equal measure.

JT, however, looked perfectly at home, and as they disembarked, hand in hand, she couldn't help but be swept up in the allure of the place. They walked through the golden streets, their fingers intertwined, their chemistry undeniable. And yet, despite the surrounding elegance, it was clear that their passionate bond had only intensified.

The evening in Monte Carlo had a certain magic about it. The Mediterranean breeze was gentle, and the stars overhead seemed to shine just a little brighter than usual. After a leisurely day spent exploring the glitzy city, JT and Drusilla were ready to step into the world of glamour and sophistication.

JT had slipped into a white dinner jacket, the crisp fabric making him look every bit the part of a suave, sophisticated gentleman. His eyes were a little wider than usual as he watched Drusilla step out of her cabin. She was dressed in a floor-length black gown, the deep neckline accentuating her graceful figure. The dress seemed to shimmer in the light. Her hair was styled elegantly, cascading in soft waves, and her makeup was flawless, her eyes sparkling with an alluring mystery.

As she entered the room, JT's breath caught in his throat. She was nothing short of stunning. He couldn't help but stare for a moment, completely captivated by the beauty standing before him. She caught the look in his eyes, the admiration written across his face, and smiled.

"You clean up well," she teased, her voice low and sultry.

"You're—" JT's voice faltered for a second, his gaze never leaving her. "You're breathtaking."

They shared a quiet, knowing look. This night would be unforgettable.

After dinner at one of Monte Carlo's finest restaurants, where they dined on exquisite seafood and decadent French pastries, they made their way to the Grand Casino. The dazzling lights of the casino reflected off the polished marble floors, and the hum of excitement in the air was palpable. The world seemed to stop as they entered, the elite patrons glancing over at the stunning couple.

JT, ever the gentleman, led Drusilla by the hand, his eyes scanning the room. The casino was a world of its own. He had been here several times and felt even more comfortable with Drusilla on his arm. She felt like a queen by his side.

They played a few rounds at the roulette tables, their laughter echoing in the air as they won and lost small amounts here and there. But it wasn't about the money—it was about the thrill, the rush of the night, the shared moments that made it all so exhilarating.

After a few drinks at the bar, where JT made sure Drusilla always had a perfectly mixed martini, they wandered out into the cool night air, hand in hand. As they walked along the streets of Monte Carlo, the night felt as though it were just beginning.

As their evening in Monte Carlo unfolds, Drusilla is captivated when JT casually mentions his family's condo nearby. Her eyes widen with surprise as he invites her to see it, and they make their way to the luxurious, understated apartment overlooking the glittering Riviera. Enchanted by the intimacy of having such a private space together, they indulge in another passionate evening, surrendering to the pull that neither of them can seem to resist. Lost in the thrill of their secluded hideaway, they miss the last shuttle back to the ship.

Ever the problem-solver, JT arranges for a private plane to take them to the next port. Drusilla, exhilarated by the spontaneity of it all, feels like she's living in a dream. This unexpected detour means two extra days alone with JT in the romance-soaked splendor of Monte Carlo—just the two of them, tucked away from the world. Drusilla thinks to herself, *being a billionaire certainly has its perks.*

Over the next two days, JT and Drusilla revel in the elegance of Monte Carlo. Without their usual attire, shopping becomes a playful necessity, turning every boutique visit into an adventure. Drusilla's face lights up as she picks out glamorous outfits, and JT, equally captivated, enjoys spoiling her with designer pieces. Each purchase feels like a piece of this unexpected, luxurious experience, and Drusilla is caught between feeling like a princess and a carefree teenager.

They lunch at charming street cafes, toast with champagne as the Mediterranean sparkles in the sun, and wander the streets hand in hand. With every passing moment, they deepen their connection, making these extra days in Monte Carlo something they'll both cherish for years to come.

JT and Drusilla indulge in every decadent pleasure the city offers—and each other. Their days are filled with the finest champagne, gourmet meals at opulent restaurants, and moonlit strolls along the water's edge. But it's each other they crave most. With no itinerary or ship to catch, they surrender fully to their passion, every glance and touch reigniting the spark between them.

Together, they laugh over delicate pastries at breakfast, share luxurious lunches with rich flavors, and end their evenings wrapped up in a blur of romance. Their time in Monte Carlo becomes a whirlwind of high living, luxurious indulgence, and an undeniable, fevered connection that neither can resist.

It's time to catch up with the ship.

The Private Plane to Florence

After their passionate days in Monte Carlo, Drusilla and JT stood at the small private airport with the warm Mediterranean breeze hitting their skin. Their time in Monaco had been a whirlwind of indulgence, but now they were ready to return to the cruise, albeit with a bit of a detour.

JT's private plane was waiting on the tarmac—a luxurious jet, its polished surface gleaming in the fading light. The pilot greeted them with a professional smile as they stepped on board, the plush interior enveloping them in comfort. Drusilla settled into a plush leather seat, feeling the excitement of the past few days still racing through her veins.

"Ready to get back to the ship?" JT asked, his voice warm but with a playful edge, as he fastened his seatbelt.

"Of course. Though I must say, I'm going to miss this view," Drusilla replied, glancing out the window, her eyes lingering on the glimmering lights of Monte Carlo in the distance.

"I'll make sure we get back on track," JT said with a wink, reaching over to take her hand. "Just think of this as an extra little adventure. We've got Florence next."

As the plane took off, the city of Monte Carlo faded into the distance. They sat side by side in companionable silence, only the hum of the engines filling the air. For Drusilla, the last few days had felt like a dream—exquisite food, champagne flowing freely, a level of luxury she'd never known. And the best part, of course, was JT. His kindness, the way he always made her feel special, had made everything feel even more magical.

The flight was short, about an hour, and as they descended toward Florence, the stunning Tuscan landscape came into view—rolling hills and vineyards stretching out under a blanket of pink evening sky.

"We'll make it just in time for dinner," JT said with a smile, his voice a low murmur as he leaned in closer to her. "Then we can explore the beauty of Florence... and each other."

Drusilla smiled, her heart racing again. Even though their time in Monte Carlo had been passionate and indulgent, she couldn't wait to experience the next leg of their journey—together.

Chapter 8

Port of Call: Florence, Italy

The plane touched down smoothly in Florence, and after a quick transfer, JT and Drusilla were back on board the cruise ship, the familiar scent of the sea air greeting them as they stepped onto the deck. It felt good to be back, though their brief escape to Monte Carlo had been nothing short of unforgettable.

"Welcome back," a steward said with a warm smile as they stepped onto the ship, leading them through the grand lobby and toward their staterooms. "It looks like the Captain is expecting you both for dinner tonight. You'll be sitting at the Captain's table."

Drusilla exchanged a surprised glance with JT.

"The Captain's table?" she repeated, her voice filled with a mix of excitement and curiosity. She hadn't been expecting such a formal affair.

JT smiled, clearly pleased by the invitation. "I guess they've heard how much fun we've been having," he said with a wink, squeezing her hand. "It'll be a new experience. Should be interesting."

They made their way to their cabin to freshen up, the evening light casting a golden glow across the ocean. Drusilla couldn't help but feel a bit giddy. She had heard of the Captain's table—the privilege of sitting there was often reserved for guests of distinction, or those who were, as the crew liked to say, 'special.'

Drusilla stood in front of the mirror, slipping into her favorite dress, the elegant black cocktail dress that JT loved. She paired it with a simple silver necklace and black heels, letting her hair fall in soft waves around her shoulders. She wanted to look stunning, but in a way that was understated and elegant.

When JT came out of the bathroom, she turned to him, feeling her heart race. He was dressed in a sharp navy suit, his tie a deep shade of crimson that complemented his dark eyes and tan skin. His hair was neatly styled, and he had a certain air about him that made Drusilla's pulse quicken.

"You look amazing," he said, his eyes roving over her body with admiration. "As always."

"Thanks," she said, twirling around to give him the total view." Stepping closer to him, "We're going to look like a couple of movie stars."

He smiled, leaning in to kiss her gently. "I think we already do," he murmured, his lips brushing against hers.

After a moment, they pulled away, and he took her hand. "Let's go make an impression."

Dinner with the Captain

The Dining Room was as grand as ever, with glittering chandeliers hanging from the ceiling, casting their soft light over the polished tables. The captain's table, however, was set apart from the rest—its cloth pristine, its place settings extravagant. There were only a few guests already seated, each of them giving the couple an appraising glance as they approached.

The captain, a tall man with a distinguished air and an easy smile, stood to greet them.

"Mr. Anderson, Miss Pennington, welcome. We've been expecting you," he said, shaking JT's hand with a firm grip before turning to Drusilla as she offered him her hand. He took her hand, leaned over and kissed it gently. "It's a pleasure to have you both join us this evening."

"Thank you, Captain," Drusilla replied, offering him a warm smile. "It's an honor."

They were seated, and the evening began with a glass of champagne, which Drusilla found herself savoring as the conversation flowed around them. The guests at the table were friendly, but

Drusilla couldn't help but feel a bit out of place. Everything was so grand, so sophisticated. And then there was JT—his effortless charm and quiet confidence put her at ease. His presence made everything feel more natural, like they truly belonged.

As the first course was served, JT leaned in slightly, his voice low but intimate. "I know this is a little different than the usual dinner we've been having," he said, his fingers brushing against hers beneath the table. "But I'm glad we're here... together."

Drusilla smiled, her heart fluttering at the touch of his hand. "I'm glad too."

They spent the evening enjoying their meal and the company, laughing and exchanging stories. But despite the formal setting, their connection never wavered. Every glance, every small touch, was a silent promise of more to come.

After dinner and several toasts given around the table, JT and Drusilla thanked the Captain for a wonderful evening and said their good byes to the others around the table. As they left the Dining Room, JT asked Drusilla if she would like to stop for a nightcap. After thinking for a minute, she said, "I'm kinda tired. Can we call it a night?"

When Drusilla's cabin door clicked behind them, Drusilla turned to face JT, her eyes filled with a mix of excitement and vulnerability. Whispering, she said, "I've enjoyed every moment with you tonight... and I don't want it to end just yet."

Without hesitation, she wrapped her arms around his neck, pulling him closer. Their lips met in a kiss that was soft at first, full of the lingering sweetness of the evening, but soon it deepened, both of them giving in to the heat and desire that had been building all day.

JT pressed her back gently against the door, his hands sliding down to her waist as the kiss became more urgent, more passionate. His body seemed to hum with the energy between them, and Drusilla responded in kind, her hands tangled in his hair as she kissed him back, her heart soaring with the intensity of the moment.

In one smooth motion, he eased her onto the bed, positioning himself above her. She was breathless, her hair spilling out around her like a dark halo, eyes wide and focused on him. For a

97

moment, they just gazed at each other, the intensity of their connection so raw it almost felt like a physical force.

Without breaking eye contact, JT rolled over, positioning her above him. His heart raced as she straddled him, a feeling of possessiveness surging through him, though he couldn't fully understand it. He just wanted her—needed her—to understand that this wasn't just about passion. This was different.

The sensation was electric. JT inhaled sharply, his hands immediately finding her hips, guiding her as she moved against him. She was warm, so impossibly soft, and every movement she made sent jolts of desire shooting through him.

His hands slid up her back, pulling her face closer to his. Without a word, his lips found hers again, soft at first—gentle. But the kiss quickly deepened, becoming more urgent, more desperate as they both gave into the mounting need.

Drusilla's fingers tangled in his hair, pulling him closer, as she deepened the kiss. The fire between them was no longer something they could control; it was all-consuming, everything else fading away as their lips and bodies moved together with an intensity neither of them had ever felt before.

JT's heart hammered in his chest. He could feel every inch of her, every breath, every movement. He pulled her closer, his hands tracing the curves of her body as she responded in kind. Their connection was fierce, magnetic, like nothing either of them had ever experienced.

Their connection was everything.

And in that moment, nothing else mattered.

The next morning

The sun streamed through the windows of the cabin, waking Drusilla with the promise of a new adventure. She stretched lazily, glancing over at JT, who was already sitting up in bed, scrolling through his phone.

"Good morning," he said, looking up and flashing her a smile that made her heart flutter.

"Good morning," she replied, still feeling the warmth of their connection from the night before.

Drusilla slid out of bed, her heart fluttering slightly as she moved toward the bathroom. Her eyes wandered over the room, and she couldn't help but smile when she saw the mess of their clothes scattered between the door and the bed. It felt real—this was no longer just a dream, but a memory in the making.

She grabbed the crisp, starched white shirt JT had worn the night before and slipped into it, relishing the smell of his cologne and the soft fabric against her skin. Closing the bathroom door quietly behind her, she freshened up, brushed her teeth, and allowed herself a moment to reflect on the night—how everything had felt so right, so natural, despite the newness of it all. This was not something that she was used to.

When she stepped back into the bedroom, JT was still in bed, reading something on his phone. The sight of him, looking so effortlessly handsome, made her heart skip a beat. She paused for a moment, noticing how the sunlight bathed him in a golden glow, before walking toward him in nothing but her white panties and his shirt.

The look on his face when he saw her made her smile, and his eyes softened as he took in the sight of her. He set the phone down and extended his hand to her, a silent invitation. She didn't hesitate. She moved into his arms, feeling the same electric connection between them as she had the night before.

They kissed gently at first, the kind of kiss that spoke volumes of what had happened between them and what might still be to come. The passion that followed was familiar but new, comforting but exciting, as they enjoyed each other once again.

Afterward, both of them, content and exhausted, fell back onto the bed. Drusilla rested her head against his chest, and JT's arm pulled her close as they drifted back to sleep, the world outside forgotten for now.

They slept late into the morning, the soft lull of the ship's gentle rocking cradling them in a peaceful slumber. When Drusilla finally stirred, she noticed the light outside had shifted, the sun now higher in the sky. She blinked a few times, stretching her arms above her head, and noticed that JT was already sitting up, pulling on his clothes. His shirt, wrinkled from the night before and now smelling like Drusilla's perfume, hung loosely on his frame, adding to the charm of his easy confidence.

"I'll head back to my cabin to shower," JT said, tossing her a smile as he stood and buttoned his shirt. "Meet you for lunch in the rooftop café?"

Drusilla smiled, still feeling the warmth of their shared morning, and nodded. "Sounds perfect."

Before he left, he leaned down to kiss her, a soft, lingering kiss. As he headed for the door, he turned and said, "See you shortly pretty girl."

She smiled, then blew him another kiss.

The Day in Florence

After breakfast, they boarded the shuttle to the city, the day ahead of them packed with possibility. Drusilla had always dreamed of seeing Florence, and now, with JT by her side, it felt surreal.

Their first stop was a stunning winery nestled in the hills outside the city. The scenery was breathtaking—vineyards stretching out over the rolling hills, the sun casting a golden light over everything. They toured the winery, sampling some of the finest wines Tuscany had to offer. Drusilla couldn't help but be impressed by the smooth, rich reds and the way JT handled the tasting. He had an appreciation for the finer things in life, but he didn't flaunt it—he enjoyed it quietly, savoring the experience.

They wandered through the Boboli Gardens, hand in hand, admiring the lush greenery and intricate sculptures. The garden was a peaceful oasis in the heart of the city, and Drusilla felt incredibly content as she explored its hidden corners with JT.

100

"What do you think?" JT asked, as they paused at a quiet spot overlooking the city.

"It's beautiful," she said, leaning into him. "I've never seen anything like it."

"I'm glad you're here to experience it," JT replied, his voice warm. His hand found hers, fingers intertwining effortlessly. He didn't need to say more; his presence alone made the moment perfect.

They continued on to the Leonardo Museum, where they marveled at the genius of Leonardo da Vinci. Drusilla was fascinated by the intricate sketches and designs, her artist's mind marveling at the brilliance of it all. JT was equally engaged, but there was something deeper in his gaze when he looked at her—something that made her heart beat faster.

The galleries they visited afterward were just as awe-inspiring. Florence was a city that had inspired centuries of artists, and it was easy to see why. The rich history and stunning art surrounding them only seemed to deepen the bond between Drusilla and JT.

As the evening approached, they grabbed the shuttle and made it back to the ship in time to freshen up and change into something casual for their Italian dinner. JT, always effortlessly stylish, looked just as comfortable in a pair of well-fitted jeans and a crisp linen shirt as he did in his white dinner jacket. Drusilla, too, chose a simple yet elegant dress—just right for the laid-back ambiance of the restaurant they'd chosen.

As they exited the shuttle boat, the evening air was filled with the scent of saltwater and the distant sound of music coming from an outdoor bar nearby.

The port was bustling with activity, the evening crowds starting to fill the streets. JT and Drusilla walked side by side, the glow of the streetlights casting soft shadows on their path. As they reached the bottom of the gangway, Drusilla slipped her hand into his, her fingers threading through his as they strolled through the bustling piazza.

"I've never felt so... free," Drusilla murmured, her voice tinged with a quiet wonder. "Florence has a way of making everything else fade away."

JT glanced over at her, his gaze softening. "I feel the same way. It's like the whole world exists in this one moment."

They reached the restaurant, a charming trattoria tucked on a quieter street. The warm, inviting light spilling out from the open door created a sense of intimacy, and the faint sounds of laughter and clinking glasses greeted them as they stepped inside

The inside was cozy, with a rustic elegance that made it feel like a hidden gem. The tables were set with crisp white cloths, and the air was filled with the mouthwatering scents of freshly prepared Italian dishes. The waiters greeted them warmly, guiding them to a small table near the window where they could look out onto the twinkling lights of the city.

As they sat down, Drusilla couldn't help but smile as she looked around, taking in the rustic charm of the place. It was simple, yet beautiful—much like the city itself.

"This place feels like it's been here forever," she said softly, gazing out at the small street.

JT leaned in, his eyes playful. "I knew you'd like it?"

The waiter arrived with the wine list, and they decided on a bottle of Chianti Classico, the deep ruby red liquid a perfect complement to the evening. As they chatted about their day, the conversation flowed as easily as the wine. They spoke about the art they'd seen, the people they'd met, and the small, quiet moments that had made Florence so magical.

After a while, the first course arrived—homemade pasta with rich sauces and fresh herbs. Drusilla closed her eyes after the first bite, savoring the simple, perfect flavors.

"This is incredible," she said, her voice full of contentment. "I don't think I've ever tasted anything like it."

JT chuckled, leaning back in his chair. "And we still have the rest of the meal ahead of us." His smile softened. "It's the perfect way to end a perfect day."

They talked through the meal, the rhythm of their conversation as easy and natural as the food that filled their plates. As the night wore on, the restaurant became quieter, the hum of conversation softer, allowing them to drift into a more intimate space.

Finally, after dessert—an indulgent panna cotta with fresh berries—they lingered at the table, their fingers entwined across the table. The wine had loosened the edges of their restraint, and as the minutes ticked by, their closeness deepened.

Drusilla looked out the window at the night sky, the stars so bright above the city that it almost seemed like magic. She turned back to JT, her voice quiet. "I don't want this night to end."

"Then let's make sure it doesn't," he said, his tone husky, a spark of something more intense in his eyes. He stood and held out his hand to her.

Drusilla smiled and took his hand, standing and letting him guide her back outside into the cool night air. They walked slowly down the cobbled streets, their hands still clasped, the world around them fading as they focused only on each other.

As they reached the edge of the piazza, with the soft murmur of the city around them, JT stopped and turned to face her, his gaze unreadable for a moment. Then, without a word, he kissed her—softly at first, a tender, lingering kiss that spoke of all the moments between them. But then it deepened, and Drusilla felt a jolt of electricity run through her, her body responding instinctively to his touch.

They'd spent the day exploring a beautiful city, but it was the moments between them that made everything feel extraordinary. The love they were sharing—spontaneous, passionate, and real—was more than they ever expected.

A Night of Reflection

The night was calm as Drusilla and JT returned to the ship after their whirlwind day in Florence. The city had been everything she'd imagined and more, and with JT by her side, every moment felt like a dream. But as they stepped back onto the ship, a change in atmosphere settled over them.

"I've got an early wake-up call tomorrow," JT said, his voice laced with a slight regret as they walked down the corridor toward their cabins. "Calls starting early. I hate to cut the night short, but I think it's best we get some rest."

Drusilla nodded, understanding. It was the first time they would be apart since their time in Monte Carlo, and although it felt strange, she knew it was necessary.

"I'll see you at lunch, then?" she asked, her voice soft.

"Definitely," JT said, as he kissed her softly, then turned and entered his cabin. She watched him disappear inside, and for the first time in days, she felt a bit of loneliness.

After a moment of hesitation, Drusilla entered her cabin. The silence felt different now, heavier somehow. She kicked off her shoes and sat on the edge of the bed, reflecting on the past few days. Her heart swelled with happiness as she thought about JT—how he made her feel cherished and wanted, how their connection deepened with every passing hour. She had never imagined such a whirlwind romance, but now that it had happened, she couldn't deny the joy it brought her.

But then, her phone beeped, interrupting her thoughts.

She picked it up to find several new messages from Sam. A knot formed in her stomach as she saw his name on the screen.

"I miss you so much, Dru. Please call me."

"I know I messed up, but we need to talk. I need to see you. Please."

Drusilla stared at the messages, feeling a rush of conflicting emotions. She had moved on. She was happy with JT, happier than she'd ever been. But a part of her, the part that had spent eight years with him, the part that had shared her life and heart with him, still felt the tug of familiarity.

Her thumb hovered over the phone screen as the urge to respond gnawed at her. She hadn't heard from him in weeks, and now here he was, reaching out like nothing had changed. She took a deep breath and made a decision.

Without thinking too much about it, she dialed his number. The phone rang once, twice, and then he answered.

"Dru?" his voice crackled on the other end, a mixture of relief and longing in his tone.

"Hi," she said softly, unsure of how to begin. "I saw your messages."

"Please, just listen to me," he said quickly, his voice tinged with desperation. "I know things ended badly, but I've been thinking about you, about us, and I just—"

"We can't do this," Drusilla interrupted gently but firmly. "I've moved on. I've met someone. Someone who makes me feel... different. Someone who makes me feel alive."

There was a long pause on the other end of the line, and Drusilla could almost hear the hurt in his silence. Then he spoke again, his voice breaking.

"Dru, I need to see you. We need to talk. Please. I know we didn't end things the way we should've. There's so much I still need to say..."

She closed her eyes, feeling the pressure of his words weighing heavily on her chest. She had never been good at letting go, especially with someone she had loved for so long. But the truth was, she was no longer in love with him. She was in love with the idea of moving forward, with JT, with something new.

"I can't," she said, her voice shaking slightly as she fought to keep her composure. "It's over. I've found someone who makes me happy. Who makes me feel... important."

There was a brief, agonizing silence, and then he spoke again, his voice almost pleading.

"I just want to see you," he said quietly. "One last time. I need to look you in the eyes and tell you how sorry I am. Please, Dru."

Drusilla's heart ached at the sincerity in his voice, but she knew deep down that seeing him again would only cause more pain.

"I'm sorry," she whispered, the words sounding so final. "But I'm not coming back. I'm done. And I need you to let me go."

She heard him sigh, and there was a long pause before he replied, "I don't want to lose you."

"You already have," she said softly, her heart breaking a little more with each word. "Goodbye Sam."

The call ended with a soft click, leaving Drusilla with an overwhelming silence. She stared at the screen of her phone, her emotions in turmoil.

She had made the right decision. She had to keep moving forward.

But even as she laid her phone down and stared out the window, she couldn't shake the feeling that part of her would always hold on to the past, no matter how far she moved into the future with JT.

Reflections and Regrets

Drusilla's eyes fluttered open a few hours later, the soft glow of the cabin light indicating the late hour. Her phone buzzed once more, the familiar name flashing across the screen. *Sam.* Her heart skipped a beat as she instinctively reached for it, half-awake and still clouded by the emotions of their earlier conversation.

She let it ring once, then twice, then answered with a quiet, "Hello?"

"Dru, it's me again," Sam's voice sounded desperate and raw, as if he had been drinking and hadn't slept at all. "I just couldn't stop thinking about our conversation earlier. I need to see you. Please."

She rubbed her eyes, the haze of sleep still clouding her thoughts. His words lingered, pulling at something deep inside her. She thought back to the good times—the late-night walks, the quiet moments they shared, the way he used to make her laugh until her stomach ached. Those were the moments she had loved.

For a moment, just a brief moment, she considered giving in. What was the harm in seeing him once more? To finally close the chapter properly? She hadn't had closure, had she? Maybe this was her last chance.

But no. She could already feel the weight of JT's presence in her heart, the way he had made her feel alive. She had moved on. Still, the pull of her past lingered.

"I'm on a cruise," she said quietly, her voice wavering as she tried to distance herself from him. "I'm in Florence right now. I can't see you."

Silence stretched between them, thick and heavy.

"I understand," Sam finally said, his voice full of resignation. "I just... I just wanted to hear your voice again."

"Goodbye Sam," Drusilla said softly, her resolve strengthening with each word. "I'm sorry, but it's over."

She ended the call quickly, placing the phone back on the nightstand, the ringing in her ears still echoing as she laid back down. But sleep didn't come as easily as before. The memories of Sam—his touch, the warmth of his embrace—played over and over in her mind like an old movie reel. She tossed and turned, her heart caught between the past and the present, the emotions she'd buried with Sam resurfacing in a jumbled mess.

That night, her sleep was restless. In her dreams, she was back with Sam, walking along a beach in the twilight, laughing with him as they reminisced about the life they had almost built. Her heart beat faster as she felt the familiar spark of connection between them, the pull that once kept her tethered to him.

But in the dream, Sam was different—more forceful, more insistent. As the dream deepened, it turned more passionate, more tangled. She felt the tension building between them, the heat of his touch sending a surge of adrenaline through her. But there was something wrong in the dream, something off. She could feel the shadows of doubt creeping in as she found herself torn between her past and her present.

Suddenly, she woke with a start, the remnants of the dream still clinging to her. Her heart was pounding, and she could still feel the lingering warmth of Sam's touch, even though she knew it was just a dream. Her body was tangled in the sheets, her head spinning with confusion.

Was she imagining things? She should have felt relief, she should have felt free, but instead, she felt conflicted, unsure of herself. She glanced at the clock—only a few hours had passed since she'd last spoken to JT. Had she really just had that dream about Sam? It wasn't what she wanted. She was with JT, wasn't she?

As the morning light filtered into her cabin, Drusilla forced herself out of bed, taking a quick shower to shake off the remnants of the dream. But by the time she stepped into the dining room for lunch, she could feel the shift within herself. She wasn't quite herself. Her movements felt slower, her thoughts disjointed. JT was already sitting at their usual table, waiting for her with a warm smile that only made her feel more uneasy.

He noticed it immediately.

"Hey, you okay?" JT asked, his brow furrowing with concern as he studied her. "You look like something is bothering you."

Drusilla forced a smile, but it didn't reach her eyes. "I'm fine," she said, her voice softer than usual. "Just a little tired, I guess."

JT didn't seem entirely convinced, but he didn't press her. He simply reached for her hand across the table, squeezing it gently as if to remind her that he was there. But even his touch didn't seem to settle her anxiety.

As they ordered their lunch, Drusilla's thoughts remained distant. The dream, the lingering feelings for Sam—it all felt so confusing. And no matter how much she wanted to push it all aside and focus on the moment with JT, she couldn't shake the remnants of her past.

Would she ever truly let go of Sam? Would her connection with JT be enough to keep her from falling back into the life she once shared with her ex?

The questions swirled in her mind, leaving her feeling more unsettled than she ever had before.

Time in Florence

The next three days in Florence passed in a whirlwind of sights, sounds, and shared moments that deepened the bond between Drusilla and JT. As they explored the historic city, they marveled at the beauty of the art, the warmth of the people, and the romance of it all. Each day seemed to pull them closer, their connection growing stronger as they discovered the magic of Florence together.

They spent their days wandering the streets, visiting museums, and taking in the spectacular views of the Arno River. But each night, they made their way into the heart of the city, sharing intimate dinners at charming trattorias and cozy cafés. They savored the simple pleasures of Italian life: the rich flavors of fresh pasta, the bold notes of Tuscan wine, and the laughter that echoed under the warm glow of streetlights.

On their final night in Florence, the city seemed to sparkle even brighter than before. They had made dinner reservations at *Enoteca Pinchiorri*, the most exclusive and celebrated restaurant in Florence. It was the perfect end to their stay—an evening to indulge in the very best of what the city had to offer, both in terms of cuisine and company.

Drusilla stood in front of the mirror in her cabin, admiring her reflection. She had chosen a sleek, form-fitting black dress the plunging neckline revealing just enough skin, while the elegant cut made it perfect for a night of fine dining. Her hair was styled in soft waves, framing her face perfectly, and she had kept her makeup simple but striking—a touch of red lipstick, a little mascara, and a hint of blush.

When she stepped out of the cabin, JT was waiting for her. He was in a sharp black suit, the crispness of his white shirt and the sheen of his cufflinks adding to his already commanding presence. The moment Drusilla saw him, her breath caught in her throat. He looked every bit the sophisticated man she had come to know, but there was also an edge to him—an energy that was impossible to ignore.

"You look absolutely stunning," JT murmured as he reached for her hand, his voice low and sincere. "Like something out of a movie."

Drusilla smiled, feeling her pulse quicken. "And you look very handsome Mr. Anderson."

They shared a brief, lingering kiss before heading out into the evening. The night air was crisp, the stars twinkling above as they made their way to the restaurant. The *Enoteca Pinchiorri* was tucked away in an elegant corner of the city, its understated façade hiding the culinary paradise within.

Once inside, they were led through the luxurious dining room, where the scent of fine wine and gourmet cuisine filled the air. The restaurant's ambiance was intimate and refined, with soft lighting casting a golden hue over everything. They were seated at a table near the window, where they could look out over the streets of Florence, the city lights flickering in the distance.

As the meal progressed, they shared laughter and stories, savoring each course and enjoying the intimacy of the evening. The world outside seemed to fade away as they became completely engrossed in each other once again. Their connection was electric, the chemistry between them undeniable, and by the time dessert arrived, it was clear that this night would remain etched in their memories forever.

After dinner, they lingered over a glass of aged Chianti, savoring the rich flavors as they watched the city unfold before them. The conversation turned quiet, the moments stretched between them, and for the first time in days Drusilla felt completely at peace. The nagging thoughts of Sam—of her past—had finally dissipated. There was no room for regret or confusion. She was with JT now, and that was all that mattered.

"Thank you for everything," Drusilla said softly, her gaze never leaving his. "These past couple of weeks have been... unforgettable."

JT smiled, his hand reaching across the table to grasp hers. "The pleasure's been all mine."

But the night wasn't over yet. After finishing their drinks, JT suggested they take a walk, and Drusilla, eager to continue the magic of the evening, agreed. They strolled through the quiet streets of Florence, the city now even more beautiful in the late-night stillness. The moonlight cast long shadows, and the sound of their footsteps echoed through the narrow alleys.

As they walked, JT stopped suddenly, pulling Drusilla closer to him. His hand rested at the small of her back as he gazed into her eyes. "You know, I've never been one to believe in fate," he said softly. "But everything about this feels like it's meant to be."

Drusilla's heart skipped a beat as she looked up at him, the intensity in his eyes matching the depth of her own feelings. "I think I believe in it now," she whispered, leaning in to kiss him.

The kiss was slow and deliberate, a reflection of the emotions that had built up between them over the past few days. It was tender, but it also carried the weight of everything they had shared. It was a kiss that said everything without needing words.

As they pulled away, Drusilla smiled, feeling the heat in her cheeks. "You're right," she said. "This feels... perfect."

They walked back to the ship in silence, each lost in their thoughts, but the bond between them was undeniable. The past had faded away completely, and for the first time, Drusilla felt truly free.

The night may have been coming to an end, but their journey together was only just beginning. As they boarded the shuttle back to the ship, they held hands, their fingers intertwined, ready for whatever the next chapter of their adventure would bring.

111

Sailing toward Rome

As the ship sailed toward Rome, JT and Drusilla spent the next couple of days relaxing. The past few ports had been a whirlwind of passion and adventure, and both were grateful for the chance to slow down. The pool deck became their sanctuary—quiet moments spent in each other's company, sunning by the pool with cocktails in hand, sometimes lost in their own thoughts, other times talking about everything and nothing.

It was the perfect time to unwind, JT stretched his legs out on the chair, his sunglasses resting on the bridge of his nose. He had been content with the quiet for a while, the comfortable silence between him and Drusilla settling around them like a warm blanket. But today, something felt different. The connection between them had deepened in ways he hadn't expected, and there was a lingering curiosity in him—an urge to know even more about the woman beside him, not just the artist he admired or the lover he couldn't resist, but the person she was beneath all of that.

"Drusilla," he began, turning slightly in his chair to face her, his voice soft but steady. "I know we've had this discussion before, but I want to know everything about you."

She glanced over at him, raising an eyebrow, a small smile tugging at the corner of her lips. "Everything?" she teased, her tone light but with a hint of curiosity.

"Yes, everything," JT said, his voice sincere. "I want to know your story—where you come from, what shaped you. All the things that made you... you."

For a moment, Drusilla was quiet. She had shared pieces of herself with JT—the glimpses of her past, the hints of her dreams—but there was something about his question that made her feel vulnerable, like she was being asked to peel back yet another layer, one she hadn't fully shown anyone before.

She let out a quiet breath, her gaze shifting to the sparkling pool in front of them as she gathered her thoughts. "I guess it all starts in Boston," she said, her voice distant at first, as though remembering a time long ago. "I grew up in a neighborhood that was... well, it was a little rough around the edges, you know? My parents didn't have a lot of money, but we had each other, and

112

we made it work. My mom was in law school, always exhausted but somehow never complaining. And my dad—well, he was a mechanic. He was the kind of guy who could fix anything, make something out of nothing."

She paused, the memory of her childhood bringing a flicker of emotion to her face.

"It wasn't a perfect childhood, but it was real. It was full of love, even if there were a lot of struggles," she continued. "My mom used to tell me I was a dreamer. I'd spend hours drawing or painting in my room, escaping into my own little world. She thought it was cute, but I think she worried that I wouldn't be able to take care of myself if I followed that dream."

JT listened intently, his gaze never leaving her as she spoke. There was something about the way she shared her past with him—open but careful, as though she was testing how much to reveal, how much to trust him with. He reached over and gently took her hand, squeezing it lightly to reassure her.

"School wasn't much better," Drusilla continued, her voice softer now. "I wasn't one of the popular kids. I didn't fit in. I was always the odd one out, the girl who was drawing or painting during lunch while everyone else was gossiping or doing whatever it is teenagers do." She chuckled to herself, the sound light but tinged with nostalgia. "I was always more comfortable with my sketchpad than with people. But I guess it was that way until... well, until I decided I wanted to go to art school."

JT smiled, intrigued. "What made you decide that?"

Drusilla's eyes softened as she thought about it. "It wasn't an easy decision. My parents, especially my mom, were worried about me going to art school. They thought it was a risky choice—'What kind of future does a painter have?' they'd ask. And I didn't have the answers. I didn't have a backup plan. But deep down, I knew it was all that I wanted to do. I couldn't imagine doing anything else. Art... painting, ceramics, it's how I understood the world. It was my way of communicating when words didn't make sense."

She paused again, her expression thoughtful. JT remained silent, giving her the space she needed to continue.

"I was the best in my high school and I got a scholarship to the Art Institute in Boston," she continued, her voice steady but with a trace of pride. "It was hard, at first. I didn't have the same kind of foundation a lot of the other students did. Everyone there was the best in their high school. But I worked my ass off, and over time, I found my voice. My work started to get noticed, and that's when I realized I could actually make a career out of it."

She looked at JT, her eyes meeting his. "That's what art school gave me—confidence, belief in myself, and a career that I'm still figuring out, even now."

JT was mesmerized by the way she spoke of her past, the way her eyes lit up when she talked about something she loved. He felt a deep respect for her journey, for the strength it must have taken to follow her passion despite the challenges she faced. But there was one more thing he was curious about, something that had been on his mind since they first talked about their past relationships.

"And Sam?" he asked, his voice gentle but insistent. "We've talked a bit about him, but how did you meet him?"

Drusilla's expression shifted slightly, the warmth in her eyes dimming just a touch. She was quiet for a long moment, clearly processing the question before answering.

"I met Sam shortly after I got out of art school," she said softly. "He was older than me, and he had this... confidence about him that I was drawn to. He was charming, funny, and he made me feel seen in a way that no one ever had. We started dating, and for a while, it was perfect. He was everything I thought I wanted."

She let out a breath, a small, rueful smile on her lips. "But over time, I started noticing things. Little things. He was always away on business, always too busy for me, and when we were together, he wanted us to do the things that he liked, like any sporting event, totally ignoring what I might want to do. He was always working out and sometimes I felt that he was more in love

114

with himself than with me. He couldn't commit, and I always wondered if he was cheating. I never had proof, but my gut told me something wasn't right. Eventually, I got tired of waiting for him to change, and we broke up."

JT could hear the sadness in her voice, though she tried to hide it. He gave her hand a soft squeeze, silently offering his support.

"And what about other relationships?" he asked, wanting to know more but not wanting to push too hard.

Drusilla looked thoughtful, her gaze drifting away as she thought for a moment. "There were a couple of guys in art school, but nothing serious though. I think I was always trying to find something... something real. But it never worked out. Maybe I was too focused on my art, or maybe I just wasn't ready for anything more." She shrugged lightly, her smile returning. "And then I went on this luxury cruise and met this most amazing guy."

JT smiled at her, his heart swelling with affection. "And here we are," he said quietly.

Drusilla laughed softly, her eyes brightening. "Here we are."

For a moment, they sat in silence, both of them processing everything that had been shared. JT realized how much he didn't know about her, but how much he now admired her resilience, her passion, and the person she had become. He felt honored that she had shared so much with him.

"I want to know everything about you, Drusilla," he said, his voice low and sincere. "Your past, your dreams, your fears. I want all of it. Because I think you're amazing."

Her smile softened, her fingers lightly brushing against his. "I think you're amazing, too, JT."

And for a moment, under the quiet sun and the gentle sway of the ocean, they were content—just two people sharing a connection, learning about each other, and allowing their bond to grow stronger with each passing conversation.

Drusilla looked up, meeting his gaze. She felt a flutter in her chest—he was making her feel seen in a way she hadn't felt in years. He seemed to really care about her and her life. "What about you, JT? What was your childhood like? Your family?"

JT leaned back in his lounge chair, his thoughts drifting for a moment. He wasn't sure he'd ever shared these details with anyone outside of family, but there was something about Drusilla, her openness, that made him want to be more honest with her.

"My parents were... well, my father had various businesses, and my mom was a homemaker. We had a good life. But it wasn't perfect. My dad purchased a farm on the outskirts of Quito. He was always focused on work, and I felt like I spent a lot of time trying to get his attention, even though he was physically there. I always had to prove myself to him, I guess. After the emerald discovery on the property, things changed dramatically. His other businesses had been successful, but nothing like this. He became more focused on the company than on me. It wasn't until he retired that I started to realize how much he actually needed me. And that's when things began to shift between us."

Drusilla nodded, understanding his struggle. "Sounds like there were a lot of expectations."

JT chuckled, a small laugh that seemed to release some of the tension he'd been carrying for years. "Yeah, a lot. I think that's why my marriage ended. I was always pushing myself to meet others' expectations, and I forgot to ask myself if I was happy. Financially, I had everything I'd ever wanted, but it was never enough. "

Drusilla felt a bit of sympathy. She knew what it was like to feel unseen. "You must have been a great husband. Your wife... she must have been someone really special for you to stay for so long."

JT's expression softened, but a shadow flickered across his eyes. "She was. But it wasn't the right fit in the end. We grew apart, and when I finally woke up to it, I knew I had to move on. She knew it too. But it wasn't easy. And I guess that's why I wasn't looking for anything like this with you." He gestured between the two of them. "I wasn't sure if I could. I didn't think I was ready."

116

Drusilla's heart warmed at his honesty, at how much he was opening up to her. She squeezed his hand, offering a soft smile. "I get it. But I think maybe we both needed something like this. Something real. Something that isn't tied to the past."

JT smiled back, his eyes lingering on her with a mixture of warmth and desire. "I think you're right."

For the rest of the afternoon, they enjoyed their quiet time by the pool, their conversation giving way to the comfortable silence that often spoke louder than words. But both knew that they had opened a door to something deeper between them, and it was something neither of them would take lightly.

As the day turned to night, the couple gathered their things and headed back to their cabins to get ready for the evening. When they reached Drusilla's cabin, the world outside seemed to disappear. In the soft glow of the cabin's lights, JT's eyes held Drusilla's with a look that spoke of everything unsaid. He moved toward her slowly, deliberately, as though savoring each moment, each step that brought them closer.

Drusilla felt a surge of warmth rush through her as he brushed his fingertips against her cheek, a silent question in his eyes. She responded, a gentle tilt of her head, her lips parting ever so slightly, inviting him closer. His touch traced the curve of her neck, sending a shiver of anticipation through her. The kiss they shared was slow, tender, as if they were both trying to memorize the feeling of being together like this.

Their hands explored each other with a kind of reverence, the weight of the moment grounding them in something far beyond mere physical desire. JT's fingers slipped down her back, finding the delicate curve of her waist, pulling her even closer. The heat between them was growing with each second.

Drusilla's breath quickened as JT's hand wandered to the small of her back, a gesture that both grounded and ignited something deep inside her. She responded by slipping her hands beneath his shirt, feeling the warmth of his skin, the hard planes of his chest. It was a sensation she couldn't get enough of. Each touch, each movement, felt like an unspoken promise, a connection deeper than either of them had experienced before.

They didn't speak as they moved together, but the language of their bodies was enough. Every kiss, every touch, was a conversation of its own, saying everything they couldn't put into words. Time seemed to slow as they enjoyed each other, their passion growing stronger, pulling them both into something entirely their own. Their connection was no longer just sex, it was soft, passionate love making. Drusilla couldn't help but think how different it was than the intimate times she spent with Sam. She felt things she had never felt before. Drusilla once again fell asleep in JT's arms, feeling comfortable and safe as the ship headed toward Rome.

The soft, golden light of dawn filtered through the cabin's curtains, casting a warm glow over JT and Drusilla as they lay entangled in each other's arms. The gentle hum of the ship and the distant sounds of waves lapping against the hull were the only sounds filling the air. As JT slowly stirred awake, he took in the sight of Drusilla, still sleeping peacefully beside him, her face softened in the glow of the morning, her tan naked body partially covered by the tangled sheet.

Drusilla's eyes fluttered open, and she smiled sleepily at JT. He brushed a strand of hair from her face, his fingers lingering on her cheek. "Good morning," he whispered, his voice tender.

"Good morning," she replied, a blush rising as the memories of their night together washed over her. Outside the cabin, the first hints of Rome appeared along the horizon, the city of romance and history awaiting them.

JT held her close for a few more quiet minutes, both of them savoring the intimacy they'd found. "Rome," he murmured, looking out the window. "Ready for a day in the Eternal City?"

Drusilla nodded, excitement gleaming in her eyes. "More than ready."

Chapter 9

Port of Call: Rome, Italy

Rome greeted them with the gentle glow of dawn, casting soft light over the horizon. JT and Drusilla lay together, their bodies intertwined as the city drew near. They shared a slow, lazy morning—savoring coffee on their cabin's deck, watching the port of Civitavecchia grow larger with each passing moment. Their quiet moments were filled with anticipation, both of them brimming with the thrill of discovering Rome together.

Their first destination was the Colosseum. JT had arranged a private tour so they could walk through the ancient amphitheater without the crush of crowds. They strolled hand-in-hand, their voices hushed as they took in the history around them. JT often leaned closer, murmuring small historical facts he'd learned, but mostly, they walked in a quiet awe. Drusilla felt a thrill whenever he brushed his hand on her back or guided her with a gentle touch, making the morning feel as though it belonged solely to them.

They next wandered to the Trevi Fountain, where JT reminded her of the famous legend. With a small laugh, she tossed a coin over her shoulder, her eyes closed in a silent wish. When she opened them, JT was watching her, his gaze filled with something deep and knowing. She blushed, suddenly aware that her wish had involved him.

Lunch was at a quaint trattoria nearby. They sat outside, shaded by a large umbrella, enjoying pasta and Italian wine. The relaxed pace and rustic food loosened their conversation, and soon they were sharing childhood memories, laughing at each other's stories. JT talked about his first big adventure as a young entrepreneur, and Drusilla opened up about her dreams of being an artist. The conversation was light yet meaningful, their connection deepening over every shared laugh and smile.

As the afternoon slipped away, they strolled through the narrow streets and admired the architecture, stopping here and there to take photos and linger in quiet corners of the city. The day ended at a small wine bar with a view of the city's domed churches and sprawling rooftops. They shared a final toast, savoring the richness of the wine and the fullness of the day.

As the sun set over Rome, casting the city in shades of warm amber, JT and Drusilla made their way back to the ship. They held hands, their fingers intertwined in a comfortable silence, each lost in thought about the day they had shared.

Once back onboard, they retreated to JT's cabin, where they shared a quiet dinner, just the two of them, away from the ship's bustling dining rooms. JT had arranged for a small table on his private balcony, where the flicker of candlelight danced over their plates as they dined on fresh seafood and a crisp salad. Drusilla kicked off her shoes, tucking her feet up on her chair, letting herself relax entirely in his presence.

After dinner, they took a walk on the deck and stood at the rail looking out across the water, then settled on the cushioned lounge chairs, watching the city's twinkling lights fade into the distance as the ship prepared to sail toward their next adventure. JT wrapped a soft blanket around them both, and they watched the lights reflecting off the water, talking quietly about everything and nothing at all.

"I don't think I could've asked for a more perfect day," Drusilla whispered, resting her head on JT's shoulder.

JT tilted his head down to kiss her hair, his arm around her. "Tomorrow's another chance to make more memories. Anything you're dying to do?"

She thought for a moment, her eyes glancing up at the sky. "I'd love to wander somewhere off the beaten path, maybe find a local artist's studio... see something unique." Her eyes sparkled with excitement. "And maybe one more little adventure?"

He chuckled softly, a smile playing on his lips. "One adventure coming up, then. I think I have a few ideas."

As they snuggled under the blanket, their hands were all over each other. They kissed passionately over and over again. Drusilla felt the warmth of JT's body rubbing against her. It was as if steam was coming off of them. As JT ran his hand under Drusilla's shirt, an older couple approached them and stood near them on the rail watching the light casting across the Rome skyline. JT suggested they call it a day and head back to his cabin. Drusilla knew exactly what he meant and they gathered up their things and scurried off, giggling like a couple of teenagers.

Inside, JT's cabin was softly lit, with the distant lights of Rome visible through the windows. The view of the city looked like a dream, leaving just the two of them in their own world. They moved toward each other, drawn together in a way that was almost magnetic, neither saying a word, but both knowing exactly what the other wanted.

Their kisses were deep, and their touches grew bolder. Drusilla felt every worry, every lingering thought about tomorrow melt away. Here, in his arms, the world seemed to shrink down to just the two of them and this moment. JT's hands traced the curves of her back, pulling her close until there was no space between them, just warmth and longing.

Their passion was as unrestrained as it was tender; they moved together with an intensity that was equal parts romance and raw need, as though every moment apart earlier in the day had only fueled the fire that now burned between them. It was thrilling and consuming, a shared experience where time seemed to lose meaning. As they took turns taking each other's clothes off, JT pressed himself against Drusilla and up against the glass doors of the balcony. The light from the moon painted the passion filled room like a Renaissance painting. The heat from their bodies left a fog on the glass as JT lifted Drusilla and carried her to the bed, breathless and content, they lay entangled in the quiet aftermath, the ship gently rocking them as they drifted toward sleep. JT wrapped his arm around her, pressing a gentle kiss to her forehead as she settled against his chest.

"Goodnight, Drusilla," he whispered, his voice barely a murmur, filled with a warmth she hadn't heard before.

She smiled, nestling closer to him. "Goodnight, JT."

With their hearts still racing, they drifted off to sleep, holding each other close, a night of passion transforming into the quiet intimacy of two people beginning to fall deeply in love.

Rome Day 2

The morning sun rose gently over Rome, casting a golden light across the ship's top deck. JT and Drusilla sat side by side at a small table, savoring a breakfast of fresh pastries, fruit, and coffee. Despite the elegance of their surroundings, they were caught up in a quiet, playful intimacy, trading glances and little smiles as they sipped their coffee and enjoyed the morning together.

Drusilla leaned in, her voice soft and teasing. "I'm not sure what surprised me more last night—the view of Rome as we sailed in or...well, everything that came after."

JT chuckled, shaking his head as he took her hand in his, his eyes sparkling with warmth. "I'm not sure I'd call that a quiet night in. Let's just say I've never been so...impressed by my own cabin before."

She laughed, glancing around to make sure no one was in earshot. "Honestly, after the day we had in the city, I didn't think I'd have any energy left. But then you..." She trailed off, her cheeks flushing slightly as she looked at him.

"Then I what?" he asked, leaning closer, a mischievous look in his eye. He loved how, even now, she could be shy with him in these moments.

Drusilla raised an eyebrow, pretending to contemplate her response. "You, Mr. Anderson, are full of surprises. I'd say I'm starting to know what to expect with you...but that would be a lie."

JT grinned, delighted by her flirtatious tone. "Well, just to keep you on your toes, I'll do my best to make sure you never know what's coming."

She laughed, squeezing his hand. "I think that's exactly what I love about you."

They fell silent for a moment, content just to sit together as the ship's soft hum and the distant bustle of Rome filled the morning air. The thrill of being in this beautiful city, along with the sweet anticipation of another day to explore—and perhaps another unforgettable night together.

To begin their day, JT and Drusilla decide to venture off the usual tourist routes to discover Rome's lesser-known art treasures. They start by visiting some hidden art galleries nestled in the winding backstreets, places that tourists rarely explore. Drusilla is enchanted by a tiny art studio where a local painter is working on a large canvas with swirls of vibrant color, and JT watches her admiration with an amused, fond smile. They discuss the pieces they see, trading insights about art and sharing little-known facts.

Next, they head to the street art in the Trastevere district, where they find stunning murals splashed across old stone walls. Drusilla insists on taking photos with each one, pulling JT in for a few candid shots of them laughing together. The day feels intimate, as though they're getting to see a side of each other that few ever do, deepening their connection over their shared love for art and new experiences.

As they wandered through a small, tucked-away art studio, a tall, slender man with wild curls and paint-streaked hands stepped forward, studying Drusilla with an appreciative eye.

"You have an artist's spirit," he said with a warm smile, his Italian accent rich and melodic.

Drusilla laughed, slightly taken aback but flattered. "Thank you. I am a painter and a potter. I'm just visiting, but I find myself drawn to every canvas here."

He extended his hand. "I'm Luca. These are my paintings. Rome has a way of calling out to creatives, doesn't it?"

"Yes, it does. I'm Drusilla." She shook his hand. "I'm from Boston in America. And yes, Rome feels like a whole new world of inspiration."

Luca tilted his head, regarding her with curiosity. "Boston—quite different from here. I bet you're seeing the city with fresh eyes. Perhaps you'd enjoy seeing more of our art scene while you're here?"

She nodded eagerly. "Absolutely. I'd love that."

"Then you must come to our gallery opening tonight." Luca leaned in conspiratorially, his tone softening. "It's a small gathering, very intimate, for those who truly appreciate art. There will be new pieces, some experimental work, and, of course, plenty of wine."

Drusilla's eyes sparkled with excitement. "That sounds incredible. We would love to come."

Luca's smile widened. "Of course! Please do. It's always better to share these things with good company." He handed her a small, intricately designed card with the gallery's name and address. "The opening starts at eight. Dress as your heart desires, though I can see you'll bring your own elegance."

Drusilla smiled, touched by his warmth and charm. "Thank you, Luca. We'll be there."

As they left the studio, she clutched the invitation, her mind racing with excitement.

Drusilla and JT returned to the ship in the late afternoon, both content from the day's adventures but excited for the evening ahead. They decided to take some time to relax by the pool. JT stretched out in a lounge chair with a drink in hand, and Drusilla sat beside him, her sketchbook open, drawing impressions of the artist's studio and the streets of Rome.

"Can't wait to see what this gallery's like tonight," JT said, glancing over at her with a smile.

"Me neither. It feels like we're getting a true taste of Rome, something off the beaten path." Drusilla's eyes sparkled with anticipation.

After a few hours unwinding, they both went back to their cabins to get ready. Drusilla slipped into a flowing, off-the-shoulder dress with a unique, artsy print—a mixture of earthy tones and abstract shapes. She paired it with a few chunky bracelets and wore her hair loosely, feeling effortlessly chic yet comfortably bohemian.

JT met her in the lobby of the ship, dressed in crisp white slacks and a vivid blue shirt that matched his eyes, the top buttons casually undone. When he saw Drusilla, he paused, admiring her look with a slow smile.

"You look perfect," he said, offering her his arm. "Like you belong in one of those galleries yourself."

She laughed, looping her arm through his. "And you, Mr. Anderson, look like you've been living in Monte Carlo your whole life."

With a warm chuckle, they stepped off the ship, making their way through the bustling streets as evening settled over Rome. The city was alive, glowing in the golden hour, and as they approached the gallery, the buzz of conversation and soft strains of classical guitar music floated out into the street.

The art gallery was tucked away on a narrow cobbled street, just off the main thoroughfare. The soft glow of candlelight flickered through the windows, casting delicate shadows across the stone façade. Inside, the atmosphere was both eclectic and refined. While an older gentleman played his guitar, the faint scent of incense curled through the air, mingling with the rich smell of fresh paint and aged paper. There was something timeless about the place, an almost nostalgic quality that reminded Drusilla of something she couldn't quite place—a 1960s California vibe, where the creativity and free spirit of the era seemed to hang in the air like a living, breathing thing. The crowd was an eclectic mix of art lovers, critics, and creators—dressed in everything from tailored suits to flowing bohemian dresses, their faces animated with that spark of curiosity that comes only from being surrounded by pure, unapologetic creativity.

As Drusilla and JT walked in, the soft murmur of conversation hushed for a moment as the room seemed to take a collective breath, then resume with new energy. Luca was standing by the entrance, as if he was waiting for them. The moment he saw Drusilla, his face broke into a wide grin, and he rushed toward her, practically twirling her around in his excitement.

"Bellissima!" he exclaimed, holding her at arm's length to inspect her outfit. "You look magnificent, Drusilla. You are like a piece of art yourself."

125

Drusilla laughed, twirling in place for him, her eyes sparkling with joy. She loved the attention, but what she loved more was that, for the first time in a long while, she felt completely herself.

Luca's smile softened as he turned toward the small crowd gathered nearby, already eager to introduce her to the people who mattered in this world. "This is Drusilla, the artist from America that I met today," he said, his voice carrying over the buzz of the room. "She has an incredible presence, and tonight, we are fortunate to have her with us."

As Drusilla was ushered into the group, JT stayed behind for a moment, leaning against a nearby wall with his hands in his pockets. He watched Drusilla with a tender smile, though he couldn't quite ignore the flicker of jealousy that sparked within him. There was something about the way Luca looked at her that made JT's chest tighten. But it was a brief moment. As quickly as it came, the feeling melted away, replaced by something else entirely—something warm, something that filled his heart with pride.

He loved how happy Drusilla looked in her element, surrounded by people who truly appreciated her. She was radiant. And that made his heart swell with affection. His gaze softened as he continued to watch her mingle, feeling a surge of warmth as she laughed, her eyes alight with enthusiasm. She belonged here, in this world, just as much as she belonged with him.

The music shifted, the scent of incense lingered in the air, and the clinking of wine glasses in the background created a melody of its own. The gallery was alive with energy, and for a moment, JT simply watched, savoring the sight of Drusilla in her element. Despite the brief pang of jealousy, he felt a deep sense of gratitude—grateful that he was here, with her, witnessing her shine.

The evening carried on with an effortless flow of conversations and clinking glasses, the kind of energy that was palpable in the air. Luca, always the perfect host, was buzzing around the room, introducing Drusilla to everyone in sight. At one point, he leaned in close to her and JT, his eyes twinkling with excitement.

"You two must come to the after party!" he insisted, his accent thick with enthusiasm. "It's at a small club nearby, and it will be *the* place to be tonight. The creative energy, the music—it's everything!"

Drusilla smiled, her hand resting lightly on JT's arm as she exchanged a glance with him. The idea of an after party—full of artists and musicians was enticing, but she knew they couldn't stay. It had been a long day, and the ship would be leaving soon.

"We would love to, Luca, but we have to get back to the ship," Drusilla said regretfully, glancing over at JT, who nodded in agreement.

"Of course," Luca replied, not missing a beat. "But you *must* come next time! Please."

Drusilla promised they would, and Luca smiled brightly before returning to his guests. As they walked through the gallery, Drusilla found herself drawn to one particular piece—an expansive painting of a vast field of bright red tomatoes, the sun casting a warm golden glow over them. It was simple, but striking. The tomatoes were so vivid, so full of life. Something about it spoke to her in a way she couldn't describe. Italy. The earth. Her connection to the land and the beauty of it all.

"This one," Drusilla murmured softly, almost to herself, standing in front of it, her eyes transfixed by the colors. "This one's... perfect."

JT stood beside her, admiring the piece, though he could tell from the way her eyes lit up that it had captured her heart. He looked at her, then at the price tag on the corner of the painting, and without thinking, he quietly pulled Luca aside.

"Luca," he said, his tone low, a quiet intent behind his words. "I'd like to buy this painting for her."

Luca's eyes widened in delight, his grin wide as he looked from JT to the painting and back. "A perfect choice! I will have it wrapped up for you immediately," he said, eager to make the arrangement.

With a few swift words in Italian to his staff, Luca made it happen. The painting was carefully rolled up and wrapped in protective paper, ready for them to take with them.

When Drusilla turned back to find him, JT was standing by the door, a slight smile on his face, the wrapped painting under his arm. Her breath caught in her throat.

"You got it for me?" she whispered, her eyes wide with disbelief, but her voice full of emotion.

JT nodded, a soft laugh escaping him. "I know it means something to you. I thought it should be yours."

Without another word, Drusilla launched herself into his arms, hugging him tight, a laugh of pure joy escaping her lips. It was like she had just hit the lottery—no, it was better. The thoughtfulness, the kindness in his gesture, made her heart swell. She pulled back just enough to look him in the eyes, then kissed him deeply, feeling every ounce of the connection between them, the depth of her feelings for him in that single moment.

"I can't believe you did this," she said, her voice filled with gratitude. "Thank you."

JT smiled warmly, kissing her back, his hand still resting on the wrapped painting. "You're welcome. I'm just happy it makes you happy."

Luca appeared just then, grinning, as he handed Drusilla a small card with his contact details on it. "If you ever need anything, you know where to find me," he said with a wink, then gently took her hand and kissed it softly.

Drusilla, blushing, smiled and tucked the card into her pocket. "I'll definitely be in touch, Luca. This has been incredible. Thank you for everything."

With that, they made their way toward the exit, Drusilla skipping along beside JT as he carried her newfound treasure. The night air felt crisp as they made their way to the ship, the excitement of the evening still buzzing in their veins. She couldn't stop smiling, a little piece of Italy now with her in the form of the painting, a reminder of this unforgettable time.

As they boarded the ship, Drusilla leaned against JT, her head resting on his shoulder, feeling more content than she had in a long time. Tonight had been magical. And the best part? It was only just beginning.

With the excitement of the night still humming between them, JT suggested with a playful grin, "Why don't we drop the painting off in your room and head to the upper deck for a nightcap?"

Drusilla smiled, the warm glow of the evening still in her eyes. "That sounds perfect," she said, glancing at him with an expression full of unspoken promises.

But once they reached her cabin, the mood shifted. The door clicked shut behind them, and the weight of their shared gaze seemed to pull them together. The painting, which had been such a thoughtful gift, was momentarily forgotten as JT set it down carefully on a side table. But his hands didn't stay idle for long.

He stepped toward her, his fingers grazing her arm, and Drusilla closed the distance with a quiet urgency. "You know," she murmured, looking up at him, "I think I may have just found my favorite thing in the whole world."

"Oh yeah?" JT replied, his voice low and intimate. "What's that?"

"You," she said simply, her breath catching as his lips met hers. It wasn't just a kiss. It was a promise. A connection that had become stronger each day they'd spent together. It was as if everything else—every other distraction, every hesitation—melted away in the heat of their embrace.

They moved together, their kisses growing deeper, their bodies pressed close as if they couldn't get enough of each other. Their hands explored, their lips never breaking contact, and the world outside her cabin faded entirely.

There would be no nightcap on the upper deck tonight. No quiet drinks under the stars. Just the two of them, consumed by the electricity that always sparked when they were close, burning bright in the privacy of her cabin

As the morning sunlight filtered into the cabin, JT and Drusilla slowly awakened, wrapped in each other's arms and with the gentle rocking of the ship signaling that they were en route to their next destination: Naples. They lay there a moment, relishing the intimacy of waking up together, before JT ordered breakfast through room service.

When it arrived, Drusilla slipped on JT's bright blue shirt from the night before, its oversized fit falling softly over her, just long enough to meet her white panties. JT, with a casual confidence, wore only his white boxers, both of them perfectly tan and looking effortlessly glamorous, like they'd just stepped out of a magazine. They lounged on the bed as they enjoyed their breakfast, exchanging smiles and lazy morning kisses over coffee, croissants, and fresh fruit.

Later, they made their way to the pool, where they found a prime spot and lay in the sun, enjoying the warmth and the peaceful rhythm of the open sea. Drusilla felt like a little girl on holiday, and JT was more than happy to share his excitement about Naples. He'd visited many times and regaled her with stories of the vibrant markets, the rich history, and his favorite local spots for coffee and pastries. Her eyes lit up as she listened, her eagerness to explore with him growing by the minute.

Their idyllic day was suddenly interrupted by the soft buzz of Drusilla's phone, lighting up with a text from Sam. She glanced at the message briefly and then set the phone face down, choosing to ignore it.

Moments later, her phone rang, the screen flashing with Sam's name. She silenced it without hesitation. Another ring. Another rejection. Drusilla's heart raced with a slight unease, but she pushed it away, not wanting anything to interfere with this perfect day. JT was nearby, absorbed in the news on his own phone, blissfully unaware of the minor interruption. With her resolve strengthened, Drusilla took a deep breath, silently vowing to focus only on the present—with JT.

As the ship docked in Naples, Drusilla and JT returned to their cabins, eager to freshen up and dress for a day in one of Italy's most historic and bustling cities. JT, effortlessly stylish, chose lightweight slacks and a crisp linen shirt, while Drusilla slipped into a breezy sundress, her hair pulled back loosely, exuding an air of effortless elegance. They met on the main deck, both smiling as if seeing each other for the first time, excitement in their eyes as they prepared to step into the heart of Naples.

They wound through the narrow streets, filled with the mingling aromas of freshly baked pastries and fragrant herbs. JT led them to one of his favorite little restaurants tucked away from the main crowds, where they enjoyed a leisurely late lunch. The menu offered everything from handmade pastas to seafood fresh from the Mediterranean, and they shared several dishes, savoring each one. JT couldn't help but notice how delighted Drusilla looked as she tried new flavors and took in the vibrant, authentic atmosphere.

After lunch, they strolled hand in hand through the bustling streets, pausing at shop windows to admire the artisanal wares—delicate ceramics, leather goods, and intricate jewelry. Drusilla pointed out every little thing that caught her eye, her childlike wonder bringing a smile to JT's face. She made JT promise not to buy her anything. She just wanted to share the time and place with him. He agreed and gave her a kiss on the cheek as they kept walking.

They found a quaint outdoor café where they ordered coffee and settled into their seats, the afternoon sun casting a warm glow over their table. People passed by, creating a moving backdrop of Italian life—locals in animated conversation, tourists admiring the scenery, children playing nearby. They shared stories, laughed, and fell quiet, simply enjoying the presence of each other in this beautiful city. For Drusilla, it was as if all the noise in her life faded, leaving only the richness of the moment and the undeniable connection she shared with JT.

After their idyllic afternoon of people-watching and exploring Naples, Drusilla and JT made their way back to the ship, feeling the warmth of the Italian sun and the magic of the city still lingering in their smiles. They returned to their cabins to relax and freshen up, taking a bit of time to recharge after the day's excitement before an evening of fine dining.

Drusilla drew a bath, soaking in the memories of their day, replaying moments in her mind—JT's knowledge of the city, his thoughtful gestures, and the way he so naturally made her laugh. Meanwhile, JT lay on his bed, closing his eyes for a few minutes, enjoying the quiet anticipation of their evening together.

As the evening hour approached, they each dressed for their dinner plans. Drusilla chose a simple but elegant black dress with delicate straps, her hair loosely curled, with a light touch of jewelry that gave her a timeless grace. JT wore a tailored jacket over a crisp, white shirt that complemented his easy, sophisticated style.

Meeting in the main foyer of the ship, they took a moment to appreciate each other's appearances, exchanging a look that needed no words. They disembarked together and strolled into the heart of Naples, where JT had reserved a table at one of the finest restaurants in the city. Nestled along a scenic street, the restaurant exuded a quiet charm, with candle-lit tables and soft Italian music playing in the background.

They were led to a table by a window, where they could watch the city unfold under the stars. The meal was a symphony of flavors, with each course crafted with the finest ingredients—fresh seafood, hand-rolled pasta, delicate pastries. They toasted to their journey, to the adventures they'd shared so far, and to the ones yet to come. The candlelight reflected in their eyes, and every touch, every glance, felt electric, and charged with the intensity of their connection.

By the time dessert arrived, they were lost in each other, the bustling world around them fading. Naples had cast its spell on them, wrapping their evening in romance and the beauty of being exactly where they wanted to be—together.

As the evening drew to a close at the elegant restaurant, JT and Drusilla shared a look that spoke volumes. Neither was ready for the night to end, and the lively streets of Naples still buzzed with laughter and music. Taking her hand, JT led Drusilla toward a small, tucked-away bar with string lights strung from olive trees, casting a warm glow over a handful of tables. The bar was just lively enough, with a few locals and the soft sound of classic Italian love songs filling the air.

They ordered limoncello nightcaps, and before long, JT took her hand, guiding her to a small dance floor under the stars. The two moved together, close and unhurried, barely noticing the few others around them. As a slow song drifted through the air, Drusilla rested her head on his shoulder, and they danced like they were the only two people in the world.

When the time came to return to the ship, they realized just how late it had become. Laughing, they picked up their pace, holding hands as they darted through the narrow streets, slipping through the port gate just before the last call for returning passengers.

Once back on the ship, they made their way to Drusilla's cabin, their laughter quieting as they crossed the threshold. The moment the door clicked shut, they moved toward each other, their lingering glances igniting into something that had been building all evening. They undressed slowly, savoring each touch, each kiss, as they tumbled onto the bed, their passion as deep and endless as the Italian night.

Afterward, they lay together in the quiet, limbs intertwined, breaths slowing in perfect harmony as they drifted off to sleep. Wrapped in each other's arms, they surrendered to the night, savoring the anticipation of what tomorrow would bring—another day together in Naples, in a city that already felt filled with memories and magic.

The next morning, JT awoke to the soft morning light filtering through the curtains. He stretched, feeling a sense of calm and fulfillment he hadn't experienced in years. Drusilla was still nestled against him, her breathing slow and peaceful. Careful not to wake her, he slipped out of bed, gave her a light kiss on the forehead, and headed back to his cabin to prepare for a scheduled video conference.

After a quick shower, JT began sorting through his notes, setting up his laptop and making sure everything was ready. Just as he was organizing his thoughts for the call, his phone rang. Seeing his best friend Robert's name on the screen, JT grinned and picked up.

"Robert! What's up?" he greeted him.

"JT, my man! How's that big, luxurious cruise of yours going? You haven't called since you left New York. Living it up?" Robert's tone was half-joking, half-genuine curiosity.

JT chuckled, unable to resist sharing the best news he had. "You're not going to believe it, Rob—I met someone."

The line went silent for a second, then Robert let out a loud laugh. "No way! On a cruise? I mean, of course you did! You are the most eligible bachelor I know. So, tell me about her. Who is this mystery woman?"

JT leaned back, a warm smile crossing his face. "Her name's Drusilla. She's from Boston, an artist—a painter and a ceramicist. We clicked right away."

Robert fired off questions, his curiosity brimming. "Okay, okay, but more details! What's she like? Is she gorgeous? Young? I mean, come on, man—what's the story?"

JT laughed, taking a moment to think of the best way to describe her. "Yeah, she's beautiful. But it's not just that, Rob. She's smart, kind, has this incredibly warm energy. And I don't know, I feel... different around her. Like I can really be myself."

Robert whistled on the other end. "Wow, JT, I haven't heard you talk like this in... well, maybe ever. Are you saying this feels real? Like, really real?"

JT hesitated, then said, "Honestly, yeah. This feels more like love than anything I've known in a long time."

Robert sounded genuinely surprised. "Man, I thought you and Sarah were great together. I mean, I was sure you'd figure things out with her."

"Yeah, it was good for a while," JT said, his voice softening, "but I don't think we were really in love anymore. We were... comfortable, but there was no spark. It was like we were just going through the motions."

Robert paused before asking, "So you're sure you're done with her? She's actually been in touch, you know. She said she was hoping you two might still have a chance."

JT shook his head. "It's over, Rob. I've moved on, and I think she should too."

The two friends wrapped up their conversation, and as he ended the call, JT took a moment to reflect. This felt like a new beginning, a chance at something real, and for the first time in a long while, he felt free. With a deep breath, he turned his attention back to preparing for his conference call, thoughts of Drusilla brightening his morning.

While JT prepared for his call, Drusilla settled into a sunny spot by the pool, savoring a light breakfast and catching up on her messages. She felt a rush of happiness as she read a sweet note from her mom, checking in to see how she was enjoying the cruise. Her friend Steven, always quick with his playful humor, had also messaged, asking, *"So, any hot guys on board?"* She chuckled and, rather than typing out a reply, dialed his number.

"Drusiiiiilla!" Steven's voice rang out with cheerful enthusiasm. "So, tell me, any swoon-worthy eye candy?"

"Oh, Steven," she laughed, glancing around to make sure no one was listening in. "I have so much to tell you. I met someone, and it's… it's really something."

There was a pause, then Steven gasped, "Oh, do tell! What's his deal? Please don't tell me he's a middle-aged dad wearing socks with sandals. I won't forgive you."

Drusilla laughed out loud. "No, no, not at all! He's—well, he's kind of amazing. His name's JT, and he's so charming, thoughtful… and, um, he's a billionaire."

"Whaaat?!" Steven shrieked so loudly she had to hold the phone away from her ear. "Girl, are you saying you're the Julia Roberts in your own *Pretty Woman* fantasy right now? Are you kidding me?"

"I swear!" Drusilla grinned, feeling like a schoolgirl sharing a secret. "He's a real-life billionaire. And I didn't even know until after we'd spent a bunch of time together. And get this— we spent two nights in his family's condo in Monte Carlo and missed the shuttle back to the ship. It was such a fairytale! He had a private plane fly us to the next port of call."

Steven gasped again. "This is too much! Private jets, luxury condos… please, please tell me he's an impeccable dresser with gentlemanly manners to boot."

135

"Oh, you'd love his style, Steven," Drusilla gushed, "He's always so put-together, and yes, he's an absolute gentleman. Opening doors, pulling out chairs… the works. Honestly, it's just such a refreshing change from Sam's chaotic energy."

"Sam's chaotic energy, bless his heart," Steven replied, "but tell me more about this JT. I need to know *everything*. How's he in… other ways?"

Drusilla laughed, her cheeks flushing. "Steven! You know good girls don't kiss and tell."

"Good girls are no fun!" he countered, laughing. "But fine, I'll let you keep your secrets— for now. Just know I'm living vicariously through you!"

They spent the next few minutes catching up, sharing little details about her travels and laughing about her incredible luck in meeting JT. Steven was one of her closest friends, and he knew all about the heartache she'd gone through over the past year. Talking to him was a comfort, as always, and she was grateful for his excitement and support.

When they finally hung up, Drusilla felt a renewed sense of happiness. She stretched out on a chaise lounge, her mind drifting through the memories of the past few days. Slipping on her sunglasses, she leaned back, her skin soaking up the warm morning sun as she wondered with anticipation what the rest of the day would bring with JT.

JT's board meeting had left him tense, the back-and-forth of corporate politics taking a toll on his mood. After a few moments of deep breaths to clear his mind, he sent a quick text to Drusilla, asking where she was. As she responded that she was poolside, he changed into his swim trunks, eager to see her and shake off the lingering stress.

When JT stepped out onto the sunlit deck, he scanned the pool area, which was buzzing with people taking advantage of the warm afternoon. As he casually strolled along the poolside, it was hard not to notice the heads turning in his direction. Many of the women watched his every step, their gazes following him as he walked, adding a subtle layer of confidence to his stride. But he only had eyes for one person.

When he spotted Drusilla, he stopped in his tracks. She was lounging in a skimpy vibrant yellow bikini, a shade so bold that it perfectly matched her tan and radiant personality. She noticed him looking and grinned, jumping up to greet him. As they embraced, he felt her toned body press against his, her warm skin electric against his chest. For a moment, he wondered how he'd gotten so lucky, and as she pulled back with a smile, he saw a few envious glances aimed her way from the other women nearby. JT couldn't help but feel a little pride in their attention.

"Mind giving me a hand with this sunscreen?" he asked, handing her the bottle. Drusilla's face lit up as she took it from him, playfully pushing him down onto his stomach on the lounge chair. She smoothed the cool lotion over his back, her hands working in slow, gentle circles, each touch melting away the last bit of tension left from his call.

Once she was done, JT rolled over, taking her hand in his as they lay side-by-side, basking in the midday sunshine. Relaxed and entirely at ease in each other's company, they stayed there, hands entwined, the warmth of the sun matching the growing warmth between them.

He turned to her with a curious smile. "So, what have you been up to?" he asked, his voice easy but with that familiar spark of interest.

Drusilla chuckled, a mischievous glint in her eyes. "I just got off the phone with my friend Steven," she said, shaking her head as if still amused by the conversation. "He's so gay. I told him all about you."

JT raised an eyebrow, intrigued. "Oh yeah?" He leaned back in his chair, crossing his arms casually. "And what did you tell him?"

Drusilla laughed again, the sound light and carefree. "I gave him the whole story, all the details. About you, about us... how we met, how we've spent so much time together. He was *so* excited. I could practically hear him jumping up and down on the other end of the line."

JT grinned, his curiosity piqued. "Really? What exactly did he say?"

Drusilla smirked, clearly enjoying the teasing. "Well, first he told me I was being way too modest. Apparently, you're 'handsome' and 'charming'—and that's just from hearing about you."

She rolled her eyes, trying to suppress another laugh. "Then he asked if you'd take him on a private jet to Monte Carlo."

JT laughed, shaking his head. "Is that all it takes? Just a little jet and he's sold?"

"Apparently," Drusilla said, her eyes twinkling. "But what really got him excited was when I mentioned that you were an entrepreneur, that you owned your own company. He was practically screaming at me, 'Tell him he *has* to take me to a fashion show in Paris! I'll design his wardrobe! I'll be his personal stylist!'"

JT chuckled, shaking his head in disbelief. "Your friend sounds like a piece of work."

Drusilla smiled, her tone fond. "Oh, he's a total character. I've known him forever, and he's always been that way—totally flamboyant, no filter, but he's got the biggest heart."

"And what else did he say?" JT asked, genuinely curious now. He was amused by the way Drusilla's face lit up as she talked about her friend. He could tell Steven had a special place in her life.

Drusilla shrugged playfully. "He kept going on about how I'm 'so lucky' and how he'd never heard me this happy before. He even said that you two would probably get along—'two faaabulous, rich men'—his words, not mine."

JT chuckled, a bit of humor in his eyes. "I don't know about all that, but I'm glad he's excited." He leaned in, lowering his voice slightly. "And what do *you* think, Drusilla? Are you happy?"

Her smile softened, and for a moment, her gaze drifted out over the horizon, the sparkling ocean stretching endlessly before them. She hesitated, her fingers lightly brushing the edge of her drink as she considered his question.

"I think..." She looked back at him, her eyes searching his face. "I think I'm happier than I've been in a long time. I feel like I'm exactly where I'm supposed to be. With you." She smiled again, her eyes brightening. "And with Steven's approval, I guess I'm doing something right."

JT's heart gave a little flutter at her words, the genuine warmth in her expression making something inside him shift. He leaned in a little closer, lowering his voice so only she could hear.

"You don't need Steven's approval," he said softly. "You've always known what's right for you."

Drusilla's smile deepened, and she reached over to rest her hand on his. The connection between them, quiet but with undeniable intensity that made her breath catch in her chest. "You're right," she said, her voice low. "But it's nice to hear someone else say it, especially someone I care about."

JT squeezed her hand gently, his thumb brushing over her skin. For a moment, they just sat there, the sound of the water and the soft hum of the ship filling the space between them. It felt like the world had quieted down just for them, and he couldn't help but feel grateful for this time, for these moments they were sharing—getting to know each other, bit by bit.

"So," he said, breaking the silence with a playful tone, "when does Steven want to meet me? Should I prepare for a full-on fashion consultation or just be ready to talk about emerald mines and jet-setting?"

Drusilla laughed again, the sound warm and infectious. "You might want to start practicing your runway walk. I think he's already planning your wardrobe for the Met Gala."

JT threw his head back, laughing with her. "I'll have to get back to him on that. But honestly, it sounds like I've got a new best friend. And here I thought I was the only fabulous one around here."

She smirked, her eyes twinkling with mischief. "You've got a lot to learn, JT. Just wait until you meet him."

The two of them sat there for a while longer, basking in the glow of shared jokes and easy companionship, the laughter still lingering in the air as they talked about everything and nothing. For JT, it was another layer to the person he was growing to care for. For Drusilla, it was another reason to smile.

As the sun dipped lower in the sky, the deck around them slowly quieted down. Yet, in their little corner by the pool, the connection between them was stronger than ever.

JT turned to Drusilla and suggested they grab a casual lunch on board rather than head into town, saving their energy for a big night out in Naples. They lingered at the ship's café, laughing over salads and seafood as the sun poured in through the windows. With the afternoon stretched out luxuriously before them, they made their way back to the pool, settling in for more sun and relaxation. Lulled by the warm breeze and each other's company, they easily fell into the rhythm of contented quiet, hands intertwined, and feeling like they had the world to themselves.

When the afternoon started to wane, they agreed it was time to head back to their cabins to prepare for their final night in Naples. But as they strolled down the hallway, they didn't make it far—Drusilla's cabin beckoned first, and they couldn't resist. The two slipped inside, and with a shared smile, they found themselves peeling off each other's swimsuits. Together, they stepped into the shower, letting the warm water cascade over them, heightening every touch and embrace. It was the first time they'd shared a shower, and the intimacy of it felt new and thrilling. They lost track of time, wrapped up in each other, until JT reluctantly realized he had to slip back to his own cabin to get ready for dinner.

With a playful wink, he slipped on his trunks and headed to his room. Drusilla, feeling the afterglow of their closeness, finished her shower, giving herself just enough time to recharge before getting ready for their night out. The restaurant they'd chosen was trendy and chic, and she wanted to match the energy. She slipped into a pair of skinny black jeans, a sleek white halter top that highlighted her tan, black heels, and silver bangles on both wrists. Her hair fell straight down her shoulders, and with a final look in the mirror, she knew she was ready.

Excited to see JT, she made her way down the hall to his cabin and tapped on the door. He greeted her with a grin and a towel wrapped around his waist, caught mid-shave at the sink. She watched him intently, admiring the way his tan contrasted with the white of the towel, the casual intimacy of the moment making her heart flutter. When he asked for her help choosing his outfit, she grinned and pulled open his closet, selecting white linen slacks, a black short-sleeved linen shirt, and black loafers. She sat on the edge of the bed, feeling like a privileged spectator, watching as he dressed, going from bare and vulnerable to polished and breathtaking.

When he was fully dressed, they shared a quiet moment, both fully aware of how perfectly they complemented each other. With a final smile, they headed down to meet their car, ready to take on an unforgettable night in Naples.

As they exited the port gate, a sleek black town car awaited, gleaming under the city lights. JT held Drusilla's hand as they slid into the back seat, excited for the evening ahead. The twenty-minute drive took them through Naples' winding streets, passing beautiful historic buildings and bustling piazzas, all bathed in the warm glow of twilight. JT pointed out some of the city's landmarks, sharing little anecdotes from his previous visits. They squeezed each other's hands as they glimpsed parts of Naples they hadn't yet explored, the anticipation building with every turn.

When they arrived at the restaurant, the valet opened their door, and they were immediately greeted by the lively beat of music drifting from the outdoor terrace—a sharp, rhythmic sound that matched the restaurant's vibrant energy. After checking in with the hostess, Drusilla turned to JT with a grin. "How about we start with a cocktail at the bar?"

JT didn't miss a beat. "Champagne?" he asked, reading her mind.

"Definitely," she replied with a gleam in her eye. JT ordered a bottle of Cristal, remembering how much she loved it. The bartender poured them each a sparkling glass and placed the bottle on ice to be brought to their table. They toasted, their glasses catching the warm glow of the bar lights as they clinked together.

"To this beautiful day and an unforgettable night ahead," JT said, lifting his glass to hers.

"To us," Drusilla replied softly, smiling as they shared a warm, knowing look. The restaurant buzzed around them, but in that moment, all they felt was each other and the excitement of the night that lay ahead.

After a dinner filled with laughter, rich Italian flavors, and the champagne, JT and Drusilla stepped out into the night, deciding to take a stroll through the lively neighborhood. They wandered hand-in-hand, savoring the last of their evening in Naples. The warm glow from nearby shops cast soft shadows along the narrow streets, adding to the city's charm. Passing by a small pastry shop, Drusilla's eyes lit up, and they went inside, breathing in the delicious aroma of freshly baked sweets. They picked out an assortment of pastries to take back to the ship, a sweet reminder of their magical night.

JT called for their car, and soon they were headed to the port, each savoring the memories they'd made that night. Once onboard, they took a detour to the upper deck, where the moon cast a shimmering path across the dark ocean. JT wrapped his arm around Drusilla, pulling her close as the cool ocean breeze brushed over them. They stood in peaceful silence, watching the waves and sharing the quiet contentment of the moment.

Finally, they headed to JT's cabin. While JT freshened up in the bathroom, Drusilla sprawled out on his bed, still dressed, and drifted into a deep sleep. When JT returned, he couldn't help but smile at the sight of her peacefully curled up on his bed. He gently grabbed a light blanket and covered her without waking her, then stepped onto the balcony with his phone, sipping a glass of brandy as he caught up on messages and gazed out at the endless horizon.

After an hour, the calm of the night made his eyes heavy. JT turned off the lights, slipped into bed beside Drusilla, and wrapped an arm around her, feeling the warmth and closeness that had become so natural. Another perfect day, another night in paradise.

Leaving Naples

As the ship eased out of the Naples harbor and set its course for Messina, an announcement came over the loudspeaker:

> *"Good morning, ladies and gentlemen. Say goodbye to Naples as we head toward Messina, Sicily. We expect to reach Messina by tomorrow morning after a scenic yet windy passage through the Tyrrhenian Sea."*

This journey to Messina promises breathtaking views as they approach Sicily—a land of ancient culture, vibrant art, and stunning landscapes dominated by the presence of Mount Etna.

142

But with a stretch of unsettled weather ahead, it wouldn't be the typical sunbathing day by the pool.

As the announcement ended, Drusilla and JT began their day in each other's embrace, savoring the warmth of a lazy morning together as the ship moved. But soon, Drusilla headed back to her cabin to freshen up, anticipating a day of excitement even without the sun.

When she opened her cabin door, however, she was caught off guard by a massive vase of red roses on the table. *How thoughtful of JT,* she thought with a smile. But as she reached for the card, her heart skipped a beat: *"I miss you... S."* Her stomach turned. These roses weren't from JT—they were from Sam. Emotions she thought she'd buried surfaced, and memories of Sam drifted into her mind. She recalled their whirlwind trip to Las Vegas when he'd surprised her with roses, just like these. Tears stung her eyes as she sat down on the bed, momentarily lost in the nostalgia.

A knock at the door broke her thoughts. When she opened it, there stood JT, his expression shifting from joy to confusion as he saw the roses and the lingering tears in her eyes.

"Who's the secret admirer?" he asked gently, noticing the card with Sam's initial. Drusilla hesitated, then leaned into him, her emotions spilling over. JT wrapped his arm around her, feeling a sudden weight. He'd tried not to think about her past, yet here it was—sitting between them in the form of roses.

As they sat quietly, JT's mind filled with doubt. Was Drusilla still connected to Sam? Did she still have feelings for him? But before he could dwell further, Drusilla straightened, wiping her eyes. She took a deep breath and explained the situation, admitting that Sam had been reaching out. Though she'd ignored most of his messages, he had managed to call her, wanting to talk. She told JT about the call she'd taken, making it clear she'd told Sam it was over.

JT listened patiently, a mix of relief and sadness. "Is that what you want?" he asked softly.

"Yes, I don't want to go back to him," she answered, her voice firm but tremulous. Tears brimmed again, and JT felt his chest ease.

"Drusilla," he began, taking her hands in his, "we're not teenagers. We each came from serious relationships, and that means baggage. But the time I've spent with you has been the most exciting, wonderful time of my life. I wasn't looking for this—wasn't looking for you. But you've become a blessing that was dropped into my life." He paused, smiling at her with raw sincerity. "I've traveled the world, I've known many women, but I've never felt this. We can handle this— Sam, Sarah—all of it. Our past brought us here, to each other. Let's move forward together."

Drusilla took his words to heart, feeling a fresh wave of admiration for JT. He wasn't just handling her past with grace; he was helping her close a door so she could fully embrace the future with him.

At JT's suggestion, they drafted a short, sincere text to Sam, thanking him for the roses and explaining that she'd moved on and hoped he would too. As she pressed *send*, she felt a weight lift from her shoulders. They embraced, and Drusilla's tears flowed anew, though now from a place of release and relief.

After a few minutes, JT kissed her forehead and suggested a change of pace. "How about we go to the casino?" he said with a grin. "We could use a little excitement after all that."

Drusilla agreed, a spark returning to her eyes.

By the time JT and Drusilla made it to the casino, the energy was building as passengers filled the tables for a lively late-morning scene due to the bad weather on deck. The hostess welcomed them with a smile and offered a drink. JT ordered two Bloody Marys, which arrived just as they found their spot at the craps table.

JT requested his pre-arranged marker, and the pit boss handed him a stack of colorful chips. Drusilla eyed the chips curiously, not fully understanding the euro values. Later, JT whispered with a smile that it was the equivalent of $5,000 USD in chips. Craps was one of JT's favorite games, and Drusilla, having played it a few times in Vegas with Sam, knew just enough to keep up.

After a few quick rounds of ups and downs, the dice came around to JT. With a grin, he handed them to Drusilla. "Shooter coming out!" he called, placing a bet on the "come" line. Drusilla blew on the dice, tossed them confidently, and the dealer shouted, "Winner 7!" Cheers erupted as the chips flowed to the players. The dice returned to Drusilla, who tossed them again. Another seven! The table came alive, players crowding closer to watch this new "gunner" at work.

For half an hour, their streak continued, with cheers and high-fives filling the air. But then, after a particularly suspenseful roll, the dealer shouted, "7 out!" and cleared the chips from the table. JT turned to Drusilla with a smile, "Nice run, pretty lady." He stacked his chips, asked the dealer to "color me up," and pocketed a handful of large yellow chips.

As they walked away, Drusilla's eyes widened at the value. "How much did we win?" she asked, her face lighting up.

"10,300 euros," JT replied with a grin, "or about $11,000."

Thrilled, they headed to the bar for a light lunch, celebrating their sudden luck and enjoying the buzz of their shared win. JT handed Drusilla the chips, and she carefully slipped them into her purse. After lunch, Drusilla suggested they try blackjack, a game she knew well. They found a table with two open seats and dove in, the rhythm of the game energizing them both. An hour passed, and they finished about even.

JT suggested they treat themselves with part of their winnings, and Drusilla's face lit up. They made their way to the ship's high-end shopping area, and the first thing Drusilla spotted was a shoe store. She looked at JT, who nodded with a grin. They browsed together, and Drusilla's gaze kept returning to a stunning silver glitter pair of Jimmy Choos.

"They're so beautiful," she murmured.

"Try them on," JT encouraged.

She requested her size, and once seated, slipped them on, her eyes sparkling as they both agreed she had to have them. Drusilla asked if they could hold the shoes for a moment, and they made their way to the cashier to cash in some of their winnings.

With $3,200 in hand, they returned to claim her prize. As they left the store, Drusilla hugged JT's arm, her heart full. "Thank you," she said, her voice warm with gratitude.

JT smiled down at her. "Don't thank me," he replied with a chuckle. "You were the 'gunner.'"

They both laughed, the thrill of their luck and new shoes making the day unforgettable.

After a few more rounds at various tables, JT and Drusilla felt the thrill of the casino wear off and decided they'd had enough for one day. Instead of taking the grand staircase up, they hopped into an elevator to head to the top deck and see what the midday scene had to offer.

The second the doors closed, JT's hand slipped around Drusilla's waist, pulling her into a heated embrace. Their mouths met in a kiss that was anything but casual—hungry and intense, like they'd waited all day for this very moment. Drusilla melted into him, her fingers tangling in his hair, and for a moment, the world outside that elevator felt distant and unimportant.

But then, the elevator dinged, jolting them out of their moment. As the doors opened, they were greeted by a small crowd waiting to get on. JT and Drusilla exchanged a quick look and broke into laughter, their faces flushed with excitement and a hint of mischief. They straightened themselves as they walked out, giggling like teenagers caught sneaking a kiss, their shared spark growing stronger by the second.

Chapter 10

Port of Call: Messina, Sicily

The next morning, sunlight slipped through the blinds, casting a warm glow over JT and Drusilla as they stirred awake. The subtle hum of the ship's engines was replaced by a soft stillness, signaling their arrival in Sicily. An announcement echoed through the room:

Good morning, ladies and gentlemen! We have arrived in beautiful Messina, Sicily. The weather is clear, with a slight breeze and temperatures perfect for exploring. Enjoy your day!

Drusilla stretched and gave JT a sleepy smile. "Good morning, handsome. Sicily, can you believe it?"

JT grinned, leaning in to kiss her forehead. "Another day in paradise, with the most beautiful woman by my side. I'd say we're doing pretty well."

After a leisurely breakfast on their balcony, overlooking the ancient port, they discussed their plans. Sicily's rich history and culture were calling, with Messina as the perfect gateway to the island's wonders. They could see the mountains in the distance, framed by the crystal-blue waters of the Mediterranean, and the view was nothing short of breathtaking.

JT suggested they spend the day wandering through Messina's charming streets, and Drusilla was immediately drawn to the idea of visiting local art galleries and finding a small trattoria for an authentic Sicilian meal.

As they prepared to head out, JT reached into his pocket and handed Drusilla a map provided by the ship's concierge, who had highlighted spots not to miss: the Cathedral of Messina, the legendary Orion Fountain, and even a few hidden gems off the beaten path.

"Ready to explore?" he asked, offering his hand. Drusilla took it, smiling as they stepped out onto the gangway, eager to dive into the vibrant streets of Messina and soak up the Sicilian charm together.

The Orion Fountain was even more spectacular than Drusilla had imagined, its marble figures standing proudly under the morning sun, the water cascading from graceful tiers with a sense of timeless elegance. She stared, mesmerized, her hand in JT's as he admired her awe-struck expression just as much as the fountain itself.

"Pictures don't do it justice," Drusilla said softly. "This... feels magical."

147

JT nodded, squeezing her hand. "It's the kind of place that seems to hold stories."

As they wandered from the fountain, they ducked in and out of small shops, each one offering little treasures—hand-painted ceramics, delicate lacework, and pieces of jewelry unique to Sicily. They picked out small mementos, sharing laughs and trying on eccentric hats and scarves, acting as if they were the only two people in the world.

Eventually, they found a cozy outdoor café with a perfect view of the bustling square. Taking a seat, they ordered two espressos and relaxed, letting the vibrant atmosphere of Messina surround them. JT leaned back, watching the locals and tourists alike as they passed by.

"Look at that couple over there," Drusilla whispered, nodding subtly toward an elderly pair walking hand in hand, moving slowly but in perfect sync. "They've probably done this a hundred times."

JT chuckled. "One day, that'll be us. Same spot, just with a little more gray hair."

Drusilla laughed, reaching across the table to squeeze his hand. "And I wouldn't change a thing."

As they sipped their coffees and shared stories, the charm of Sicily worked its way into their hearts, and for that moment, they felt truly at home, surrounded by history, beauty, and the intoxicating sense of being completely in love.

As they sat there, the soft hum of Sicily surrounding them, Drusilla asked, "Have you ever thought about living abroad?"

JT looked at her, then out across the busy street. "You know, I did get a taste of that in Ecuador when I was a teenager. My family's there, but... somehow, I never thought of living anywhere else as an adult. New York is just... New York. It's hard to leave."

Drusilla nodded, smiling. "I get that. But I could live anywhere, honestly. I've always thought Copenhagen would be a dream. I'd want a studio on a top floor, big windows, a view of the city. The people there seem wonderful, and they say it's one of the best places to live."

JT took this in, imagining her in a sunlit studio in Copenhagen, paints scattered everywhere, overlooking the bustling squares. Then he looked back at her, his voice soft but serious. "How about Manhattan?"

Her smile broadened at the thought, and her eyes sparkled as she caught on to the meaning behind his question. "You never know. I do love the theater... and you can't beat Mr. Chow's."

JT laughed, feeling the warmth of possibility settling in. "Good answer. One day, maybe I'll show you the view from my place."

They both knew they were treading new ground, and as they sipped their coffee, a quiet understanding passed between them. For the first time, they were imagining a future together—whether it was Copenhagen, Ecuador, or New York City, it seemed a whole world of options was open. And that feeling, the sense of a shared path yet to come, brought them even closer in this sunlit Sicilian morning.

Drusilla's mind wandered briefly, as if a faint shadow of doubt had crept in. She had been swept up in the whirlwind of this incredible experience—the romance, the luxury, the places she'd never thought she'd visit, let alone enjoy so intimately. But now, in the quiet moments as she sat with JT, she couldn't help but wonder if it was all just... *the fantasy.*

Was it just the allure of his wealth, his confidence, and the high-flying lifestyle he'd introduced her to? Or was it him—*Jonathan*—the man who had shared parts of his life with her, the man who cared enough to listen, to be there, to support her in moments of vulnerability?

As they continued talking, Drusilla's fingers absently traced the rim of her coffee cup. JT had just finished talking about a business venture, his eyes lighting up as he spoke. She smiled and nodded, but her thoughts were miles away.

What did she really want? And how much of what she felt for him was because he was this larger-than-life figure—a man with a past, a future, a world that seemed so far beyond hers?

She felt the cool breeze from the ocean, trying to ground herself in the present, but the question lingered. What if she was falling for the *idea* of him and not *him*?

JT noticed the quiet in her eyes as she stared out at the busy square. "Drusilla?" he asked gently, his voice pulling her back to the moment.

She looked at him, his brow furrowed in concern. She smiled, trying to shake off her inner conflict, but there was a slight hesitation.

"I'm fine," she said, though she wasn't sure if she believed it herself. "Just thinking about everything. This... us... I just don't want to be caught up in something that's more about the lifestyle than the real connection."

JT, ever perceptive, didn't push but his expression softened, understanding that there was more beneath the surface. He reached across the table, gently covering her hand with his. "I get it," he said quietly. "But, Drusilla, what we have... it's not just the places or the things. It's us. You and me."

For a moment, all her doubts seemed to melt away. His words were simple, but in them, she could feel the sincerity. He wasn't just the billionaire businessman, the man of luxury. He was *there*, looking at her, hoping she would see him for who he truly was. The man who had shared his vulnerabilities and desires with her, just as she had with him.

And yet...

She took a breath, her heart pounding a little harder. She wasn't sure what would happen next, or where this would all lead, but one thing was certain—she wasn't just living in a dream. The feeling she had when she was with him, the moments of real connection, the laughter, the shared silences—they felt real.

She squeezed his hand, her smile returning, albeit a little shakier. "You're right. I guess I'm just... a little overwhelmed by everything. But maybe that's a good thing. Maybe I'm exactly where I'm supposed to be."

And with that, her doubts quieted, for now. She wasn't sure if it was love or the allure of this incredible adventure, but maybe it didn't matter. What mattered was that for the first time in

150

a long time, she wasn't thinking about *what-ifs*. She was in this moment, and whatever it was, it felt like it was meant to be.

After their quiet conversation, Drusilla and JT stood up from the café, stretching their legs as they decided to take a walk through the charming streets of Messina. The air was warm, the sunlight soft as it filtered through the trees, and the whole town seemed to hum with the energy of people enjoying their day.

They wandered aimlessly, enjoying the simplicity of just being together, no plans, no pressure. As they strolled, they passed by little boutiques and artisan shops, the kind that sold handmade jewelry and local crafts. Drusilla stopped to admire a hand-painted ceramic plate with vibrant hues of blue and green. She smiled, tracing the designs with her fingers, before JT gently nudged her forward.

"Come on, I know you're getting ideas for your own studio," he teased, his eyes warm with affection.

"I might take that home as inspiration," she laughed, the playful back-and-forth easing her mind even more.

As they continued their walk, they spotted a cozy little café tucked between two buildings, with a small terrace filled with people enjoying the breeze. They decided it was the perfect spot to relax and have a light lunch. The café's charm was undeniable—simple wooden tables shaded by vines, and the smell of freshly brewed espresso filled the air. They found a quiet table where they could watch the people passing on the bustling street.

The waiter arrived, and after a brief exchange of smiles and broken English, they ordered two glasses of chilled white wine and a couple of light antipasti plates—bruschetta, a small serving of Sicilian olives, and some perfectly ripe tomatoes drizzled with olive oil and balsamic.

As they sipped their wine and nibbled on the food, they talked about everything and nothing—JT shared a funny story about his first business trip to Italy, and Drusilla told him about a few of the more bizarre experiences she'd had during her travels. They were both so comfortable together, the laughter came easily, and for a while, they just enjoyed the simplicity of being in each other's company.

"I'm glad we took the time to do this," Drusilla said, sitting back in her chair, her eyes soft with contentment. "It feels like we've been running around doing everything, but this is nice. Just the two of us, relaxing."

"I agree," JT smiled, leaning back with a satisfied look. "It's good to take a moment, even when everything around us feels like it's moving so fast."

After lunch, they paid the bill and set off toward their next destination. They walked through the streets of Messina, the sun now lower in the sky, casting a golden glow over the town. Drusilla noticed that people were starting to gather near the famous *Piazza del Duomo*, and they followed the crowds, eventually arriving at a spectacular sight—the Cathedral of Messina, with its stunning facade and impressive architecture. The church was built in the 12th century and stood as a testament to the city's rich history. Drusilla marveled at the intricate carvings on the stone walls and the bright blue sky overhead.

"It's breathtaking," Drusilla said, her voice filled with awe as she gazed up at the church's bell tower.

"I told you," JT grinned, clearly pleased to be sharing these experiences with her. "Sicily has so much to offer. You'd never guess what's around the corner until you see it."

They spent some time exploring the area, taking in the sights and snapping a few photos. JT stood beside her, his arm around her shoulders as they admired the view together. As they walked back to the ship, their conversation shifted to their plans for the evening—dinner in the ship's upscale restaurant, followed by a night of dancing and cocktails.

By the time they reached the ship, the sun had begun to set, painting the sky in warm oranges and pinks. They went to their separate cabins to shower and get ready for dinner, both feeling refreshed and content after their day exploring Messina.

Drusilla stood in front of the mirror, brushing through her hair as she thought about the day. She hadn't felt this at peace in a long time. She was so thankful for everything that had happened so far—her unexpected connection with JT, the adventures they'd shared, and the man he was showing himself to be. She smiled to herself as she finished getting dressed, excited to see where the night would take them.

Drusilla chose a stunning midnight blue dress that shimmered softly under the lights of the ship. The fabric hugged her curves, with delicate lace detailing along the neckline and sleeves. The dress fell just below her knees, and the subtle pleats added an elegant movement when she walked. She paired it with her new Jimmy Choos—silver glittering heels that sparkled as she moved. Her hair was styled in soft waves, cascading over her shoulders, and once again, her makeup was understated but enhanced her natural beauty. She looked effortlessly chic, the perfect blend of grace and allure.

Meanwhile, JT was already dressed in a crisp white shirt with open collar, sharp black suit, his hair perfectly styled. As he stood in front of the mirror, adjusting his cufflinks, he couldn't help but think about how much he looked forward to spending more time with Drusilla. He wanted to make tonight special for her—another night to remind them both of the magic they had together.

When they met in the hallway outside their cabins, they exchanged smiles, both equally pleased with the day they had shared and anticipating the night ahead.

"You look beautiful", JT whispered as he reach for her hand.

"Ready for dinner?" he asked, his voice warm with affection.

"Definitely," Drusilla replied, her eyes sparkling. "I'm so excited."

As they approached the restaurant, the maître d' paused to greet them with a warm smile. He noticed how perfect they looked together and asked if they would like a photo before dinner. Drusilla, always thoughtful, agreed. She wanted to capture the moment, so she could share it with Steven back in Boston, the friend she'd confided in about her journey.

With the soft glow of the restaurant lighting behind them, JT stood beside her, a perfect gentleman as always. Drusilla beamed, her arm linked with his, both of them looking every bit the power couple, the kind of scene you'd expect to see in magazines. The photographer clicked the camera, and after a few moments, handed them a printed photo. Drusilla smiled, her heart fluttering at how good they looked together.

She quickly took out her phone, snapped a photo of the picture, and sent it to Steven with the message:

"A picture from tonight... thought you'd like to see what Mr. Perfect looks like. ☺"

Within seconds, Steven's reply lit up her phone.

"Ugh, I can already see it—he's that kind of handsome. The one who looks like he should be on a yacht sipping champagne while telling you he's 'too busy' for a relationship. Does he have a trust fund, or is that just the 'I know I'm hot' energy I'm picking up? Anyway, tell him he looks great, but I'll need to see his personality before I approve. ☺ Does he have a younger brother?"

Drusilla laughed aloud at Steven's sassy response. His humor always cut through any doubt, and it made her wonder once again—was she really caught up in the fantasy, or was she starting to see the real JT beneath the polished surface?

As they were finishing their appetizers, the Captain himself made his way over to their table, his tall figure standing out in the dining room. With a warm, welcoming smile, he greeted them.

"Good evening, Mr. Anderson, Miss Pennington," he said, extending a hand to JT first, then to Drusilla. "I just wanted to make sure you two are enjoying your time with us here aboard the ship. Is everything to your liking? The weather's been perfect, and I do hope you've had a chance to experience some of the sights and activities on shore."

JT stood up, shaking the Captain's hand. "Everything's been fantastic, thank you. We've been having a great time. The cruise, the ports... it's been more than we expected."

Drusilla nodded with a smile. "It's been incredible. We've had the most wonderful time exploring the cities, and the service here has been exceptional. Thank you for such a memorable experience."

The captain smiled, clearly pleased by their response. "That's what we strive for. If there's anything at all you need, don't hesitate to let us know. We want you to feel special—enjoying every moment of this adventure."

He lingered for a moment longer, before tipping his hat and excusing himself. "Enjoy your dinner," he said, with a final smile, "and I hope you'll find even more surprises in the days ahead." Little did he know the "surprises" they have been enjoying.

As they settled into their dinner, champagne flute in hand, the bubbles danced merrily in the glass as they toasted to another perfect day on their journey. The dinner started with a beautiful antipasti, then a crisp bib lettuce salad. For their entre, they shared a large Maine lobster, having the waiter crack and serve them. The tender and succulent lobster paired beautifully with the crisp champagne, adding to the sense of luxury that surrounded them.

Their waiter, a young man with a clear New York accent, prepared the lobster tableside, placing it in front of them with a professional grace. "Everything good so far?" he asked, a warm smile on his face.

Drusilla smiled back. "Everything's wonderful, thank you."

JT raised his glass and leaned in with interest. "Where in New York are you from?" he asked, curious.

The waiter's grin widened. "Born and raised in Manhattan. I'm working here on the ship for a bit, just taking a break from the city hustle. It's a whole different vibe."

"Small world," JT said, amused. "I'm from Manhattan too." He glanced at Drusilla, adding, "But she's from Boston. A Red Sox fan."

The waiter chuckled. "Oh, so we've got a mix of East Coast energy going on at this table. I love it." He refilled their glasses, his New York pride evident. "If you two are thinking of dessert, I'll go ahead and get your soufflé started so it's perfect by the time you're finished with dinner. Takes a little time, but it's worth it."

"I'll take you up on that," Drusilla said with a smile. "Can't wait."

As the waiter left to put in the order, Drusilla glanced at JT, the connection between them deepening with each shared moment. "It's funny, you two both coming from Manhattan and me being a Boston girl. How did you know that I'm a Red Sox fan?" JT shrugged and said "just a lucky guess."

They continued their meal, savoring every bite, every sip, and every lingering moment of the evening, knowing that the journey ahead was still full of possibilities.

After finishing their luxurious dinner, Drusilla and JT decided to continue the evening's celebration at the ship's nightclub. The vibrant pulse of music echoed from the entrance as they approached, the promise of more champagne and dancing enticing them into the dimly lit space. The energy was contagious, with couples twirling on the dance floor and the sound of laughter and clinking glasses filling the air.

A hostess greeted them at the door, showing them to a plush, intimate table by the dance floor. "What can I get you this evening?" she asked, her voice soft but cheerful.

Drusilla smiled at JT. "Champagne," she said, already feeling the thrill of the night in her veins. JT nodded in agreement, his hand gently brushing hers across the table. JT looked at the young hostess and said, "we'll have a bottle of Cristal please and a bottle of still water."

When the champagne arrived, they toasted once more—this time to the spontaneity of their adventure. The bubbles made their way to Drusilla's head quickly, the music and lights only heightening the mood. She stood up and offered her hand to JT. "Dance with me?"

156

JT chuckled, rising from his seat and taking her hand. "Of course, but I warn you, I'm not the best dancer."

Drusilla grinned, her eyes twinkling. "No worries. Neither am I, but that's never stopped me before."

As the first notes of a slow song began to play, they swayed to the music, the world outside their little bubble fading away. The champagne had loosened their inhibitions, and the warmth of the room, the closeness of their bodies, and the chemistry between them made the night feel impossibly perfect. Drusilla rested her head on JT's shoulder as they moved together, a contented sigh escaping her lips. It felt right, being here with him, even in this grand, impersonal space—it felt intimate, like they were the only two people on the ship.

"How's this for a night?" JT murmured, his voice low and warm in her ear.

Drusilla smiled, lifting her head to look at him. "Perfect," she whispered back, as they continued to dance, lost in the magic of the moment.

As the last of the champagne bubbles danced on their tongues, Drusilla and JT exchanged a look—one that said everything without a single word. The night had been perfect: the dinner, the laughter, the dancing. But now, the only thing they wanted was to be alone with each other.

"Shall we?" JT said, his voice a low murmur, his hand resting lightly on the small of her back as he led her away from the table.

Drusilla didn't need to ask what he meant. She could feel it, too—the electric pull between them, the unspoken desire that had been building all evening. They both knew what would make this evening truly unforgettable. A night of mad passion, no interruptions, just the two of them and the moonlight spilling through the window as their bodies intertwined.

JT signed the check and with a quiet chuckle, guided her through the club, and without looking back, they made their way toward the elevator. The door slid open, and they entered, the air between them thick with anticipation. As soon as the doors closed behind them, JT pulled her to him, his lips finding hers in a kiss that was hungry and desperate, as if they'd been starved for each other.

Drusilla's breath quickened, her hands threading through his hair, tugging him closer. They pulled away for just a moment, the only sound between them their shared breaths, before JT kissed her again, his hands wandering all over her body, pulling her closer still.

The elevator dinged softly as they reached their floor. They gathered themselves and walked down the corridor, their steps quick and determined, hearts racing with excitement. When they reached the door to JT's cabin, JT fumbled with the keycard, but the moment it clicked open, they were inside, the door shutting behind them with a soft click.

As the lights dimmed and the curtains swayed gently in the breeze from the open balcony, they stood there for a moment—locked in a gaze that spoke volumes.

Unlike the romantic passionate times they had spent before, this was more like two lovers that had been separated for months. JT's hands already moving to the buttons on her dress as she fumbled with the buttons on his shirt. Within a minute, the two lovers were grasping each other's bodies as if they couldn't get enough of each other. JT sat in the soft oversized chair as Drusilla straddled him, arms wrapped around his neck, as she pressed her body against his. Their lovemaking moved to the bed where the moonlight shined across the room and the waves splashed against the hull of the ship. After what seemed like hours, they fell back, both drenched in each other's sweat, their hearts beating wildly. Drusilla thought to herself, I think I'm falling in love with this man. I can't get enough of him. They laid together, neither one saying anything. JT rolled over, kissed her on the neck and said, "I think I'm falling in love with you Drusilla." Just then, Drusilla rolled over on top of him and said "I love that you are falling in love with me. I feel the same about you." They kissed and made love again, this time softer and gentler, then fell asleep in each other's arms. Another day in paradise.

The sun hung high in the sky as JT and Drusilla found themselves lounging by the pool the following morning, the gentle hum of the ship's engines and the soft splash of water creating a serene backdrop to their exhausted state. Both still wore the aftermath of the previous night—a mix of satisfaction, contentment, and just a hint of a hangover from the champagne and the passion they'd shared. JT lay back on a lounger with his sunglasses on, his face relaxed, his legs stretched out, while Drusilla sat on the edge of the pool with her feet dipped in the cool water. She looked at him occasionally, her heart fluttering at the memory of their night together, but the weariness in her bones was undeniable.

She reached for her phone to call her mother, something she had been meaning to do for a few days. As the phone rang, she waited for the familiar voice on the other end.

"Hi, Mom," Drusilla said with a tired but happy smile, her fingers lightly tracing the edge of the pool.

"Oh, darling, you sound like you've been having too much fun," her mother teased, the sound of background noise filtering through the phone. "How's the cruise? Tell me everything!"

"It's been incredible," Drusilla replied, her voice soft. "Thank you so much for this gift. I'm so glad I came. I needed this more than I even realized." She paused, then added, "And... I met someone."

There was a slight silence on the other end before her mother spoke again, her tone warmer now. "Oh, sweetheart, that's wonderful! Tell me about him."

Drusilla smiled, her eyes flicking over to JT, who had propped himself up on his elbows to listen to her talk, a lazy grin playing on his lips. "His name is JT. He's... well, he's incredible. We met at the launch party and have spent the entire time together, and I think—I think I'm falling in love with him, Mom."

Her mother's voice became a little more cautious. "Falling in love already? Darling, you just met him. Are you sure about this?"

Drusilla sighed, leaning back against the pool's edge, her fingers twirling through the water. "I know it sounds crazy, but it feels different. We've been talking, and... I don't know, Mom. It just feels right. I never thought I'd feel this way again."

159

Her mother took a moment to respond, as if processing Drusilla's words. "I understand, darling. You know I want the best for you. Just be careful. Make sure this is what you want, not just the excitement of the moment. Relationships take time to really know someone."

"I know," Drusilla said softly, her gaze lingering on JT. "I just... I don't know how to explain it. I feel like I'm exactly where I'm supposed to be. With him."

"Well, I'm happy for you, sweetheart, but take things slow. Trust your heart, but also make sure you're seeing everything clearly." Her mother's voice softened again, the warmth coming through. "But for now, enjoy yourself. Have fun, and don't worry about tomorrow just yet."

Drusilla smiled, her heart swelling at her mother's support. "I will, Mom. Thanks for everything."

"I love you, sweetheart. Take care."

"I love you too," Drusilla replied, then hung up, her thoughts swirling as she gazed out at the vast ocean before her. When she looked back at JT, he was sitting up now, his eyes watching her with quiet curiosity.

"You okay?" he asked, a hint of concern in his voice as he sat up fully on the lounger.

She smiled, tucking her phone into her bag. "Yeah. Just checking in with my mom. She's happy for me, but she's also a little cautious. I think she's just worried it's all happening too fast."

JT gave a soft laugh, his eyes twinkling as he leaned back. "Well, if you're falling in love, I'd say you're doing it the right way... with someone who knows how to treat you the way you deserve to be treated."

Drusilla felt a warmth spread through her chest. "Yeah," she murmured. "I think so, too."

Leaving Sicily

The loud horn sounded as the ship set sail from Messina, the warm Mediterranean breeze stirred the air as JT and Drusilla found a quiet table by the pool for a leisurely lunch. The scene was perfect—gentle waves lapping at the ship's hull, the sun casting a golden glow on the sparkling water, and the soothing hum of the ship's engines in the background. Drusilla, still a little hazy from their champagne-filled night, relished the calm and the beauty of the view as they sailed away.

Her excitement was intense as she gazed out toward the horizon. "Venice," she said with a soft sigh, her voice full of wonder. "I've always wanted to go. The canals, the architecture, the gondolas... It's like stepping into a dream. I can't believe we're actually going there."

JT watched her, his lips curved into a smile as he listened to her excitement. She was glowing, and for a moment, he couldn't help but feel a twinge of guilt. Venice meant something to him too, but it was a memory he wasn't ready to revisit yet. He kept his gaze on the horizon, the thought of his honeymoon there with Sarah lingering at the back of his mind. He didn't want to bring it up, not now, especially not with Drusilla so excited.

"Venice is magical," he said, his tone warm, but measured, trying to keep his thoughts focused on the present. "You'll love it."

Drusilla grinned, her enthusiasm undimmed. "I can't wait to see everything! I've heard it's one of the most romantic places on Earth. I'm just so excited to finally see it in person. It's going to be amazing…with you."

JT nodded, his smile a little tight. He had been there before, but it was a different time, with a different person. His memories of Venice with Sarah were bittersweet. He didn't want to spoil the magic of the moment by sharing those memories, so he kept them locked away for now.

As the ship sailed for the two-day trip toward Venice, Drusilla leaned back in her chair, her eyes closed for a moment as she let the sea breeze wash over her. She was falling for JT, there was no denying it. And she had a feeling that Venice—this magical city—might just be where everything fell into place.

161

Chapter 11

Port of Call: Venice, Italy

As the sun dipped toward the horizon, the distant skyline of Venice began to take shape. Drusilla leaned over the ship's railing, her eyes shining with excitement as the city's domes and bell towers grew larger, shimmering in the warm, amber glow of twilight. She sighed in awe, barely able to contain her excitement.

"Venice," she whispered, more to herself than to JT, as if saying it aloud would make the moment even more real.

JT watched her, his face a blend of anticipation and something unspoken. Venice had been a part of his past, yet here, seeing it again through Drusilla's fresh wonder, it felt as though the city was revealing itself anew.

"I think I've been waiting my whole life for this," she said softly, her voice filled with awe. "I always dreamed of coming here someday."

"Well, Venice awaits," JT said with a warm smile. "But first, what do you say we clean up and get ready for dinner?"

Drusilla nodded, tearing her gaze away from the skyline to meet his eyes. "I'm so excited," she said, her voice barely containing her excitement.

They walked back to their cabins, sharing a final glance as they parted ways, each swept up in a sense of possibility. Venice lay ahead of them, waiting to unfold its charm, mystery, and romance.

Opting for a more relaxed evening on board, JT and Drusilla chose a casual dinner at one of the ship's cozy bistros, where they dined on fresh pasta and shared a simple bottle of red wine, enjoying the unhurried pace and the anticipation of the night ahead.

As they sipped their last glass, an announcement came over the intercom: they'd be docking in Venice within the hour. Drusilla's eyes lit up at the news, but before she could even ask what they should do, JT leaned in with a mischievous grin.

"Let's go ashore," he whispered. "We'll have about two hours, and I know just the place to take you."

Intrigued, Drusilla smiled back, her heart racing with the thrill of the unknown. They finished their meal and made their way to the main deck, watching as the ship glided slowly into the Venetian port, the ancient city sparkling under the moonlight. The narrow canals, glistening like silk, beckoned them closer.

As soon as they were able, JT led Drusilla off the ship and into the winding, narrow streets. They moved swiftly through the alleys, JT keeping their destination a surprise as he led her over quaint bridges and past quiet piazzas. Finally, they arrived at a hidden little wine bar tucked into a corner of a canal-side street, its terrace illuminated by flickering candlelight and overlooking a view straight out of a painting.

"This," JT said, "was always my favorite spot."

He pulled out a chair for her, and she settled into the romance of the moment, Venice unfolding like a dream before them. With glasses of rich, Venetian wine, they toasted to the night, to adventure, and to finding something unexpected in each other. Time seemed to slow as they shared a quiet connection, making the most of their precious two hours in the city of love before they'd have to return to the ship.

The following morning, Drusilla received a message from the ship's crew: she had a visitor waiting on the dock. Curiosity mixed with unease as she made her way down. When she reached the dock, her heart skipped a beat—there was Sam, looking like he'd crossed half the world just to find her.

"Sam! What...what are you doing here?" she asked, shock and a trace of old emotions flickering in her voice.

"I had to see you, Dru," he said earnestly. "I still love you, and I needed to tell you that in person." He pulled her into a hug, and although she tensed at first, she allowed it, feeling the weight of their history settle between them.

They talked for a few minutes, and Sam pressed her to take a walk with him, to hear him out. Hesitant but realizing this was her chance to bring closure, she agreed. As they walked toward the famous Danieli Hotel, Drusilla rehearsed the words in her mind, ready to tell Sam it was over.

But JT, standing on the upper deck, spotted them. His chest tightened as he recognized the man beside her—he'd seen photos of Sam when she showed him once, thinking nothing of it at the time. Now, his stomach dropped. He hurried down from the deck, staying just far enough behind to watch them without being seen, following as they entered the opulent Danieli.

Through the window, JT saw them settle into the bar. Sam leaned close, his face full of warmth as he talked to Drusilla, who seemed deep in thought. JT felt his heart splinter, each moment feeling like a betrayal. Unable to bear it any longer, he returned to the ship, his mind swirling with doubt and heartbreak. Back on board, he sat by the pool where they'd spent so many mornings together, staring blankly at the horizon, fighting the lump in his throat.

Hours passed. Finally, he looked up to see Drusilla coming toward him. She scanned the deck, clearly searching for him, with an anxious, vulnerable look he hadn't seen before. JT stood as she approached, her face full of turmoil.

"Where have you been?" he asked, the hurt in his voice evident. "I texted you—no response."

Drusilla took a deep breath, her gaze dropping to their joined hands. "I…I need to tell you about Sam. He showed up this morning. He said he still loved me, and I thought maybe I owed it to him to listen."

They sank into two lounge chairs, sitting across from each other, their hands still entwined. Drusilla took another deep breath. "I was confused, JT. For a moment, I thought I still had feelings for him…so I agreed to hear him out." Her voice was trembling, her eyes glassy. "But, sitting there with him, I realized that part of my life was done."

JT was quiet, processing her words, then nodded, sadness deepening in his expression. "I understand," he said, his voice subdued. "But, Drusilla, you could have told me, given me a heads-up. This feels like…like you're slipping away." He paused, the pain evident in his face. "I need some time to think."

He got up and walked away, leaving Drusilla alone, tears slipping down her cheeks. She stayed there, staring at the spot he'd vacated, feeling the weight of what she might have just lost. Eventually, she returned to her cabin, curling up on the bed, her body racked with quiet sobs. The hours ticked by, and her phone remained silent until finally a message from JT arrived:

"I'll have dinner in my cabin tonight. You take care."

She replied,

"I understand. Can I see you tomorrow?"

But there was no response.

Heartbroken and exhausted, she finally cried herself to sleep, uncertain if their romance could survive the heartbreak of that Venetian morning.

The following morning, Drusilla got up, showered, and made her way to the top deck for breakfast. As she arrived, she saw JT sitting alone, reading his phone and sipping his coffee. She approached him, and when he looked up, he thought of how beautiful she looked, even after everything. He stood up, and she softly asked, "May I join you?"

By now, JT had taken the time he needed to reflect, realizing that if this was real, he would need to give her the space to find her answers. He smiled and replied, "Of course," pulling out her chair. Drusilla felt a wave of relief wash over her as she reached out and placed her hand over his, already apologizing. The waiter arrived, and she told him, "I'm not sure that I'm staying," looking curiously at JT. JT glanced up at the waiter and said, "She'll have a latte and a chocolate croissant." Drusilla's heart swelled—he wanted her to stay.

They sat across from each other, talking and crying, then talking even more as she poured her heart out to him. She admitted that when she first saw Sam, she felt a rush of old feelings. She hadn't seen him in over a year, and he looked good, and he seemed sincere when he said he still loved her. It made her wonder if there was a chance for them, if he had truly changed, and if they could pick up where they left off. She shared with JT that it was a difficult moment, a "big girl" moment, realizing she was in the middle of a love triangle—of all places, in Venice.

However, the more she listened to Sam, the more her thoughts kept drifting back to JT. She'd changed since then; she no longer wanted the life she had with Sam. She valued the time they'd shared but had come to realize that her future was different now. Sam had tried to persuade her to go up to his room to talk privately, but she knew that if she went, his charm might tempt her, and she could end up surrendering to old feelings. Instead, she leaned over, kissed him on the cheek, and told him goodbye before heading back to the ship, almost running back to JT. The thought of losing him had begun to break her heart.

As she finished, she looked into JT's eyes, filled with worry and hope. JT sat quietly, processing her every word, and then leaned forward, gently cupping her chin as he had that first time he'd kissed her. He gazed into her eyes and softly said, "I love you, Drusilla. I don't want to lose you. My heart felt like it was breaking too, afraid you'd go back to him."

Then he kissed her deeply, holding her as if he'd never let go. Drusilla wrapped her arms around him and whispered, "I love you too, JT. I want to be with you more than anything. Please, please forgive me."

JT smiled, brushing a tear from her cheek, and said, "You don't have anything to apologize for."

They stayed like that for a few moments, and as her breakfast arrived, they settled into a peaceful quiet, both knowing they'd weathered something that had brought them even closer.

166

After breakfast, JT suggested they go into Venice, grab lunch, and explore the city together. He knew his way around well, though Drusilla didn't realize why—Venice held a hidden significance for him. During lunch, JT grew quiet, gazing at Drusilla with a serious expression. Finally, he took a deep breath and said, "I have something to tell you. A bit of a confession..."

Drusilla's heart skipped a beat, caught off guard and nervous about what he might reveal. JT explained that he had spent his honeymoon with Sarah in Venice, and they'd even returned two other times during their marriage. After the divorce, he'd come to hate the idea of coming back. "It was *our* place," he admitted, and when Drusilla first mentioned Venice, he'd felt a surge of reluctance. He hadn't even remembered it was on the itinerary until she brought it up. And then, with Sam showing up, he felt like the city was playing tricks on him, as if he were doomed to relive painful moments from his past.

Drusilla was both shocked and relieved. The last thing she wanted now was more drama or shadows from the past. Smiling, she took his hand and said, "There's no such thing as a curse. Now we have the perfect reason to make this *our* place. Screw the past. We're here now—together, in love, and free from it all."

JT felt a wave of gratitude and love, reaching across the table to take her hand, bringing it to his lips and kissing it gently. "That's why I love you, my little Red Sox fan."

They both laughed, the tension broken, and began to make new plans for the rest of the day. JT smiled and said, "I have to take you to Murano. It's where the finest glass in the world is made, and we'll need to take a boat to get there. It's a little island just off Venice."

Drusilla's face lit up with excitement, her earlier worries forgotten. Their adventure was back on track, and the day ahead felt full of promise.

The trip to Murano felt straight out of a romance film. They climbed into a sleek wooden boat, captained by a young Venetian in a black-striped shirt, embodying Venice's timeless charm. As they set off across the water, Drusilla and JT sat in the back, nestled together as they watched the city's skyline fade.

With JT's arm wrapped around her, Drusilla tilted her face up to meet his, and he kissed her softly. One kiss became two, then three, until their restraint melted away in the gentle waves and their kiss deepened, full of urgency and passion. Lost in each other, they barely noticed the world around them. The boat driver caught a glance of their embrace, then quickly turned his gaze forward, smiling slightly. He'd seen this scene play out many times before—the passion of new love under the spell of Venice.

As they neared Murano, JT pulled back just enough to meet her eyes, his smile promising more of the same once they stepped onto the island. Drusilla could barely wait; her heart raced with the thrill of this new adventure, both with him and in this magical place. Venice was becoming *their* city, one kiss at a time.

As they strolled through the charming streets of Murano, the more they immersed themselves in the sights and sounds of the island, the more the magnetic pull between them intensified. The air was thick with unspoken desire, and they found themselves stealing lingering touches whenever they thought no one was looking. JT's hand would brush against hers, fingers grazing lightly, and sending electric currents through her skin. When he hugged her close, her lips would graze his ear, and she couldn't resist biting it softly, her breath warm against his skin.

The tension between them built with every step, and neither of them could ignore the heat rising between them. The way their bodies gravitated toward one another felt inevitable, as if the world around them had faded away, leaving only the undeniable pull of attraction.

JT and Drusilla strolled through several foundries, each more captivating than the last, as artisans expertly blew glass into intricate shapes and vibrant colors. When they entered the Chihuly studio, JT pointed out, "This is the artist behind that famous ceiling at the Bellagio in Vegas."

Drusilla's eyes lit up. "I've stayed there a few times—always admired that ceiling! Isn't he the artist with the eye patch?"

"Yep, that's him," JT replied with a grin. They admired the colors and shapes, and Drusilla couldn't resist finding a memento. With JT's guidance on prices, she eventually settled on a pair of beautiful red and blue tinted vases—one for herself and one as a thank-you gift for her mother.

As they continued browsing, JT pointed to a large glass chandelier on display, sharing a memory. "Sarah and I bought a chandelier just like this on our honeymoon. It still hangs in *her* house," he chuckled.

Drusilla gave him a playful pout. "Then I'll skip the chandelier," she said, feigning a sulk.

They both burst into laughter, and JT pulled her close, brushing a kiss on her forehead. Their laughter and ease continued as they explored, and Drusilla found herself more deeply captivated by JT and their shared experience in this beautiful, art-filled corner of the world.

Finally, JT broke the silence, his voice low and purposeful. "Let's head back to the ship and get ready for a nice dinner in Venice."

Drusilla's heart raced at the thought of a quiet evening in Venice with JT. "Absolutely," she said without hesitation. She was already anticipating the night ahead—the romance, the passion, the unrestrained intimacy. They made their way to the dock, hands brushing again, before they climbed aboard the water taxi back to *their place*—the place that felt more like "theirs" with every passing moment.

As the taxi moved across the water, their eyes met, and there was no more need for words. Their chemistry was undeniable, and they both knew exactly what awaited them once they were back on the ship.

Returning to the ship

As they step back onto the ship, they walk hand-in-hand, the warmth of the sun and the thrill of their Murano adventure still lingering in the air. They briefly pause to take in the views of the Venetian lagoon from the deck, enjoying the sight of the city in the distance, with its stunning canals and architecture bathed in the fading golden light of the day. The peaceful moment feels like a snapshot of their romance—a perfect pause before the evening's festivities.

Once back in their cabin, they drop off their shopping bags from Murano, including Drusilla's beautiful vases. They share a few playful glances and smiles, both eager to get dressed up for their evening out. They don't have a lot of time, and when Drusilla goes into the bathroom,

169

JT hears her start the shower. "JT, will you help me for a minute," As JT walks into the bathroom, he sees Drusilla already in the shower, her beautifully tanned naked body calling out for him. He doesn't hesitate, strips off his clothes and joins her. Their embrace is the crescendo to what they had been toying with all day. The showers on a ship are small and forced the new lovers to stay pressed against one another as the hot water poured over them. Steam from the hot water fogged the glass door and all that was visible was Drusilla's back pressed up against the glass. They found the passion they longed for all day.

After their shower, a sense of relaxed intimacy between them continued, and neither was in a rush. JT pours them each a glass of wine to sip as they unwind for a moment before heading off to their separate wardrobes. Drusilla runs her fingers through her hair, smiles at her reflection, and contemplates the evening ahead.

Before getting dressed, they sit down for a few moments on the balcony. JT lights a cigar as they talk about their day—how much fun they had exploring Murano and all the fascinating things they saw. Drusilla mentioned the glass-blowing demonstrations, the beautiful pieces, and her surprise at JT's connection to Chihuly, which adds another layer of depth to her understanding of him.

This quiet, comfortable time together lets them connect even more deeply after their steamy lovemaking session in the shower, but also builds up a sense of anticipation as they prepare for a romantic dinner and a fun evening out in Venice. Music from the upper deck playing in the background, as they enjoy the gentle rocking of the ship while sitting in the soft glow of the cabin lights.

For their chic night out in Venice, both JT and Drusilla dress in elegant, sophisticated styles that reflect the city's romantic and stylish atmosphere.

Drusilla chooses a stylish, tailored white blouse made of silk—something light and breezy to complement the warm Venetian evening. She tucks it into a high-waisted, wide-legged pair of black trousers, creating an effortlessly chic silhouette. To add a touch of her artistic side, she adds a delicate gold necklace with a small pendant. For shoes, she opts for simple strappy sandals in metallic gold that highlight her tan. She carries a small leather crossbody bag—functional but still stylish. Her makeup is fresh and natural, with just a hint of blush and a soft red lip to stand out against the evening air. Her hair is loosely styled, a few waves framing her face, with a small hairpin to keep a strand in place.

JT, ever the stylish yet understated gentleman, chooses a crisp, button-down shirt in a soft, light blue that contrasts subtly with his dark, tailored jeans. The shirt is slightly unbuttoned at the collar, allowing for an easy, laid-back vibe but still sharp enough to look polished. His shoes are leather loafers in a rich brown, combining comfort and class. He wears a thin leather belt and a watch with a simple, elegant face—nothing too flashy, but it speaks to his taste for the finer things. His jacket is lightweight and unstructured, a perfect fit for Venice's mild evening temperatures. JT's hair is neatly styled, and he keeps the look fresh with a light spritz of cologne.

Once they are both dressed and looking absolutely stunning, they meet again in JT's cabin. There's a moment of admiration from both sides as JT looks Drusilla over with a twinkle in his eye, and she gazes at him with a mix of admiration and desire. They share a kiss, and then, with one last check in the mirror, they head out to enjoy their evening in Venice, ready to take on the night together.

Drusilla slips her arm through JT's as they walk down the hall, both of them moving with a fluid ease, as if this had become second nature to them. She smiles up at him, feeling a rush of excitement for what's to come. His gaze on her is appreciative, and there's something in his eyes that tells her he's just as eager to be with her tonight as he was the first time they met.

The soft glow of the hallway lights reflects off the polished wood, and they pass crew members who greet them with warm smiles, their excitement clearly visible as they make their way toward the gangway. JT gives a polite nod to the staff, but his attention is focused entirely on Drusilla, her beauty making his heart race just a little faster. The crew members can't resist watching her as she walks by in admiration.

They step off the ship and onto the dock, the fresh evening air of Venice greeting them like a long-lost lover. The city, with its twinkling lights and romantic ambiance, seems to come alive in the night, its canals reflecting the colors of the city's ornate buildings and the fading sunset. The gondolas gently rock in the water nearby, adding to the magic of the evening.

Drusilla, with her arm still linked with his, feels a surge of warmth as she looks around at the city she's come to love. But it's not the city she's focused on right now—it's JT. Tonight, this adventure, this moment, is about them. The thought of their quiet dinner, followed by the excitement of exploring Venice's nightlife together, makes her heart flutter.

JT, sensing her excitement, leans in and whispers, "Tonight's all about us, Drusilla. Let's make it unforgettable."

They walk down the narrow streets, the sound of their footsteps a rhythm to the beating of their hearts. JT's hand rests lightly on the small of her back, guiding her through the winding streets toward the restaurant he's chosen. It's a place tucked away from the crowds, with an intimate atmosphere that perfectly matches the vibe of their evening.

As they approach the entrance of the restaurant, the warm glow from the windows spills out onto the sidewalk, drawing them in. JT opens the door for her with a gentleman's grace, and Drusilla steps inside, her senses immediately engulfed by the cozy ambiance—soft lighting, flickering candles, and the savory scent of Italian cuisine wafting through the air. The maître d' greets them with a welcoming smile, and they are led to a table in a quiet corner, perfect for the intimate dinner they've been looking forward to.

They settle into their seats, and Drusilla smiles across the table at JT, feeling more at ease with him than she ever has before. Their connection, strong and undeniable, only grows as the night progresses. With a glass of fine wine in hand, they raise a toast to their time together, to Venice, and to the adventure they've shared so far.

Dinner is filled with laughter, meaningful conversation, and the occasional flirtatious glance. They talk about everything—from the joys of exploring Venice to their dreams for the future, and everything in between. The easy camaraderie between them is obvious, as though they've known each other for years, rather than just a matter of weeks.

As the night goes on, the chemistry between them builds, and the idea of exploring Venice's nightlife after dinner seems even more enticing. But for now, they savor the moment—together, in this magical city, with the promise of more to come.

After dinner they head out to explore the city's nightlife. They wander through narrow, winding streets lined with antique shops, and stop at an intimate, upscale bar that overlooks the Grand Canal. It's a beautiful, private location, where the city's soft lights shimmer across the water. The atmosphere is elegant but relaxed, with smooth jazz playing in the background. The place is not overcrowded, providing a quiet, intimate spot where they can enjoy each other's company.

After enjoying their perfect martinis, they head to an iconic Venetian lounge known for its chic atmosphere. From the outside, it seemed unassuming, but as they stepped through the door, they were greeted by a pulsating beat that instantly swept them into its rhythm.

The club was a blend of sleek modern design and the historic charm of Venice, with dark leather booths lining the walls and flickering lights illuminating the dance floor. The crowd was a mix of locals and tourists, all caught up in the intensity of the night. But for JT and Drusilla, it felt like just the two of them existed in this moment. The heavy bass of the music thudded in their chests, a deep, relentless pulse that felt almost primal.

They found two seats the bar and JT quickly ordered a bottle of Cristal, as the bartender poured them both a glass, his eyes never left Drusilla's. "To us," he said, his voice low but full of promise.

They clinked their glasses, and as the first notes of a powerful dance beat reverberated through the room, JT pulled her into his arms. Drusilla's eyes lit up with excitement as she followed his lead, feeling the heavy rhythm pulse through her body. The crowd around them faded away, and it was as if the music existed solely for them. The heat from the dance floor, the flashing lights, and the intoxicating pull of the night wrapped around them, drawing them closer.

JT was completely in sync with her, his body moving effortlessly to the rhythm. Drusilla felt her pulse race, matching the beat of the music, her body swaying and spinning with a newfound freedom. There was an electric tension between them, the way their bodies aligned, the way his hands moved over her as they danced together. She could feel the heat rising between them as they pressed closer, their movements becoming more fluid and intoxicating.

173

With each beat, it was as if the world outside the club disappeared. The music wasn't just heard—it was felt, vibrating through their bodies, syncing them into a single force of nature. JT's hands grazed her back, pulling her tighter to him as their movements became more intimate, more sensual. The sound of the music, the bass, the pulse, was like an extension of the chemistry between them.

As the night deepened, the atmosphere in the club grew hotter, the beats heavier. The champagne flowed freely, the lights blurring with each turn and spin on the dance floor. JT and Drusilla were lost in the moment, in each other, their bodies moving to the beat.

At one point, JT leaned in close, his breath warm against her ear, "This is the best time I've ever had in Venice," She turned her head, meeting his eyes, her heart racing. She wanted to say something, anything, but the music, the moment, made words seem insignificant. Instead, she kissed him, pulling him deeper into the dance, the world spinning around them as their bodies collided in rhythm.

They danced for what felt like hours, the music never stopping, the beat going on and on, thundering through their chests. They didn't want it to end. But eventually, the music slowed, and the crowd began to thin out. They left the dance floor together, hands still entwined, hearts still racing.

As they made their way back out into the Venice night, the moonlight bathed them in a soft glow. The night had been perfect—filled with passion, laughter, and a connection neither of them could deny. JT's arm around Drusilla's waist, and her head resting against his shoulder, they walked in comfortable silence, knowing that no matter where the night went next, they were exactly where they were meant to be—together.

After leaving the nightclub, the streets of Venice felt quieter, the sounds of music and chatter from earlier fading into the distance. The moon hung high in the sky, casting silver light over the canals and the city seemed to be holding its breath in the stillness of the night. JT and Drusilla, their hands intertwined, walked leisurely through the narrow streets, each step in sync with the lingering beat in their veins.

As they rounded a corner and headed toward the dock, JT glanced at his watch. His eyes widened. "Oh no," he said, his voice tinged with surprise. "It's after midnight!"

He looked over at Drusilla, his lips curving into a playful grin. "Looks like we've missed the ship's curfew," he said, as if it was no big deal.

Drusilla frowned slightly, looking at the lit-up ship docked in the distance. "Does this mean we're stranded here?" she asked with a half-joking tone, though the thought of being stuck in Venice after hours wasn't exactly as appealing as it sounds.

JT gave her a reassuring smile, his confidence never wavering. "Not a chance," he said. "I've got this."

They approached the security checkpoint near the gangway. A guard, standing in front of a barrier, looked up as they neared.

"Sorry, folks. The ship's closed for the night. You'll have to wait until morning," the guard said, holding up his hand to stop them.

JT, with his usual easy charm, stepped forward and flashed the guard a friendly smile. "Hey there, we just got caught up in the nightlife here in Venice. Didn't realize the time," he said, keeping his voice casual and warm. "Is there any way you could help us out? We're just looking to get back on board."

The guard glanced at them for a moment, clearly sizing them up. JT reached out as if to shake the guard's hand and calmly palmed him a folded $100 bill. "I'd really appreciate your help, my friend," JT added with a knowing smile.

The guard glanced at what JT had put in his hand, then at JT, and with a resigned sigh, he took it. "Alright, just this once. I'll let you in through the lower deck, but don't make a habit of this. Captain's orders, no one after midnight."

JT smiled broadly, his charisma working its magic. "We won't make a habit of it. Thanks so much."

Drusilla's eyes widened slightly as they moved past the guard, impressed by JT's effortless charm. "You are amazing," she whispered under her breath.

JT shrugged with a playful grin. "Sometimes a little charm…and a crisp Benjamin… goes a long way.

They made their way through the quiet, dimly lit hallways of the ship's lower deck, the sounds of the kitchens and crew members moving quietly around them. The atmosphere was hushed, a stark contrast to the buzzing energy they had just left behind.

As they reached the back stairwell that led up to their cabin, Drusilla couldn't help but laugh softly. "I'm really starting to think you can talk your way out of anything."

JT chuckled, pulling her a little closer. "When I want something, I go after it," he said, his voice low and filled with meaning. "And tonight, all I want is you."

They reached Drusilla's cabin door, and JT unlocked it, glancing over at Drusilla. "Shall we continue our adventure?"

Drusilla smiled, feeling the warmth of his words wrap around her like a blanket. She couldn't resist. "Lead the way," she said, the excitement of the night still buzzing in her chest.

As the door closed behind them, they both knew the night was far from over. In fact, it felt like it was only just beginning.

Drusilla places her handbag down on the small table by the door and turns to face JT. Her eyes meet his, and in that moment, everything feels both electric and serene. The playful banter from the evening still lingers in her smile, but now there's a deeper, more intimate connection between them—an undeniable pull.

JT steps toward her, his hand lightly grazing the side of her face, his touch as gentle as the sea breeze that just swept through their earlier walk by the canals. Drusilla tilts her head slightly, her breath catching as she leans into his touch, allowing herself to fully feel the warmth and affection that radiates from him.

176

Without breaking eye contact, he lowers his lips to hers, the kiss slow at first—soft, exploratory, and almost teasing. Her lips part as he deepens the kiss, and in that moment, their mutual longing surges. The kiss becomes more urgent, more passionate, as if everything they've been holding back all evening is now being released in a tidal wave of desire.

She pulls him closer, feeling the strength in his arms as he responds, his hands tracing the curves of her back. A soft gasp escapes her, and he takes that as a cue, lifting her effortlessly as if nothing else mattered but this perfect moment between them. She wraps her legs around him, feeling his body press against hers, both of them needing the closeness as they move toward the bed.

Clothes quickly become an afterthought, tossed aside as they explore each other with a raw intensity that feels both new and deeply familiar. JT's hands, once so carefully restrained, now seem to know exactly where to touch to make her feel alive. Her fingers trace his jaw, moving to his chest, feeling the beat of his heart match her own.

The room is filled with the soft sounds of their breath, the shuffle of sheets, and the quietest whispers of their names. Everything else fades away as they lose themselves in each other, every kiss, every touch an expression of the desire and passion that has been building all evening.

Afterward, they lay tangled in the sheets, bodies still connected, but now in a softer, more peaceful rhythm. Drusilla rests her head on JT's chest, listening to the steady beat of his heart, a small smile tugging at her lips. JT's hand lightly brushes through her hair, and for a moment, there's nothing but the quiet sound of their breathing, the perfect ending to a night that has been nothing short of magical.

In that silence, they both know something has shifted—this is no longer just a fling, but something far deeper. Their connection has moved beyond physical attraction, toward something more meaningful.

Chapter 12

Heading to New York

The next morning, as the ship's horn sounded, Drusilla and JT stood at the edge of the deck, the golden light of dawn reflecting off the calm sea. The ship is starting its journey back to New York, the distant skyline of Venice gradually disappearing behind them, replaced by the vast, endless ocean ahead. The excitement of their time in Italy—the passion, the late nights, the adventures—was slowly giving way to the reality of the return voyage. With only eight days left together, they would spend the time planning what was next in their relationship. Drusilla was scheduled to stay two nights in New York before heading back to Boston. JT was a bit anxious to get back and deal with corporate issues that were delayed while he was on holiday.

Drusilla rested her head against JT's shoulder, her fingers lightly brushing against his hand as they both watched the horizon. There was a sense of bittersweetness in the air. Venice had felt like a whirlwind, a brief but intense escape from the complexities of their pasts. Now, the ship was carrying them back to the world they had left behind, but somehow, it felt different. They had changed. They had found something in each other that neither had expected, but that they both desperately needed.

"It feels strange, doesn't it?" Drusilla murmured, breaking the silence between them.

JT turned his head to look at her, his hand gently brushing through her hair. "Yeah," he said quietly. "But I think... I think it feels like the right kind of strange."

She smiled up at him, her eyes meeting his with a mixture of tenderness and excitement. "I don't want to go back to the way things were," she said, her voice low but resolute.

JT squeezed her hand, his voice filled with warmth and sincerity. "You don't have to," he replied. "We're starting something new, Drusilla. Something real. Something that has been lacking in both of our lives."

They stood there for a long moment, the sound of the ocean filling the space between them. For the first time in what felt like forever, Drusilla felt at peace. The chaos of her past was behind her, and as they sailed toward New York, she realized that what she had with JT wasn't just a fleeting escape—it was the beginning of something lasting, something she hadn't even known she was looking for. But the uncertainty of what comes next weighed heavy on her heart.

Later, as the ship cruised through the open waters, JT and Drusilla sat together at one of the outdoor cafes, sipping on iced drinks and talking about everything they had experienced. They joked about the future, about their plans when they got back to New York, but in the back of their minds, both knew they were embarking on a new chapter that was far more promising than either had ever imagined. They had major decisions to make during the next eight days.

Their time on the cruise had been filled with romance, laughter, and passion, but now, with the ship heading home, there was an undeniable sense of anticipation in the air. The real test was just beginning. How would they navigate life once they were back in the real world? Would the chemistry and connection they had found in the midst of a whirlwind escape survive the pressures of their pasts and the reality of their daily lives?

For now, though, there was no rush. They had each other, and for the first time in a long time, that was enough.

After a quiet morning and Venice out of sight, Drusilla and JT decide to spend the afternoon unwinding by the pool. They head back to their cabins, change into their bathing suits, and meet at their favorite spot by the pool. The sun is shining brightly, casting a warm glow over the ship as they settle into lounge chairs, side by side.

Drusilla stretches out in the sun, feeling the warmth against her skin, sporting a bright white bikini while JT relaxes with his sunglasses on, occasionally glancing at her, admiring her beautiful body. They chat about everything—the easy banter of a couple completely comfortable with each other, enjoying the moment. The poolside is busy but not crowded, with the gentle hum of the ship beneath them and the sound of waves lapping against the hull.

They order lunch poolside, opting for light fare: fresh salads, chilled seafood, and cold drinks to cool off in the afternoon heat. JT lifts his glass toward Drusilla, toasting to the perfect day. "To us," he says with a grin, and she laughs, clinking her glass against his.

179

As the day goes on, the sun beats down, and they both feel completely at ease in each other's company. JT keeps a hand on Drusilla's back when she reclines, occasionally brushing her arm or leaning in to kiss her softly when no one is looking. Their connection is intense, like an electric current between them.

By late afternoon, they decide to head back to their cabins to get ready for the evening. JT's cabin is a bit larger than Drusilla's, and he suggests they have dinner on his balcony. It's a romantic setting, with the ocean stretching out before them. The evening breeze is a refreshing change after the hot sun, carrying a faint sea breeze that ruffles Drusilla's hair just a little. They're both dressed casually, comfortable yet stylish in a way that feels effortless, perfect for a quiet evening together.

Drusilla wears a soft, flowy sundress in a muted pastel color—its fabric swaying gently in the breeze. The dress is simple, with a flattering A-line cut that hugs her waist and cascades down to her knees. She wears a small pair of gold hoop earrings and a thin bracelet on her wrist. Her feet are bare, relaxed as she leans against the balcony railing, watching the view.

JT is equally laid-back, opting for a crisp long sleeve white t-shirt and light, relaxed-fit khaki shorts. He has a pair of well-worn loafers that he's slipped off, letting his feet enjoy the coolness of the floor. His sleeves are rolled up just enough to show his forearms, and the relaxed look suits him perfectly, giving him the appearance of someone who is confident without needing to try too hard.

The evening feels intimate and peaceful, a rare moment of quiet between the two of them as they sit on the balcony, sipping on chilled glasses of white wine. They share light conversation—about the day's adventures, their dreams, the soft laughter of the passengers on the deck far below—but the quiet hum of the ship and the lapping of the waves is the dominant soundtrack to their evening.

As they talk, room service arrives—a delicious spread, perfect for their low-key dinner. A waiter, in crisp white uniform, wheeled in a tray with a variety of dishes: a fresh seafood salad with lemon vinaigrette, grilled vegetables, a delicate risotto with saffron, and a perfectly seared tuna steak for JT, paired with roasted chicken for Drusilla. There's also a basket of warm, freshly baked bread and a small plate of olives and cheeses.

180

The waiter sets everything up on the small outdoor table, then quietly leaves them alone, the door to the suite softly clicking shut behind him.

The two of them dive into the meal with an easy enjoyment, taking in bites of the food and savoring both the flavors and the peacefulness of the evening. Drusilla leans back in her chair, closing her eyes for a moment, letting the sun's warmth fade into the cool of the evening air. "I'm so glad we're doing this," she says softly, her gaze resting on the horizon, where the last streaks of daylight are beginning to fade.

JT glances over at her, a quiet smile playing on his lips as he takes a sip of his wine. "Me too," he says, his voice calm, content. "Sometimes it's nice to just enjoy the moment."

They share a comfortable silence, their hands brushing occasionally as they reach for more food or pour more wine. As the night stretches on, the conversation turns to deeper things—talk of their lives back home, the hopes and dreams they each carry, and how this time together feels like the start of something that could last.

The view from the balcony is breathtaking, the sky now painted in shades of purple and pink as the stars begin to emerge, and they both know that this is the kind of moment that will stay with them. As the evening winds down, the shared meal, laughter, and easy conversation will become another cherished memory in what is slowly becoming the most unforgettable journey of their lives.

After dinner, they decide to go to the ship's casino for a little while. The energy is different now: the lights are dimmed, and the sound of coins and chatter fills the air as they walk through the casino doors. The place is buzzing with excitement, and they both feel a rush of energy, a sense of thrill that's heightened by the intimacy of the night.

Walking arm in arm through the casino, Drusilla and JT find themselves standing before a bustling craps table, the crowd around it lively with anticipation. The sound of the dice rattling, the cheering, and the occasional groan fill the air. JT leans against the table, watching the scene unfold with amusement, while Drusilla's eyes light up as she recognizes the familiar rush of the game.

181

"Shall we try our luck?" JT asks with a grin, his hand resting lightly on her back.

Drusilla smiles back, the sparkle in her eyes betraying her excitement. "You know how much I love this game," she teases as she reaches in her purse and hands JT eight yellow $500 chips. "Let's use these." JT smiles as he forgot that she kept her winnings from their last trip to the casino.

She steps forward, and JT follows, positioning himself behind her, his hand brushing her shoulder in a way that sends a pleasant shiver down her spine. Before the dealer calls for the next round, JT tosses two of the yellow chips on the table and requests change from the dealer. Drusilla stands confidently, eyes narrowing with focus. JT watches her with amusement. The last time they played together, she rolled the dice with a fierce intensity and earned the nickname "Gunner." She was back for more.

"Alright," she says, rolling her shoulders back, preparing for her turn. "Here we go."

The crowd around them grows quiet, all eyes on Drusilla as she picks up the dice. She glances at JT with a playful smile, her fingers curling around the dice, blows on them, then leans across the rail, her breasts almost falling out of her dress, shoots him a wink and with a smooth motion, she throws the dice down the table. The crowd watches in suspense as the dice tumble and spin across the green felt.

"Come on, baby!" she mutters under her breath, her eyes locked on the dice.

JT leans in, watching the dice roll with her. The moment stretches out before them, an almost intimate tension in the air. The dice finally come to a stop....WINNER 7, the dealer shouts. The crowd erupts in cheers as Drusilla's lucky streak continues. She throws her arms up in victory, grinning ear to ear, her excitement contagious.

JT laughs, clapping her on the back. "Impressive as always, Gunner," he says.

She tosses him a teasing glance, her fingers still tingling from the touch of the dice. "I have my moments," she says with a wink. Then, as if the magic of the dice hadn't left her, she rolls again, and again, landing perfect shots each time, building a small but enthusiastic following of gamblers around them.

JT is half-amused, half-impressed as he watches Drusilla. She's in her element, and the chemistry between them is undeniable. Every time she hits the mark, he can't help but feel a little proud of her. But it's more than that—it's the way she takes charge, with such grace and confidence, that leaves him captivated.

By the time she finally hands the dice over to the next player, the table has erupted into applause for the pretty girl from Boston. JT's heart beats a little faster. He knew Drusilla was special, but seeing her in her element, so carefree and full of life, only makes his feelings for her grow stronger.

"I guess that's enough excitement for tonight," he says, as he stacks his chips on the felt and asks the dealer to color him up. He hands the chips to Drusilla, takes her hand and leads her away from the table. "You were amazing, as always."

Drusilla laughs, her eyes dancing. "I told you, JT. It's all about the luck of the roll."

As they walk away from the table, she squeezes his hand, her smile lingering, the thrill of the game still fresh on her face. For a moment, it feels like nothing else matters—just the two of them and the unspoken connection they share.

As they exit the casino, they walk past a little nightclub, Drusilla tugs at JT's arm and pulls him inside and onto the dance floor, where a jazz band plays a soft, smooth tune. The vibe is relaxed but electric, the perfect contrast to the earlier, more energetic casino atmosphere. They sway together, lost in the rhythm, feeling closer than ever.

When they leave the club and head down the quiet hallway, there's an obvious energy between them—charged, magnetic, and undeniable. Their footsteps are light but deliberate, and the brief exchange of glances, the soft smiles shared, speak volumes. It's as if they both know exactly what's coming next.

183

"How about a nightcap?" JT suggests with a playful glint in his eye. He's already imagining what the night could become, and from the way Drusilla's lips curl into a knowing smile, she's thinking the same thing.

"A nightcap?" she teases, raising an eyebrow as they approach her cabin door. "Is that what we're calling it now?"

JT laughs, the sound rich and warm, but there's a hunger in his voice as they approach Drusilla's cabin. "You know exactly what I mean."

The door clicks shut behind them, and in the instant it closes, the air in the room shifts. The world outside disappears. They're alone, together, and every inch of space between them feels like a thousand miles, pulling them closer. The music left playing from earlier in the day is the only thing that remains—a steady, rhythmic beat.

Drusilla steps toward him, her breath quickening, and without a word, they're wrapped in each other's arms. JT pulls her closer, his lips crashing onto hers with an urgency that has been building between them all night. It's a kiss that says everything, a kiss that speaks of longing, of need, and of the heat that's been simmering just below the surface.

Drusilla responds with equal fervor, her hands threading through his hair, tugging him deeper into the kiss. As their clothes come off and are tossed about the room, Drusilla knows what comes next. The night has led them here—every moment, every touch, every laugh—it's all been a prelude to this. She can feel his desire, his strength, the way his body reacts to hers, and it only fuels her own.

With a sudden, swift motion, JT sweeps her up into his arms, carrying her naked body to the bed. Drusilla's heart races, but she doesn't protest. She pulls him down on top of her, their lips never leaving each other's as they tumble onto the bed together. The world outside doesn't exist. There's only the heat, the passion, the way their bodies seem to fit together so perfectly.

Their bodies move in rhythm to the music, with a hunger that's been quietly building all day, the chemistry undeniable. The kiss deepens, and JT's hand traces the curve of her back then

184

to the softness of her thigh, sending a shiver through her. Drusilla feels her pulse quicken, her skin alive with electricity at the touch of his fingers.

As their bodies press together, the passion takes over, fierce and powerful. Drusilla loses herself in the sensation of him—his touch, his kiss, the way he makes her feel more alive than she's ever felt before. And with each passing moment, JT is consumed by the same desire, his need for her matching hers in a way that only deepens their connection.

They don't speak—there's no need for words when everything they've been feeling is expressed in the heat of their embrace, in the way their hands move over each other's bodies, in the way they breathe in sync.

It's a nightcap like no other, the kind of night that leaves no room for anything but the two of them, lost in the rush of desire and the loving intimacy they've found together. Another day in paradise.

Eight days to New York

Day two of the trip back to New York started with the early morning light filtering softly through the cabin's curtains, Drusilla stirred in JT's arms, her head nestled against his chest. The gentle rhythm of the ship's movement seemed to set the tempo of their breathing, and before long, she felt JT's fingers brush slowly down her back, pulling her closer. She opened her eyes to find him already awake, looking at her with a warm, sleepy smile.

Without a word, Drusilla rolled over on top of JT, their embrace gentle at first but soon full of passion, picking up from where the night before had left off. Drusilla sat up on JT, the morning sun painting her tan body. The world beyond the cabin faded away as they lost themselves in each other once more, their connection deeper with each touch and whispered word.

When they finally lay tangled together, both blissful and content, they lingered in the quiet moment, soaking in each other's presence. Eventually, JT propped himself up, giving her a lingering kiss before reaching for the phone to call for breakfast.

"Croissants, fresh fruit, and coffee sound good?" he asked, a twinkle in his eye.

"Perfect," Drusilla replied, tracing a line down his smooth chest with her fingertip. "And we can enjoy it out on the balcony?"

"Absolutely."

When breakfast arrived, they slipped into their robes and took their meal out onto the balcony. They savored each bite in comfortable silence, watching the sun climb over the endless horizon. With Drusilla's feet resting on JT's lap, the two lovers enjoyed the thought of what was to come today. The ocean stretched wide around them, the soft sound of waves below matching the calm they felt together.

Later, they changed into swimsuits and made their way to the pool, ready to enjoy a sun-drenched day, grateful for these quiet, perfect moments shared between them.

As JT reclined with his sunglasses on and a book in hand, Drusilla picked up her phone to call Steven. She could practically see his face lighting up when he answered.

"Darling!" Steven's voice was immediately bright and effervescent. "Well, if it isn't the elusive Drusilla Pennington! Are you calling me from the deck of your love yacht?"

"Sort of," Drusilla laughed, rolling her eyes at his dramatic tone. "How'd you know?"

"Oh, please," he drawled, "I'm living vicariously through your romance novel life. Now, tell me everything—start with Mr. Wonderful."

Drusilla glanced over at JT, who was quietly engrossed in his book, but somehow, she was sure he was listening.

"He's... perfect, Steven. I mean, he's gorgeous, he's smart, a total gentleman—"

"Gorgeous and smart?" Steven interjected with a gasp. "A dashing, rich gentleman? You found yourself a real unicorn."

"Oh, it's too much," Steven sighed, pretending to swoon. "Alright, so, are we talking real love, darling? Are you getting swept off your feet?"

Drusilla's voice softened as she looked out over the water. "I think so, Steven. I feel different when I'm with him—he's everything I didn't even know I needed."

There was a pause before Steven replied, his voice unusually serious. "Then I think you've found someone worth holding on to, Drucy. You deserve this, you know? I loved the picture you sent. You are such a cute couple."

Drusilla blinked, a little taken aback by the unexpected emotion. "Thanks, Steven. Really."

"Now," he said, his tone snapping back to its usual liveliness, "if he's *truly* perfect, bring him back to me for my approval. A full inspection is in order. Got it?"

She laughed. "Got it. I'll keep you posted."

As she hung up, she felt a newfound sense of joy and certainty. She glanced over at JT, who smiled and held her hand, asking, "How's Steven?"

"Oh, you know, full of opinions, as usual." She grinned, squeezing his hand. "But I think he'd like you."

"Then I'm already winning," JT replied, pulling her closer as they leaned back, enjoying the warmth of the sun and each other's company, the ocean stretching endlessly around them. "Let's grab lunch."

They decided on the Café. As they settled into seats near the ship's railing, the gentle ocean breeze and sparkling waves set the perfect backdrop for lunch. JT ordered for them both—a light seafood platter to share—and Drusilla smiled at his easy confidence, feeling a deeper warmth for him.

After a few bites, JT leaned back with a mischievous grin. "How about a game of 20 Questions?" he suggested. Drusilla's eyes lit up, and she agreed with a playful laugh. It felt like the perfect way to discover new layers to each other, blending humor, curiosity, and a dash of intrigue.

187

"Alright," JT began, leaning in with a smile. "What's your dream job if you weren't an artist?"

"Professional cat whisperer," she joked, making him laugh. But then she softened, thinking for a moment. "Actually... I'd love to own a small art gallery—maybe in New England. Somewhere cozy and full of charm."

Drusilla followed with her own question: "Okay, Mr. Anderson—what's something you've always wanted to try but haven't yet?"

JT rubbed his chin thoughtfully. "You'll laugh, but ballroom dancing. My mother used to dance around the house, and it always looked like such a beautiful way to express yourself. One day..."

They volleyed questions back and forth, touching on everything from favorite childhood memories to silly quirks—JT admitted his odd fascination with classic detective novels, and Drusilla confessed to her "secret" stash of Polaroids she took in her studio when a painting came out just right.

The conversation flowed so easily that time seemed to disappear. By the time they glanced at their watches, they realized they'd been sitting together for over two hours. The cafe was quieter, the lunch crowd having mostly dispersed, and they shared a look of realization.

"We need to do this more often," Drusilla said, reaching for his hand. "I love these moments with you." JT squeezed her hand gently. "Agreed."

They both laughed, feeling that familiar spark between them deepen with each passing question and answer.

After their long lunch, the two decided some cool air and downtime sounded perfect. They headed to JT's cabin, looking forward to a lazy, air-conditioned break from the midday sun. Inside, JT put on some soft music and they changed out of their swimsuits, enjoying the easy comfort between them. But as Drusilla slipped out of hers and JT took in the sight of her tan, graceful form, he couldn't resist.

188

With a playful grin, he swept her into his arms and began to ballroom dance around the room, their bare bodies moving together with a lighthearted elegance. They laughed, twirling together with carefree abandon, and as JT's hand slipped to the small of her back, the playful moment turned into something more. They fell onto the bed, their laughter fading into quiet, intimate whispers, and soon, they were lost in each other once again, the sunlight streaming through the balcony and casting a warm glow around them.

Their lovemaking lasted, a slow and sensual connection that lingered, blending passion and tenderness. When they finally drifted off afterward, wrapped around each other beneath a light sheet, the afternoon felt perfect, a world reduced to just the two of them. The soft ocean breeze from the open balcony filled the room, lulling them both into a peaceful sleep.

As Drusilla slipped out of bed and wrapped herself in a plush robe, she glanced back at JT, still sprawled out on the bed, peacefully dozing. Smiling, she quietly made her way back to her cabin to shower and prepare for the evening ahead. They'd agreed on the ship's steakhouse for dinner tonight, and she was already thinking about picking something chic, a little daring—an outfit that would catch JT's eye.

Under the warm cascade of the shower, Drusilla's thoughts drifted. This cruise had started as a simple escape, a way to clear her mind and refresh her spirit. But since that first coy meeting with JT, everything had shifted. She'd gone from looking for solitude to finding something entirely unexpected. Now, she couldn't help but wonder where it all might lead. Could this be the beginning of something lasting? Was this real love, or just the heady rush of a whirlwind romance and passionate sex? Her mind spun with questions—what if JT was the one she'd been waiting for, even when she didn't know she was waiting? Did he feel the same way? Would they want the same things beyond the thrill and the passion?

The questions echoed, blending with the steady rhythm of the water. She took a deep breath, letting the warmth settle her racing mind, then turned off the water, ready to leave the wondering behind for now. Tonight was about enjoying the moment with JT, savoring each second they had together. She reached for two towels, wrapping one around her hair and the other around her body and let her thoughts shift to the excitement of the evening—selecting the perfect outfit, imagining how the night might play out, and hoping to see that familiar, enchanted look in JT's eyes the moment he sees her.

JT awoke from their nap, blinking at the empty space beside him. Drusilla was gone, and he realized with a start that he didn't have much time to get ready for their dinner reservation at the steakhouse. He rubbed his eyes, the memory of their romantic afternoon and nap lingering, and swung his legs over the side of the bed. He loved the steakhouse on board—the service, the ambiance, and the lobster, which was as succulent as any he'd tasted back in New York.

He turned up the music, something smooth and upbeat to wake himself up fully, and headed into the shower. As the hot water streamed over his shoulders and back, his thoughts drifted to Drusilla and the evening they had ahead. He imagined her smile, her laughter, the way she would look across the table at him. He wondered what she'd wear tonight, knowing she'd look stunning no matter what. The anticipation of sharing this quiet, intimate dinner with her sent a thrill through him. He couldn't get her out of his mind.

Once he was out of the shower, JT wrapped a towel around his waist and strode over to the closet. He pulled out a pair of black slacks, crisp white shirt, and his favorite black sport coat—classic, understated, but sharp enough to match the level of elegance he was sure Drusilla would bring to the evening.

As he buttoned his shirt, he remembered the small package that had arrived in Venice, courtesy of his assistant. He crossed the room to his suitcase, unzipping it and retrieving the slim, black velvet box inside. Opening it, he admired the emerald necklace within, the stones gleaming with a deep, captivating green that reminded him of the richness of his family's history and homeland in Ecuador. The necklace was special—crafted with emeralds from his family's mines. It was for Drusilla. He hoped she would like it, but more than that, he hoped she would understand what it represented to him: a part of his life he had only recently felt ready to share.

After buttoning the last button and slipping into his jacket, JT tucked the velvet box into his pocket and gave himself a quick once-over in the mirror. His hair was perfectly in place, his shirt smooth and crisp, the open collar revealing the top of his tan chest. Satisfied, he turned down the music, dimmed the lights with a thought of how he hoped the evening would end, and took a deep breath. With a slight grin, he headed to Drusilla's cabin, the box pressing against his chest as a reminder of all that he was about to reveal to her.

Drusilla stood in front of the mirror, adjusting the strap of her black dress, its low-cut neckline showcasing a hint of cleavage. The short, figure-hugging fabric emphasized her toned body, and the slit on the side of the dress gave just the right amount of allure. She slipped into her black heels, and her diamond studs sparkled softly as she secured them in her ears. With a quick glance at herself, she couldn't help but feel a surge of excitement. Tonight was important. She wanted everything to be perfect.

Just as she was about to grab her clutch, there was a soft tap at the door. Her heart skipped a beat. She opened it, and there stood JT—his tall frame impeccably dressed in black slacks, a white shirt, and his signature black jacket. His eyes immediately found hers, and she could see the appreciation in his gaze.

"You look absolutely breathtaking," JT said, his voice low and full of admiration.

Drusilla smiled, feeling a flutter in her chest. "So do you," she replied, taking a step forward into his arms. He pulled her close, their bodies fitting together naturally, and their lips met in a sweet, lingering kiss. The heat between them was undeniable, and she felt his presence, solid and comforting.

When they broke apart, Drusilla stepped back, smoothing the front of her dress. JT took a moment to admire her once more, his expression softening with affection.

"I'll be right back," she said, heading toward the mirror to brush her hair.

As she straightened her locks, making sure every strand was in place, she felt the warmth of JT's presence behind her. He came up close, his hands resting lightly on her shoulders. She could see his reflection in the mirror as he leaned in, his breath warm against her skin.

"I have something for you," he murmured, his voice a tantalizing whisper in her ear.

191

Before she could respond, she felt his hands gently brush her hair aside, his fingers warm against the back of her neck. She gasped softly as he placed the necklace around her neck. She glanced down to see the stunning emerald necklace, its deep green stones glowing against her tan skin, knowing immediately the significance of emeralds.

Drusilla turned quickly, her heart racing, and before she could say a word, she threw her arms around JT's neck, pulling him close. "Oh my God," she breathed, her voice thick with emotion. "It's beautiful."

She kissed his face, her lips grazing his cheek, his jaw, his forehead—each kiss more desperate than the last. "I can't believe this," she murmured between kisses. "It's perfect, JT. I love it. I love *you*."

JT smiled, his hands resting on her back as he held her tightly. His heart swelled with the moment, the joy of seeing her so happy. "I'm glad you like it," he whispered. "I wanted to give you something that meant something to me."

"The emeralds…" JT began, his voice filled with emotion. "They come from my family's mines in Ecuador. I had my assistant overnight it to me while we were in Venice. I wanted you to have something special, something that connects you to where I come from."

Drusilla felt her eyes misting as she looked up at him, touched beyond words. She smiled, her hands still wrapped around his neck, the emeralds now resting softly against her skin. She was overwhelmed, both by the gift and by the man who had given it to her. And as they stood there, their foreheads touching, the rest of the world seemed to fall away, leaving just the two of them, connected by something more than just the necklace around her neck.

As JT and Drusilla approached the entrance to the steakhouse, the soft murmur of conversation and soft music filled the air. The maître d' recognized them immediately, offering a warm smile as he greeted them. "Good evening, Mr. Anderson, Miss Pennington," he said, his tone respectful but friendly. "My, that's a beautiful necklace Ms. Pennington. Would you like another picture taken before you're seated?"

Drusilla's eyes lit up, and without hesitation, she replied, "Yes, please!" She wanted to capture every moment of this magical evening, to hold onto the memory of it long after the night had passed.

JT smiled, loving how enthusiastic she was, and they stepped closer together, ready for the snapshot. Just as the camera clicked, Drusilla kicked up her right heel leaning her body toward JT's shoulder in a playful, effortless move. Her laugh was soft but bright as the flash went off, capturing the sweet, carefree moment between them. It was the perfect picture—a moment of joy, spontaneity, and connection.

Once the picture was taken, they exchanged a glance and decided to enjoy a drink before heading to their table. They found two seats at the polished bar, and before he could even ask Drusilla what she wanted, she interrupted with a confident smile.

"Champagne," she said, her eyes twinkling with a sense of celebration.

JT chuckled, nodding in agreement. "Champagne it is," he said, already thinking how right it felt to be sharing this evening with her, toasting to their connection.

As the bartender poured their glasses, they clinked their flutes together, both silently acknowledging that this wasn't just another dinner. This was a special night—a moment in time they'd remember forever. And as they sipped their champagne, leaning slightly toward each other, the world seemed to fade away, leaving only the warmth of the evening, the promise of more to come, and the undeniable pull of the growing bond between them.

When they moved to their table, it felt as though the entire room held its breath. The conversations around them quieted momentarily, and a few heads turned to watch the couple as they made their way across the dining room. JT, ever the gentleman, pulled out Drusilla's chair, and as she sat down, she caught her breath, glancing at him with a playful sparkle in her eyes.

"Oh my god, JT," she said, her gaze fixed on him. "I can see the reflection of my necklace in your eyes. I love it."

193

JT chuckled, deeply pleased, his smile growing as he looked at her. The emerald necklace stood out beautifully against her black dress, a perfect accent to her elegance and charm. "I'm glad you like it," reaching across the table to give her hand a gentle squeeze.

They turned to the menu, finally deciding on a decadent feast to match the night. They ordered a chilled shrimp cocktail to start, followed by two Caesar salads prepared tableside with fresh ingredients. For the main course, they chose an enormous lobster, cracked and served right next to them by the attentive waiter.

The server poured their first glass of Cristal, and they savored the champagne's crisp bubbles alongside the buttery richness of the lobster. The pairing was perfect, with each sip enhancing the flavors of the seafood.

After a pause in their conversation, Drusilla looked at JT and asked, "Do you mind if I ask you about the necklace? Where did it come from? When was it made? How long have you had it? What were you planning to do with it? I'm sorry, I love it and I want to know all about it.

"I don't mind at all. I was planning to tell you all about it. This particular necklace is made from emeralds from the first major discovery my father and his team found. It's part of a collection that he had made into jewelry for my mother when they were celebrating the success of the mine. He gave her the first piece on their anniversary, and she wore it every year after that."

JT takes a breath, a touch of vulnerability slipping into his tone. "When my mother passed away, I inherited the necklace. It became a part of me—not just a reminder of her, but of my family's journey. And of my father's belief in something bigger. It's why I kept it all these years."

He looks down at the necklace admiring how it looked on her tan décolleté, its green stones catching the soft light from the candles, and then back up at Drusilla, his gaze earnest.

"I thought you'd appreciate it. The story. The history. Not just the emeralds themselves, but what they represent."

Drusilla is quiet for a beat, processing the layers of history, love, and sacrifice that JT just shared. Her heart swells with admiration for him—not just for his wealth or status, but for the family legacy he carries, the pride he feels in his father's dream, and the depth of emotion he shows when mentioning his Mother.

"Do you mind if I ask why you didn't give it to Sarah?"

JT explained, "By the time my Mother died, the connection had faded between Sarah and I. I hadn't thought about it for a long time. Then when I met you, I thought immediately about it and thought it would be a perfect gift for you, for someone that is now so special to me."

Finally, she reaches across the table, her fingers brushing his gently. "It's beautiful, JT," she says softly, her voice thick with meaning. "I can see why it's so important to you—it's a piece of your family's heart. I will treasure it forever."

JT squeezes her hand, his smile warm and genuine. "I wanted you to understand," he says simply, "because you've become such an important part of my story, too."

In the quiet that follows, the weight of his words hangs in the air between them—no longer just a moment shared over dinner, but something more. Something lasting. And as the sun fully sets, they both know that this connection—this bond—is only deepening.

Just then, the waiter noticed their glasses were almost empty and refilled them both, emptying the bottle. JT didn't hesitate, he caught the waiter's attention and ordered another, grinning as he looked at Drusilla. "Who orders just one bottle of champagne?" he said with a laugh, his eyes gleaming with mischief.

She laughed along with him, their joy infectious as they clinked glasses once more. As they enjoyed each bite of the lobster, the champagne flowed, heightening the warmth between them. It was a night of laughter, exquisite food, and the kind of sparkling connection they both knew was rare.

With a smile, Drusilla propped the picture of them up against the vase in the center of the table. Once she'd wiped the butter from her fingers, laughing at herself, she pulled out her phone to snap a quick picture. Her mother had been asking nonstop about JT, and this seemed like the

195

perfect moment to share a little glimpse of the evening—and to show off the beautiful necklace he'd given her.

She hit send, and within moments, her mom replied, her response as enthusiastic as Drusilla had expected.

Oh my, Drusilla! He is one handsome man. And where did you get that necklace?

Drusilla grinned and typed back a quick response, explaining it was a gift from JT, with stones from his family's mine in Ecuador. She added a little heart emoji and sent it off, feeling a surge of joy as she thought of how meaningful it was that he'd given her such a special gift.

Her mom's next reply came quickly:

Well, he sounds like a real gentleman! I'm so happy you're happy, sweetie.

A moment later, her mother sent a photo of herself at home, holding Drusilla's beloved cat, Cynthia. Drusilla laughed softly, showing JT the picture of her mom with the kitty. She felt a wave of warmth at seeing Cynthia's familiar face, her mom beaming beside him.

"It's so good to see her," she murmured, eyes lingering on the screen.

JT leaned closer, smiling at the image. "You'll see her soon," he reminded her gently, giving her hand a squeeze.

For now, she was exactly where she wanted to be, enjoying every moment with the man beside her, the laughter, and the special night that she knew she would treasure forever.

As the last plates were cleared and the table was left pristine, the waiter brought them each a warm wet towel to clean their hands and asked if they were ready for dessert. JT and Drusilla exchanged a knowing look, both feeling too satisfied to even consider dessert. Instead, they lingered, savoring the final sips of their champagne, the warmth of the evening settling around them like a shared secret.

196

After a while, they decided to take a stroll toward the front of the ship, where the breeze was cool and the stars seemed closer—a secluded, romantic spot with only a few couples dotting the rail. Feeling a touch tipsy, Drusilla clung to JT's strong arm as they walked, giggling softly when she stumbled slightly. He steadied her, his own eyes sparkling with amusement and the unmistakable glow of affection.

At the rail, they gazed out at the moonlit ocean, watching as the ship's slow glide made the water shimmer beneath the night sky. JT noticed Drusilla shiver slightly from the breeze and, ever the gentleman, slipped his jacket off, draping it over her shoulders. The gesture felt intimate, his warmth lingering on the fabric as she pulled it closer.

Turning to face him, Drusilla's eyes were bright, her lips parted in a soft smile. They embraced, their connection deepening as their lips met in a passionate kiss that seemed to hold all the feelings neither could put into words. JT's hand drifted to her side, sliding down to where her dress parted at the slit, his fingers grazing the warm smooth skin of her thigh. Drusilla felt a thrilling shiver race up her spine as he held her there, close, his touch igniting something raw and undeniable between them.

In that moment, the world around them faded away, and it felt as if they were the only two people alive, wrapped in each other and the magic of the night. The thought of making love right there, under the stars with no one caring or noticing, sent a rush of heat through them both.

After a few breathless minutes, JT's voice was low and filled with desire as he whispered, "Should we head to my cabin?"

With a soft laugh and a nod, Drusilla agreed, leaning into him as they made their way, step by step, back through the ship toward the elevator. Their journey was filled with teasing glances, naughty touches, and laughter as they both knew what awaited them when they finally reached his cabin.

When they arrived at JT's cabin door, anticipation thick in the air, JT patted his pockets and felt an immediate twinge of realization. His key card was nowhere to be found. This minor

197

setback couldn't have come at a worse time, with their shared excitement bubbling over. Drusilla laughed softly, amused by the sudden twist in their evening.

JT, ever quick on his feet, glanced down the hall and spotted a butler nearby. Raising his hand, he called him over, explaining his predicament with a smile. The butler, recognizing JT, gave him a knowing nod and promptly unlocked the door for them. JT slipped him a generous tip, earning a polite smile before the butler quietly departed, leaving them in privacy.

As they stumbled through the door, both laughed at JT's forgetfulness.

"I was so wrapped up in giving you that necklace," he explained, grinning, "I didn't think twice about my key card."

Drusilla gave him an affectionate look, her eyes warm. "Well, it was worth it," she replied, her fingers brushing the emeralds at her neck. "But let's make sure you don't lose your head along with your key next time."

With laughter still echoing in the room, they closed the door behind them, the last traces of amusement mingling with the building tension, leaving them exactly where they'd wanted to be all night: alone, with nothing but each other to focus on.

Still giddy from all the champagne and laughter, JT and Drusilla fell back onto the bed, lying side by side with matching, contented sighs. The room filled with a comfortable silence as they listened to the soft music JT had left on, the melodies wrapping around them like a lullaby. Eyes closed, they lay there, a warm glow of happiness settling over them, and in no time, the evening's excitement gave way to drowsiness.

Without a word, both drifted off, fully dressed, their fingers just barely touching as they lay side by side, hearts full and minds quiet. They'd built the night to such a fever pitch of romance and anticipation, only to let sleep steal them away.

When morning came, they'd both wake up, their clothes wrinkled from the night, and laugh at themselves. For all the romantic excitement, their evening had ended in the most innocent of ways—side by side, simply content to be together.

As the early morning light seeped into the cabin, JT blinked awake, realizing they'd drifted off fully dressed. Smiling at the memory of the night, he slipped out of bed and shed his clothes before reaching for a plush white robe. He glanced over at Drusilla, still softly sleeping, and headed quietly to the bathroom.

Moments later, Drusilla stirred, stretching luxuriously. As she got up, she caught a glimpse of herself in the mirror and paused, her fingers touching the emeralds around her neck. A wave of emotion washed over her as she thought about how deeply she loved JT, the gift he'd given her, and the quiet joy they shared. Hearing the sound of the shower, she slipped out of her dress, leaving herself in just her black bra and panties, and walked toward the bathroom, her steps soft.

When she reached the glass shower door, she paused, leaning one arm against the wall and the other one on her hip as she admired JT through the misted glass. He turned, catching sight of her, and his breath hitched—she looked like an angel, so beautiful, so sensual, so sexy. He opened the shower door, extending his hand, and when she slipped her hand into his, he drew her in, not giving her a moment to remove her remaining clothes.

The warm water cascaded over them as they embraced, hands exploring and rediscovering each other in the close quarters of the shower. Pressed together, their bodies moved in perfect rhythm, their passion finally igniting in the intimacy of the small space. Drusilla felt swept up in a love that was new yet felt timeless, every touch deepening her feelings, every kiss a promise.

When their passion ebbed, they stood together, letting the water wash over them in silence, savoring the moment. JT stepped out first, grabbing a towel, and, ever the gentleman, left Drusilla to finish her shower in privacy, a tender smile on his face as he closed the door. Six days until they return to New York.

Seven days to New York

Day three of their sail back to New York dawned bright and sunny, with a gentle breeze drifting over the ocean. JT and Drusilla enjoyed breakfast on his balcony, soaking up the morning sun and the warm afterglow of their fun evening and intimate morning. As they sipped coffee and indulged in fresh pastries, they talked about doing something "different" that day, something to add a bit of adventure.

"What about pickleball?" JT suggested with a grin.

Drusilla laughed, surprised and intrigued. She hadn't played in a while, but the idea sounded like a fun way to shake things up. "Pickleball it is," she agreed, her eyes sparkling with excitement. They each had a little experience—she from her gym back in Boston with Sam and he from his club. It was settled: they'd lounge by the pool after breakfast, then change for their 1:00 game on the courts at the ship's stern.

After sunbathing for a while and cooling dips in the pool, they strolled over to the café for a light lunch, keeping it simple to save their energy for the upcoming match. Over salads and iced tea, they teased each other about who might win and reminisced about their previous attempts at the sport. By the time lunch wrapped up, they were both eager to see who'd come out on top. With laughter and a bit of friendly competition sparking between them, they headed back to their cabins to change for their afternoon on the court.

Arriving at the pickleball courts just before 1:00, JT and Drusilla chose their paddles, each of them exchanging playful banter about what they planned to do to the other on the court. JT, always a gentleman, started out taking it easy, thinking it'd be a fun, lighthearted match. But within minutes, he realized Drusilla was far more competitive—and skilled—than he'd expected. Her quick reflexes and strategic shots caught him off guard, and he couldn't help but admire how effortlessly she played, looking so cute in her white shorts and fitted tank top.

The match was heating up, and after about 15 minutes, they were tied at 9-9, each laughing and fully engaged. Drusilla had the serve, and she locked in, winning the next two points with ease, claiming victory at 11-9. She flashed him a triumphant grin as they met at the net, extending her hand with a playful gleam in her eye.

"Do you lose at anything?" JT asked, chuckling and shaking his head in disbelief.

Drusilla laughed, tossing him the ball as she teased, "Loser serves!"

After two more competitive games, JT managed to win the second, but Drusilla took the deciding match, sealing her pickleball victory. She grinned, thrilled at the new material for teasing him the rest of their trip. As they strolled back to their cabins, sweat glistening on both of them, JT glanced over and smirked, "You know I let you win, right?"

With a mock gasp, Drusilla swung her towel playfully at him, muttering a few choice words under her breath. They both laughed, trading playful jabs and teasing each other all the way down the hallway. Outside their cabins, they agreed to take a quick break to freshen up and meet in the café for high tea at 3:00.

Back in her cabin, Drusilla took a deep breath, relishing a moment of peace after their spirited match. She showered and dressed, already looking forward to their next rendezvous, while JT did the same, grinning as he thought about her competitive spirit. The friendly rivalry had only brought them closer, and high tea promised to be a lovely, lighthearted follow-up to their energetic afternoon.

The warm sunlight streamed through the large windows of the café, casting a soft glow over the polished wood tables. JT and Drusilla arrived a few minutes apart, both dressed casually yet elegantly for the afternoon. Drusilla walked in first, her eyes immediately catching JT's across the room. He smiled, a look of quiet admiration on his face. The air between them still carried that electric charge, though now it was tempered by the comfort of their shared moments and growing connection.

Drusilla made her way over, and they exchanged a quick kiss on the cheek before sitting down.

"You're looking stunning as always," JT said with a playful grin as he pulled out her chair and watched her settle in.

Drusilla chuckled, smoothing out the edges of her skirt. "I could say the same about you. Who would've guessed you'd be the most stylish man I've met on this ship?" she teased.

JT raised his eyebrows. "That's because you haven't met everyone else, Drusilla," he said with a wink. "But I like to think I make an exception."

She laughed, rolling her eyes. "Right. You're so modest."

A waiter arrived, placing a delicate teapot on the table with two fine china cups. He poured the tea with practiced grace before stepping aside, leaving them to enjoy their quiet moment.

"So, what's the plan for tonight?" Drusilla asked, her eyes meeting his. "I thought we'd do something special, since it's been such a perfect day."

JT leaned back in his chair, thoughtfully swirling his tea. "I was thinking dinner on the deck. I know you like the quiet out there, and it's such a beautiful evening. Just the two of us. The sunset's supposed to be spectacular, and I want to enjoy it with you."

Drusilla's heart warmed at his thoughtful gesture. "That sounds lovely. You've been full of surprises, haven't you?"

He smiled softly. "I like to keep you guessing."

She tilted her head slightly, her curiosity piqued. "Are we dressing up or going casual for dinner?"

JT's grin widened. "Let's do casual tonight and maybe dress up and hit the steakhouse tomorrow night."

She raised an eyebrow, teasing. "I like how you think?"

Drusilla loved the moment and the way he looked at her made her feel seen, cherished. She smiled softly, reaching for the delicate scones, but the moment hung between them, a promise of more.

After finishing their afternoon tea, JT and Drusilla stepped out of the café into the warm, golden light of the late afternoon. The sun was still high, casting long shadows across the polished deck as they walked side by side. The sea breeze gently tousled Drusilla's hair, and she tucked a loose strand behind her ear with a soft laugh. The world seemed far away as they strolled, the hum of the ship's engines and the soft murmur of other passengers fading into the background.

It had been such a beautiful day—filled with laughter, flirtation, and moments of unexpected connection. But now, as they walked at a leisurely pace, the quiet between them felt different. It was comfortable. The kind of silence that came with knowing someone deeply, even after only a short time.

JT looked out toward the horizon, his gaze distant for a moment, then glanced at Drusilla. She noticed the way his jaw tightened, like he was carefully weighing his words.

"You know, I've been thinking," he began, his voice almost introspective.

Drusilla tilted her head toward him, smiling softly. "About what?"

"How crazy it all is," he said with a slight shake of his head. "I mean, we met, what? A few weeks ago? And yet here we are. Walking around the ship, just... completely at ease with each other."

She laughed softly. "I know, it's wild. We're like two people who were meant to bump into each other at exactly the right moment. It's like we were both just... waiting for something or someone to show us a new direction."

JT's lips curled into a half-smile as he looked down at her. "I wasn't looking for anything. I was just looking to get away. To recharge."

Drusilla nodded. "Me too. My last relationship... it was suffocating, to be honest. I just needed space, needed to be alone, and then my Mom saw this cruise as a chance for me to clear my head. She thought a week of solitude and maybe some art would do it for me."

"I get that," JT said, his voice growing softer. "I've been so focused on work and keeping everything running smoothly. I didn't expect to find... this." He paused, looking at her with an intensity that made her heart skip a beat. "You. I didn't expect to meet someone like you."

203

Drusilla's smile softened as she turned her gaze to the horizon, feeling a swell of warmth in her chest. "I didn't either."

JT chuckled, the sound low and genuine. "You know, I think I fell for you the moment I saw you at that departure reception in New York. When you walked in, I couldn't take my eyes off of you. There was something about the way you carried yourself—confident but with a quiet grace. I thought for sure that you were with someone."

Drusilla stopped walking for a moment, her heart beating faster as she turned to face him. His words caught her off guard, but in the best way. There was no pretense, no hesitation—just pure honesty.

"You're telling me," she said, her voice soft but teasing, "that the moment you saw me, you knew? You knew you'd fall for me?"

JT stepped closer, his expression serious but warm. "I'm not saying I *knew* anything would happen this fast. But there was this feeling. Like something clicked. I was drawn to you. And everything about this, about us—this connection—is more than I could have imagined."

Drusilla's heart swelled in her chest, and she felt her lips part in surprise. She hadn't realized how much she needed to hear that. To hear that it wasn't just her, that he felt the same pull, the same bond.

"I feel it too," she said quietly, her voice barely above a whisper. "I'm not even sure how we got here, but I'm glad we did."

JT reached out, gently taking her hand in his. His thumb traced a gentle circle on her skin, a tender gesture that made her heart flutter. "Me too, Drusilla. And I look forward to seeing where this goes."

She looked up at him, their eyes meeting in a quiet exchange, the kind that spoke louder than words. It was true—they weren't looking for love, but here it was, unfolding right in front of them, just as they needed it most.

204

They walked in silence for a moment, simply enjoying the closeness between them. The ship rocked gently beneath their feet, and the sound of the ocean became a soothing background to their quiet steps. Drusilla smiled, the weight of the world falling away as she walked with him.

"This feels like a dream," she said, half-laughing as she squeezed his hand.

JT grinned. "A good one, I hope."

"Definitely a good one," she replied, smiling up at him as they continued walking.

After their walk, Drusilla returned to her cabin, feeling content and basking in the afterglow of an afternoon spent with JT. She stepped inside and let out a long breath, appreciating the quiet hum of the ship around her. She had some time before dinner, and she was looking forward to a little private moment to unwind.

She immediately kicked off her shoes, took a deep breath, and headed to the bathroom, eager to shower after the warm sun and the gentle breeze. The cool water of the shower felt heavenly as it hit her skin, washing away the tension from the day. She closed her eyes, letting the water cleanse not just her body, but also her mind. Her thoughts briefly drifted back to JT—his touch, the way he'd looked at her, the deepening connection between them.

The water eventually grew cold, snapping her out of her thoughts. With a sigh, she turned off the shower and stepped out, wrapping herself in a soft, plush towel. The steam from the shower filled the bathroom as she dried off, but she felt alive and energized, ready to slip into something chic yet comfortable for their dinner on the deck.

As she moved to the closet, she flicked a glance at the bed where she had laid out her emerald necklace earlier. She decided it wasn't right for tonight and put it safely in her overnight bag. It felt like more of an "occasion" piece—one to save for the steakhouse dinner tomorrow. Tonight would be more casual, more laid-back, but still stylish. She pulled out a pair of sleek black pants, their fabric light enough for the evening air. Then, she reached for a flowing white blouse, one that felt feminine but effortless. She could already picture the soft drape of the fabric against her skin as she slipped it on, the simple elegance of the look.

205

She laid the clothes out on the bed, a few stray strands of wet hair falling over her face as she sat down on the oversized chair, ready to relax for a moment before continuing her preparations. As she grabbed her phone, her mind wandered for a second, and her fingers instinctively tapped Steven's name into her contacts. He was the friend she could always count on for entertainment, drama, and endless gossip. The perfect way to kill time.

She opened up the chat and typed out a message with a grin:

> "Girl, you are NOT going to believe the day I've had. Time with JT has been so awesome. I love spending time with him. Can't wait to tell you all about it. Also, send me your latest gossip, you know I need it. Miss you!"

She hit send and reclined back in her chair, tapping her fingers to the beat of the music she had playing. Within seconds, Steven was texting back, and she didn't waste a second before opening his reply:

> "Yassss, girl. You better be having the time of your life! I'm obsessed with your new romance already. Tell me EVERYTHING. And you know I'm not going to hold back on my doings. I've been keeping my eye on my own Mr. Right at the gym... but THAT'S for later."

Drusilla giggled to herself, loving the way Steven's text always seemed to sound just like him—sassy and full of flair. It was one of the things she missed most about being away. They had this dynamic, where they could chat for hours about nothing and everything. She laughed out loud as she typed her reply:

> "Oh lord, Steven, you KNOW I need all the details! But also—hold on. I've got this serious situation here. I think I've fallen in love. Crazy right? It's been one amazing day after another!"

She glanced at the clock next to the bed, reminding her that dinner with JT was soon approaching. She had a moment of hesitation, but after a few more texts with Steven that were full of drama and playfulness, she put the phone down. Time to finish getting ready.

Drusilla stood up and glanced at herself in the mirror one last time before getting dressed. As she slid on her sleek black pants and the flowing blouse, she felt confident, relaxed, and more herself than she had in weeks. The white blouse felt perfect for tonight—effortlessly chic, with just the right amount of casual elegance. The black flats added comfort to the outfit.

With her outfit complete, she opened her jewelry case grabbing her diamond studs and quickly putting them on. She glanced at the emerald necklace again, a bittersweet smile tugging at her lips. She was dying to wear it, but she knew tonight wasn't the night for it. Tomorrow's steakhouse dinner would be the perfect occasion for the beautiful necklace.

As she finished getting dressed, she sent one last message to Steven before slipping her phone into her purse.

> *"Alright, I gotta run, but I'll fill you in on everything when I get back. Keep me posted on your drama. Love you girl!"*

She stood up, feeling a rush of excitement for the night ahead. Dinner with JT on the deck was just what she needed to unwind, and she couldn't wait to see what the evening would bring.

JT closed his laptop with a satisfied sigh, his conference call wrapping up right on schedule. As he turned on the shower, the soft hum filled the room, waiting for it to warm, he reached for his phone, his thoughts immediately drifting to Drusilla. Without hesitation, he typed a quick message:

> *"I'm thinking about you."*

The reply came almost instantly, bringing a smile to his face.

> *"I can't stop thinking about you,"* she wrote.

He felt his pulse quicken as he typed back,

> *"I'm jumping in the shower. I'll see you shortly. It's going to be a fun night."*

Tossing the phone onto the bed, JT stepped into the bathroom, the steam curling around him. The warm water cascaded over his tanned body, washing away the day. He leaned against the cool tile for a moment, letting the anticipation of the evening build. Tonight felt special— different. He wanted everything to be perfect.

After his shower, JT wrapped a towel around his waist and leaned over the sink, wiping the fog from the mirror. He reached for his razor, running it methodically over his day-old stubble. The sharp scent of aftershave stung his freshly shaven skin, waking him up further. He ran a hand along his jawline, satisfied with the smooth result, and caught a glimpse of his reflection. His thoughts lingered on Drusilla's smile, the way her eyes lit up when she looked at him. He wanted her to look at him like that tonight.

Walking over to the closet, JT slid the door open, fingers skimming over the neatly hung clothes. He paused, considering his options. Something simple yet striking. Something to match her beauty. He finally settled on a pair of tailored black slacks and a luxurious black silk T-shirt that fit his toned body perfectly, the soft fabric clinging lightly to his chest and shoulders. He slipped on his silver watch, its gleam catching the light, the only contrast to the all-black ensemble. Running his hand through his hair, he admired the effect in the mirror—sleek and understated, his sun-kissed skin standing out against the dark tones.

As he spritzed his neck with cologne, JT found himself hoping Drusilla would approve. A small smile tugged at the corner of his lips as he grabbed his phone from the bed, glancing at their earlier messages. Tonight wasn't just about the dinner—it was about her. And he couldn't wait to see her face when she opened the door to her cabin.

With one last look in the mirror, JT grabbed his room key and stepped out into the hall, ready to make the night unforgettable.

JT walked the short distance to Drusilla's cabin, his heart beating a little faster with each step. He paused at her door and tapped twice. Moments later, the door opened, and there she stood, a vision in her sleek black pants and flowing white blouse, her diamond studs catching the light. For a brief second, neither of them spoke, simply taking each other in.

208

Drusilla's breath hitched as her eyes swept over him. Dressed in all black, with the perfect fit of his silk T-shirt highlighting his broad shoulders, JT looked like he'd just stepped out of the pages of *GQ*. Every time she saw him, it took her breath away.

"Come in, handsome," she said, her voice soft but filled with warmth.

JT stepped inside, the door clicking shut behind him. Before either of them could say more, they were in each other's arms, their lips meeting in a slow, passionate kiss. The world seemed to fade away for those precious moments, their connection undeniable.

When they pulled back, JT cupped her face gently, his dark eyes fixed on hers. "Ready for a fun night, pretty girl?" he asked, his voice low and inviting.

Drusilla smiled, her cheeks warming. "Absolutely," she replied, her excitement clear.

They turned to the full-length mirror by the wall, standing side by side, and admired their reflection. Drusilla couldn't help but think how perfect they looked together—her prince charming and his artist muse. She smoothed the front of her blouse, while JT watched intently, a faint smirk playing on his lips.

"You clean up pretty well," she teased, nudging him gently.

JT laughed, wrapping an arm around her waist. "You're one to talk. You're stunning."

With one last glance in the mirror, they turned toward the door, ready to make their way to the deck. JT held it open for her, his gentlemanly nature never failing to charm her. As they walked side by side toward dinner, the promise of an unforgettable night hung in the air.

The setting for dinner on the deck was nothing short of magical. The sun hung low on the horizon, casting a fiery orange and pink glow across the sky. Its reflection danced on the gentle wake of the ship, creating ripples of light that seemed to follow them. A soft contemporary beat played in the background, blending seamlessly with the calming rush of the ocean.

As they approached the hostess stand, JT smiled at the young woman behind it. "Anderson," he said, his voice confident yet warm.

The hostess nodded and picked up two menus, leading them to their table—a prime spot right at the ship's rail. The view was breathtaking, the kind of scene that seemed almost too perfect to be real. JT, ever the gentleman, pulled out Drusilla's chair, waiting until she was seated before taking his own.

Drusilla glanced around, her eyes wide with wonder. "I think we've got the best table on the ship," she said, her voice filled with awe.

JT leaned in slightly, his gaze fixed on her. "Only the best for you."

Within moments, their waitress appeared, her cheerful demeanor matching the vibrant setting. "Would you like to start with a cocktail?" she asked, her notepad ready.

JT deferred to Drusilla with a slight gesture. She smiled and said, "I'd like a cosmo, please."

JT chimed in after her, "Crown on the rocks, lots of ice."

As they waited for their drinks, JT reached across the table, his hand gently covering Drusilla's. She looked up at him, her heart skipping a beat at the intensity of his gaze.

"You are so beautiful," he said softly, his thumb tracing circles on her hand. "I love spending time with you."

Her cheeks flushed, and she squeezed his hand in return. "You're not so bad yourself," she teased, though her voice was filled with sincerity. "This is perfect. You make everything feel so special."

Their drinks arrived, and they raised their glasses in a quiet toast, their eyes locking over the flickering candle on the table. As they sipped their cocktails, they began to discuss their plans for the rest of the evening, their conversation flowing as naturally as the ocean around them.

Drusilla leaned back slightly, a contented on her lips. The night felt electric, the kind of evening that made time seem to stand still. Little did they know, the calm would soon give way to unexpected turmoil.

After sharing the light dinner under the stars, they decided to keep the night alive with dancing at the ship's nightclub. The evening was still young, so instead of heading straight to the club, they strolled to the nearby bar for a glass of champagne. Neither wanted to be the first on the dance floor.

The golden bubbles fizzed in their glasses as they clinked a quiet toast. They lingered, hands intertwined, talking and laughing softly until Drusilla nudged JT. "Ready?" she asked, her eyes sparkling with excitement.

"Let's do it," he replied, standing and offering his hand.

They walked hand in hand to *Waves*, the ship's nightclub. As they stepped through the wide double doors, they were immediately immersed in a swirling cloud of fog, illuminated by colorful strobe lights slicing through the haze. The deep bass of the music reverberated in their chests, a pulse that seemed to sync with the rhythm of the night.

JT looked around, then turned to Drusilla with a grin. "Well, we're in it now."

She laughed, gripping his hand tighter. "Lead the way."

A hostess appeared and guided them to a private table tucked in the corner of the VIP section, its elevated position offering a perfect view of the pulsing dance floor below. JT motioned to the waitress and, with an effortless charm, ordered a bottle of Cristal.

Minutes later, the arrival of the champagne was a spectacle in itself. Three young servers sashayed through the crowd, holding sparklers that fizzled and popped, illuminating their path as they made their way to the table. The crowd turned to watch as the girls danced up to them, the music crescendoing with their steps.

One of the servers expertly popped the cork, the sound lost in the thumping beat of the music, and poured two glasses of the golden liquid for the couple. The show only added to the electric energy of the night.

Drusilla leaned closer to JT, laughing as she gestured toward the retreating servers, raising her voice so he could hear her. "Do they do that for everyone?"

JT smirked, tilting his glass toward hers, leaning over so she could hear him. "Only for guys with pretty girls."

She rolled her eyes playfully but couldn't stop the blush that spread across her cheeks. Leaning into him, she brushed her lips softly against his in a lingering kiss before they both raised their glasses.

"To another night in paradise," JT said. "whaaat?" Drusilla yelled, trying to talk over the music. "To another night in paradise," JT repeated a bit louder. Drusilla ran her hand over his face and smiled.

"To us," Drusilla added, her eyes holding his as they sipped the champagne, savoring the perfect blend of luxury and connection.

As the music swelled, they felt the night pulling them toward the dance floor, ready for the next chapter in their unforgettable evening.

They danced, drank champagne, and danced some more, the night blending into a dizzying haze of laughter, music, and the magnetic pull between them. Each song seemed to draw them closer, their bodies moving in perfect sync. Champagne glasses clinked as they toasted to the moment, only to be swept back onto the dance floor, losing track of time and space.

As the night reached its peak, JT leaned in, his lips brushing Drusilla's ear to be heard over the pulsing beat. "Let's get out of here," he suggested, his voice deep and warm.

Drusilla smiled, her cheeks flushed from the dancing—and the champagne. "I thought you'd never ask," she teased, slipping her hand into his. JT signed the check and they headed for the door.

Even as they exited the club, the music seemed to echo in their ears, the thrum of the bass still vibrating in their chests. They walked toward the grand staircase, JT's arm resting protectively around her waist. When they reached the landing, he stopped and grinned. "How about we take the elevator this time?"

Drusilla laughed. "Smart man," she replied, leaning into him as they waited for the lift.

When they arrived at JT's cabin, he pulled out his key card, flashing it playfully. "Didn't forget it this time," he joked.

The moment the door clicked shut, JT wasted no time. He grabbed Drusilla by the waist and pressed her against the door, his lips trailing fiery kisses along her neck and collarbone. She gasped, her fingers tangling in his hair, pulling him closer. Their movements were frantic, fueled by a night of desire and champagne.

Hands roamed freely, clothes slipping away piece by piece as their passion consumed them. JT lifted Drusilla, carrying her toward the oversized chair by the window, where the moonlight poured in, bathing the room in a soft glow.

Their bodies moved together in a rhythm that felt as old as the ocean outside, their connection transcending words. The world outside the cabin disappeared, leaving only the two of them, illuminated by the silvery light.

As they collapsed into each other, breathless and satisfied, Drusilla lay across JT, her head resting against his chest. Their sweaty bodies gleamed in the moonlight, the stillness after their passion almost as intoxicating as the act itself.

For several minutes, they didn't speak, letting the quiet intimacy of the moment envelop them. Finally, Drusilla murmured, her voice soft and dreamy, "Another unforgettable night with Prince Charming."

JT kissed the top of her head, his arms tightening around her. "Unforgettable," he agreed.

Little did they know, the night would hold surprises yet to be discovered?

Drusilla was the first to wake, the soft light of dawn filtering through the cabin's sheer curtains. She blinked slowly, a lazy smile spreading across her face as she pieced together the events of the night before. The champagne-induced haze was a small price to pay for the memories that flooded her mind—dancing, laughter, and the passion that had swept them into the early hours of the morning.

Turning her head, she glanced at JT, who was still sound asleep, his chest rising and falling in a steady rhythm. The sheet lay draped across his waist, leaving his toned upper body exposed, the soft morning light accentuating every line and angle.

She couldn't help but smile, warmth blooming in her chest at the sight of him. Quietly, she rolled over, nestling her head against his chest. The sound of his heartbeat was steady and comforting. JT stirred slightly, his arm instinctively wrapping around her shoulders as a soft murmur escaped his lips.

Drusilla tilted her head and kissed his chest, her lips lingering on his warm skin. A sudden spark ignited within her, and before she could think twice, she shifted, crawling on top of him. JT's eyes fluttered open, still heavy with sleep, but the moment he looked up at her, a slow, knowing grin spread across his face.

As she sat up on him, the morning light painted her skin in golden highlights, casting an ethereal glow that took his breath away. "Good morning, beautiful," he whispered, his voice a bit husky.

Drusilla smiled down at him, her fingers brushing the hair from his forehead. "Good morning," she replied, leaning down to kiss him.

As she moved against him, their connection from the night before reignited, this time slower, softer, but no less consuming. JT's hands roamed her back, holding her close as she arched above him, their bodies moving together as if the sunrise was meant to witness their union.

214

When they finally collapsed against each other, their breathing ragged but content, they tangled together in the sheets. JT pulled her into his arms, pressing a kiss to her temple.

"Thank you," he whispered.

Drusilla laughed softly, her head resting on his shoulder. "That was amazing."

Wrapped in each other's warmth, they drifted back to sleep, the world outside their cabin forgotten for just a little while longer.

Six days to New York

Over breakfast, accompanied by much-needed caffeine, Drusilla and JT mapped out their plans for the day. The ship edged ever closer to New York, and both felt the bittersweet tug of their journey nearing its end.

"How about we hit the pool for a while?" Drusilla suggested, stirring her coffee. "It's not too hot yet, and we can soak up some sun."

JT nodded, his easy grin spreading across his face. "Perfect idea. Let's do it."

After finishing their breakfast, they parted ways to change, agreeing to meet in JT's cabin in thirty minutes.

JT didn't think twice, grabbing the first pair of trunks he found—navy blue with a subtle pattern he barely noticed. A quick glance in the mirror, and he was ready. Drusilla, on the other hand, took her time.

She stood in front of the open closet in her cabin, contemplating which of the six bathing suits she'd packed would suit the day. Finally, she decided on the bright orange one-piece, knowing the vibrant color would accentuate her sun-kissed skin. She smiled to herself, recalling the way JT had complimented her tan during one of their walks.

After slipping into her suit, she layered a semi-sheer white cover-up over it, its light fabric flowing around her as she moved. A pair of gold sandals completed the look, along with her oversized sunglasses tucked into her pool bag. Satisfied, she glanced in the mirror, gave a quick nod of approval, and headed out the door to meet JT.

As she approached his cabin, her heart skipped a beat, the anticipation of spending another carefree day together lighting her mood.

As they lounged by the pool, the sun warm against their skin and the sound of the ship's wake a soothing backdrop, JT and Drusilla chatted lazily about the day ahead.

"Where should we do lunch?" JT asked, glancing at Drusilla over the rim of his sunglasses. "Your call this time."

Drusilla thought for a moment, twirling the corner of her beach towel between her fingers. "How about the Asian restaurant near the nightclub? I've heard great things about it."

JT nodded without hesitation. "Sounds perfect."

Lunch became another enjoyable part of their day, filled with flavorful dishes and lighthearted conversation. Afterward, they made their way back to the pool for a couple more hours of relaxation.

Drusilla lost herself in her book, her sunhat shielding her face as she reclined in her lounger. JT, meanwhile, caught up on the news on his phone, occasionally sharing an article or comment with her.

By late afternoon, both agreed they'd had enough sun for one day. They packed up their things, laughing about their rosy cheeks and sun-kissed noses, and headed back to their cabins to cool off and prepare for the evening.

"We're still on for the steakhouse, right?" Drusilla asked as they lingered by her cabin door.

"Absolutely. I'll meet you in my cabin at 6:30?" JT suggested.

She smiled. "Perfect. I'll be ready."

The minute JT stepped into his cabin, the comfort of the cool, darkened room beckoned. He kicked off his shoes, stretched out across the bed, and drifted into a peaceful late afternoon nap.

Meanwhile, in her cabin, Drusilla stood before her open closet, the soundtrack of her internal fashion debate accompanied by the soft hum of her playlist. She started with the essentials: her new silver sparkly Jimmy Choos heels and her emerald necklace. From there, the options seemed endless.

She tried on dress after dress, then switched to sleek trousers, only to circle back to dresses again. She wanted tonight to be perfect—a memorable evening with JT, with only four nights left to savor their time together on the ship.

After an hour of indecision, Drusilla collapsed into the oversized armchair, defeated. With a huff, she reached for her phone and tapped Steven's number.

"Darling! To what do I owe this pleasure?" Steven answered with exaggerated excitement, his voice like a warm hug over the phone.

"I need help. I'm staring at my closet, and it's staring back. I can't decide what to wear tonight," Drusilla confessed, exasperated.

"Oh, honey, this is *my* moment. Let me save you. Face chat me *right now*," Steven demanded with mock urgency.

Moments later, Drusilla's phone beeped as Steven's face filled the screen, his excitement palpable. "Let's see the options! Show me everything. We'll make magic happen."

Together, they went through her wardrobe, Steven delivering his opinions with flamboyant flair. "No, no, no—too serious! You're not a CEO at a board meeting. And *that*? Too casual. You're dressing for *romance*, darling!"

Finally, after much deliberation, they landed on the perfect ensemble: her cute white Donna Karan baby doll dress, light and flirty, paired with the shimmering Jimmy Choos and the stunning emerald necklace as the centerpiece.

217

"You'll look divine, trust me," Steven declared with satisfaction.

"You're a lifesaver," Drusilla said, laughing.

"Oh, and add some fishnets," Steven suggested with a mischievous grin.

"Steven, I'm not 20 years old," she replied with an eye roll, but her tone was warm.

"Fine, fine. Keep it classy, darling. But if JT doesn't propose tonight, I'm flying to wherever you are to have *words* with him."

Drusilla laughed and blew Steven a kiss through the screen. "Thanks for the help, fashion guru."

"Anytime, my love. Now go knock his socks off."

As Drusilla hung up, she looked at her outfit spread across the bed and smiled. This was going to be another night to remember.

JT woke from his nap feeling refreshed but groggy. He grabbed a quick shower, letting the cool water wake him fully. As he dried off, a sharp knock at the door pulled him from his routine. He wrapped the towel around his waist and opened the door to find the valet holding his freshly pressed black suit and crisp white shirt.

"Thank you," JT said, taking the garments and hanging them neatly in the closet.

Feeling the need to unwind for a moment before getting ready, he turned on some music and stepped out onto the balcony. With the warm breeze brushing against him, he lit one of the Cuban cigars he'd purchased during their stop in Barcelona. The rich aroma mingled with the salty ocean air, helping to clear his mind as he admired the endless horizon.

His phone buzzed on the table behind him, breaking the tranquility. He put down the cigar and grabbed the phone. "Hey, beautiful," he said with a smile.

"JT, my necklace is gone!" Drusilla's voice was strained, cutting through his greeting.

"What do you mean, gone?" he asked, his tone immediately serious.

"I keep it in my jewelry wrap with my other pieces, and it's not there! I've turned this cabin upside down. It's just gone."

"I'll be right there," JT said without hesitation. He threw on a pair of shorts and a T-shirt, grabbed his room key, and was out the door in seconds.

When JT arrived, Drusilla was pacing the cabin, her face a mix of worry and frustration. "I don't understand," she said as he walked in.

"Let's look together," JT said calmly, placing his hands on her shoulders for a moment to steady her.

They scoured every inch of the cabin—opening drawers, checking under the bed, rifling through her luggage. JT even moved the furniture to check behind and underneath. The necklace was nowhere to be found.

Drusilla sank onto the edge of the bed, her hands clasped tightly. "I know I had it last night," she said, her voice quivering. "I remember seeing it when I picked out my diamond earrings. It was right there."

"Could it have fallen somewhere, or maybe you took it out and forgot?" JT asked, crouching down to meet her gaze.

"I've been so careful with it," she whispered, tears welling in her eyes.

JT wrapped an arm around her shoulders, pulling her close. "We'll find it. I promise," he said softly. "Let's retrace every step from last night, talk to the crew if we have to. It'll be okay."

Drusilla nodded, leaning into him. "I just can't believe this."

"We'll figure it out," JT assured her. "For now, let's take a deep breath and keep looking.

Drusilla sighed, her anxiety easing slightly under JT's steady presence.

With nowhere else to look, they both came to the gut-wrenching realization that the necklace must have been stolen. What else could have happened? Drusilla's distress was obvious, her hands trembling as she wiped at her eyes, trying to stay calm.

JT took charge, his voice firm as he spoke. "I'll be right back. Stay here." He gave her a quick, reassuring look before rushing out of the cabin, his mind already turning over the possibilities. He knew he needed to get to the security office immediately.

He filed the report with the duty officer, and after a few questions, the officer suggested they check the key card log to see if anyone else had entered Drusilla's cabin. The last entry was when she returned from the pool. But there was something off about the entry from "last night." The door was opened at 7:47 p.m.

JT's heart skipped a beat. That was the exact time they were sitting down to dinner. He felt a surge of urgency.

He asked, "Are there security cameras in the hallways? Can we check to see who was in the area around that time?"

The officer nodded and typed into the system. "We've got cameras everywhere except in the cabins. Let's check the footage."

The screen blinked to life, showing the hallways near Drusilla's cabin at 7:47 p.m. The footage revealed a white male, appearing to be in his fifties, with a hat pulled low over his face, entering her cabin. He stayed inside for exactly six minutes before leaving.

JT's eyes widened, his jaw tightening. "That's him," he muttered under his breath. "That's the guy who took it."

The officer zoomed in on the footage, and JT leaned forward, scrutinizing every detail. The man's movements were quick and deliberate—too quick. JT could feel his pulse racing, his mind already racing to figure out how this had happened.

The officer then pulled up the footage after the man left. "We've got him exiting and disappearing up the upper deck. Looks like he went out of view right after that."

JT's frustration boiled over. "That's it? He just disappears?"

The officer nodded, and JT could see the same helplessness in the man's eyes. The cameras had no coverage on the upper deck, and the thief had vanished into the dark.

"Is there anything else we can do?" JT asked, feeling a surge of protectiveness over Drusilla. "Can we track where he went next? Can we follow him after he left?"

The officer quickly pulled up more recordings, trying to track the man's movements. "He disappears into the dark up top. I'll see if I can get a better angle when we dock and check with the authorities."

JT stood there for a moment, clenching his jaw. This wasn't over. He wasn't going to let this man just walk away with something that meant so much to Drusilla.

He looked at the officer. "I need everything you can give me. Let me know if you find anything else."

As he walked back to Drusilla's cabin, he felt the weight of the situation settling on him. The thief was still out there, and Drusilla was beside herself with worry. JT burst into the cabin, his eyes immediately finding her.

Her face was pale, her eyes wide and anxious.

"I talked to security," JT said, his voice firm. "The guy who took it—he entered your cabin while we were at dinner. The footage shows it all."

Drusilla's eyes filled with tears again. "But why? Why would someone steal it?"

JT put his arm around her, pulling her close. "I don't know yet, but we'll get it back. I'll make sure of it."

Drusilla let out a shaky breath, clinging to him. "I can't believe this is happening."

"It'll be okay," JT reassured her. "We're going to find him. We're not letting this go."

The officer's investigation was still ongoing, and JT wasn't about to rest until they had more answers. But right now, the most important thing was making sure Drusilla felt safe—and that they got her necklace back.

JT looked at Drusilla, his voice steady and reassuring as he spoke. "We're in the middle of the ocean. No one's going anywhere, and we'll find this guy. I promise you."

Drusilla took a deep breath, her nerves settling a little under JT's calm authority. His words gave her some relief, and she felt grateful for how he took charge. She was also relieved that it wasn't something she had done, some careless mistake that had caused the necklace to go missing.

He gave her a soft, encouraging smile. "Let's get ready for dinner. We can talk about this more then."

Drusilla hesitated, still shaken by the events, but finally agreed. "I need a drink," she said with a small, tired laugh. "I'll be ready in twenty minutes."

JT didn't want to leave her, knowing she was still upset. "Gather your outfit and anything else you need. Let's go to my cabin to get ready.

When they got to JT's cabin, Drusilla sat down on the edge of the bed, staring at her reflection in the mirror. The missing necklace seemed to ruin everything—her outfit, her mood, even the evening. She picked up her phone and called Steven, her voice frantic as she explained what had happened.

Steven's voice was instantly full of concern, but with his signature flair. "Wait, WHAAAT?! First, you meet Prince Charming, and now you have a mystery on the high seas? What a life you're leading, girl!" He paused dramatically. "Okay, listen to me—ditch that white dress. It's bad luck now. Go with the little black dress. Stick with the new shoes, and those stud earrings. The little black clutch will work perfectly. You'll be HOT AF."

Drusilla felt the corner of her mouth twitch into a smile. "But I wore that outfit at the steakhouse last time."

Steven scoffed. "And? It works. You look amazing. Shut up, put it on, and go please your man. That's an order!"

Drusilla laughed, feeling a little lighter despite everything. They blew each other kisses before hanging up, and Drusilla immediately told JT they needed to go back to her cabin to change dresses. She hung the white dress in the closet and grabbed the black one. She slipped it on, doing a quick re-touch on her makeup to cover the puffiness around her eyes, a side effect of her earlier distress. JT couldn't help but admire the way she was handling things.

By the time she was finished, she looked into the mirror and felt a surge of confidence. Maybe the necklace was gone, but she still had the night ahead of her.

They went back to JT's cabin so he could finish getting ready. When he came out of the bathroom, she was hit by how perfect he looked. He was dressed to the nines, his suit fitting him flawlessly—he looked like a million dollars. Or, in his case, a billion dollars.

"Wow," she whispered, letting her gaze linger on him for a moment before he pulled her into a warm embrace.

"You look incredible," JT murmured, holding her tightly. "This is just a thing. We'll deal with it. It's not worth ruining our night."

She nodded, letting his words sink in. "You're right. We'll deal with it."

Drusilla smiled up at him, suddenly feeling lighter, and he smiled back, relieved that they were both on the same page. He offered her his arm, and together they left the cabin and made their way to the steakhouse, the evening ahead of them still full of promise.

As they walked down the hallway, JT's arm around her waist, Drusilla felt a quiet sense of gratitude for the man beside her. Despite the stolen necklace and the unsettling situation, they were together. And that was enough for now.

223

As they enjoyed their meal, the atmosphere around JT and Drusilla was more relaxed, but still tinged with the tension from the earlier events. The wine flowed, and conversation shifted to lighter topics. Drusilla was trying her best to push the disappearance of the necklace from her mind, focusing on the present moment with JT.

But as dessert arrived, JT's phone buzzed on the table, interrupting their conversation. He glanced at the screen, excusing himself briefly. "I'll be right back," he said to Drusilla, his voice calm but with a note of seriousness that made her raise an eyebrow.

Drusilla watched him step away from the table and didn't think much of it. But a few minutes later, JT returned, a bit more focused than before. He slid back into his seat, still wearing a calm expression, but Drusilla could tell something had shifted.

He didn't say anything right away, but he took out a piece of paper from his jacket pocket— what looked like a blurry printout. He set it gently on the table, the paper crinkling slightly under his fingertips.

Drusilla looked at it curiously. "What's that?"

JT glanced at the image for a moment before meeting her eyes, carefully masking any emotion. "The duty officer just gave me this photo. It's the man who entered your cabin," he said quietly.

Drusilla leaned forward, scrutinizing the image. It was a grainy picture, the man's features distorted by the poor quality of the shot, but something in the back of JT's mind clicked. He thought he recognized the face. He thought he had seen it before. The man on the printout—he looked so familiar. The timing hit him like a punch in the gut: he had seen him just a month ago, during a major business deal that went south. A failed transaction involving their businesses.

JT's mind raced, but he kept his voice steady. "I think I might know who this is," he said under his breath.

Drusilla frowned, looking up at him. "Do you? Who is he?"

JT hesitated, unsure of how much to share, especially in the midst of dinner. He didn't want to ruin the evening. "I'm not entirely sure," he said, his voice low, "but I think this man may be connected to a business deal I had a while ago. A really big deal that went wrong."

Drusilla's curiosity piqued, but JT held up a hand. "I don't want to spoil the night. Let's enjoy dinner. We'll figure this out after."

She nodded, though her mind raced, trying to piece together the puzzle.

After a brief pause, JT took out his phone and snapped a picture of the printout, quickly composing a message. He sent the blurry image to Robert Ash, the head of his security team back in New York, along with a brief note.

> Subject: Urgent—Possible ID of suspect
>
> *"This man may be involved in the theft of a necklace from a guest on the cruise. His image was caught entering her cabin. See if you can identify him—possibly the Colombian involved in the failed transaction from last month. Please make this a priority."*

JT hit send, then leaned back in his chair, eyes still on his phone as he waited for a reply.

Drusilla, sensing his focus had shifted, took a slow sip of wine, trying to remain composed. She didn't press him further about the business connection, knowing there were things he didn't want to burden her with just yet.

"Let's finish our meal," JT said softly, his eyes meeting hers again, trying to reassure her. "We'll get to the bottom of this. But tonight, we'll focus on enjoying our time together. You are staying with me for the rest of the trip."

Drusilla smiled faintly, trying to push aside the unease, and agreed, not wanting to be alone in her cabin with this guy on the loose.

When JT and Drusilla returned to his cabin after dinner, the mood had shifted. JT could feel the weight of everything that had happened, but his mind was focused on solving the mystery. He walked over to the desk, saw the blinking light on his phone, and grabbed it. The message was from his office.

As he dialed the number and the call was connected, he motioned for Drusilla to sit on the bed, signaling her to stay close. He hit the speakerphone button so she could hear the update, and she nodded in acknowledgment.

"JT, Ash" a calm, authoritative voice came through the speaker. "We have news on the theft."

JT sat up straighter, his pulse quickening as he leaned in.

"We've identified the perpetrator," Ash continued. "It's Juan Alvarez from Alvarez Mining Corporation, the same guy who stormed out of your office last month when he realized they had lost out on the merger with Sampson."

Drusilla's eyes widened, and she glanced over at JT, who was already processing the information.

"Wait, you're telling me the man who stole Drusilla's necklace is the same guy from the failed merger?" JT asked, his voice tight with both shock and anger.

"Yes," Ash confirmed. "And there's more. We also received a message that was left with your secretary. It's meant for you. It simply reads,

'You took something from me, now I'll take something from you.'

No signature."

Drusilla's face fell, her hand instinctively reaching for JT's as she processed the chilling words. The message was direct and ominous, like something out of a movie.

226

"Do you think he's threatening more than just the necklace?" JT asked, his voice steady, though his mind was racing.

"We don't know," Ash replied. "But it's clear that he's targeting you. We were able to learn that Alvarez arrived in New York the day before you left for the cruise. It's possible he's been planning something like this for a while. He is apparently traveling under an assumed name with false travel documents. We've been in contact with the cruise line and there is no Alvarez on the manifest."

Drusilla looked at JT, worry in his eyes, but he kept his composure. "What are you doing about it?" he asked.

"Sir, I need you to know that you could be in danger. If he went through the trouble of traveling to New York and boarding your ship using false documents, then stealing the necklace, we can't rule out what he might do next. To ensure your safety, I've been in contact with security on the ship. I've arranged for a plainclothes security officer to shadow you for the rest of the trip. His name is Leonard, and he'll be stationed near your cabin when you're inside and be close wherever else you go. They are also issuing a new key card with special security measures. I suggest you meet him as soon as possible."

Drusilla's hand tightened around JT's, and he could feel the tension in her grip.

JT thought for a moment before replying, "I appreciate the caution, Robert. But this... I mean, it seems like a lot. Isn't it a bit much?"

"I understand, sir," Ash replied, "but it's what we're trained for. You're not just any guest on this cruise. You are the head of a major international corporation. You have a responsibility to your family and your shareholders to protect yourself. You're a target now, and our priority is to make sure you're safe. Leonard will be discreet, and he'll be close if anything goes wrong. My team will meet you at the port when you return to New York."

JT sighed, rubbing the back of his neck. He didn't want to turn his vacation into a security operation, but the reality was that he was dealing with a serious threat. "Alright, I'll meet with Leonard," he said reluctantly. "I trust you, Robert. Keep me posted if anything changes."

"We'll keep you updated Sir," Ash said before ending the call.

The room was silent for a moment. Drusilla looked at him, her expression a mixture of fear and concern. "What now?" she asked softly, her eyes searching his face.

JT stood up and walked toward the window, looking out at the dark ocean. The weight of the situation was settling in. "Now, we do what we can to stay safe. I'll meet Leonard, and we'll figure out how to deal with Alvarez. But you're right here with me. I'm not letting you out of my sight. We'll get through this."

Drusilla nodded, though she could still feel the gnawing worry in the pit of her stomach. It wasn't just about the necklace anymore—it was about something much bigger, and much more dangerous.

"We'll stay calm," JT added, turning back to her. "And we'll stay together. I promise you, I'll take care of this." He pulled her into a tight embrace, the security of his arms around her offering a small comfort amid the uncertainty.

Drusilla breathed in deeply, trying to shake off the unease that had settled over her. "I just want it to be over," she murmured, her heart racing.

"I know," JT said softly, his lips brushing her forehead. "We'll get it sorted. I promise."

Five days to New York

The next morning, JT woke up early, his mind still heavy with the events of the previous day. After a quick breakfast, he made his way to the ship's security office to meet with Leonard and the head of security, Major Hayes. They'd already made arrangements to put the crew on high alert, but JT wanted to ensure everything was moving forward.

When JT arrived at the office, Leonard was waiting for him, along with Major Hayes, a tall, broad-shouldered man who looked like he was used to handling high-pressure situations. He stood up when JT entered and extended a hand. "Good morning, sir. We've already distributed Alvarez's photo to the entire crew."

JT nodded, feeling reassured that they were taking the situation seriously. "Good. I want him found as quickly as possible. He's already targeted Miss Pennington once, and we can't let that happen again."

Major Hayes gave a firm nod. "We're on it. The photo's gone out to everyone—from the front desk to the housekeeping staff. We're keeping an eye out for him in all areas of the ship."

Leonard added, "We've already started searching the cabins of male passengers traveling alone. We've got a list, and we're going through it now. Some of these cabins are being checked as we speak."

JT felt a small weight lift off his shoulders, but he knew this was only the beginning. "Good," he said, his jaw tightening. "I want everyone to stay vigilant. If anyone sees something suspicious, I want them to report it immediately. I don't care how small the detail is."

"We'll keep our eyes wide open, sir," Leonard replied. "And I'll personally follow up with the crew to ensure nothing falls through the cracks."

Major Hayes interjected, "We'll have more patrols around the public areas, and we'll ensure no one is lingering in places they shouldn't be. We've got all the right people on it."

JT glanced at the two of them, feeling a bit more at ease but still focused on the bigger picture. "I'm trusting you both with this. Keep me updated every step of the way."

Leonard nodded. "Understood. You'll hear from us as soon as we have anything new."

"Good," JT said. "And if you need anything from me—my team in New York is standing by. Don't hesitate to reach out."

With a final handshake, JT left the security office, a plan in place to ensure Drusilla's safety and get to the bottom of what was happening. He couldn't shake the feeling that this wasn't just a simple theft—Alvarez had a motive, and JT had a sinking feeling that it wasn't just the necklace he wanted.

When he got back to his cabin, he updated Drusilla, filling her in on the latest. "They're putting a full team on it," he reassured her. "They've started searching cabins and they're watching for him. We'll find him, Drusilla. I promise."

Her voice was still shaky, but she appreciated his calmness. "I just want it to be over, JT."

"I know. And it will be. Soon."

The tension of the day hung in the air even as the night settled around them. After everything that had happened—the theft, the worry, the uncertainty—neither JT nor Drusilla felt like going anywhere or doing anything more. They both needed the quiet, the comfort of just being together.

Drusilla glanced at the clock on the wall of JT's cabin. It was early, still not even ten, but they both felt the exhaustion creeping in, the emotional toll of the day finally catching up to them. She sat on the edge of the bed, her body still aching from the strain of the events, but her mind even more so.

JT stood by the window, watching the moonlight reflect off the ocean's surface. His mind racing. He turned to her with a reassuring smile. "Then let's call it a night. No need to go anywhere. Let's stay in and just... rest."

She nodded gratefully. "That sounds perfect."

JT walked over to the bed and sat next to her, then gently pulled her into his arms. She didn't resist; instead, she let herself relax against him, her head resting on his chest, listening to the steady rhythm of his heartbeat. His arms wrapped around her, offering a sense of safety and warmth.

She closed her eyes and inhaled the scent of him—clean, strong, and steady. It was a comfort to be held like this after everything they'd been through.

"I'm here," JT whispered, his voice a soft promise in the quiet of the room. "You're safe."

And with that, the quiet, soothing presence of JT wrapped around her like a blanket. She felt her muscles relax, the last remnants of stress slowly melting away as the warmth of his embrace did what no words could.

It wasn't long before Drusilla's breathing deepened, the rhythm of her breath matching JT's as she drifted off to sleep in his arms.

JT stayed awake for a while longer, watching the slow rise and fall of her chest as she slept soundly. The weight of the day's events still pressed on his mind, but knowing she was safe, here with him, helped ease some of that burden. He gently brushed a strand of hair from her face and kissed the top of her head, the quiet promise to himself that he would protect her—whatever it took.

And with that, JT closed his eyes, holding Drusilla close as his mind wandered.

It had been a long, exhausting day, but tonight, they had each other.

The room was quiet accept for the soft rhythm of Drusilla's breathing as she slept peacefully in his arms. Yet, despite the calm around him, JT couldn't seem to quiet the thoughts swirling in his mind. His mind drifting back to the conversation he'd had with Ash just before he left New York.

As head of his security team, Ash had always been a practical man—calculating, methodical. He'd pressed JT hard before his departure, urging him not to go on the cruise without at least a small security detail.

"Boss, I know you're used to doing things your way," Ash had said, his voice firm, "but you're not just anyone. People know who you are. And when you travel alone, you're a target. Remember what happened to your father."

But JT had brushed him off, as he always did. He'd been insistent. This cruise was supposed to be a break from the pressures of the world, from the constant watchfulness. He wanted to be free of it all, even if only for a short time. He needed to recharge after the difficult divorce with Sarah and the toll it took on them both. So, he insisted: no security, no bodyguards. I need to be alone for a while.

Now, as he lay in the dark, his thoughts tangled with regret.

The theft of the necklace had shaken him more than he let on. He should have known something was off, should have been more careful. The thought that he may have put her in danger—that he hadn't taken Ash's advice to heart—gnawed at him.

If I'd had security with me…

It was a rare thing for him to doubt himself, but tonight, with the weight of what had happened pressing on him, he couldn't help it.

The guilt tugged at him, a heavy knot in his stomach. In that moment, he realized Ash had been right. His life, his world, was too complex, too exposed to the kind of risks that came with travel without protection. And now Drusilla—who had nothing to do with his world—was pulled into it.

JT ran a hand over his face, trying to shake the feeling of helplessness. He had just wanted to get away and have some peace and quiet. The constant strain of his father's legacy, the company, the reputation, Sarah,—was, creeping back into his thoughts.

He glanced down at Drusilla, sleeping so peacefully beside him, unaware of the turmoil in his mind. She deserved better than this. Better than a world where she had to worry about things like this.

A heavy sigh left his chest as he shifted in the bed, careful not to wake her. He sat up, leaning against the headboard, staring out at the moonlight.

He couldn't undo what had happened, but he would do everything in his power to make sure nothing like this would ever happen again. To her. Or to him.

As the minutes ticked by, JT's thoughts slowly quieted, the pull of sleep taking over. But before he drifted off, one last thought lingered in his mind.

Next time, Ash, I'll listen to you. That's what I pay you for.

With a final glance at Drusilla, he closed his eyes, hoping tomorrow would be a better day.

Juan Alvarez

Juan Alvarez was born in Bogotá, Colombia, into a powerful and wealthy family. His father, Antonio Alvarez, was a self-made man who founded Alvarez Mining Corporation (AMC) in the 1970s, focusing on the extraction of valuable resources such as gold, silver, and emeralds. The company quickly expanded across Latin America, becoming one of the biggest players in the mining industry.

Juan grew up with the constant expectation to succeed, watching his father run the company with a mixture of awe and resentment. Antonio was an imposing figure, strict and demanding, expecting nothing less than perfection from his son. The pressure to live up to his father's legacy weighed heavily on Juan. While his father imparted business knowledge, it was often at the cost of emotional connection. As a result, Juan's formative years were filled with intense study, strict discipline, and a clear sense that the family's fortune was his to protect and expand.

His early academic success led him to study at a prestigious business school in the United States, where he gained a reputation for being highly intelligent and strategic. There, he honed his skills in business management, finance, and international relations. He mastered English and became well-versed in Western business practices, which proved invaluable as he navigated AMC's international dealings.

Despite his achievements, Juan's relationship with his father remained distant. He felt constantly overshadowed by Antonio's larger-than-life persona. The pressure to fill his father's

233

shoes grew heavier as he neared adulthood, but it also sparked a deep ambition in Juan. He returned to Bogotá after his education, eager to prove his worth and take AMC to new heights.

At the age of 29, Juan's life took an unexpected turn when his father passed away suddenly from a heart attack. The loss left Juan reeling, but it also thrust him into the role of CEO of AMC far earlier than expected. While his father's death was devastating, it allowed Juan to finally chart his own course. Under his leadership, AMC expanded even further, acquiring smaller mining companies and solidifying its position in the Latin American market.

However, Juan's approach to business was much more aggressive than his father's. While Antonio had focused on maintaining stability and conservative growth, Juan's strategy was to take risks, push boundaries, and crush the competition. He was ruthless in negotiations and willing to take shortcuts, often leveraging political connections and manipulating situations to ensure AMC came out on top.

Despite his success, Juan never felt entirely satisfied. The cutthroat world of mining and business continued to consume him, leaving little room for personal happiness or family life. He became a solitary figure, known for his hard edge and complete focus on business.

AMC was involved in negotiations with The Sampson Group, a very large mining company in Argentina to acquire Sampson in a deal worth over 47 billion dollars. After working with the principals of Sampson for over six years, the two companies were set to merge and AMC would become the surviving entity, with Juan as it's Chairman/CEO. They had worked on the deal for over a year. Just when it looked like the deal would finally close, the Latin American Mining Authority stepped in and would not sanction the transaction. Two months later, Sampson successfully merged with JT's company. Everyone in the industry suspected foul play and Alvarez vowed to get even, even if it took his entire life.

JT's ex-wife, Sarah was the youngest daughter of the Vice President of Colombia and Alvarez respected her family and it wasn't until JT and Sarah were divorced that he planned to hurt JT and start taking things from him.

Alvarez sat in the cramped, dimly lit crew quarters, feeling the weight of the emerald necklace pressing against his chest in the pocket of his uniform. It was almost too much to bear—the fact that he had successfully stolen it was only the beginning and the anger inside him festered.

JT Anderson, the name felt like a bitter taste on his tongue. His company had lost the merger with Sampson, but that wasn't the worst of it. It was the way JT's company had maneuvered, how they were suspected of using underhanded tactics to destroy his deal, driving his own company to the brink. They had used every dirty trick in the book to outbid them, including using influence, connections, and—he suspected—money. *And that goddamn necklace was now part of it.*

Alvarez remembered the meeting that had sealed their fate. JT had sat there, calm and collected, while his team made moves that pushed Alvarez's company into a corner. There was no way out. He had stormed out of that meeting, knowing it was over. But the real sting wasn't in the loss. It was in the way JT had gloatingly brushed it aside. *No one humiliates me like that,* Alvarez had sworn that day.

Alvarez had heard whispers that JT was taking a cruise, a perfect opportunity to settle a score. And when the necklace arrived for Drusilla—*of all people*—it felt like a golden opportunity to strike. The jewels had come from the very mines that his family had worked for decades in Ecuador, mines that had given them their wealth. To Alvarez, stealing the necklace wasn't just about the value—it was a declaration of war, a reminder that Juan had not forgotten their rivalry. He also planned to steal more from JT, taking everything of value he could, as a way to strike back at the man who had humiliated him.

However, things have spiraled out of control. Juan's initial plan was to target JT's wealth and assets, but he has now found himself unexpectedly drawn to Drusilla. His emotions are clouding his judgment, and his need for revenge is escalating. He feels trapped by his own anger and resentment, and it's driving him to consider more extreme actions, potentially involving Drusilla in ways he hadn't planned.

Alvarez's plan had always been bigger than a necklace. The jewel was merely the first part of his scheme. He had carefully crafted his cover as Hector Villalobos, bribing his way onto the crew as a low-level employee. He had remained invisible, staying out of the way, biding his time. He had watched as JT and Drusilla grew closer, seeing how the two of them were practically inseparable, and it sickened him. He hadn't planned on Drusilla being part of the equation, but now that she was, the stakes had gotten higher.

Drusilla wasn't just some trophy for JT. Their relationship had become a complication. He had watched her and JT together, their connection so obvious it made him want to choke on the very thought of it. The plans he'd made for stealing from JT now felt inadequate. The necklace was just the beginning. If he wanted to truly hurt JT, he would have to hit him where it hurt most— and that was Drusilla.

But no, he thought. *Not yet.*

The problem was that he had limited options of moving forward. The crew had been instructed to stay out of the way for the time being. No one knew his true identity. But that wouldn't last forever. As he thought more about it, he began to see how he could use Drusilla to his advantage. If he took her, if he threatened her, JT would do anything to get her back. He was convinced of that.

But I can't just take her, he thought, pacing the small cabin. *That would be too simple. Too quick.*

The only question now was: how long could he stay hidden before the noose tightened around him? How long before security found him?

He stared out of the small porthole, watching the endless stretch of ocean. There were no land stops until they reached New York. He had time, but that time was running out.

His heart raced as he plotted his next move, every possibility crossing his mind like a series of dominoes. The necklace had already served its purpose. Now, he would increase the pressure...but how?

What if I just take her? The idea lingered in his mind like a tempting whisper. *Take her now, put an end to this. Force JT to face the consequences.*

236

He imagined the confrontation—the look on JT's face when he realized what was happening. He could practically see it: the panic, the desperation. The way he would bend to Alvarez's will to get her back.

But then, a more rational voice cut through the haze of rage. *You can't just take her.*

He had to wait. He knew that.

The ship was too isolated. With no land in sight for the next three days, trying to hide Drusilla would be nearly impossible. Even if he managed to subdue her, the ship was crawling with security and surveillance cameras. There was no way to escape without being caught. He couldn't risk taking her now. There was no plan in place. No network of people to help him. He'd be on his own, and his chances of getting away would be slim.

No, he thought, clenching his jaw. *I'll wait until we're in New York.*

New York was different. The city was a labyrinth, full of places to disappear, full of people willing to do anything for the right price. Alvarez knew the city, knew the underworld that thrived there, and he had people he could call on. *That's when I'll take her. When I have everything set up. When I can make sure nothing goes wrong.*

But even as he thought this, he could feel the anger bubbling up again. The rational part of his mind—always the one to plan, to think things through—was being drowned out by his emotions. His hatred for JT, the humiliation of losing the merger, the sense of powerlessness after everything had been taken from him. He wasn't thinking clearly anymore. The deeper he got into this plan, the more the lines between revenge and something darker blurred.

It was too late to stop now. He had already made his choice. But he would wait and let time go by--- Letting him believe it was just about the necklace.

Four days to New York

As the sunlight filtered through the curtains, JT woke up first, the events of the previous day still weighing heavily on his mind. He turned his head slightly to see Drusilla, curled up beside him, her hair fanned out across the pillow. She looked peaceful, even after all the stress. JT's chest tightened; he couldn't let this Alvarez situation cast a shadow over her—or over them.

When Drusilla stirred and opened her eyes, he greeted her with a soft smile. "Morning," he said, his voice warm but resolute. "Let's take back our day. We'll have breakfast on the balcony, soak up some sun by the pool, and forget all this bullshit. Alvarez is a lowlife. We're not letting him ruin another second."

Drusilla blinked at him, still groggy but touched by his determination. She smiled faintly and nodded. "You're right. I'm done letting him live in my head rent-free."

JT chuckled and kissed her forehead before slipping out of bed. He ordered a room-service breakfast—eggs, bacon, toast, and jam—and by the time Drusilla had freshened up, their meal had arrived. They carried the plates out to the balcony, where the view of the endless blue ocean stretched to the horizon. A gentle breeze rolled in, carrying the scent of salt and the promise of a better day.

The conversation over breakfast was light and easy. They avoided any mention of Alvarez, focusing instead on sharing stories about their past travels, their pickleball match, and even debating who made the better cup of coffee. Drusilla's laugh came more freely as JT teased her about being a coffee snob, and by the time they'd finished eating, she felt like the weight of the previous day was finally starting to lift

After breakfast, they changed into their swimwear. JT opted for his usual black swim trunks and tee shirt, while Drusilla selected a sleek black bikini that accentuated her toned tanned figure. She layered it with a sheer cover-up that fluttered around her legs as they walked. JT paused when she stepped out of the bathroom, his eyes lingering on her longer than necessary.

"You look amazing," he said sincerely, his voice low.

Drusilla blushed and rolled her eyes playfully. "You're just trying to score extra points after yesterday."

JT smirked as he reached out for her. Not one to miss an opportunity to feel her warm skin against his. "Always," he replied.

They each made a drink to bring along—JT mixed a crisp gin and tonic, while Drusilla prepared a healthier green drink to ease in to the day. Armed with their glasses, they headed to the pool deck. Leonard, their newly assigned security detail, was already nearby, blending in seamlessly as he trailed a few steps behind. JT had spoken to him earlier, ensuring he would keep a low profile but remain within sight.

The morning passed in blissful quiet. Drusilla scrolled through her messages, catching up on emails from friends and updates on an art show she was planning back in Boston. JT worked through a few work-related emails, but he made sure to keep the phone calls to a minimum.

"Anything exciting?" Drusilla asked, peeking over her sunglasses as she sipped her mimosa. Any jewel thieves in our future?"

"Stop," JT replied, leaning back in his chair and crossing his legs at the ankle. "That crap is over. I'm dealing with worrisome board members making small fires seem like explosions. Nothing I can't handle."

Drusilla smirked. "You make it sound so glamorous."

He chuckled and turned his head toward her. "What about you? Anyone back home dying for your attention?" "

Just my gallery manager. She wants me to confirm some dates for the spring opening," Drusilla said. "But I told her she'd have to wait. This is my time to recharge." She paused, her gaze softening. "Our time."

JT reached over and took her hand, giving it a gentle squeeze. "Exactly."

Leonard lingered in the background, his watchful eyes scanning the area as he sipped a bottle of water, staying unobtrusive but vigilant with is aviators on. The knowledge of his presence gave JT some peace of mind, though he didn't let it distract from the serene moment he was sharing

239

with Drusilla. He was used to having security around. It made him relax, knowing that someone had his back.

They spent the next hour basking in the sun, chatting intermittently, and occasionally dipping their feet into the cool water of the pool. It felt like a return to normalcy, a chance to reconnect without the specter of Alvarez looming over them. For JT, seeing Drusilla smile and relax was all he needed to reaffirm his resolve to keep her safe and happy.

But in the back of his mind, a small voice reminded him that the danger wasn't over yet. Still, for now, he pushed those thoughts aside. They had the rest of the day to enjoy, and he wasn't going to let anything spoil it. He wanted to protect Drusilla, he didn't want her to worry.

As the late morning sun climbed higher, JT decided to check in with Leonard and the ship's security team before they continued their day. Drusilla lounged by the pool, scrolling through her phone while JT stepped aside to make the call. After a brief discussion, Leonard reassured him that everything was quiet and under control, though the security team remained vigilant.

Satisfied, JT returned to Drusilla and perched on the edge of her lounge chair. "So, what are you thinking for lunch?" he asked, brushing a strand of hair from her face.

Drusilla tilted her sunglasses down and looked up at him, her expression light. "I was thinking about that Chinese restaurant we went to the other day—The Noodle House. Remember? That noodle soup was incredible."

JT smiled. "I remember. I'd never seen someone get so excited over dumplings. Sounds like a plan."

They spent a little more time by the pool, enjoying the warm breeze and people-watching. When the sun began to feel too intense, they decided to head inside. Tossing on their cover-ups, JT in a loose linen shirt and Drusilla in her sheer black wrap, they gathered their things and made their way to *The Noodle House* on the middle deck

240

The restaurant had a relaxed ambiance, with soft instrumental music playing and the faint aroma of soy, garlic, and ginger wafting through the air. They were quickly seated near a window with a view of the glistening ocean.

Drusilla scanned the menu eagerly, her finger trailing over the selections. "I think I'm going for the chili garlic noodles this time," she said, glancing up at JT. "What about you?"

"I might stick with the wonton soup," JT replied, setting his menu aside. "It's hard to beat something classic."

Their server appeared moments later, and they placed their orders along with a pot of jasmine tea. As they waited, the conversation flowed easily. They discussed everything from their favorite cuisines to their dream travel destinations. Avoiding any discussion of Alvarez.

"You've traveled so much for work," Drusilla mused. "But what about just for fun? If you could go anywhere without a schedule or meetings, where would you go?"

JT leaned back, considering her question. "That's a tough one," he admitted. "But maybe Patagonia. The idea of wide open spaces, mountains, and just being completely off the grid—it sounds perfect. What about you?"

Drusilla smiled, resting her chin on her hand. "I'd love to explore Kyoto in the spring. The cherry blossoms, the temples, the art—it's been on my bucket list forever."

"Sounds like we might need to make both happen," JT said, his tone light but his expression sincere.

When their food arrived, the conversation paused as they savored each bite. Drusilla's eyes lit up at the first taste of her noodles. "Oh, this is even better than I remembered."

JT chuckled. "I'll take your word for it, noodle expert."

As they ate, the atmosphere around them felt calm and comforting—a stark contrast to the tension of the previous day. It was a reminder of why they had come on this cruise in the first place: to escape, to connect, and to enjoy life.

JT, however, couldn't completely let his guard down. Every so often, he glanced toward the entrance or scanned the room, his instincts sharp. He knew Leonard was nearby, keeping a quiet watch, which gave him some peace of mind.

For now, he was content to focus on Drusilla, her laughter, and the way her eyes sparkled when she spoke. Alvarez and his schemes could wait. This was their time.

After lunch, while Drusilla lingered at the table, enjoying the last of the jasmine tea, JT excused himself briefly to make a quick call. He stepped out into the quiet corridor, pulling out his phone.

"Ashley," he said when his assistant answered. "It's JT."

"JT! Everything okay?" Her tone was crisp but concerned.

"Yes, everything's fine—well, almost," he said, glancing around to ensure no one was within earshot. "Listen, I need you to do something for me. It's personal, not business."

"Of course," Ashley said immediately. "What do you need?"

"I need another emerald necklace, identical to the one you sent to the ship in Venice. Same cut, same setting, everything. It needs to be ready as soon as possible and sent directly to my office in New York. No delays. There is a picture of it in my insurance file.   "

Ashley hesitated only for a second. "OK. I'm on it. I'll get in touch with our jeweler in Ecuador right away and make sure it's expedited. How soon do you need it?"

"We return to New York in three days. I need it there then. Call me if there are any issues."

"You've got it boss," Ashley replied confidently.

"Thanks, Ashley. I owe you."

As he hung up, JT exhaled slowly, leaning against the wall for a moment. He didn't want Drusilla to feel like she'd lost something so meaningful, he wanted to replace it as soon as possible, thinking it would help ease her mind.

When he returned to the table, Drusilla looked up, smiling softly. "Everything okay?"

"Yeah," he said, settling back into his seat. "Just tying up a few loose ends. How about we take a walk on the deck before heading back to the cabin?"

Drusilla nodded, grateful for his effort to keep things light and normal. Whatever JT had been doing, she trusted that he had her best interests at heart.

Hidden away in the crew quarters, Alvarez paced the narrow space like a caged animal. His nerves were frayed, his thoughts racing faster than he could keep up with. His crew uniform was rumpled, and his hair, usually neatly combed, was disheveled from running his hands through it repeatedly. The hideout was far from the luxury he was used to, but it served its purpose—keeping him out of sight.

He held his phone tightly, his fingers trembling slightly as he typed out an encrypted message to his contact in New York.

> *"It's JA. Docking in NY in 3 days. Assemble a team. Be read to move on my command. Critical. Cash for your group. Details to come."*

After pressing send, he wiped sweat from his brow and muttered under his breath in Spanish. "Maldita sea, cálmate, Juan. Focus. Think."

He knew he was unraveling, and he hated it. A man of his stature—owner of one of Latin America's largest mining companies—shouldn't be reduced to skulking around a cruise ship like a petty thief. But JT Anderson had humiliated him, destroyed years of work, and left his reputation in tatters. The necklace was supposed to be a warning, but his anger burned hotter with each passing hour.

The plan was evolving, growing darker by the minute. Alvarez's new objective was Drusilla, the woman JT seemed to treasure so deeply. The thought of taking something JT valued so much gave him a twisted sense of satisfaction.

But he needed to keep his head clear. Any slip-up now would ruin everything. He'd carefully bribed his way onto this ship, using forged documents and a back-channel payment to a crooked hiring officer. So far, his cover had held, but he couldn't risk being seen too often. Some of the other crew members had started to notice his odd behavior, his tendency to avoid socializing, and his frequent disappearances when searches were done.

Alvarez tapped out another message, this one more specific:

"Have vehicles ready. Discreet location. Need immediate transport upon docking."

He stared at the screen, willing his contacts to respond. He couldn't afford their hesitation or incompetence. Everything depended on precision.

Two and a half days. That was all he needed to endure. If he could just keep his head down and avoid detection until they reached New York, the real plan could begin.

"Focus. Survive. Wait. Revenge will come."

Three days to New York

As the soft morning sun filtered through the curtains, JT stirred, his internal clock waking him just as the first light touched the horizon. Drusilla was still curled against him, her breathing steady and peaceful. He gently shifted, careful not to disturb her, and slipped out of bed.

Grabbing his phone from the nightstand, JT made his way to the bathroom, closing the door behind him with a quiet click. He turned on the shower, letting the water run to heat up, and perched on the toilet to check his messages from the night before.

A flood of emails and updates awaited him. Most were from his assistant, confirming the arrangements for the replacement emerald necklace.

"The jeweler confirmed the piece is identical. Delivery to your New York office is scheduled. Let me know if any changes are needed."

JT nodded to himself, satisfied that part of the ordeal was being handled. But other messages demanded his attention too—updates from Leonard, the ship's security, and even a flagged report from Ash in New York.

"Ran a deeper background check on Alvarez after your call. His financials show significant recent withdrawals, and there's chatter he's been trying to hire mercenary-level help in NY. Will tighten surveillance on known associates. Recommend heightened precautions upon arrival in NY. Our team will meet you at the dock. Call at your convenience for details."

JT frowned, the weight of the situation pressing on him. Alvarez wasn't just lashing out—he was calculating, dangerous, and now possibly coordinating something far more serious.

He leaned forward, rubbing his temples, the gravity of it all seeping into his thoughts. He hated the idea of Drusilla being caught in the crossfire of this feud. She deserved better than this chaos, better than the threats Alvarez posed.

The shower's steam filled the room, fogging the mirror as JT composed a quick reply to Ash.

"Understood. Keep me updated on any developments. Have a security detail ready for our arrival in New York. I will text you when we dock. Plan is to take us to the apartment, then wait for further instructions. I'll call you shortly to go over details."

He sent the message and stood, peeling off his clothes as he prepared to step into the hot spray of water. A part of him wanted to shield Drusilla from the depth of Alvarez's potential plans, but another part knew she deserved the truth.

This was no longer just about him or his business. It was about keeping her safe. He would share what he knew over breakfast.

245

Drusilla stirred as the sunlight crept through the edges of the curtains, warming her cheek. She reached out instinctively, her hand searching the bed for JT, but the space beside her was empty, the sheets cool. Blinking her eyes open, she turned to see his phone was gone from the nightstand, the faint sound of running water coming from the bathroom.

She sighed, sinking back into the pillows. Her mind, still hazy with sleep, began to churn with everything that had happened over the past few days. The theft of the necklace. The revelation about Alvarez, the danger, the mystery, and JT's calm but determined presence through it all.

She rolled onto her side, staring out the window at the endless expanse of ocean. How had she ended up here? A few weeks ago, she had boarded this cruise to heal, to escape, to find herself again after the collapse of her last relationship. She had never imagined meeting someone like JT—intense, magnetic, and deeply caring.

But now, she was caught in the whirlwind of his world, and it was nothing like the quiet life she had imagined. There were stolen emeralds, shadowy enemies, and security teams. It felt more like a thriller novel than reality.

Her heart twisted at the thought. Was this... normal? Was this what loving JT would always be like—danger lurking in the background, secrets to be uncovered, crises to be managed?

And yet, she adored him.

She thought back to the way he had held her last night, his arms strong and protective, the steady rhythm of his breathing lulling her into the first real sleep she'd had since this ordeal began. He was the kind of man who would move mountains for the people he loved, and she knew without a doubt that she was one of those people.

But she couldn't ignore the questions clawing at her mind. Was he worth it? Could she handle this? Was this the way she wanted to spend her life?

Drusilla ran her fingers through her hair, trying to push the doubts away. As bizarre as it was, she wanted to put the necklace theft behind them, to move on, to focus on the connection they

246

shared. The moments of laughter, the quiet conversations, the passion—they were all real. She wanted that life with him again, not this chaotic, high-stakes drama.

Her eyes shifted to the bathroom door as it creaked open. JT emerged, a towel slung around his waist, his hair damp and dripping onto his shoulders. He gave her a small, soft smile that melted some of the tension in her chest.

"Good morning," he said, crossing the room to meet her. As they embraced, his towel fell to the floor and she let her hands run all over his body. "You are so beautiful Mr. Anderson. I just love putting my hands on you. Please tell me that everything is going to be ok today?" JT, now suddenly aroused, looked her in eye and said, "nothing is going to interfere with our time together." He reached out and kissed her softly on the lips. She grabbed his head and extended the kiss, not wanting it to end. It didn't.

"How about something relaxing this morning?" she asked, her voice soft. "There's a meditation group meeting on the rear deck at ten. I think it could be good for both of us."

Now standing naked in front of her, JT laughed and said, "That's not what I had in mind, but let's do it. Meditation, huh? Can't say I've ever tried it."

Drusilla smiled faintly, a flicker of light breaking through her concern. "It's transcendental meditation. It helps clear your mind. I've been practicing for years—it's helped me get through a lot."

He looked at her, taking in her serene determination. Even after everything, she still carried a grace that both humbled and intrigued him. "Well, there's a first time for everything," he said as he put on a pair of shorts and tee shirt. "Let's do it."

By ten o'clock, they were seated on plush mats on the rear deck, the sound of the ship cutting through the waves blending with the soothing instructions of the meditation leader. The sun was warm but not oppressive, the gentle breeze carrying the salty tang of the ocean air.

247

Drusilla, in her sleek Lululemon pants and tight fitting top, sat cross-legged, her hands resting on her knees, her posture perfectly aligned. JT did his best to mimic her, though he couldn't quite match her effortless ease.

The instructor, a woman with a calming voice and flowing robe, guided the group through breathing exercises, encouraging them to focus on a single mantra. Drusilla fell into the rhythm quickly, her breath slowing, her shoulders relaxing as she surrendered to the moment.

JT, on the other hand, found it hard to quiet his mind. His thoughts jumped from Alvarez to the necklace to the way Drusilla looked in that outfit. He shifted slightly, earning a sideways glance from her. She reached over and placed her hand gently on his knee, a silent reminder to stay present. He smiled, as if to conform.

He closed his eyes, inhaling deeply, and let the words of the instructor wash over him. For the first time in days, he felt a small crack in the tension that had gripped him.

When the session ended, they remained seated for a few moments, soaking in the calm that lingered.

Drusilla turned to him, her eyes brighter than they had been earlier. "What did you think?"

JT stretched his legs out in front of him and gave her a crooked smile. "I think I need more practice. But I'll admit, it wasn't bad. It felt... grounding."

She chuckled softly. "That's the point."

"I can see why you're into it. You've got this inner calm I wish I could bottle up."

Drusilla tilted her head, her smile softening. "It's not something that comes naturally. It takes work. But it's worth it."

JT nodded, making a mental note to add meditation to his growing list of new things to explore with her. Whatever challenges lay ahead, he wanted to face them with the same clarity and strength she seemed to embody.

248

"Alright," he said, standing and offering her a hand. "What's next on today's relaxation agenda?"

She laughed lightly, taking his hand. "Let's see where the day takes us."

Back at JT's cabin, they slipped off their shoes and stepped into the cool, quiet space. "You take the first shower," JT offered, grabbing his phone from the desk. "I need to make a few calls."

Drusilla nodded, gathering a towel from the closet. "Don't take too long," she teased lightly before disappearing into the bathroom.

The sound of the water running filled the room as JT sat down on the edge of the bed, dialing Ash's number. The line clicked almost immediately.

"Talk to me," Ash said, his voice sharp and efficient as always.

JT recounted the latest updates, ensuring Ash had everything he needed to coordinate with ship security and the team waiting in New York. Ash reassured him they were prepared, but the conversation did little to ease the knot in JT's stomach.

"Thanks, Ash," he said before ending the call. He set the phone down and exhaled deeply, rubbing his temples.

Standing, JT stripped off his tee shirt and shorts, tossing them onto the chair in the corner. The sound of the shower and the faint scent of Drusilla's shampoo called to him. As he walked into the bathroom, steam enveloped him, turning the small space into a warm, misty haven.

He paused at the fogged-over mirror, wiping a small circle clear to catch his reflection. A smirk tugged at his lips as an idea struck.

Moving to the glass shower door, JT slowly drew a heart on the misty surface with his finger.

Inside, Drusilla noticed immediately. She grinned and drew a matching heart.

He chuckled softly, drawing another heart beside the first.

She responded in kind, mirroring his every move until the door was filled with their playful exchange. Then, without hesitation, she wiped a clear patch of steam from the glass.

Through the opening, her eyes met his. He stood there, completely bare, his confident posture softened by the tenderness in his gaze.

For a moment, neither of them moved. The heat from the shower and the shared intimacy of the moment made the rest of the world fall away.

Drusilla's smile widened. "What are you waiting for?" she murmured, sliding the glass door open.

JT stepped inside, the hot water cascading over both of them as he closed the door behind him. He wrapped his arms around her, pulling her against his chest as the spray drenched them.

Their lips met, the kiss slow and deliberate, filled with unspoken promises. The stress, the tension, the fear—all of it dissolved in the heat of the water and the closeness of their embrace.

Drusilla ran her fingers down his back, her touch light and teasing, while JT cradled her face, his thumbs brushing her cheeks. They moved together, their connection unhurried but consuming, as if this moment was all that mattered.

She sighed softly, her head resting against his shoulder, the water streaming over her back. "I wish this could last forever," she whispered.

JT tilted her chin up, looking deep into her eyes. "As far as I'm concerned, it can."

They lost themselves in the rhythm of their bodies, the gentle rush of water against their skin amplifying their every touch. For a time, there were no stolen necklaces, no lurking threats, no unresolved questions—only the two of them and the sanctuary they found in each other.

When at last they stepped out of the shower, the world seemed brighter. Wrapped in fresh towels, they smiled at each other, knowing that no matter what lay ahead, they would face it together.

As they dressed, the comfortable, passionate, post-shower atmosphere lingered between them. They slipped into their robes and looked at each other with a shy smile, not wanting the feeling from the shower to end.

"So," JT began, glancing at her, "how about sushi for dinner?"

Drusilla's face lit up with instant approval. "Absolutely. I've been craving something fresh and light. Perfect choice."

"Great," JT said, as he grabbed his watch from the nightstand, glancing at her again. I'll make a reservation.

The afternoon passed in a peaceful, easy rhythm. Classical music played softly in the background—Drusilla's choice. They both slipped into their own little worlds, the hum of the music enveloping the cabin, and the moments passing without urgency.

JT sprawled on the sofa, scrolling through emails and news updates on his phone. Drusilla settled by the window in a chair, her legs tucked beneath her as she went down a rabbit hole on Instagram.

Every now and then, one would glance at the other, a soft smile exchanged, or a remark made about a random discovery. The silences were comfortable, each moment with the other feeling more like a continuation of their last conversation.

At one point, Drusilla looked up from her phone, catching JT's gaze on her. "What?" she asked, her voice light.

"Nothing," JT said with a small, affectionate smile. "Just... admiring you."

Drusilla's cheeks flushed slightly, and she gave him a playful eye-roll, extended her bare leg to run along his foot.

JT chuckled, but his eyes remained soft as they lingered on her.

They continued on like this, drifting between their own playful activities and the rare moments of sharing a piece of content that made them laugh. JT showed her a funny meme, and Drusilla pointed out an intriguing piece of art from Instagram. Every so often, their hands would brush, and they'd pause, exchanging a smile before going back to what they were doing. The memory of their sensual afternoon shower remaining in their minds.

JT looked over at her again—her hair, the way the light caught her face. The thought of how *right* everything felt between them tightened in his chest. She wasn't just beautiful—she was captivating.

"Are you sure you didn't come on this cruise to make me a classical music fan?" she asked, glancing up from her phone as the volume of the music shifted with a new piece.

JT reached over and turned the volume up a bit. "Maybe," he said with a smirk. "It's working, isn't it?" He laid his phone down, got up, scooped her up and laid her gently on the bed, within seconds, they were in a lovers rhythm and nothing else mattered. Afterwards, they both drifted off, satisfied. Their love was real.

After another shower, they were both ready for dinner. What was better than making love twice before dinner? Following it with a fun dinner with the one you love.

Drusilla suggested they dress casual for dinner. "Who dresses up for sushi?"

JT put on his white slacks and a red polo. Drusilla slipped into white jeans and a flowery blouse.

They left the cabin, side by side, their connection growing deeper with every passing moment.

The morning light filtered softly through the curtains as Drusilla woke first, her usual early riser instinct kicking in. Quietly, she slipped out of bed and headed for the bathroom, leaving JT to sleep soundly. The gentle sound of water soon filled the room as she stepped into the shower, the steam beginning to rise and mix with the morning air.

JT stirred as he heard the faint sound of the shower door closing. He blinked a few times, trying to shake off the remnants of sleep. Rolling over, he grabbed his phone from the nightstand and checked his messages. One from Ash caught his eye:

> *"Everything quiet, Boss. No movement on this end. I've been communicating with Leonard. They are still searching for Alvarez."*

JT exhaled slowly, his mind still racing from the events of the past days. Maybe it was over. Maybe Alvarez had just wanted to make a point—grab the necklace, try to scare them. The tension in his chest eased just slightly. There were almost back in New York. They would be back in the safety of his team's protection, and whatever game Alvarez had been playing would finally end.

Sighing, he sat up in bed, his mind still running through the possibilities. After a moment, he decided to get ready for the day. He slipped out of bed, grabbed his robe, and made his way to the bathroom.

The sight of Drusilla in the shower was something JT had grown accustomed to—her silhouette outlined through the steamed-up glass, the curve of her body reminding him just how lucky he was. He stopped for a moment, his thoughts softening as he took her in. A slight smile tugged at his lips.

"Good morning," he called gently, though not expecting a reply.

Her soft hum from the shower acknowledged him, and with that, he brushed his teeth, wiped his mouth with the towel, then closed the door behind him and gave Drusilla privacy to get ready for the day.

His thoughts lingered on the message from Ash, and the quiet that had settled in. Perhaps the threat had passed. He hoped it had. He wasn't used to feeling so out of control.

The morning unfolded gently as JT and Drusilla settled into their routine. Fresh from their showers, they discussed their plans for the day. They were determined to make the most of their time together. He masked his stress with a calm demeanor, unwilling to let Drusilla sense the unease bubbling under the surface. She had so many questions about Alvarez, and he didn't want those concerns to overshadow their remaining time on the ship.

Over coffee and juice at the café, Drusilla broke the silence. "Why would Alvarez steal the necklace? Why does he hate you so much?" she asked, her brows furrowed with concern. "And how did he even get on the ship? Is he dangerous, JT?"

JT reached across the table and squeezed her hand gently. "Honestly, I don't have all the answers yet. But I do know that we're being careful, and we have people watching out for us." He offered her a reassuring smile, though he wasn't sure if he entirely believed his own words.

Their poached eggs and bacon arrived, and JT dug in eagerly. "Let's hit the pool after breakfast," he suggested between bites. "We can relax for a bit and figure out what we want to do the rest of the day."

Drusilla nodded, sipping her juice. "I'll need to stop by my cabin to grab a few things. Now that I'm staying with you, my stuff is all over the place," she said with a chuckle, trying to lighten the mood.

When they returned to JT's cabin, he put on some soft music, setting a laid-back vibe as they got ready for the pool. JT grabbed his dependable black trunks, while Drusilla opted for a vibrant orange bikini that contrasted beautifully with her skin. She tossed on a sheer white cover-up and grabbed her pool bag. JT pulled on a plain tee shirt over his trunks, and with everything in place, they headed out together, eager to let the sun and water wash away the tension of the past few days.

As JT and Drusilla made their way to the pool, Leonard approached with a firm but composed demeanor. "Mr. Anderson," he began in a low voice, nodding politely to Drusilla before continuing, "just wanted to give you an update on the Alvarez situation. We haven't located him yet, but we're confident we will. With 2,000 people on board, it takes time to comb through everyone while respecting their privacy. For now, we've kept the situation under wraps. No announcements have been made, so there's no risk of panic among the passengers."

JT nodded, appreciating Leonard's professionalism. "Thanks for letting me know. Keep me posted on any developments," he replied, his tone steady but his mind racing. The thought of Alvarez still lurking on the ship was unsettling, but JT knew Leonard and the ship's security team were doing everything they could.

When they arrived at the pool, they found their usual spot and settled in. JT pulled out his phone and dialed Ash in New York.

"Ash," he said once the call connected, "Leonard just updated me. Still no sign of Alvarez, but they are continue to look for him."

Ash's voice came through, calm and reassuring. "Got it, boss. I'll make sure a full security detail is waiting for you when the ship docks in New York. Alvarez won't have a chance to get close to you or Miss Pennington once you're off that ship."

JT exhaled deeply, comforted by Ash's competence. "Thanks, Ash. I'll check in later."

Ending the call, JT leaned back in his chair, the warmth of the sun beginning to relax him. Drusilla glanced at him, her expression soft yet questioning. "Everything okay?" she asked.

"Yeah," JT replied with a small smile, reaching for her hand. "Ash is arranging a security detail to meet us when we dock. We're covered."

Drusilla nodded, nervous, but reassured by his words, and the two settled into their chairs. For now, they let the tension ease, the sun's rays and the gentle sound of the ship slicing through the water offering a brief respite from the storm looming on the horizon.

As Drusilla lounged by the pool, the warmth of the sun and the soothing sound of the ocean lulled her into a light nap. Her dreams, however, were anything but peaceful. In her mind, shadowy figures pursued her, their intentions menacing and unclear. She was running, her heart pounding, desperately seeking safety but finding none.

She woke with a start, her breath quick and shallow, her body tense. JT noticed immediately, setting his phone aside and leaning toward her. "Drusilla?" he asked gently, concern etched across his face. "Are you okay?"

She sat up, brushing her hair from her damp forehead. "I—I was dreaming," she stammered. "It felt so real. Someone was chasing me... trying to hurt me."

JT reached for her hand, his grip firm and reassuring. "Hey," he said softly, his voice steady. "It was just a dream. You're safe, I promise. Nothing's going to happen to you. Not while I'm here."

She looked into his eyes, finding solace in his unwavering confidence. "I know," she whispered, though her heart still raced. "It's just... everything that's happened. It's hard not to feel on edge."

JT moved closer, wrapping an arm around her shoulders. "I get it," he said, his tone earnest. "This whole Alvarez thing is enough to shake anyone. But I need you to trust me on this—Leonard, Ash, the ship's security, and I—we've got this under control. No one is going to touch you."

Drusilla leaned into him, feeling the strength of his embrace. "Thank you," she whispered. "I don't know what I'd do without you right now."

JT kissed the top of her head, holding her tightly for a moment before pulling back to look at her. "We're almost back in New York. Once we're there, this whole nightmare will be behind us. Until then, let's just focus on each other and enjoy these last couple of days."

Drusilla managed a small smile. "You're right," she said, trying to push the lingering unease from her mind.

JT reached for her drink on the small side table and handed it to her. "Here, sip on this. It'll help."

She took the glass, grateful for his thoughtfulness, and together they settled back into their loungers. JT's presence beside her was enough to chase away the shadows of her dream, if only for a while.

Hiding in plain sight

Alvarez paced in his crew quarters, the faint hum of the ship's engines vibrating through the walls. His nerves were frayed, and his phone was his only lifeline to the outside world. He had already missed two meals but didn't dare venture out, knowing that any misstep could expose him.

For the past two days, he had been moving in the shadows, slipping into areas rarely patrolled by staff and avoiding public spaces entirely. The ship was massive, but Alvarez knew how to blend in—he had a knack for becoming invisible when necessary. Dressed in his maintenance attire, he walked with purpose whenever he had to traverse the corridors, acting as though he belonged. So far, it had worked.

Sitting on an overturned crate, Alvarez dialed a number he knew by heart. His contact in New York answered on the second ring.

"Villalobos," the voice on the other end said, using the alias Alvarez preferred. "You're cutting it close. I got your texts, but need details."

"I know," Alvarez hissed, his frustration evident. "But I need you to listen. We'll be docking in two days. I need you to assemble a team—two, maybe three people. I'm working on something delicate, and I'll need backup. Money isn't an issue. I'll pay whatever it takes."

There was a pause before the voice responded. "What exactly are we dealing with?"

Alvarez glanced around the dimly lit space, ensuring he was alone. "A loose end that needs tying up. I'll explain everything when we meet at the dock. Just be ready. I can't risk discussing this right now. I'll send you the details."

"You sound heavy," the contact said, his tone tinged with caution.

"I'm handling it," Alvarez snapped. "Just do your part. Be at the dock, and bring the others."

The call ended abruptly, and Alvarez leaned back, closing his eyes for a moment. He had no choice but to trust his contacts in New York. His pride wouldn't let him admit how badly this operation had gone off the rails.

The theft of the necklace had been only the beginning—a way to strike at JT, the man who had always been one step ahead in the mining industry. But now, Alvarez was in over his head. His anger had clouded his judgment, and the simple plan to steal and humiliate had turned into something far more dangerous. He wasn't even sure what his endgame was anymore. All he knew was that he wanted to hurt JT, to take something (or someone) from him.

For now, Alvarez remained vigilant, sticking to the shadows and plotting his next move. He had learned the ship's schedule, waiting for moments when the corridors were quieter. He raided the crew kitchen late at night, grabbing enough food to sustain himself and retreating back to his quarters.

His thoughts raced as he mapped out the final days of the voyage. They will be back in New York soon, he reminded himself. Then he could make his move. Until then, he would stay hidden, biding his time like the predator he believed himself to be.

JT and Drusilla settled into the rhythm of the pool's gentle waves. The sun glistened on the water's surface as JT swam with powerful strokes, his lean body cutting through the water effortlessly. Drusilla, meanwhile, waded in gracefully, savoring the cool sensation as it enveloped her inch by inch.

"Come on, slowpoke!" JT teased, splashing a small wave toward her.

Drusilla laughed, shielding her face. "Some of us like to enjoy the process!"

Eventually, they both ended up in the deep end, gripping the smooth edge of the pool as they floated lazily, the sounds of laughter and splashing surrounding them. The Bloody Marys JT ordered hadn't arrived yet, so they savored the moment—just the two of them, untethered from the tension of the last few days.

Drusilla swam toward him, her face alight with mischief. She grabbed onto his broad shoulders, feeling the strength beneath her hands. Without a second thought, she wrapped her legs around his torso, pulling herself closer. Her lips met his in a kiss that was tender but deep, a silent reassurance that she was still with him despite everything.

JT's free arm slipped around her waist instinctively, pulling her closer. His heart raced—not just from her touch but from the awareness that they weren't alone. He felt the eyes of nearby swimmers and sunbathers on them, a mix of curiosity and envy. Despite that, he couldn't resist her.

"Drusilla," he murmured against her lips, his voice low and playful, "you're going to make a scene."

"Let them watch," she whispered back, her eyes locked on his, sparkling with defiance and affection.

JT chuckled softly but maintained his restraint. He shifted them slightly so they were partially hidden by the pool's ledge, leaning in closer while still keeping things respectable. The weight of the past few days seemed to lift in the buoyancy of the water, replaced by the simple joy of being together.

The arrival of the server with their drinks snapped them out of the moment. "Two Bloody Marys Mr. Anderson," the attendant announced with a polite nod, placing the tray on a small table by their lounge chairs.

Drusilla smiled and unwrapped herself from JT, pushing off toward the pool steps. "Saved by the drinks," she quipped, glancing back at him with a teasing grin.

259

JT climbed out of the pool, water cascading down his toned and tanned body, grabbed his towel and tossed one to Drusilla, and followed her to their chairs. He handed her one of the Bloody Marys before taking a long sip of his own.

"To forgetting everything but this," he said, raising his glass toward hers.

Drusilla clinked her glass against his. "To us."

The rest of the afternoon was theirs—relaxed and carefree, a much-needed reprieve from the storm still brewing around them.

As they sipped their drinks, the late-morning sun shimmered across the pool deck. JT casually checked his messages, scrolling through updates from Ash and the ship's staff. Meanwhile, Drusilla snapped a few selfies, framing the pool and ocean as her backdrop, then texted her mom. She attached a few photos from their adventures, assuring her that she was having a wonderful time.

"Sending proof of life?" JT teased, glancing at her screen.

Drusilla smirked. "Something like that. Mom loves updates. It keeps her from calling me a hundred times."

"Smart move," JT chuckled as he swiped through his notifications.

With lunchtime approaching, they decided on something light by the pool. JT flagged down a waiter, ordering two Caesar salads and—of course—French fries.

"French fries?" Drusilla teased, rolling her eyes. "You're such a creature of habit."

"Don't knock them," JT said with a grin. "They're perfect with everything."

Lunch arrived quickly, and the two ate leisurely under the umbrella. Drusilla sprinkled a bit of extra parmesan on her salad while stealing one of JT's fries, a mischievous smile on her lips.

"You're lucky I like you," JT said, mock-serious as she stole another fry.

"I know," she shot back, winking.

As they finished their meal, Drusilla suggested, "What do you think about taking that yoga class we saw on the schedule earlier?"

JT arched a brow, "if it's with you in yoga pants, I'm in."

"I'll sign us up." She said as she jumped up and headed to the bar to use the phone and reserve their spot.

After lunch, they returned to JT's cabin to change. Drusilla slipped into a pair of bright yellow yoga pants and a matching tank top. JT, already dressed in his shorts and tee, paused when she emerged. His eyes swept over her appreciatively, a smirk tugging at the corner of his mouth.

"You look incredible in everything you wear," he said, his voice low and full of admiration. "My God, come here."

Drusilla laughed as JT pulled her into an embrace, his hands lingering on her waist. His lips grazed her neck, and for a moment, she felt herself giving in to the warmth of his touch.

"We've got a class to catch, big boy."

JT groaned dramatically. "You're killing me."

"Grab your towel," she quipped,

Laughing, they headed out the door, Leonard discreetly following behind. As they made their way through the ship's corridors, Drusilla felt a bubbling sense of anticipation—not just for the yoga class but for the peace and joy she had found in JT's company. Whatever challenges lay ahead, she liked the fact that they were together.

As they walked back to the cabin, JT couldn't keep his eyes off Drusilla. Her yellow yoga pants hugged her cute body, and the way her ponytail swayed with each step drove him crazy. She had her towel draped over her shoulder, her face still glowing from the yoga session.

"What now, Miss Pennington?" JT asked, his voice low and teasing as he shot her a sly grin.

Drusilla turned to him with a smirk. "I know what *you're* thinking, Mr. Anderson," she said, snapping her towel playfully at him.

He dodged with a laugh and caught her by the waist, pulling her close. "And what's wrong with that? A warm shower sounds like just the thing after yoga."

Drusilla raised an eyebrow, pretending to consider it. "Well... I suppose we're both a little sweaty," she said, her tone dripping with mock seriousness.

Back in the cabin, JT locked the door behind them and started peeling off his shirt. Drusilla raised her tank top over her head exposing her firm tan body. She tossed her towel onto the chair and sauntered toward the bathroom, glancing back at him over her shoulder with a mischievous glint in her eye. "You coming, or are you just going to stand there?"

He didn't need to be asked twice.

In the bathroom, the steam quickly filled the space as the hot water poured from the showerhead. Drusilla stepped under the stream first, sighing as the warmth washed over her. JT followed, his strong arms wrapping around her waist as he pulled her close under the spray.

She leaned into him, tilting her head back to meet his gaze. "Is this your idea of saving water?" she teased, her voice soft and playful.

JT chuckled, brushing a strand of wet hair from her face. "It's my idea of spending as much time with you as possible."

Their lips met in a slow, lingering kiss as the water cascaded over them. JT ran his hands along her back and down her thigh, savoring the feeling of her warm skin beneath his fingers. Drusilla responded in kind, her fingers trailing down his chest as she melted into him.

The playful mood turned more passionate as their bodies moved together in the tight intimate space. The water wasn't the only thing heating up the room as they lost themselves in each other, forgetting about everything beyond the walls of the cabin.

When the water finally began to cool, JT reached over to turn off the shower. Drusilla wrapped her arms around his neck, resting her forehead against his.

"See?" he said, a satisfied smile on his face. "A warm shower really *was* the perfect idea."

Drusilla laughed softly, her cheeks still flushed. "Okay, you win."

They dried off together, stealing kisses between laughs as they each slipped in to their plush robes and headed to the balcony to relax and plan the rest of the day.

With only two days left on the cruise, JT leaned back in the chair, sipping his coffee, and suggested, "Let's make tonight unforgettable. Get all dolled up. Fine dinner, champagne, dancing—the works."

Drusilla, sitting with her legs in his lap, tilted her head thoughtfully. A slow smile spread across her face as she got up, swinging her leg over him, straddling his lap. She slid her robe higher as she settled herself facing him, her knees pressing into his thighs.

"I love the idea," she murmured, her voice low and sultry. Her arms draped over his shoulders, pulling him closer as she pressed a kiss to his lips, slow and deliberate.

JT ran his hands up her sides, resting them just beneath her robe. "You're making it really hard to focus on tonight," he said, his voice husky, his lips brushing against her ear.

Drusilla giggled, pulling back just enough to look into his eyes. "Focus on this, then," she teased, giving him another lingering kiss before hopping up with a playful bounce.

She strode over to the closet, her robe slipping off one shoulder as she began rifling through her options. "What do you think?" she asked, holding up a shimmering silver dress that sparkled even in the dim cabin light.

JT leaned back, watching her with unabashed admiration. "I haven't seen that one," he said, grinning. "It'll turn every head in the room—especially mine."

She tossed the dress onto the bed and twirled toward him. "Good. I only care about one pair of eyes tonight."

JT stood, crossing the room to where she was standing. He wrapped his arms around her waist, pulling her close once more. "You sexy thing, you're making it very hard to wait until tonight," he said, his voice low.

Drusilla smirked, tracing her finger along his jawline. "Then you'd better get ready, Mr. Anderson. Because tonight, you'll need to keep up with me."

With that, she spun away, laughing, and began laying out accessories for the evening ahead. JT watched her, a mix of amusement and desire in his expression, knowing tonight was going to be another one to remember.

As soft jazz played in the background, the cabin felt more like an intimate haven than just another room on the ship. JT had ordered a charcuterie plate and sparkling water for them both, and the delicate spread of cheeses, cured meats, and fruits was a perfect touch for the moment. They were savoring the quiet before the evening ahead, each enjoying the peace of the moment, the sounds of the music mingling with the gentle rocking of the ship.

Drusilla, standing by the window, stared out at the ocean, her reflection mirrored in the glass. The sky was a blend of purple and orange as the sun began to set, and she felt a wave of gratitude for this rare slice of tranquility. JT had been right—she needed this. They both did.

She turned back to find JT lounging on the couch, eyes studying her with that intense, warm look that had been impossible to resist since they met. He caught her gaze and gave a small, inviting smile.

"Everything okay?" he asked, his voice low and easy, as if there were no weight in the world.

264

Drusilla smiled, walking over to him. She sat beside him, the cushions sinking under her weight. "Perfect," she replied, curling into his side. "I needed this... quiet time."

JT's arm wrapped around her, pulling her closer. "Me too. No rush, no stress. Just... us."

For a moment, they both sat in contented silence. The ship was still, and so were they. There was no talk of plans, no mention of the impending return to New York. In that moment, everything seemed right.

"I love the idea of another fun night out," Drusilla said softly, her fingers brushing against his. "Let's not let the time slip away." She looked up at him, eyes twinkling.

JT met her gaze with a thoughtful smile, brushing a strand of hair from her face. "That sounds perfect," he agreed, his voice warm with affection. "We can forget about everything else— just you and me. No worries, no stress.....and maybe a run at the crap table?"

Drusilla stood up, feeling a surge of energy. "That's a great idea. I'm going to make tonight unforgettable," she said, already moving toward the closet.

JT, still lounging on the couch, chuckled. "You always make everything unforgettable. "I'm already looking forward to it."

As she disappeared into the bathroom, JT leaned back, staring out at the ocean, feeling a rare sense of peace. The world outside their bubble seemed distant, irrelevant. It was just the two of them now, and for tonight, that was all that mattered.

As the balcony door slid closed behind him, JT took a deep breath, the lingering aroma of his cigar mixing with the salty sea breeze. His thoughts swirled with unanswered questions about Alvarez. The man's actions defied logic—an influential corporate leader resorting to petty theft and prowling around a cruise ship? JT's instincts told him there was more to this puzzle, and whatever it was, it likely wasn't good.

A light tapping on the door pulled him from his musings. JT stubbed out his cigar, set the ashtray aside, and made his way across the cabin. Opening the door, he saw a young valet standing there, Leonard close behind, his eyes scanning the corridor. The valet handed over JT's pressed shirts with a polite smile.

"Thank you," JT said, slipping the young man a generous tip. He gave Leonard a knowing nod before shutting the door behind them.

JT draped the shirts across the back of a chair and glanced at the clock. Tonight was their chance to forget the chaos for a while, to enjoy each other's company and the last couple of days of the cruise. He wanted the evening to be perfect.

The sound of the shower stopped. He smiled, imagining Drusilla stepping out, her hair damp, her skin glowing, as she prepared for their evening. He thought of joining her, but decided to give her some privacy and wait to shower she comes out. He turned up the music, poured himself a few fingers of Crown, opened the balcony door, re-lit his cigar and enjoyed his own bit of privacy.

As Drusilla steps out of the bathroom, steam trailing behind her, she pauses for a moment, soaking in the music playing in the cabin. Wrapped in the plush white robe, her hair secured in a towel, she glances toward the balcony where JT sits, deep in thought. She smiles to herself, feeling a surge of affection for him.

After laying out her outfit for the evening—a stunning silver dress that shows off her perfectly toned body—she moves to the vanity. She starts applying a light moisturizer to her face, letting the cool lotion soothe her skin. As her hands glide over her cheeks, she hums softly along with the music.

Drusilla's eyes catch her reflection, and she decides to spend a few extra moments on her makeup tonight. She pulls out her makeup bag and selects her favorite products: a touch of shimmering eyeshadow to complement her dress, a bold eyeliner to make her eyes pop, and a soft, rose-colored lipstick. Each stroke is deliberate, almost meditative. She can't decide on undergarments. She wants it to be perfect, knowing that she will most likely end the night in them. She chooses sleek white panties and thin white bra, managing to put them on without taking her robe off completely. She glances in the mirror and is pleased with the choice, thinking JT will like them.

Once she's satisfied with her look, she walks over to her jewelry wrap and sifts through her collection. She picks out a pair of silver chandelier earrings and a delicate bracelet, holding them up to the light to admire their sparkle.

As the music shifts to a slower, jazzier tune, Drusilla feels a sudden whim to dance. She sways gently in front of the mirror, the rhythm guiding her movements. Her robe swirls around her as she twirls, her laughter breaking the silence of the cabin.

Finally, her gaze falls on the bottle of cologne JT left on the nightstand. She picks it up, spraying a little on her wrist, letting the scent mix with her own. Smiling, she looks out at the balcony again, watching him for a moment, his silhouette outlined by the fading light.

With a deep breath, she decides to grab her phone and snap a few pics, capturing the growing excitement for the evening ahead. She considers sending one to her mom but instead decides to keep them for herself—little reminders of this magical, unexpected chapter of her life.

Satisfied with her preparations and feeling a little mischievous, she slips in to her Jimmy Choos, the silver glitter shining in the light. She tiptoes toward the balcony door. JT has his back to the room as he looks out over the ocean. She taps gently on the glass with her fingernails. As JT turns around, she lifts her arm over her head and rests it on the door frame, letting her robe fall to the floor, exposing her beautiful tanned body, the white panties and bra, and the glittering shoes. JT shakes his head in disbelief. He feels like the luckiest man alive. As he smiles and reaches for the door handle, she presses her finger down and locks it. She mouths "do you like it?" JT moves his head up and down slowly, joining the little game. She laughs, opens the door and says, "You better be ready to sweep me off my feet tonight. I'm feeling lucky. JT steps into the room, slips his arm around her, then picks up her robe and drapes it over her shoulders. "I'm ready my dear. We can go out or we can stay right here. It will be fun either way." Drusilla pushes him away playfully and says, "get ready, and we can do both."

JT headed to the bathroom to take a quick shower and shave, taking a fraction of the time Drusilla takes. When he comes back out, a towel around his waist, Drusilla is sitting in front of the mirror, drying her hair. He opens the top drawer and stares for a moment. She turns off the hair dryer and asks what he's looking at. "Just trying to pick out the perfect pair of undies. It seems like that's important tonight." Looking at her with a sly grin on his face. He picks out the white Tommy Johns boxer/briefs, drops his towel and slips them on as Drusilla watches him in the mirror. "White seems to be the color for the night," he says, lifting his eyebrows. Drusilla looks at him in the mirror smiling and says, "White looks good in the moonlight."

With that thought in mind, the two of them began getting dressed, sharing the mirror and swaying to the music. While Drusilla slid in to her cute little silver dress, JT opted for his tailored black suit. A crisp tailored white shirt with French cuffs was accented with a black Brioni tie. He reached into his travel case for his signature white pocket square but hesitated. Tonight wasn't just about tradition; it was about matching Drusilla, complementing her in every way. He replaced the white square with a sleek silver one, folding it neatly before sliding it into place. He held out a handful of cufflinks and asked Drusilla to pick out a pair. She didn't hesitate and grabbed the silver pinwheels, sticking with the theme of the evening.

As they finished getting dressed, the cabin was alive with an air of anticipation. JT adjusted his tie in the mirror one last time, running a hand over the sleek lines of his black suit. Drusilla sat on the upholstered stool to put her silver heels on, the final touch to her dazzling outfit. She gave a small twirl in front of the mirror, the shimmer of her dress catching the light.

"Perfect," JT said as he turned to look at her, his voice filled with admiration. "You look absolutely stunning."

"And you," Drusilla replied with a sly smile, "look like you just walked out of a Bond movie."

They both laughed, and JT held out his hand, pulling her into a gentle embrace. The moment felt quiet and intimate, a calm before the evening's festivities.

Before heading out, Drusilla suggested they have a quick toast to set the tone for the night. JT agreed, reaching for the chilled bottle of champagne they had in the minibar. He popped it open with a satisfying *pop*, pouring two glasses.

"To an unforgettable night," JT said, holding his glass up.

"To us," Drusilla added, clinking her glass against his. They sipped the champagne, savoring its crisp taste as they exchanged a knowing look, excitement bubbling between them.

After finishing their drinks, JT walked over to the speaker system and switched the music to an upbeat jazz tune. "One quick dance before we go?" he asked, extending a hand to Drusilla.

"Why not?" she replied, taking his hand.

They swayed to the rhythm in the middle of the cabin, laughing as JT spun her around dramatically. For a moment, it felt like they were the only two people in the world, wrapped in their own little bubble of joy.

As the song came to an end, JT checked his watch. "We should probably head out before they give away our table."

Drusilla grabbed her silver clutch from the bed, and JT slipped his wallet into his jacket pocket. As they made their way to the door, JT stopped and looked at her, his expression soft.

"Whatever happens tonight, just know…" he said, pausing for a beat. "You've made this trip something I'll never forget."

Drusilla smiled, her eyes sparkling. "I feel the same."

With that, JT opened the door, offering his arm. Drusilla looped hers through his, and together they stepped out into the corridor, ready to take on the night.

As they exited the cabin, their laughter echoed softly in the corridor. She held onto his arm, the sparkle of her silver dress matching the twinkle in her eyes. JT couldn't help but smile, her happiness infectious.

But as they stepped into the hallway, JT's gaze flicked to the side, catching sight of Leonard standing a few steps away. His sharp suit blended with the shadows, but his watchful eyes missed nothing. The sight of him was a jarring reminder—a contrast to the lightness of the moment.

JT's jaw tightened briefly as his mind snapped back to the lurking danger. *Alvarez.* The name hovered in his thoughts like a dark cloud. He forced himself to stay composed, not wanting to dampen the mood for Drusilla.

Leonard gave him a subtle nod, a signal that everything was still under control—for now. JT returned the nod with a slight one of his own, silently grateful for the man's presence, even as it underscored the risks they were still facing.

"What's on your mind?" Drusilla asked, tilting her head to look up at him as they walked.

JT smiled, masking his unease. "Just thinking about how lucky I am to have you on my arm tonight."

Drusilla's smile widened, and she gave his arm a playful squeeze. "You're quite the charmer, Jonathan."

As they reached the elevator, JT pressed the button, stealing one last glance over his shoulder. Leonard was still there, a silent guardian in the background.

Just two more days, JT thought to himself. *We can make it.*

The elevator doors opened with a soft chime, and as they stepped inside, JT resolved to push the worry aside for the evening. Tonight was about celebrating their time together, and he wouldn't let Alvarez or anyone else take that away from them.

The maître d' greeted them with a warm smile as they stepped into the dimly lit steakhouse. "Good evening to my favorite couple. Welcome back," he said, his voice smooth and full of charm.

JT and Drusilla exchanged smiles, both feeling like VIPs as the maître d' led them inside.

"We'll grab a cocktail at the bar before dinner," JT said.

270

"Of course, Mr. Anderson," the maître d' replied with a knowing nod, motioning for the hostess to escort them.

The hostess guided them to two seats at the far end of the bar, a cozy, semi-private corner where the amber glow of the lights reflected off rows of glistening glassware.

Drusilla slipped onto the barstool, smoothing her silver dress as she crossed her legs. JT, looking sharp in his black suit, sat beside her, leaning in just slightly to catch her scent—a mix of jasmine and something uniquely Drusilla.

The bartender approached with a smile. "Good evening. What can I start you off with?"

"We'll have a bottle of Cristal," JT said confidently, knowing it was her favorite and a special treat for the evening.

The bartender returned swiftly, placing two gleaming champagne flutes before them, popped open the champagne and poured a taste for JT. "Perfect," he said as he nodded to the bartender.

As they clinked glasses, their smiles mirrored each other's.

"To us," JT said, his voice low but full of meaning.

"To us," Drusilla echoed, taking a sip and savoring the luxurious bubbles on her tongue.

After finishing two glasses of bubbles, the host reappeared, ready to lead them to their table. They followed, hand in hand, until they reached a quiet two-top in the corner near the window. The table was perfectly situated, offering a view of the ocean bathed in moonlight.

JT pulled out Drusilla's chair, and she slid into it gracefully, murmuring, "Thank you, kind sir."

He took his seat across from her, and for a moment, they simply took in the ambiance— the soft hum of conversation, the faint clink of cutlery, soft music, and the glow of the candlelight casting flickering shadows.

271

"This," Drusilla said softly, meeting JT's eyes, "is perfect."

As the waiter approached with menus, JT and Drusilla exchanged a glance, both already knowing this would be an evening to remember. JT looked up at the waiter and asked for him to put another bottle of Cristal on ice." The waiter nodded and slipped away.

JT and Drusilla turned their attention to the menus, though the energy between them made it hard to focus on the words.

"I think I'm going with the steak," JT said, glancing up at her over the top of his menu.

Drusilla smiled, her fingers lightly tracing the edge of hers. "Then I'll have the lobster tail."

JT chuckled softly, setting his menu down. "Perfect pair—just like us."

Drusilla tilted her head, her smile playful and warm. "You're smooth tonight, aren't you?"

"Only for you," JT replied, his voice dropping to a lower, more intimate tone.

As he reached across the table and placed his hand over hers, Drusilla's foot found its way to his leg. Slowly, she slid her bare leg up his calf, her eyes locking with his as a coy smile played on her lips. The thought that someone might see them, made the playful move even more exciting.

JT's hand tightened ever so slightly around hers, his composure flickering as he felt the unmistakable intent behind her touch. "You're trouble, you know that?" Leaning in slightly, his voice just loud enough for her to hear over the quiet hum of the dining room.

She leaned in too, her voice soft and teasing. "You don't seem too upset about it."

JT laughed under his breath, his eyes gleaming with anticipation. "Upset isn't the word I'd use."

The Sommelier returned with their bottle of Cristal holding it for JT to see and approve. JT nodded and the waiter expertly opened it and poured two fresh glasses. The moment was broken only briefly as the waiter arrived and took their orders, then stepped away.

272

As they sipped the chilled champagne, the spark between them grew hotter, their smiles and glances carrying promises for the hours ahead.

Meanwhile, at the other end of the ship, Alvarez sat in a dimly lit corner of the crew lounge, far away from the main activity of the ship. He had chosen the spot deliberately, ensuring privacy while maintaining a clear line of sight to the entrance. His demeanor was calm, almost too calm for someone with so much at stake.

On the small table in front of him lay a laptop, its screen casting a faint glow. He wasn't looking at typical crew tasks or entertainment—he was monitoring encrypted messages from his contact in New York. His fingers flew over the keyboard as he typed:

"Everything's on schedule. Be ready at the dock. This is bigger than we planned, but the payoff will be worth it."

A reply came within moments:

"You sure it's clean? Last thing we need is heat."

Alvarez smirked, his confidence unwavering. He responded:

"Trust me. The distraction is working perfectly. No one suspects what's coming."

He closed the laptop and leaned back, reaching into his pocket to pull out a worn photo of a man and a young boy standing in front of a massive corporate building. His jaw tightened as he stared at the image.

"This isn't just business, JT," he muttered under his breath, his voice low and venomous. "This is personal."

He tucked the photo back into his pocket and stood, straightening his uniform. He had avoided detection so far by sticking to areas where staff turnover was high and faces blurred into anonymity. Every interaction with passengers was brief, every movement calculated. He was aware that his photo had been distributed to some onboard and had to be careful, not showing his face any more than necessary.

Alvarez checked his watch. He had just enough time to visit one last secured area before his shift officially ended. He needed to retrieve a small item hidden in an inconspicuous part of the ship's maintenance deck—a flash drive containing information he'd gathered during his time aboard. Information that wasn't just valuable but dangerous in the wrong hands—or the right ones, depending on your perspective.

As he exited the lounge, he blended seamlessly into the flow of crew members, his movements practiced and unremarkable. The faintest smile played on his lips as he thought of JT and Drusilla, blissfully unaware of the storm gathering on the horizon.

"This isn't over yet," he whispered, disappearing into the maze of corridors that led to the ship's underbelly.

After savoring the last bites of their decadent meal, JT looks at Drusilla with a mischievous smile, his eyes twinkling. "The night's still young. Shall we try our luck?"

Drusilla grins, her lips curling in that playful way he's come to adore. "I'm feeling lucky."

They make their way to the casino, the air thick with anticipation. The soft clink of glasses and the hum of chatter greet them as they step inside, the vibrant lights casting a warm glow over the sea of tables. Drusilla's gaze flits from one to another, but it's the *baccarat* table that catches her eye—a game of high stakes, perfect for the mood of the night.

As JT and Drusilla sat at the busy baccarat table, JT gave her a quick lesson on the game. After signing his marker and receiving his chips, the dealer began the next hand.

JT adjusted his cufflinks as the dealer dealt the cards. The green felt of the baccarat table gleamed under the warm lights, and the hum of the casino filled the air—laughter, the shuffle of cards, the soft chime of slot machines. Drusilla sat beside him, her slender fingers resting lightly on his arm as she observed the game.

The dealer announced, "Place your bets, ladies and gentlemen."

JT slid a neat stack of chips forward, nodding to indicate he was betting on the *Player*. Drusilla, curious but cautious, decided to observe for the first round. She was fascinated by JT's calm demeanor, the slight arch of his brow as he studied the cards.

The dealer dealt the cards:

Player: 6
Banker: 5

JT's lips curved into a confident smile. The dealer revealed the next cards, and the total stood:

Player: 9
Banker: 8

"Player wins." The dealer pushed JT's winnings forward, and Drusilla clapped softly.

"Good start," JT said with a grin, stacking his chips with practiced ease.

Drusilla leaned closer, her lips brushing his ear. "You're dangerous when you're confident. Should I be worried?"

He chuckled, turning his head slightly to meet her gaze. "Only if you plan to bet against me."

For the next few hands, Drusilla joined in, placing small, playful bets. She surprised herself by winning twice, though JT's luck held steady. He never bet too aggressively, but his knack for reading the game was evident.

As the evening unfolded, the pit boss looked over the dealer's shoulder and asked JT if they would like a beverage. JT nodded and mouthed "Cristal". The pit boss called a waitress over, whispered to her and within minutes, they were sipping on the cold champagne. "Compliments of management," the pit boss said softly. "Enjoy." JT smiled and placed his next bet. The glimmer of the bubbly drink matched the sparkle in Drusilla's eyes as she leaned into JT, thoroughly enjoying the experience.

When a rare streak of losses hit, JT leaned back with a relaxed smile, signaling the dealer to pause his bets.

"Taking a break?" Drusilla asked, her tone teasing.

"Just letting the game breathe," he replied smoothly, turning to face her. "Besides, I'm much more interested in you right now."

She laughed, her cheeks flushed with the warmth of champagne and the thrill of the game. "Let's see if I can win the next one for us."

She slid a few chips forward, choosing the **Banker** this time. JT leaned back, sipping his champagne, watching her play with a mixture of pride and admiration.

"Good choice," he murmured as the dealer revealed the cards.

And just like that, she won.

JT raised his glass in a toast. "To my lucky charm."

Drusilla clinked her glass to his, her heart fluttering at the way he looked at her. The connection between them was growing stronger with each passing moment. They were ready for the next part of the evening.

After their thrilling time at the baccarat table, the tension between JT and Drusilla is palpable—each glance, each shared laugh, only deepening their connection. As they step away from the casino, the cool night air feels refreshing, but it's nothing compared to the heat simmering between them.

"How are you feeling, lucky?" JT asks, a playful gleam in his eyes as he walks beside her, their hands brushing with every step.

Drusilla smiles, the corner of her mouth curving up sensually. "I'm definitely feeling lucky... but not because of the cards," she says, her voice a little lower, a hint of something more intimate in it.

JT's heart skips a beat, his pulse quickening as they continue walking down the ship's quiet, candle-lit corridor. The soft sound of their footsteps is the only noise that surrounds them.

"Is that so?" he asks, his voice a little husky now. He lets his fingers graze hers before gently lacing them together. "What exactly are you feeling lucky about?"

Drusilla turns to him, her eyes dark with intent, the flirtatious banter between them slipping into something more serious. "Maybe it's the company I'm keeping," she says, the words hanging between them with undeniable desire.

They pause in front of his cabin, the door just ahead, but neither seems eager to break the spell of the moment. JT stands close enough to feel the warmth of her body, his chest rising and falling with each breath.

"I can't think of anywhere else I'd rather be right now," JT says softly, his gaze locked on hers, each word filled with sincerity.

Drusilla looks up at him, the intensity of the connection between them so strong it almost feels like they're the only two people in the world. Her lips part slightly, her breath catching as her heart beats faster. The chemistry between them is undeniable.

With a soft laugh, she leans in closer, her hand moving to rest on his chest. "Then let's not waste any more time."

Without another word, she opens the door to his cabin, and they step inside. The room is dimly lit, the soft glow of the bedside lamp casting shadows over the luxurious furnishings. JT's cabin feels like a sanctuary, but the real comfort is the way their bodies feel drawn together, like magnets.

With that, the world outside disappears, leaving only the two of them—unspoken words, unbridled passion, and the promise of what's to come.

As the door to JT's cabin clicked shut, the soft glow of the message light on the phone caught JT's eye. He quickly walked over to the desk and pressed the button to retrieve his messages.

There was one from Ash. It was brief, a reminder to call him for an update on security. JT knew this call would be important. He glanced over at Drusilla, who had already started slipping off her shoes and taking off her earrings. She smiled at him playfully, and he gave her a quick nod before picking up the phone.

"I'll just be a minute." He stepped out onto the balcony for privacy and dialed Ash's number.

"Good evening Boss," Ash's voice came through the line. "I've been working on the details for your return to New York. The security team will be in place when you arrive. I'll have the specifics for you in the morning."

JT rubbed the back of his neck. "Thanks, Ash. I appreciate it. I'm really concerned about Alvarez. I have a bad feeling that something might happen once we get off the ship."

Ash paused for a moment. "We're on it, Boss. You're not alone in this. We'll be there with a full team to escort the two of you."

"Good. Keep me posted." JT's voice was calm, but his mind was racing. After a few more pleasantries, he ended the call and took a deep breath, trying to push aside the lingering worry.

When he came back inside, Drusilla, tipsy from all the champagne, was having a little trouble getting out of her dress.

"Unzip me," she said softly, her eyes mischievous.

JT crossed the room with a grin, his fingers moving easily to the zipper on her dress. As the fabric slid down, she stepped out of it and tossed it into a heap on the chair nearby.

She turned toward the bathroom, heading in to brush her teeth and prepare for bed.

JT paused for a moment, staring at her as she walked away. He removed his cufflinks, placing them next to her earrings.

After a few moments, the bathroom door opened and Drusilla, dressed only in her white panties and bra skipped across the room and hopped in to bed.

JT laughed and stepped in to the bathroom to brush his teeth and wash his face, his thoughts briefly drifting back to the security plans Ash had discussed. Trusting that his head of security for the past 15 years had things under control.

Once done, he returned to the bedroom wearing just his white shirt unbuttoned part way and his white boxers. The sound of the waves outside filled the room, the soft breeze from the balcony carrying the scent of the sea.

Drusilla, already settled in bed, smiled at him as he entered. Her eyes tracked his every movement. JT walked over, undid the last button of his shirt, and tossed it onto the chair, turning off the light. He noticed her watching him with a look of admiration.

"God, you look *so* good," she said in a champagne induced, sultry voice, low and full of desire.

JT smiled, feeling the excitement between them rise as he crawled in next to her.

Drusilla rolled over on top of him, wrapping her arms around him as their lips met in a slow, deep kiss. The world outside seemed to disappear. They only had each other in that moment, and it felt as if time had stopped.

After enjoying each other for what seemed like hours, exhausted, they fell asleep in each other's arms as the dim light of the moon shined across the room.

279

As the morning sun came across the cabin, JT and Drusilla shielded their eyes with the sheet, wanting a little more time to sleep off the feeling you have the morning after three bottles of champagne.

JT slowly opened his eyes, the dim light from the curtains filtering into the room. His head throbbed, but the weight on his chest wasn't from the hangover—it was the gnawing sense that something was wrong. He turned to see Drusilla, still asleep beside him, her breath soft and steady. Her hair was sprawled across the pillow, the same way it had been when they fell asleep.

Alvarez. The name haunted him, a reminder that things were far from over. His threat to "take things from him" seemed all too real. Stealing the necklace was just the beginning, he feared.

He rolled over and glanced at the clock—almost 8 a.m. The ship would be docking in New York the following morning. He hadn't slept much, his mind running in circles, but now there was no time to waste. Ash said he would provide him with an update on the security plans for their arrival in NY. He was anxious to get it.

Carefully, JT slipped out of bed, trying not to disturb Drusilla. He walked over to the desk and reached for his phone. There was an unread message from Ash, JT's pulse quickened as he opened the message:

> **Ash:** *We'll be ready for your arrival, but there's something you need to know. There is chatter that Alvarez has been in contact with someone in the city, and we have reason to believe he may be planning something upon your arrival. I've arranged for an extra security detail and we are finalizing our plans now. I'll update you soon with the details.*

JT clenched his jaw. Alvarez wasn't going to get away with this. He needed to protect Drusilla, and he couldn't afford to let his guard down now. He took a deep breath, mentally preparing himself for the confrontation that was inevitably coming.

He heard a rustling sound behind him, and when he turned, Drusilla was awake, her eyes still heavy with sleep but focused on him.

"What's going on?" she asked softly, sensing his shift in mood.

JT didn't want to worry her. Not yet. But he couldn't lie either. I had a message from Ash," he said quietly, walking over to sit beside her. "Alvarez has to still be on the ship. Ash is concerned that he might be planning something for when we dock."

Her expression shifted to one of concern, but she didn't pull away. "What do we do?"

"I'll have the details shortly," trying to stay calm for Drusilla's benefit. "Ash is the best at what he does. We don't have to worry. There will be a plan in place. Unfortunately, we've been through things like this before. I should have accepted his suggestion to bring security with me, but I just wanted to be alone."

JT gave her a tight hug and assured her that she was safe, though the weight of what was to come hung heavily in the air. He had to keep her safe. Whatever it took.

After breakfast was delivered to the cabin, JT and Drusilla sat together on the balcony, enjoying the morning air and the gentle sway of the ship. They chatted about the next couple of days—Drusilla's time in New York before she headed back to Boston. There was a feeling of calm between them, but it didn't last long.

As they sipped their coffee, JT's phone buzzed on the table. He glanced down at the screen and saw Ash's name.

"It's Ash," JT said, a knot forming in his stomach. He picked up the phone and set it on the table, switching it to speaker so Drusilla could hear the update, too.

"Boss," Ash's voice came through the speaker, steady and professional. "I'm in the office with some of my team. The plan is finalized. We'll be ready when you dock. I'll walk you through it."

JT leaned forward, his attention fully on the phone as Ash continued.

"We're putting a dozen guys on the dock when you arrive. We'll form a secure perimeter. Two of my team will pick up your luggage, Leonard is making sure it's the first to come off the ship. He'll make sure everything goes smoothly there."

JT nodded, relieved that everything was being handled. But Ash wasn't done.

"If Alvarez is planning anything, my men will have eyes on the main gangplank. But I've arranged an alternative exit for you and Miss Pennington," Ash said. "You'll leave via the loading dock. I'll have six of my team there waiting for you. They'll escort you directly to the limo."

Drusilla glanced at JT, her brows furrowed, but JT squeezed her hand reassuringly.

"The limo will take you five blocks to the helipad, where the copter will be waiting. It'll take you straight to the roof of our building. We'll have men outside the building and additional men stationed outside your condo, just in case."

JT sat back, his mind processing the plan. It was tight. He appreciated Ash's thoroughness—nothing was being left to chance.

"Sounds like everything's in place," JT said, his voice steady, though he could feel the weight of the situation. "Thanks, Ash. I'll keep you posted if anything changes."

"Of course," Ash replied. "We're ready for anything."

JT ended the call and sat back, looking at Drusilla.

"We'll be alright," he said, though the anxiety still lingered in his chest. "Ash is the best at what he does. He'll make sure nothing goes wrong."

Drusilla nodded, but JT could see the tension in her eyes. She wasn't naïve—she understood the danger, too. "I'm not used to this kind of thing JT. I know you have things under control, but it's still scary as hell."

"We'll stick to the plan," JT said, trying to give her a reassuring smile. "Let's try to enjoy the rest of the morning. We have time before the ship docks, and we can't let this guy ruin that."

She gave him a soft smile and nodded, but inside, both of them knew their peaceful morning was slipping away with each passing moment.

Meanwhile, deep in the bowels of the ship, Alvarez paced the narrow confines of the crew quarters. The air was stale, and the dull hum of the ship's engines did little to soothe his fraying patience. His burner phone buzzed in his hand—it was Juan Carlos, his contact in New York.

Juan Carlos: "The plan is set. Gangplank at 0900. We need to know what they will be wearing as soon as you know in the morning. We have a picture of him, but one of the two of them would be helpful."

"I'll let you know what they are wearing before we dock. I'll get a pic if possible." Alvarez smirked, though there was a cold calculation in his eyes. His plan was falling into place. If there was one thing he wanted more than money, it was to watch JT suffer. That emerald necklace had been a message, a reminder that no matter how high JT rose, Alvarez could always bring him crashing down. "La venganza viene (revenge is coming)" he said under his breath.

His men in New York had come at a cost. They demanded one million US dollars to execute the operation—a steep price, but one Alvarez was willing to pay for revenge. He had already arranged to wire a substantial portion of the funds as a deposit, ensuring their loyalty. The rest would come after they had Drusilla.

He tapped out a quick reply:

> *Alvarez: "Los fondos se transferiran esta noche" (the funds will be wired tonight). Confirm when received."*

Alvarez knew better than to dirty his own hands. The last thing he needed was to set foot on U.S. soil and risk arrest. This crew, ruthless as they were, would carry out the kidnapping and vanish before anyone knew what had happened.

The plan was simple yet brutal: the van, posing as transport for another passenger, would roll up to the gangplank just as JT and Drusilla disembarked. Having no security with him, four men would leap out, two overpowering JT while the other two grabbed Drusilla. They'd shove her into the van and speed off, leaving chaos in their wake. The instructions were not to harm JT.

The van's destination was another dock just two blocks away, where a boat would be waiting to whisk them across the Hudson. Drusilla would become Alvarez's bargaining chip, a tool to squeeze JT into giving up the businesses that Alvarez had lost to him. Terrorizing JT while holding Drusilla captive would be the ultimate payback.

Alvarez glanced at the clock on the wall. The ship would dock in the morning. There was no turning back now.

Satisfied, he tossed the burner phone onto the small cot and leaned back against the wall. He could almost taste victory. He had no idea there would be resistance.

"Enjoy your last peaceful moments, JT," he muttered under his breath. "Tomorrow, your world comes crashing down."

Packing

Their last day passed in a mix of quiet anticipation and underlying tension. JT and Drusilla worked side by side, gathering her belongings from her cabin and moving them into his. The intimacy of packing together felt oddly grounding, as if combining their lives into a few suitcases might keep the looming threat at bay.

The soft notes of a jazz playlist played from JT's phone, an attempt to set a calm atmosphere. Drusilla folded clothes while JT carefully wrapped her ceramic travel souvenirs in layers of tissue.

"Do you think we've got everything?" Drusilla asked, glancing around.

JT smiled faintly. "If we missed anything, I'll buy you ten more when we get to New York."

Drusilla chuckled softly, but the worry in her eyes betrayed her forced lightheartedness. They both knew the thought of Alvarez was lingering like a storm cloud over the horizon.

A knock at the door interrupted their quiet moment. JT looked at Drusilla, then went to answer. Leonard stood in the hallway. His face was calm but serious.

"Mr. Anderson, may I have a word?" Leonard asked, glancing briefly at Drusilla in the background.

JT stepped into the hallway and closed the door behind him. "What's the update?"

Leonard kept his voice low. "The ship uses facial recognition for security purposes—passengers and crew are scanned as they board or leave the vessel. We've been cross-referencing those scans with the picture of Alvarez that Mr. Ash sent us."

JT's eyes narrowed. "And?"

Leonard nodded slightly. "We're narrowing it down. Alvarez's movements have been erratic, but we know he's still on board. We're confident we'll locate him before we reach New York tomorrow morning."

JT exhaled, relief mixed with residual tension. "Good work. Keep me updated."

"I will," Leonard assured him. "And don't worry—we've got extra personnel patrolling the restricted areas and monitoring the exits. He's not getting off this ship unnoticed."

JT clapped Leonard on the shoulder before re-entering the cabin.

Drusilla looked up from where she was folding a dress. "What's going on?"

"They're using facial recognition," JT said, walking over to her. "They're cross-checking scans against a picture of Alvarez that Ash sent them. Leonard says they're confident they'll find him before we dock."

285

Drusilla's shoulders visibly relaxed, though her fingers still fidgeted with the fabric in her hands. "That's good news."

"It is," JT said, taking her hands in his. "They're on top of it. And so are we. We'll get through this, Drusilla. Tomorrow night, we'll be eating dinner and drinking champagne at Mr. Chow's."

She smiled at him, a flicker of gratitude breaking through the tension. They returned to their packing, trying to focus on the mundane task and not the what-ifs that hovered in the back of their minds.

The anticipation weighed heavily on everyone, though they each carried it differently.

JT and Drusilla decided to step away from the tension for a while. After spending the day packing and planning, they made their way to the ship's sushi bar for an early dinner. The restaurant was tucked into a quiet corner of the ship, its ambiance marked by dim lighting and the soft murmur of other diners.

Drusilla scanned the menu but struggled to focus. She could feel JT watching her, his steady presence a reminder that, despite everything, they were in this together.

"Let's start with a sake flight," JT suggested, his tone light.

Drusilla smirked. "Are we sure we've recovered from the champagne last night?"

He chuckled. "Fair point. Maybe just green tea, then."

The meal passed with a mix of forced normalcy and genuine moments of connection. They talked about the places they wanted to visit during Drusilla's two days in New York—art galleries, a quiet dinner, maybe even a stroll through Central Park if time allowed. But every so often, the conversation would lapse, and the unspoken tension would settle between them like a shadow.

After dinner, they returned to JT's cabin, agreeing to spend the evening quietly. Drusilla settled onto the plush couch with her tablet, catching up on emails and reading through messages from friends back home. JT sat nearby, his laptop open, scrolling through updates from Ash and reviewing news about Alvarez's business dealings, trying to glean any insights that might prove useful.

Occasionally, they'd share a comment or a smile, but the focus was mostly on their devices. It was a practical way to pass the time, but also an unspoken attempt to distract themselves from the looming uncertainty.

Meanwhile, in the crew quarters, Alvarez kept to himself. His tiny room felt more confining than ever, the walls pressing in with each passing hour. He'd spent most of the day reviewing his plan, double-checking his communications with the New York crew, and ensuring the payment transfer was ready.

As night fell, his nerves only grew sharper. He avoided the common areas, worried that any misstep or accidental glance could betray his presence. Instead, he paced his quarters, muttering reassurances to himself.

"Tomorrow," he whispered under his breath, clenching his fists. "Tomorrow, Anderson will learn what it's like to lose."

Chapter 13

New York

The low, resonant sound of the ship's horn echoed through the cabin, pulling JT and Drusilla from sleep. It wasn't a gradual awakening but a sharp jolt, a reminder that the day they had been anticipating—and dreading—had arrived.

Drusilla stirred first, her eyes fluttering open as the reality of their arrival in New York settled in. She turned to find JT already awake, lying beside her with his arms behind his head, staring at the ceiling.

"The horn," she murmured groggily, her voice thick with sleep. "We're here."

JT nodded, his expression unreadable. "Yeah," he replied, his voice steady but low. "We've arrived."

The ship's gentle rocking was now replaced by the faint hum of the engines slowing to a stop, mingled with the distant sounds of crew activity preparing for docking. Drusilla sat up, brushing her hair from her face, her gaze shifting to the window where the New York skyline peeked through the curtains.

JT swung his legs over the side of the bed and stood, stretching. "How are you feeling?" he asked, glancing over his shoulder at her.

"Honestly?" She gave him a small, nervous smile. "I'm trying not to feel anything. Just... focus on getting through it."

He walked over to her side, brushing a hand gently against her cheek. "We'll get through this," he said firmly. "Ash and his team have everything covered. I trust them completely,"

Drusilla placed her hand over his, squeezing it lightly. "I trust you."

They moved through their morning routine in silence, the weight of what was ahead hanging in the air. As they dressed and packed the final few items, the ship's intercom crackled to life, announcing the docking process and reminding passengers to prepare for disembarkation.

JT glanced at his phone. A message from Ash flashed on the screen:

> **Ash**: *"We're in position. Everything is running smoothly so far. All quiet here. Let me know when you're ready to disembark."*

JT showed the message to Drusilla. "See? Everything's under control."

She nodded, but her eyes lingered on the phone a moment longer. "Let's just get this over with."

Outside the cabin, Leonard was already waiting. His presence, as usual, was stoic and reassuring. "Morning," he said with a polite nod. "The ship's security team confirmed they've completed their facial recognition sweeps and are reviewing the data as we speak."

"Thanks, Leonard," JT replied. "We'll be ready soon."

As the horn sounded once more indicating they had one hour before they disembark, the sense of finality set in. They were here. And if Alvarez was planning anything, it was time to face it.

With just an hour remaining before disembarkation, JT paced the cabin, his phone in hand. Every few minutes, he checked the time, the seconds crawling by. Finally, he turned to Leonard, who stood near the door, ever watchful.

"Leonard, can you call for the porter to handle the luggage?" JT asked, his tone calm but edged with urgency.

Leonard nodded and stepped into the hall to make the call. JT turned to Drusilla, who sat on the edge of the bed, her hands clasped tightly in her lap.

"Everything's running smoothly," he assured her. "The bags will be offloaded first, just like Ash planned. His team is already waiting at the dock."

Drusilla managed a small smile. "I'm glad someone knows what they're doing. I'd probably just curl up in the luggage cart and hide."

JT chuckled, the sound a welcome break from the tension. He moved to sit beside her, taking her hands in his. "We're not hiding from Alvarez or anyone else. We're walking off this ship and not stopping until we get to my place. I promise you—you're safe."

Leonard re-entered the cabin, his phone in hand. "The porter's on his way," he informed JT. "And I've confirmed with Ash that his team has secured the luggage area. They've got a black Escalade waiting to load everything as soon as the porter brings it down."

"Good," JT replied. "What about the limo?"

"It's already in position," Leonard said. "It's parked at the far end of the ship, near the loading dock. No one from the main gangplank area will see you or Drusilla when you disembark."

Drusilla stood, smoothing her dress and taking a deep breath. "What happens after the limo?"

JT answered, his voice steady. "The limo takes us five blocks to the helipad. From there, we're on the helicopter straight to the roof of my building. Once we're there, Ash's team will escort us to my condo. And that's it. We'll be home."

Leonard's phone buzzed. He glanced at the screen. "The porter's on the way up now."

JT nodded and rose to his feet. "Let's get this done."

The porter arrived promptly, his uniform crisp and his demeanor professional. He handled their luggage with care, stacking the bags neatly onto the cart. JT reached into his pocket, pulling out a generous tip and slipping it into the porter's hand.

"Thank you for everything during the cruise," JT said, offering a firm handshake.

The young porter's face lit up. "My pleasure, sir. Safe travels."

As the door clicked shut behind him, JT and Drusilla were left with a quiet thirty minutes before they were set to disembark. They stepped out onto the balcony, the cool morning air brushing against their faces as they took in the breathtaking view of the New York skyline.

"It's always good to come home," JT said softly, his eyes on the towering buildings and bustling harbor. Then, turning to Drusilla, he wrapped his arms around her, pulling her close.

Drusilla leaned into him, her arms finding their place around his waist. They kissed—a long, passionate kiss that spoke of everything they had been through and the connection they had found.

For a few moments, they held each other in silence, their foreheads met, and they smiled.

"It's been quite an adventure," JT said, his voice low and filled with warmth.

Drusilla laughed softly, her gaze meeting his. "It's not at all what I expected when my mom treated me to this cruise. But I wouldn't change a minute of it."

JT raised an eyebrow, his expression teasing. "Not even the part where you lost your emerald necklace?"

Drusilla swatted his arm playfully. "OK, maybe that," she said. "But I gained so much more." Her smile softened. "I can't believe I fell in love on a cruise."

"You haven't seen anything yet," JT replied, a mischievous grin spreading across his face.

Just then, JT's phone buzzed on the table inside the cabin. He stepped away to answer it, leaving the balcony door ajar.

"Hello?"

"Boss," came Ash's steady voice. "Your driver will be wearing a black suit and a red tie instead of the usual black one. I wanted to make sure you can confirm it's him. Leonard will escort you to the loading dock. We'll talk when you are in the limo."

"Thanks, Ash," JT replied, glancing back at Drusilla, who watched him with curiosity. "See you soon."

He hung up the phone and stepped back onto the balcony, his hand reaching for hers. "It's almost time."

Drusilla nodded, her fingers lacing with his. "Let's do this."

In the dimly lit confines of the ship's lower deck, Alvarez paced back and forth, his phone pressed tightly against his ear. The faint hum of machinery filled the air, but his focus was solely on the conversation at hand.

"I'm counting on you, JC. Don't let me down," Alvarez hissed, his voice low but intense.

On the other end of the line, Juan Carlos's tone was steady, almost cocky. "Relax, amigo. We're ready. My men are in position, and the van is already parked near the gangplank. Everything's set. Did you get a picture of them this morning?"

Alvarez paused, "no I wasn't able to. You know what he looks like. It's obvious who the girl is with him. "You better be ready. I've paid a lot of money to make this happen. I want them separated—her in the van, him left scrambling."

"It'll go like clockwork," Juan Carlos assured him. "The van's close enough to the ship to blend in, but far enough to avoid suspicion. When the moment comes, we'll strike fast. They won't know what hit them."

Alvarez exhaled sharply, a mix of anxiety and anticipation coursing through him. "And the boat? It's ready at the second dock?"

"Ready and waiting. As soon as we have the girl, we'll be out of there in minutes. You'll have what you want, and he'll have nothing."

For a moment, silence hung between them, the weight of the plan pressing on Alvarez's shoulders. Finally, he said, "Good. Don't mess this up, JC. If anything goes wrong..."

"It won't," Juan Carlos interrupted confidently. "You'll get your revenge, amigo."

Alvarez ended the call and slipped the phone back into his pocket. He allowed himself a brief, grim smile. Revenge wasn't just a dish best served cold—it was about to be delivered with precision.

Still, as he stood alone in the belly of the ship, he couldn't shake the unease that gnawed at the edges of his confidence. Everything was riding on this plan, and failure was not an option.

As the announcement echoed through the ship that passengers were free to disembark at their leisure, there was a firm knock at JT's cabin door. He exchanged a quick glance with Drusilla, who was seated on the edge of the bed, before walking over to open it. Standing in the hallway were three men in black suits, their serious expressions immediately setting the tone.

One of them stepped forward, extending his hand. "Mr. Anderson, I'm Agent Ruiz with Interpol. Pleasure to meet you," he said, his voice calm but authoritative.

JT shook his hand, noting the firm grip. "Agent Ruiz. What's going on?"

Ruiz motioned for the group to step inside. "We've been aboard since the ship docked three hours ago. After the ship's security finished cross-referencing the facial recognition data the picture of Alvarez, they contacted us. Through Interpol's database, we've positively identified him. We knew he traveled to New York, but he disappeared. Now we know where he's been hiding—posing as a crew member on this ship. A team is en route to his quarters as we speak." JT called Ash immediately and informed him what was happening.

As he hung up, one of the other agents' phones buzzed. The man stepped away to take the call, his expression tightening as he listened. When he returned, his face was resolute.

"They've got him," the agent reported. "Alvarez has been arrested. We've confiscated his phone and laptop, and... there's more. We've uncovered an elaborate plan to kidnap Ms. Pennington. Four men are waiting in a van outside the gangplank to grab her when you leave the ship, and there's a boat at a nearby pier for a quick getaway."

Drusilla's hand flew to her mouth in shock, and JT's jaw clenched, his protective instincts kicking in.

Ruiz raised a calming hand. "Please, have a seat. We've already contacted the port authority and NYPD. They're on their way."

JT and Drusilla reluctantly sat down, though the tension in the room was palpable. JT held Drusilla's hand tightly, offering silent reassurance as the agents coordinated the next steps.

Thirty minutes later, the sound of sirens blared outside. JT and Drusilla moved to the balcony and saw six NYPD squad cars and two unmarked vehicles screech into the port, a police helicopter hovering above. Ash's team saw several officers quickly surround the van, guns drawn, and within moments, four men were pulled out, handcuffed, and taken into custody.

Meanwhile, another team descended on the nearby pier. There, they arrested three more of Alvarez's associates who had been stationed with the getaway boat.

Just then, JT's phone buzzed. It was Ash.

"It's over," Ash said, his tone filled with relief. "Alvarez and his crew are in custody. Everyone's safe."

JT exhaled deeply, his grip on Drusilla's hand tightening. "Thank you, Ash."

As they hung up, the cabin door opened again, and one of the agents who had apprehended Alvarez stepped in. He held a small object wrapped in a washcloth.

Approaching Drusilla, he said with a kind smile, "I believe this belongs to you."

Drusilla hesitated, then unwrapped the cloth. Her emerald necklace sparkled in the soft cabin light, its beauty undiminished despite the ordeal. Her breath caught, and tears welled in her eyes as she clutched the necklace to her chest.

"It's over," she whispered, her voice trembling with relief. JT pulled her into a tight embrace, his lips brushing against her temple.

"It's just beginning," he whispered, holding her tight as the weight of the past few days finally lifted.

"I love you Drusilla." Drusilla with tears still running down her cheeks, buried her head in his chest, then looked up, "I love you too JT."

A New Chapter Begins

After the agents left and the tension began to dissolve, JT and Drusilla found themselves alone in the cabin. The morning sun streamed through the window, casting a golden glow over the room. Drusilla held the necklace in her hand, its weight feeling different now—no longer a reminder of fear, but of resilience and triumph.

JT took her hands in his, his blue eyes steady as they met hers. "Drusilla, I know this cruise didn't exactly go as planned," he began with a soft smile, "but I've never been more certain of anything in my life. Meeting you... it's changed everything for me."

Drusilla smiled, her cheeks flushing as she squeezed his hands. "It wasn't the cruise I expected, that's for sure," she replied, "But I wouldn't change a single moment of it. Not if it means I wouldn't find you."

Their shared laughter broke the last of the tension, and for a moment, it felt like the world was theirs again.

JT pulled her into one last embrace on the cabin's balcony. "This is just the beginning," he promised, his voice low but filled with conviction. "I want you to come to New York. Stay with me for a while. Let's see where this goes."

Drusilla tilted her head up, her heart racing as she searched his face for any hesitation. She found none. "I'd like that," she said softly, her voice barely above a whisper.

They disembarked together, flanked by Ash and his team, the weight of Alvarez's threat now a memory. The limo swept them away to the helipad. As the helicopter lifted off, Drusilla looked down at the cruise ship, a bittersweet smile on her face.

She turned to JT, who was watching her with quiet affection. "So," she said, her voice teasing. "What's next, Mr. Anderson?"

JT grinned, leaning closer. "Whatever we want, Drusilla. Whatever we want."

As the helicopter turned and soared over the skyline of New York City, the future lay wide open before them—a blend of uncertainty, adventure, and the promise of love.

To be continued....

Epilogue

One month later

The late afternoon sunlight streamed into Drusilla's Boston studio, casting a warm glow across her latest painting. Swirls of emerald green and deep blue dominated the canvas, evoking memories of the sea and the way it shimmered under the Monte Carlo sun. She stepped back, brushing a stray strand of hair from her face, and studied her work with a smile.

Behind her, JT's familiar voice broke the silence. "Still working on that masterpiece, I see." Surprised, she turned to see him leaning casually against the doorway, a bouquet of wildflowers in one hand and a small leather folder in the other. His tailored shirt hinted at the Manhattan meeting he'd just returned from, but his relaxed stance reminded her of the man who had shared moonlit strolls on the ship's deck.

"It's almost done," she replied, crossing the room to meet him. "But don't call it a masterpiece yet. It still needs something."

JT grinned, handing her the flowers. "You always say that. What do you call it?" She smiled and looked into those beautiful blue eyes and said, "The Emerald Voyage."

He kissed her lightly on the forehead, and she felt the same rush of warmth that had started weeks ago on the cruise. Their lives had intertwined effortlessly since then—splitting time between her sunlit studio in Boston and his penthouse overlooking Manhattan. They both knew this was just the beginning, though neither of them was in a rush to define it.

She nodded toward the folder in his hand. "What's that?"

JT's grin widened as he handed it to her. She opened it and found an itinerary on his company's letterhead clipped to a sleek boarding pass. Her heart skipped a beat as she read the destination: Quito, Ecuador.

"I thought it was time you saw where it all began," JT said softly. "The mines, the land, the legacy... and maybe a few secrets I haven't shared yet."

Drusilla raised an eyebrow, half-teasing. "Secrets, huh?"

JT chuckled. "Only the good kind." He took her hand, intertwining his fingers with hers. "The jet's fueled and ready whenever you are."

She stared at the itinerary, feeling a rush of excitement and anticipation. There was so much she still didn't know about him, layers he'd yet to reveal. She loved that their story was still unfolding, an adventure that promised more twists, turns, and passion.

"I guess I'd better finish this painting before we leave," she said, glancing back at the canvas.

296

"Take your time," JT replied. "The plane won't leave without us."

As they stood together in the studio, the faint sound of a distant church bell drifted through the open window, marking the hour. Drusilla looked at the boarding pass again, imagining the view from JT's jet as they crossed the sky toward their next adventure.

This was only the beginning. Their journey wasn't over, and something told her that Ecuador would reveal more than either of them expected.

To be continued....